BY NICOLE CUFFY

O Sinners!

Dances

o sinners!

ONE WORLD
NEW YORK

o sinners!

A NOVEL

nicole cuffy

Published in the United States by One World, an imprint of Random House,
a division of Penguin Random House LLC, New York.

ONE WORLD and colophon are registered trademarks of
Penguin Random House LLC.

Library of Congress Cataloging-in-Publication Data
Names: Cuffy, Nicole, author.
Title: O sinners! : a novel / by Nicole Cuffy.
Description: First edition. | New York, NY: One World, 2025.
Identifiers: LCCN 2024018387 (print) | LCCN 2024018388 (ebook) |
ISBN 9780593597446 (hardcover; acid-free paper) |
ISBN 9780593597453 (ebook)
Subjects: LCGFT: Novels.
Classification: LCC PS3603.U48 O85 2025 (print) | LCC PS3603.U48 (ebook) |
DDC 813/.6—dc23/eng/20240506
LC record available at https://lccn.loc.gov/2024018387
LC ebook record available at https://lccn.loc.gov/2024018388

Printed in the United States of America on acid-free paper

oneworldlit.com

1st Printing

First Edition

To the burning ones, the seekers, the tigers

o sinners!

today

THE FRIGID AIR burned Faruq's nose; when he blew it later, he would find that the city's dirt had made its way inside him with the cold. Cars passed him sleepily, their headlights murky streaks in the early morning gloom. He wore only a thermal shirt, gloves, and running tights. His muscles were warm, though. His body moved exactly as it needed to. Beneath him, the East River, still semi-frozen, chugged icily. Gray slush slapped up from the bridge onto his ankles, some of it hooking into the thin strip of bare flesh between his running tights and his socks, one of which had slipped down a little. He was still on an incline and the deeper his breath, the lighter he felt—less weight to carry uphill before the glorious downward slope off the bridge, where he'd fly with no effort, letting gravity carry him down onto Centre Street, through the crowded heel of Manhattan. He took another deep breath. *Don't you stop*, he told himself. *Just keep going.*

When his father was still here, the morning ritual was different, less quiet. His father would expect Faruq to do morning prayers with him, and then he'd sit at the table with his newspaper, commenting disapprovingly on what he read there. Now, Faruq had a quick, post-run granola bar at the kitchen counter, the news blaring distantly from the television in the living room. Muezza yawned as Faruq scratched behind his ears. The cat liked to act like he was unaffected by Faruq's comings and goings, but whenever Faruq returned home after being gone long, Muezza followed him around the brownstone like a new kitten. This—Faruq's scratching, Muezza's indifference, the morning news—was their morning ritual now.

Muezza stalked off, tail held high, as Faruq went into the living room to turn off the television. He ran his fingers over a groove in the wall between the living room and the dining room—a thin black mark like a dead vine from when his mother used to push the heavy coffee table up against the wall so they could dance. *Dance with me, puttar,* she would say, holding out her arms, bouncing rhythmically from one foot to the other. And he would laugh because she always danced like a Bollywood starlet, whether they were listening to Nazia Hassan or Rick James. Her smile would be so wide he could see the yellowish glint of her back teeth. She never smiled that wide in front of his father. They never danced in front of his father, either. This mark on the wall in this dim room was their little secret. Faruq's father either never noticed it, or he pretended not to.

He switched off the television just as the weatherman made his appearance on-screen. *It's gonna be a cold one, folks . . .* In the new silence, Faruq could hear his own breathing over the sound of his footsteps as he headed upstairs to take a shower. But even the silence here was crowded, like static; echoes of his parents, himself. Sometimes he'd wake up and feel a weight, as though someone were sitting on his chest. He didn't believe in ghosts, not literally, but the place was as haunted as he believed a place could be—stale energy, what the dead leave behind.

The water came out cold and stayed that way for a good minute, so Faruq gritted his teeth until, finally, warm water poured through the old pipes. He kept his shower quick, economical. Better to not get too comfortable right before heading out into the cold. When he stepped out of the shower, he froze. The house was so quiet these days that even the slightest out-of-place noise rang through like a foghorn. Someone was in the house.

Wrapping his towel around his waist, he grabbed the nearest thing to a weapon—the plunger—and stalked out into the hall. The noise was coming from downstairs. Footsteps, crinkling, the snap of something, a door opening. Faruq crept down the stairs, trying to remember where he'd left his cell phone. Shit. The kitchen. And that's where the noise was coming from. The best he could do was rely on the element of surprise and hope the burglar didn't have a gun. On the third step before the landing lay his father's abandoned AirPods. They had lain there for the better part of a year now. He avoided brushing them with his foot as he passed, as he always did. When he reached the landing, he froze. Before he could fully flesh out his plan of attack, the intruder suddenly came into the hall. Faruq jumped up, brandishing the plunger.

"Holy shit," he panted, relief undoing the tension in his muscles once he saw who it was. "Auntie, I thought you were a robber."

Auntie Naila raised an eyebrow and put a hand on her sharp hip. "Oh? And what were you going to do with that?" she asked, nodding toward the plunger.

Now that the adrenaline was dissipating, irritation flooded into its place. "Auntie, I was taking a shower. I was *naked*." He tried to keep his tone gentle, though this was the third time this month she'd let herself into the house with no notice. It was infantilizing. Still, he knew she was only doing what she thought was best for him. Even if he hated it. Even if it was stifling.

She shrugged. "I've raised three boys. I used to give all of you baths together when you were children."

"Still," said Faruq, getting more annoyed—she was missing the point. "Remember, I asked you to call first? And knock?"

"This is my brother's house," she said firmly.

Faruq ran his free hand over his forehead. She'd never done this when his father was still alive. "Auntie, it's my house now."

His auntie pursed her lips in disapproval. "I was just coming to check on you."

"It's not even eight in the morning."

"And I'm glad I did," she continued, tsking. "It's a mess. No food in the refrigerator, stuff all over the floor." She pointed to the AirPods.

He stepped over to block them from her view.

She raised an eyebrow but made no further comment. "I was just going through some old clothes to donate, and look what I found." She held out a turquoise silk scarf. "It was your mother's. She lent it to me I don't even know how long ago. I never got to return it." She didn't quite meet his eye as she said this.

Faruq was slightly hesitant to touch the scarf. He reached out but his hands didn't quite meet the material. Auntie Naila noticed.

"Bismillah," she said, quietly.

"Thanks, Auntie," he said, taking the scarf. "It's not like it's cursed."

She scoffed. "Of course not. Maybe it will give you luck."

"Don't know if I believe in luck, Auntie."

"Well, what do you kids say? It will surround your bases."

"*Cover* your bases."

She waved a hand in the air. "Whatever. You have always been very logical, Faruq. There is a place for logic. But remember that not everything in the world is logic."

"What's the rest of it, then? Magic?"

"Rude boy. The rest of it is Allah, subhanahu wa ta'ala."

Faruq suppressed any further argument.

"Alhamdulillah, I didn't accidentally donate that scarf. Keep it near you, Faruq."

He ran a thumb over the silky fabric. "I was just getting ready to leave for work, Auntie." Which she knew. She knew enough of his daily routine by now that he had to figure her timing wasn't an accident. He suspected she'd intended to come in after he'd already left, because he was running late.

She crossed her arms. "You're kicking me out?"

"Look, I'll visit this weekend or something."

She huffed. "Don't bother. Rude boy. What would your father say?"

Faruq closed his eyes briefly, and Auntie Naila swept back toward the kitchen. She cursed him in Urdu before slamming the back door shut on her way out. He sighed. He knew she didn't mean it. He didn't want to hurt her feelings, either, but the house was beginning to feel like it was made of greenhouse glass—hot, stinking, offering no real protection from the outside. When his father was alive, he'd always felt scrutinized here, his father watching, and Faruq ever careful not to slip up and let his lack of faith show. Now his father was gone, but the scrutiny wasn't. *Rude boy.* He couldn't escape.

A few months after his father died, Faruq had the locks changed. Too many people had had access to the house. He wasn't even sure who had a key anymore, and he couldn't stand the surprise visitors. But it wasn't long before Auntie Naila found his spare and had copies made for all the other aunties before he'd even noticed it was missing.

The walk to the subway was brisk—late February in New York was gray and soggy. His earphones were in, but he could still hear the traffic, the people on the street, the squelch of his shoes in the gray slush on the sidewalks. The train wasn't much better. Faruq was lucky enough to find a seat, but the car he'd landed in smelled of damp clothes and body odor. *When I die, fuck it, I wanna go to hell,* Biggie rapped into his ear. He'd been shocked by those lyrics when he'd first heard them—shocked and thrilled. The idea that hell was something one could welcome, that one could defy by welcoming it. That he could disregard something his religion told him to fear. It made him wonder if he could disregard everything Islam had been telling him. Which, he supposed in retrospect, was exactly why his father didn't like him listening to this kind of music.

Two kids entered at Hoyt–Schermerhorn, their clothes loud and their voices louder. They were laughing at each other, but for everyone else. Faruq remembered being like them, him and his friends thinking they were so much more interesting than anyone else. He felt embarrassed for them, and also strangely old.

The taller boy saw Faruq looking and stopped his performance long enough to stand straight and hold up a hand. "Salami leakum, brother," he said.

Faruq stiffened. His breath came as though through a straw. A psychologist he'd stopped seeing years ago had called this trauma.

It came from those post-9/11 years, when the notice of strangers was dangerous, especially in New York.

"Leave that A-rab nigga alone," the other kid laughed.

Faruq's shoulders relaxed with tingling relief. He rolled his eyes; his parents had been from Pakistan.

He ignored the boys until they got off at Jay Street–MetroTech. Their kind of ignorance annoyed him but didn't frighten him. It was the other kind—the kind that entered with the finance folks around Fulton Street with their concerned white faces watching him out the sides of their eyes while they spoke to each other, their eyes checking him every few minutes from behind their self-help books, the way they scanned his beard, his coat, his pockets. If they saw something they'd certainly say something. They'd say something even if they saw nothing.

Faruq got out at Thirty-Fourth Street and walked to his office. He nodded in greeting to Gary, the intern, who was holding Anita's macchiato.

"Zaidi," Anita called from her office, "that you? Get in here." He took the macchiato from Gary and walked into Anita's office, where she was seated behind her massive, cluttered desk. Anita looked up at him behind her bright pink glasses, and he handed her her coffee.

Faruq first met Anita when he was at Columbia's Graduate School of Journalism. He had been her TA. She was quirky and personable, and she and Faruq bonded over being first-generation Americans—she had immigrated from Ecuador. They often went to dinner together in Washington Heights after lectures; Faruq met her husband, Dave, who was nice enough, but who Faruq suspected of exoticism.

In the early aughts, Anita resurrected a dying magazine by bringing it into the twenty-first century, offering a print edition that focused on the arts, fiction, and poetry, and a digital edition that featured longform articles and think pieces. By the time she and Faruq met, the magazine was one of the most respected publications for art and culture. When Faruq graduated, she gave him a job.

Over the past six years, Faruq helped to draw a larger millennial audience with pop culture critiques—Anita joked that he brought the "cool" back. And he'd written a few career-making pieces—an analysis of Black pop culture dynasties and stardom that went viral, the piece on failure and freedom, and his coverage of a police brutality case in Louisiana and its aftermath, which had won him a couple of awards.

Faruq was no longer a fumbling rookie journalist. Though, despite the nearly limitless creative freedom she gave him, Anita was still his boss, and though she'd never dropped the habit of calling him by his last name, she was one of his closest friends, included among Muezza, his cousin Danish, some high school buddies he still played basketball with, and a network of friends from college, which had shrunk over the years due to marriages, kids, and overdoses.

"Morning," he said.

"You excited? Ready to head west?"

In just a few more days, he would set out for his next longform piece. He was flying out to California to immerse himself in a community that called itself "the nameless," which had recently been propelled into the public eye thanks to a documentary about their clash with a small, fundamentalist Texas church.

"Almost."

"Almost?"

"I have a feeling I've got a few more hoops to jump through before they take me to their leader."

Anita laughed. "I'm kinda jealous you get to meet this Odo character. He's like a rock star at this point."

"A rock star with a cult."

Even getting to this point had been a bizarrely circuitous journey. He'd started, a few months ago, by reaching out to the New York chapter of the nameless movement. He'd introduced himself, the magazine he was from, told them about the piece he wanted to write about Odo and his followers. They'd invited him right away to the "house of the nameless" in Brooklyn, their flagship. Like all houses of the nameless, it was painted entirely white, the windows whitewashed as well, with only an empty square outlined in gold above the front door. There, he'd been treated like a long-lost and well-loved relative—they touched him when they greeted him, held his eyes with their own, said his name like it was a magic word. He'd been taken on a tour by a woman named Jenny, and afterward, she'd held both of his hands, her face full of saintly compassion. *I can see that you're hurting. We're waiting for you, when you're ready.*

It took six more visits before Faruq was granted permission to enter what some of the followers had begun calling the Forbidden City, where Odo had retreated into California's redwoods and where the center for the nameless was formed. It had greatly unsettled Faruq that he was never able to find former followers—all the members seemed not to have left. At least none that were willing to come forward. But now he was being granted the opportunity to see everything for himself.

"Now Zaidi," Anita said. "I want you to remember that this is also about giving you time. Please, try to rest also."

Faruq hadn't taken time off when his father died. The magazine had been in the middle of expanding its digital edition, and Faruq was in the middle of two stories he'd fought to get ahold of. He'd thought it best to power his way through his complicated grief. But eight months later, Faruq, for the first time in his life, began to burn out. When he'd first pitched the nameless piece to Anita, she had suggested he take it as a kind of working vacation. She knew he'd never fully stop; he could at least slow down. She was prepared to give him six weeks.

"Yeah, yeah," he said. "You read over my brown role models piece yet?"

"I did. Awful, just awful. You'll have to rewrite the whole thing."

Faruq laughed, flicking Anita off as he walked out of her office and to his desk. It was largely bare except for a thinning notepad, a coffee can full of pens, paper clips, magnets, and other miscellany, and a sketch of Muezza from Danish. He took a moment to open Instagram for what had become a daily ritual. He opened the nameless's Instagram page, scrolled through their carefully curated, colorful feed. There was a new post: a photo of a bunch of followers laughing and holding hands, all of them wearing cerulean blue. Faruq pulled his laptop from its bag and set it on the desk, opened it. He leaned back in his chair for a moment, looking up toward the industrial ceiling. Rest. A nice thing if you could afford it. He looked down at the glowing screen, the bright white portal, an escape.

Danish came bearing his mother's haleem. "She's still pissed at you," Danish told him. "She said, 'I *should* let that rude boy starve.'" Faruq shrugged, though he was amused. He recognized his aunt's version of an apology. They sat at the old dining table, its olive-green formica faded and stained in spots. Faruq had always loved his aunt's cooking—the stew was warming, comforting, the lentils well seasoned and the meat tender. Muezza nuzzled Danish's leg, hoping he would share his food. When it became clear he would not, Muezza stalked off balefully, tail held high.

"I ought to just take the cat to my place," Danish said with his mouth full. "Even with me stopping by every day, won't he be lonely with you gone so long?"

"He's a cat," said Faruq. "He'll be overjoyed."

"Hm."

"If you're so worried, you can just stay here while I'm gone."

"Nah, man. This place gives me the creeps. I don't know how you live here. Why don't you get your own place?"

"I have a brownstone in Brooklyn. I'm not going anywhere." But Faruq knew what Danish meant. The brownstone was still sodden with his father's presence. The ghosts of resentment, disappointment, stifling devoutness. His mother. But what could he do? He'd never afford another place like it, not in the city. He was stuck here, with all his memories.

"Then at least redecorate. Get rid of some of Uncle's things."

"Why is this family's response to death to act like the person never existed?"

Danish went quiet for a moment. "We're not trying to act like Uncle never existed. We all miss him. You know that, Faruq."

"I was talking about my mother."

Danish put down his spoon and ran a hand across his brow like he'd suddenly broken into a sweat. "It's—it's hard to talk about. But no one's forgotten her."

Faruq continued eating with no further comment.

"Well," said Danish after a while. "You don't have to get rid of anything, then. But does it have to be a shrine? It's maudlin, man."

"'Maudlin'? Now there's an SAT word."

"Fuck you," Danish laughed.

They finished their dinner and Muezza hopped into the sink to lick their dishes as Danish gathered his things. Danish clapped Faruq on the back as they walked to the door and stepped out onto the stoop, but then paused, turned to look at his cousin.

"Take it easy out there, right?"

"It's basically a big commune in the redwoods." Faruq smiled, hoped it was reassuring. "This is gonna be a vacation." He borrowed Anita's phrase. "A working vacation."

Danish raised an eyebrow. "You know everyone's gonna have questions, man. And if they find out you're out there with that cult . . ." Danish let out a dramatic breath.

Danish often acted as the gatekeeper between Faruq and an intrusive pack of aunties from his father's side.

"It's not like I haven't been on long assignments before. Just tell them I'm in California."

"California?" Danish said, mocking his own mother's voice. "What's he doing out there? Tell him to come home and visit."

Faruq laughed. "Keep it vague. They know my job."

Danish shook his head. "Well. Allah ki Rehmat rahe tumhare saath."

Faruq rolled his eyes.

"Oh, just take it," Danish said. "Heathen."

When Faruq closed the door, he was once again alone with Muezza. And all the ghosts.

. . .

Quiver, whose name used to be Annie Frankel, had met Faruq in a café in Crown Heights two weeks before he'd received an invite to California. He had found her by going down a rabbit hole of TikTok posts about the nameless. She was herself a follower, who came from old Upper East Side money, and he wanted to know what would make a New York heiress leave her comfortable life and give her trust fund away to a Vietnam War vet with a penchant for coming up with catchy phrases that sounded like wisdom.

He'd recognized Quiver as soon as he walked into the café, not because of the photos he'd found of her—all of the photos online were from her old life, and she looked quite different now—but because she was dressed in flowing cerulean blue, and the shaved half of her head contained a tattoo of an empty square. She turned as he approached her, and she was, as he'd found most of the followers he'd encountered so far, very attractive. Wide brown eyes offset by glowingly pale skin, and the cascade of brown hair that fell down her left shoulder was a glossy chestnut.

"I ordered you a drink," she said as he sat down. "I hope you don't mind. I'm good at guessing people's coffee order."

He looked down at his mug. It looked like an Americano. Way off. He took a sip anyway and tried not to cringe. "Do you mind if I record our conversation?" he asked, taking out his phone.

"Not at all," said Quiver. "I'm so curious what you want to talk to me about."

Faruq began to record. "I'm curious about you and your experience with the nameless. What attracted you to this—movement? organization? religion?"

Quiver laughed warmly. "It's not a religion."

"But how can it not be? It has a theology. You have a god."

"Faruq, when you go to a yoga class, you do poses named after gods—hanumanasana after Hanuman, natarajasana after Shiva. But yoga is not a religion."

"Then is the nameless a practice, then? Like yoga is a practice?"

She thought about this for a moment, and then her smile widened. "Yeah, I dig that. A practice."

"All right then, what drew you to this practice?"

Quiver took a delicate sip of her tea. "The philanthropy. The nameless has a philosophy of giving that I really vibed with. And once I started getting involved that way, the rest of this beautiful *practice* began singing to me too."

"Forgive me," Faruq said, charitably taking another sip from his mug, "but your great-grandfather founded one of the foremost banks on the East Coast. Why would you need to be a follower of the nameless to get into philanthropy?"

Quiver nodded like a doctor nods at a patient describing banal symptoms. "I come from a family with a lot of money. People with money think philanthropy is just throwing money around. But I wanted to get involved. I wanted my giving to mean more than bragging rights and a tax write-off."

"And how did the nameless provide that for you?" Faruq asked. There was a stringy redheaded teenager seated at a table behind Quiver. Faruq found his presence odd. He couldn't remember the last time he'd seen a teenager hanging out in a café alone.

"Sacrifice. It's one of the 18 Utterances. You can't just give, you have to give something of yourself too."

"What are the 18 Utterances?"

"They're the series of commands Odo received when he got hipped in Vietnam."

"'Hipped'?"

"To get hipped is to be awakened. Everyone gets hipped when they join the nameless. Usually Odo hips you, in person or otherwise."

"How does he do it if not in person?"

Quiver laughed. "Faruq, we don't live in an analog world."

"So, what, he's converting people over Zoom?"

"Hipping."

"Okay." Faruq took a breath. "What does hipping look like?"

Quiver smiled an enigmatic smile. "You have to be careful not to overwhelm people. You walk around with sunglasses on your whole life, and then you rip them off . . . you'd go blind. So we start slow. We start by asking questions."

"What kind of questions?"

"We start by simply asking people what it is they want. What they think they're missing. Usually they'll say some variation of love or money. Maybe both. It's what everyone wants." Small laugh. "And then we start asking them what's *underneath* that want. *Why*, for an example, do they want to be loved? *How* do they want to be loved? And, most importantly, *what* or *who* is stopping them from receiving that love?"

"And what's the most common answer? What's stopping people?"

Another small laugh. "Well, Faruq, people always have a lot of answers for that—their parents fucked them up, they're too busy, dating culture sucks, blah blah blah. But there's only one true answer."

"Distortion?"

"Distortion. And once someone realizes that, they're ready to hear about Vutu and the World."

"How long does it take for them to understand distortion?"

"Sometimes days. Sometimes months. As long as it needs to take."

"And who 'hipped' Odo?"

"Vutu Theyself."

Across the café, the ginger-haired kid was eating a muffin by tearing off tiny pieces at a time and crumbling them into his mouth. Faruq felt Quiver's resistance. He needed to get around it, but gently. "All right, so sacrifice is written into these 18 Utterances, which came directly from your god. Is that why you gave away your trust fund to the nameless?"

Quiver shook her head. "That was no sacrifice. What do I need a trust fund for? That was a gift."

"To Odo or to the nameless?"

She laughed, shaking her head again. "Money like mine helps the nameless to grow. We can build villages with it. We can make beauty. Another of the Utterances, by the way."

"But did you have to give it away? Like, was it a condition of becoming a follower?"

"Nobody made me, Faruq. I wanted to."

"But did you make your check out to Vutu or to Odo?" He smiled to soften the question.

"That's not the important part, Faruq."

The teen briefly glanced up and met Faruq's eyes and held them before going back to his muffin. "I guess I just find it remarkable," Faruq said, "that everyone who joins the nameless seems to end up giving away their worldly goods. Thought it might be part of the philosophy."

"Not exactly," said Quiver. "It's just that we're a community that believes in holding each other up. We work as a collective to clear the world's eyes of distortion. Fear, hate, greed, war—that's all distortion. When you belong to a community like that, you don't need to hoard. You share because it's what you believe in."

"So you're like communists?" he joked.

Quiver shrugged. "More like socialists, but we're not a government, Faruq."

"I know," he said. Quiver's tone hadn't been reproachful, but he still felt a bit chastened. "What does that symbol mean?" he asked her, gesturing to her head. "I saw it on the house of the nameless too."

She nodded. "They all have it. Above the front door. It's like an empty text-box, a blank space where a word for the nameless would go, if any word were sufficient."

"I see. Kinda like a placeholder for language." The ginger teen met his eyes again. "Hey, do you know that kid?" Faruq asked, nodding in the teen's direction.

Quiver glanced over her shoulder. When she faced Faruq again, she was smirking. "You're not feeling paranoid, are you?"

He laughed and shook his head, but noted that she didn't say no.

"What is it you're looking for, Faruq?" she asked. She was looking directly into his eyes.

"I want to know more about the nameless. I want to understand why its followers love Odo so much they'd devote themselves to him, to building him an entire city."

"If you met him, you'd understand."

"I hope to meet him."

"Oh, I'm sure he'd love to talk to you. He'd like you. I like you."

The ginger teen got up from his table and stalked, gangly, toward the door. His eyes met Faruq's one more time before he left. Most of his muffin was still on the plate.

"And do you think I would like Odo?" he asked Quiver.

She lifted her chin a bit, as though she were appraising Faruq. "You're gonna love him."

JFK was never calm. Faruq had staked out a seat in a corner near his gate, all his belongings for the next six weeks stuffed into a duffel bag. His computer was on his lap as he reviewed what material he had so far. He knew what the documentary, *Nero*, had covered regarding the origins of the nameless, but his own research had taught him that they were basically a monotheistic religion that refused to refer to itself as a religion. They followed a god they called "Vutu," and they were known for their (sometimes controversial) activism and occasionally parading through the streets naked.

What disturbed Faruq was that, through some extensive digging, he had found that they had a network of very wealthy and very powerful donors. Several art collectors, celebrities, and tech millionaires, a former governor from Vermont, two senators, and a few relatives of former presidents—probably how they were able to build an entire city, Faruq assumed.

And then there was Odo. A charismatic leader if ever there was one. From what Faruq could gather from his research, Odo had a way of speaking to exactly what each individual follower needed, of finding the holes in people and filling them with himself and his philosophy. Odo had retreated out into the redwoods a couple years ago, refusing for a while to speak, and his followers had built up a city around him. Faruq was meeting two followers who lived in San Francisco. He hoped they'd take him to that city, to Odo.

He glanced up from his laptop's screen. He could swear that, ever since he'd gotten to the airport, people had been staring at him, watching him when they thought he wasn't looking. Absently, he fiddled with the silk scarf he'd stuffed into his pocket last minute. He didn't know why he'd brought it. He took it out and lifted it to his nose. It didn't smell like his mother, only aged fabric. He tucked it away again, looked back down at his screen. In his notes, he kept capitalizing "Nameless," treating it like a proper noun. But that wasn't really what they wanted. In their own documents, they never capitalized the *n*. They were called the nameless because they refused to label themselves as an organization, a movement. A cult.

Faruq looked up again. At another gate across from his, a woman sat in a row of chairs by the windows. She was pretty— petite with thick, dark hair, fresh-faced. She was facing Faruq, watching. As his eyes met hers, she smiled. Faruq didn't typically have trouble meeting women—he was tall, athletic, and his job demanded that he be good at socializing. But this seemed oddly bold—he met women at parties, at bookstores, through friends, even once on the subway. Rarely did he receive this kind of unapologetic attention.

A garbled announcement blared, breaking his focus on the woman, the voice indecipherable over the crackling speakers, more than likely announcing boarding for a flight, though not his. When he looked again, the woman had pulled out a book and was reading. She never glanced up again. At least not that Faruq saw. He closed his laptop and put in his earphones. He listened to nothing, watched everyone. Maybe he was being paranoid. But if not, if they wanted to look at him, he'd look back.

Instagram Post # 378

@thenamelessmvmnt: A portrait in dramatic monochrome; Odo with a cap on, his eyes shadowed darkly by its brim, a bright white mug contrasting starkly against his large, dark hands. The steam billows white and voluminous, reaching up to writhe against Odo's mouth.

#shadowandlight #haveteawithme #Odo

18,061 likes | 109 comments

Nero

INT. GEORGETOWN OFFICE—CLOSEUP—FATHER SCHUYLER'S HANDS

Father Schuyler's hands fidget in his lap.

                                        FADE TO BLACK.

BLACK SCREEN

TITLE: "NERO"

                                             FADE IN:

INT. GEORGETOWN OFFICE—MED. SHOT—FATHER SCHUYLER

Father Schuyler is sitting in front of a heavy desk
that is cluttered with stacks of books and papers.
SUPER: "Father Schuyler, SJ, PhD"

              FATHER SCHUYLER
        So, Nero: Nero Caesar was a Roman emperor;
        54 to 68 A.D. And he was actually the last
        emperor of the Julio-Claudian dynasty.

INSERT—IMAGE

Statue of Nero and Agrippina. ZOOM in to Nero's face.

              FATHER SCHUYLER
        He takes the throne at only 17, and for the
        first 5 years of his rule, despite rumors of
        ordering his 13-year-old stepbrother
        poisoned, he's actually seen as a pretty
        fair—even generous—ruler.*

                                        DISSOLVE TO:

Nero at Baiae, by Jan Styka. SLOW ZOOM.

              FATHER SCHUYLER
        But that all changes in the year 59, when he
        has his mother, Agrippina, killed. He starts
        spending huge sums of money on self-
        indulgence, starts staging public

_____
* Music: faint, Piano Sonata in B Minor, S. 178 (Liszt)

performances as a poet and lyre player,
which was seen as incredibly taboo for
someone of his class.

DISSOLVE TO:

Bust of Nero at the Capitoline Museum, Rome. SLOW ZOOM.

FATHER SCHUYLER
And he starts executing rivals, anyone who
criticizes or questions him. In 64, you have
the Great Fire of Rome.

DISSOLVE TO:

The Fire of Rome, by Karl von Piloty.

FATHER SCHUYLER
Many believed that Nero started it to make
room for his villa, Domus Aurea.

DISSOLVE TO:

Fire in Rome, by Hubert Robert.

FATHER SCHUYLER
We don't know how many people died, but
something like 70% of Rome was just
destroyed.

At the time, Christianity is still a new
religion—Christians are a minority in Rome.

DISSOLVE TO:

Nero's Torches, by Henryk Siemiradzki.

FATHER SCHUYLER
Who better to blame for the Great Fire? So
Nero begins torturing and persecuting
Christians.

Meanwhile, Nero moves ahead with his plans
to build Domus Aurea.

DISSOLVE TO:

Nero Caesar, by Abraham Janssens van Nuyssen. SLOW ZOOM
on Nero's face.

           FATHER SCHUYLER
To finance it, he's selling positions in
public office, taking money from temples,
increasing taxes, seizing property, and,
ultimately, devaluing the currency.

                          DISSOLVE TO:
Bust of Roman Emperor Galba, Antiques Museum in the
Royal Palace, Stockholm.

           FATHER SCHUYLER
An assassination conspiracy in 65 leads to
the execution of a bunch of aristocrats. But
then, 3 years later, another group of
conspirators, including Servius Galba,
organize against him, and even Nero's own
bodyguards abandon him.

                          DISSOLVE TO:
The Remorse of the Emperor Nero after the Murder of his
Mother, by John William Waterhouse.

           FATHER SCHUYLER
When he gets word that the Senate has
condemned him to death, he commits suicide.

INT. CHRIST THE WORD EVANGELICAL CHURCH (CWE)—DAY (HOME
VIDEO)*
Will Roy delivers a sermon on Matthew 5:1-15
(Beatitudes, salt of the earth, righteousness, etc.)

Afterward, Will Roy greets and laughs with his
congregants.

                          FADE TO BLACK.

                          FADE IN:

INT. CWE NAVE—MED. SHOT—WILL ROY†
Will Roy is seated sideways on a chair at the front of
his church, the altar behind him.

_____

* Music: Gnossienne No. 3 (Satie)
† Silence.

SUPER: "Pastor Will Roy, Christ the Word Evangelical
(CWE), Texas"

                    WILL ROY
'And the beast was given a mouth to utter
proud words and blasphemies. It opened its
mouth to blaspheme God. It was given power
to wage war against God's holy people.'
That's John's Revelation.

Nero persecuted the Christians. He fed them
to dogs, crucified them, used them as torches
to light the streets of Rome.

CLOSEUP—WILL ROY'S FACE

                    WILL ROY
His name is the number of the beast.

                                   DISSOLVE TO:

INT. GEORGETOWN OFFICE—MED. SHOT—FATHER SCHUYLER

                    FATHER SCHUYLER
Arabic numerals weren't introduced to the
West until about the 12th century. That's
why in Latin, letters themselves have
numerical value.

So if you translate 'Nero Caesar' into Greek,

                                   BLACK SCREEN:
SUPER: "Neron Kaisar"

                    FATHER SCHUYLER
and then translate that into Hebrew,

                                   BLACK SCREEN:
SUPER: "nrwn qsr"

                    FATHER SCHUYLER
and then add up the numerical value of each
letter, keeping in mind, of course, that
Hebrew is read from right to left,

BLACK SCREEN:

SUPER: "rsq nwrn"

SUPER: "100 + 60 + 200 + 50 + 200 + 6 + 50"

FATHER SCHUYLER
you get the number of the beast, 666.

BLACK SCREEN:

SUPER: "666." SLOW ZOOM.

DISSOLVE TO:
The Remorse of the Emperor Nero after the Murder of his
Mother, by John William Waterhouse. SLOW ZOOM on Nero's
face.*

WILL ROY
When Nero committed suicide, a lot of people
believed he would come back. And three
imposters appeared, claiming to be Nero
resurrected. They were all of them proved
false. But that doesn't mean the
resurrection wasn't coming. As far as I'm
concerned, 'Nero' means 'Antichrist.'

FADE TO BLACK.†

MINH-AN
(laughter)

FADE IN:

INT. GREENHOUSE—MED. SHOT—MINH-AN

Minh-An is seated on a stool, surrounded by greenery.
SUPER: "Minh-An, Follower of the Nameless"

MINH-AN
Well, 'Nero' has many meanings. It comes
from an Old Latin word that means 'man.' It
means 'genius' in Finnish. In the ancient
Sabine language, it meant something like

---

* Music: faint, Piano Sonata in B Minor, S. 178 (Liszt)
† Silence.

'brave.' It means 'water' in Greek, 'to
sleep' in Japanese.

CLOSEUP—MINH-AN'S FACE
Minh-An raises an eyebrow.

                    MINH-AN
        In Italian, it means 'black.'

                                          CUT TO:

INT. CWE NAVE—MED. SHOT—WILL ROY

                    PRODUCER (O.S.)
        So, do you think that Odo, the leader of the
        nameless, is a resurrection of Nero Caesar?

Will Roy nods.

                    WILL ROY
        I believe that Nero was the antichrist, and
        Odo is the antichrist returned.

INT. HOUSE OF THE NAMELESS, BROOKLYN—DAY (HOME VIDEO)*

Odo, in a red beanie and black sweater, holds the hands
of one of his followers. He is looking into her eyes
and speaking, smiling. She is smiling as well, and
crying.
CLOSEUP of their clasped hands, his elegant and brown,
long-fingered like a trumpet player's; hers pale and
veined.

                                      DISSOLVE TO:
CLOSEUP—SOLDIERS IN THE VIETNAM WAR (HOME VIDEO)
Four Black soldiers are laughing together, flashing
straight, white teeth. One soldier's dark eyes are
focused on something outside of the shot, something to
the right of the camera.

                                      FADE TO BLACK.

_____
* Music: Gnossienne No. 4 (Satie)

before: 1969

UNDER THE CHOPPER'S BELLY, the beaten orange earth pulsed up, loose dirt and the carcasses of grass and dead weeds scampering out and away. Preach stood smoking, watching the thing land. The helicopter's wind sucked his cigarette smoke up and whipped it around like spun sugar.

They were told the chopper carried four replacements, one of them Black, what the brothers called a blood. This replacement watched the earth while Preach watched the sky, the knot in his drawers digging into his back. The blood and the others were there to replace men who were either dead or back home with their children, their wives, their mothers, their sisters, their girlfriends—though he was still green, the new blood already knew that it was the women you missed the most.

Having heard that the bird was coming, Silk and Crazy Horse joined Preach as he flicked aside the first cigarette and lit a second. The three of them stood silent, waiting; they could feel themselves creaking like ancient trees in the artificial wind. The bird was bringing not just the replacements, but also the things the soldiers needed—letters and food and malaria tablets and pep pills and morphine and *Playboy*s and the brand-new cassette recorder somebody had ordered and a few harmonicas and a new guitar for one of the bloods; the old one had been broken over somebody's head. This deed had gone unpunished, which irked some of the men who'd fought in wars before this one—but Vietnam was chaos, it seemed to them, anarchy. They were on their own out here.

As he hopped out of the chopper, the new blood half expected the ground to evaporate beneath his feet, for everything to have been an illusion all along, and really, he was spinning, weightless, through a black void. But when his feet hit the ground it held him, the burnt dust already clinging to his boots. He looked around the landing zone and saw the clusters of gathering men. He saw the three brothers, could tell by their eyes that it was a dead soldier he was replacing, not a discharged one.

Preach, Silk, and Crazy Horse kept their silence as they watched the new blood. Preach went to light a third cigarette, Silk swiped it from his fingers and lit it for himself. They were all thinking the same thing. That this new blood, stepping unsteadily from the bird like a newborn foal, was only a kid. That his mouth was still wet with his mama's milk. That they didn't want to see him die. They were far, far older than him, though the oldest among them—Silk—was not yet twenty, but time didn't simply move forward in this fragrant, blighted land, but rather hurtled in every direction at once.

The new blood stared at the three brothers as they stared at him. He was unsure, he didn't know what their stares meant. Didn't know whether it was a challenge or an invitation. He thought about waving, but then decided that was something a schoolboy would do on his first day of junior high. So he nodded, lifted his chin so slightly it was barely a movement at all. For a long time the brothers did nothing, and he began to think he really hadn't moved. But then one of them nodded back, and the other two warily followed.

The new blood turned to follow the other three replacements, and Preach, Silk, and Crazy Horse watched him walk off, the three of them swaying in the dirt-laden wind.

None of the brothers talked to him—not the three he first saw or any of the others—until his second day at the camp, when one of the brothers approached him, a joint in one hand and the other extended. Hey brother, where you from? he'd said. The new blood had taken the offered hand, shook it. Chicago, he told him. But he'd gotten something wrong. The brother tilted his head, the joint dangling from a corner of his mouth, looked at him like he was strange and audacious and walked away without saying anything. Now the new blood was on his third day and none of them had spoken to him since.

He could feel them watching him now, sly-eyed, as he stood in line, waiting to be served a sloppy ladleful of chow, which he would eat while trying to remember the taste of his mother's cooking; her sugared grits, her johnnycakes, her stewed peas, her biscuits with sour cream. The chow was hot, and when it was ladled into his canteen cup some of it glopped out and onto his hand, onto the base of his thumb, where it burned in the relentless sun. He made no move to wipe it off. It would toughen him, he thought.

As the line shuffled forward, with the sun burning, the new blood stumbled into the soldier in front of him, a large white man, the back of his neck marbled in reds and yellows. The large soldier spun around, almost eager.

Watch it, nigger.

He put down the canteen cup, the little metal plate that held his slice of white bread, took off his soft cap and licked the hot chow off his hand. The big white soldier looked on with a funny smile, like he was admiring a woman undress before inviting him to bed.

The staff sergeant made his way over in four leisurely steps, snatched the new blood back by the elbow before he could throw his first punch.

Eager to see that guardhouse already? Cool it, Kentucky. Go on, now.

The big white soldier growled, stalked off. The new blood didn't struggle in the sergeant's grip, not even when he tightened it, but the sergeant could feel the heat of anger where his palm pressed against the kid's sharp elbow.

Where you from, boy?

Chicago. And I sure wouldn't be here if I was a "boy." Sir.

The staff sergeant laughed, but tightened his grip even more.

Listen. This is as much trouble as I want from you until the gooks get you, hear? And I haven't decided yet whether I'm going to rip this arm off, but you got the other one free to salute me with proper.

Yessir.

The new blood waited as long as he dared before lifting his free hand up into a salute.

Good. And you're in Vietnam, not some soul brother club. Cut your bush. That's a fuckin order.

Silk, who had been watching this exchange with a bemused smirk, saw that the new blood was about to answer with something other than "Yes sir," and so he came up alongside the new blood, propped his elbow up on the kid's shoulder like they were easy old friends.

Hardly that, sir.

Hardly what?

A soul brother, sir.

Silk roughed the top of the new blood's head, which he knew would irritate him a little. Better the kid get irritated with another brother than with his staff sergeant.

I'll cut his bush, sir.

The staff sergeant shook his head.

Finney's the barber.

Naw. You know I can't let Finney cut a brother's hair.

The staff sergeant rolled his eyes, but the new blood thought he could see something soften somewhere around the man's shoulders. He let go of the kid's elbow.

Fine. But do it now. And I mean *right* now, soldier.

Yes sir.

Yessir.

As the sergeant walked off, Silk turned to face the new blood, looked him up and down, less to see him and more to make a point.

Don't you know you here to fight the *Vietnamese*, cherry?

That's what I came here for. Not any of that.

The new blood gestured toward the white soldier's back. Silk grimaced.

You one of them Panthers or something? Let the brothers at home fight *that* war, and we'll do whatever we doing over here. Let's go.

The new blood began to follow, relieved at the brother's peculiar brand of warmth, but Silk stopped him, shaking his head.

Get your shit outta the dirt, man.

As the new blood bent over to collect his food and his cap, Silk shook his head again, mumbled to himself.

Cherries.

Silk led the new blood over to where Preach and Crazy Horse were sitting, introduced him and them. Crazy Horse grinned at Silk in a way that made the new blood think they were making fun of him.

Word is you're from Chicago.

Yes, that's right.

Crazy Horse chuckled.

Relax, brother. You talk like you educated.

The new blood puffed up a bit, nearly preened like a cat.

I've got a semester at the University of Chicago.

Preach nodded approvingly, an unlit cigarette held between two fingers.

My, my, my.

Silk raised an eyebrow.

Just the one semester? What happened? Draft interrupt you?

The new blood was less puffed up now. He lowered his eyes, fingered the spot where the chow had burned. It was still red.

Ran out of money. Figured I'd volunteer, go back home, and finish on the G.I. Bill. Figured it was the only thing I could do.

The other three men nodded solemnly. They could see it now, the scars of poverty just beneath the skin. Silk held the clippers in his hand, scanning the new blood's head with one eye closed, making a mental blueprint for shaping the kid's hair.

We ought to call you Bigger.

Crazy Horse squinted balefully up at the glaring sun.

Bigger?

Yeah, man. Bigger. You read *Native Son*? That Wright cat?

Preach lit his cigarette, took a long pull, his eyes half closed.

Ain't that a book about Chicago?

The new blood, feeling like a child with Silk standing over him and the three of them discussing what to call him, shifted a bit, coughed.

It's about a bit more than just Chicago.

They ignored him. Silk held the clippers up high.

Bigger Thomas. That's the kid's name in the book. Bigger. Because you come from Chicago.

The new blood tried again.

Things didn't turn out too well for Bigger Thomas, in the end.

Preach blew a stream of smoke up.

Ain't no omens. The spirit God gave you does not make us timid.

Bigger watched the other two nod.

Well I can see why you're called Preach. But why Silk? Why Crazy Horse?

Silk leaned down toward the kid, smirked.

I think you just saw why they call me Silk. That white boy, Finney, would've mangled you. And as for Crazy Horse—well, you'll see once we're out in the field.

Nearby, Bullwhip, a reed-thin Indian from South Dakota, rolled his eyes at the bloods. Crazy Horse didn't have a lick of Indian in him, and he for sure didn't know a damned thing about Tȟašúŋke Witkó.

I'm still waiting to see why them call him that myself.

Crazy Horse grinned goofily.

What you want them to call me, Squanto? Jim Crow?

Bullwhip laughed and lifted his middle finger in Crazy Horse's direction. Crazy Horse leaned toward Bigger but spoke loud enough for Bullwhip to hear.

Imagine that—got a nigger named after an Indian, and an Indian named after a whip.

Truth was, Crazy Horse had been nicknamed when he too was a cherry, by another Indian soldier called Howler (a name given to him after his reaction to his first kill), when he'd caught a trembling Crazy Horse crumbling tobacco between his fingers the night before his first mission.

What you wasting good tobacco for? Howler had asked.

They're sending us out there to fuckin die, Crazy Horse had said, and Howler, kindhearted enough to mistake Crazy Horse's rage for fear, had told him, Not you. Nah. You got something in you. They give you a name yet? I'll call you Crazy Horse.

Nearby, Bullwhip had scoffed. Does he look like *Crazy Horse* to you?

Howler had smiled. It's not about the outside.

Bullwhip smirked. Right. I'm sure you got Indian in you, huh, kid? You all do. Lemme guess: Cherokee? A grandmother?

Crazy Horse ignored Bullwhip. Howler told him, *You're a warrior*. Crazy Horse believed him. Two days later he watched Howler be thrown to the ground by enemy fire. They hadn't even reached the jungle yet.

Silk switched the clippers on and began on Bigger's hair. Preach started on another cigarette, and Crazy Horse watched as black clumps of Bigger's hair fell, thick as flesh, and then were carried away by a wind he didn't feel.

The woman they called Mama-san was in fact only twenty-eight, but she looked far older. She watched the American soldiers warily from the door of the photo shop. They had a way of walking, like they were trying to make the earth move, like it was theirs to command. It was a kind of surety she couldn't trust. They claimed to be the good guys, but it was Americans who'd burned her village, leaving her with nothing but her body, and a scrap of a soul.

She'd met an American soldier once, a long time ago now, who, with so much kindness in his eyes, had asked her why a nice girl like her would sell herself. She'd pretended not to understand, because she knew he wouldn't. Because of them she'd sold herself; and because of them, because of this fake town, which they'd built up within the perimeters of their camp, which opened at eight and closed at seven, she could process their photos for money instead, watch in the darkroom as her own country came into focus through foreigners' eyes.

She thought of her three brothers, two dead and one probably not alive, wondered how we can ever forgive ourselves, because it's not only that you forget the small things you'd thought unforgettable, but also that you remember the minutiae you'd thought entirely unremarkable. What was she already missing, right now, as she developed the memories of these American soldiers?

Two soldiers approached, their faces bright pink, their eyes covered with sunglasses. Sometimes, if she squinted hard enough, she could see them as one of those plants you find deep in the jungle, something the highlanders might dip the tips of their arrows in.

How I help you?

One of them tossed her a roll of film, asked how long it would take her to process it.

You come back tomorrow.

The other soldier leaned in close to her, so that she could smell the menthol on his breath, and, faintly, the sickly-sweet perfume of opium.

I see some of the boys come in here sometimes. You take em to the back. Whaddaya got back there, huh?

She pretended not to understand.

To-mor-row. Twenty-four hour. Ok yes thankyousomuch.

They shrugged their shoulders and turned to go. She took the film inside, labeled it carefully, put it on the shelf with the other rolls waiting to be developed. In her darkroom, put up haphazardly with scavenged plywood, the cracks stuffed with rags to keep the light out, the soldiers' pictures hung. In the dark, the pictures emerged from mottled grayness—soldiers grinning, their arms slung around each other; sepia shots of the camp itself, jagged green mountains in the distance; smiling Vietnamese girls in shining, fringed shirts and go-go boots; a dead tiger, shot somewhere out in the field; a trio of children, staring with haunted eyes; an officer, grinning, lunging toward a small and shriveled mama-san, who appeared to be either laughing or screaming; rows of dead Vietnamese men—boys—some of their faces seeming to hold the hint of a smile.

She heard someone step into the shop.

Hey there, Mama-san. You here?

That you, brotherman?

She walked out to find Silk and Crazy Horse and a new Black soldier she'd never seen before. There was something about this one that reminded her of Thien, her youngest brother, who had died shortly after the Viet Cong forced him into their black pajamas. That's what she liked about the brothermans—they almost looked like they belonged here.

Silk and Crazy Horse clasped their hands in front of their chests and bowed. She bowed back.

Who's your friend?

This here is Bigger. Just a little cherry.

Bigger had seen some Vietnamese men and women around the camp—interpreters, some of them servants for the NCOs. He'd even seen some of the brothers dapping the Vietnamese men— a complicated handshake consisting of slaps and claps and fists and twitching thumbs that Silk had taught him. *You don't just shake a brother's hand here, man.* But until now, Bigger hadn't spoken to a local, and he found he wasn't sure what to say. Mama-san shocked him by dapping him. He stared at their hands as they performed the complex series of movements. It was almost as if he had nothing at all to do with it, as if his own hand weren't involved. Mama-san grinned, and he saw that several of her teeth were black.

You boys hungry?

Crazy Horse slipped a couple packs of Kools into her hands, which she'd sell later on the black market—it was this that brought her the real money, rather than the soldiers' photos. Silk rubbed his dry hands together.

What you got?

Mama-san waved at them to follow her and led them to the

back, to the little tin room with the cooler, the hot plate, the mismatched chairs that you had to settle your weight into carefully because they were all broken.

I got some chicken. I'm gonna fry it up for you like your mama at home. Some other brotherman brought me some cornmeal, so I made some cornbread. It's there. Eat, eat.

She waved to an inverted nón lá in the corner, covered with a white shirt. Underneath the shirt was the cornbread. The men took some and ate while Mama-san pulled seasoned and floured chicken out of the cooler, heated oil in a wok on the hot plate. The cornbread didn't taste quite right, but it never really could have—to Bigger it was too sweet, to Silk too dry. To Crazy Horse it had a strange complexity of flavor, something that reminded him of what this war had snatched him from. It angered him, made him hungry for more. Mama-san threw the first pieces of chicken into the oil, and the sound of the sizzling bounced off the metal walls.

How's that cornbread?

Silk gave her a thumbs-up.

Tastes just like home.

Crazy Horse took another piece.

Where are the girls at, Mama-san?

She sucked her aching teeth.

What do you need to buy a girl for, eh? Don't you boys have girlfriends?

Crazy Horse pulled a sweating beer out of the cooler.

How can we have girlfriends if we over here? We need a nice Cambodian girl for the cherry over here.

Silk leaned in toward Bigger.

They make sure the girls in here are clean. Only downside is you got to do your business by seven.

Mama-san laughed, poking at a chicken leg with a chopstick.

No Cambodians here, brotherman. You have to go to Saigon for that.

They sweated as they ate the cornbread and the chicken straight from the wok in the hot room, carefully balanced on the groaning chairs, wiping the grease from their fingers on the knees of their pants.

Just like home.

Just like home.

today

AS FARUQ FLOATED up into consciousness, he could feel the dream clinging to him like cobwebs. Or like arms, reluctant to let him go, straining either to be brought up with him or to pull him down. The dream itself was already an indiscernible ghost to him. Something about his mother, about his father, all of it strangely noiseless, like the moments immediately after a great and terrible shock.

Upon waking, Faruq did not recognize his surroundings right away. This was not the cluttered and groaning Brooklyn apartment he shared with an old cat and, until a year ago, his father. Several mildly panicked moments passed before he remembered that he was on the other side of the country, in the very white guestroom of a neurotically modern mansion outside of San Francisco. The broad, bare window displayed a pastel pink sky, redwood-spiked hills, the glittering sliver of the Pacific.

Out of habit, he reached over and grabbed his phone. Nothing new on the nameless Instagram account, but someone had posted a TikTok video of a pair of slender women harvesting vegetables from a lush garden Faruq presumed was in the Forbidden City. The video had over thirty thousand likes, and even Faruq had to admit there was something soothing about watching their basket fill with bounty. He dressed, crept downstairs, hoping to sneak out for an early morning run, but Clover, one half of the couple hosting him, was already up and seated in the living room. She had her veined hands wrapped around a mug that was sending tendrils of steam up into her face and looked straight ahead, alert, like she was waiting for him. Clover was a middle-aged brunette, beautiful, as all followers of the nameless were.

"Morning," she said. "Did you sleep okay?" Clover smiled brightly, inclined her head. She was perched on the white linen sofa, her feet tucked underneath her, and she was wearing a kind of Asian-style pajama set, elaborately embroidered and undoubtedly handmade.

"Good morning," said Faruq. "I did, thank you. And thanks again for all your hospitality."

Faruq had been staying with Clover and Aeschylus for two days now, and he had the sense that they were constantly trying to manage his perception of them. It was just after six in the morning, and Clover's face was already made up, her hair carefully arranged, a book—Thoreau's *Walden*—set open on the coffee table, as though hastily set aside upon his coming down the stairs, though her fingers were pink from the hot mug.

"Well, I'm glad you're well rested. Aeschylus and I have a big day planned for you, Faruq."

He joined her on the couch. He would not be going for his run, had not been able to since he'd arrived. In addition to the deliberate way in which they presented themselves, Clover and Aeschylus had a knack for not letting him out of their sight, while making it seem as though their watchfulness was a kind of loving, even parental, attentiveness, instead of what Faruq knew it was: suspicion.

"Do you?" he said. "Are we headed up to the redwoods today, then?"

Clover only smiled again.

"Come on," said Faruq. "Why all the mystery?"

Clover's smile didn't budge. "Strip down, Faruq."

Nameless jargon. He'd heard this and phrases like it dozens of times over the past several months, and he was convinced they meant nothing. Little verbal green screens onto which you could project anything you wanted, anything that suited you. The truth, Faruq suspected, was that they were assessing him, trying to determine whether he was worthy of meeting Odo.

Clover and Aeschylus had reached out to him on their own, while he was still searching for answers in New York. One night, his phone had rung at eleven o'clock, just as he was getting into bed. No one called him at that hour during the week unless it was an emergency, so he'd answered the phone with a dull sense of dread. *What more could happen?* he'd tried to reason with himself. Both of his parents were already dead. When he answered, he didn't recognize the man's voice on the other end of the line.

"My name is Aeschylus," the man had said. "I'd like to extend an invitation to you."

"Aeschylus," Faruq said dubiously.

"Yes." The man sounded like he was smiling. "We'd like you to come to California."

"'We'? Are you with the nameless?" Faruq asked, sitting up straighter.

"That's right."

"Okay. I'm sorry—how did you get my number again? It's late. Who, exactly, is *'we'*?"

Aeschylus laughed. "Apologies, Faruq. It isn't late here—I'm in San Francisco. There are no secrets among the nameless. We've heard of your . . . curiosity from other followers. My partner, Clover, and I would like to invite you to our home and then we can take you to the heart of the auspicious redwoods."

"The redwoods? You mean to the Forbidden City?"

"Yes, Faruq."

"Odo would talk to me?"

Another laugh. "He's not a recluse."

"Okay, but did Odo himself say he'd speak with me?"

"You've been asking questions. Odo will answer them. You're hesitating, Faruq. Why?"

"I guess this is just out of the blue. I'm catching up."

"That's a matter of perspective, Faruq. Come see me and Clover and we'll take you to the redwoods. Stay in the Forbidden City awhile. I think you'll find what you're looking for. Clover and I will buy your ticket."

"Oh no, I couldn't accept that. I'll pay my own way."

"As you like it, Faruq."

When they'd hung up, Faruq had been excited, if a little un-settled. This would either be the greatest piece of immersion jour-nalism of his career, or a suicide mission.

"All right," he said now as Clover picked up her copy of *Walden*. "Let me go change."

He made his way back upstairs into the guestroom and closed himself inside. He pulled his cell phone out and called Anita. It was after nine back in the City, and he knew she would be at her desk, on her second macchiato of the day.

"How goes it, Zaidi?" Anita's voice was always gentle, soft, but there was a kind of force behind it.

"To be honest, I'm not sure."

"What do you mean? Are you in the Forbidden City?"

"They haven't taken me yet. They're sizing me up."

Anita paused. "Didn't Odo already *agree* to let you come?"

"Strip down, Anita."

"What?"

Faruq laughed, holding the phone between his ear and shoul-der as he struggled into presentable clothes. "That's what they say when I ask questions they don't want to answer. I'm telling you, these people are . . . I don't even know what."

He froze when he thought he heard someone in the hall. He was keeping his voice down, but part of him wouldn't be sur-prised if the room was bugged.

"You need to earn their trust, Zaidi," said Anita. "Remind them that you're just there to write their story."

"Trust me, I'm trying."

He heard Anita set her espresso mug down on her desk. She hesitated, took an audible breath, and launched into the story about her husband, who, when he was a young, rising star of a photojournalist, had been sent on an assignment to capture the soft underbellies of LA gang members. How he'd had guns—*guns*—pulled on him at first, but then he managed to gain their trust, had even earned a nickname: El Rubito.

Faruq zoned out. He'd heard this story several times before, and he found it nauseatingly colonial, like Dave had discovered a "lost" tribe or something. And Faruq was not a blond-haired, blue-eyed white man entering into a culture so disenfranchised by people who looked like him that, with a kind of elated relief, they'd embrace him once he proved he wasn't there to take anything from them. Faruq was a brown ex-Muslim entering a world of beautiful people, many of them rich—and white—who were devoted to an enigmatic guru whose name, Clover had explained to him, meant nothing and everything at the same time.

"You know what's weird?" Faruq said, before Anita could get into the awards Dave had won for the LA gang photos. "No one's even mentioned the documentary."

"So what? You're not there about the documentary. That story's already been told." Faruq heard a knock on the door, and quickly got off the phone.

He straightened his shirt and opened the door to find Aeschylus, shoulder-length silver hair meticulously gelled, holding a steaming mug and smiling beatifically. "Coffee, Faruq?" Aeschylus called. Faruq wondered if he had been listening at the door. He took the mug, genuinely grateful—he doubted that it was a coincidence that they served their coffee in the Pakistani way: whipped, milky, and sweet, with cardamom and cinnamon. It was blatant pandering, but it was delicious.

"Clover's making scones," said Aeschylus. "We have a big day planned for you."

"I heard," Faruq said, following Aeschylus downstairs.

The early spring weather in San Francisco was cool, though it was warmer here than it was in New York. There, you could still find the odd patch of snow clinging to some sunless square of sidewalk. The warmth was a welcome change.

Clover and Aeschylus picked him up from the airport and went right into escorting Faruq around San Francisco—first to a house of the nameless, where they joined a group meditation and volunteered to clean the floors and wash the windows; then to a rare book dealer in the Mission, where Aeschylus coolly procured a slightly worn first edition of *Gray's Anatomy* for several thousand dollars; then to the Tenderloin, where they handed out twenty-dollar bills to the homeless, held their hands and asked their names, and, in the case of one relatively young homeless couple, invited them to the house of the nameless; and finally, to an art gallery featuring the work of a follower—intricate smears of bright, vertiginous color that Aeschylus explained were supposed to correspond to the later compositions of Shostakovich.

The artist's name was Joaquin, and he greeted Faruq with a complicated handshake. Usually these were reserved for intra-follower greetings, so Faruq was taken aback, but tried to follow Joaquin's lead. Joaquin's nails were painted a neon orange, and there was an empty square tattooed in white on his wrist.

"What do you think of the art?" Joaquin asked Faruq. He spoke with a heavy accent.

"Very complex. I like it. Were you inspired by Kandinsky?"

Joaquin smiled a broad smile, and shook a finger at Faruq. "This guy, he knows his art."

"Your accent—where are you from?" Faruq asked.

"Figueres," he said. "Like Dalí."

"What brought you to the United States?"

"Odo did," Joaquin said, closing his eyes for a moment as he said Odo's name.

"You came here for the nameless? How long ago was that?"

"Oh, eight years now, I think? I saw Odo's videos online. I watched him talk about art and the universe, and creating beauty. I wanted to learn more, so I came here. I had forty dollars in my pocket when I came to the U.S."

Faruq raised an eyebrow, interest piqued. It wasn't very often that he spoke to a follower who wasn't wealthy when they joined the nameless. "How did you survive?"

"I start by selling my work on the street. I spent all my money to go see Odo speak." He nodded toward Clover and Aeschylus, who were nearby pretending not to listen. "I met those two by chance, and they took me in for a while. That's when I really started to learn more about the nameless."

"You got hipped."

"Yes, Faruq. I got hipped. And you know what? My art got better." He swept out a hand, indicating the entire gallery. "Everything I have, I owe it to the nameless."

"And you've met Odo?"

"Oh yes," said Joaquin. "That is a beautiful man. He will like you, I think."

"What makes you say that?"

Joaquin laughed. "*I* like you. You are smart, and you know how to look. If you let him, Odo can help you *see*."

"Mmm," said Faruq. "I don't think I know what that means."

Joaquin threw an arm around Faruq's shoulders. "I mean this: This world is full of suffering, you agree? But what if all that suffering was just a kind of blindness? We call it a distortion. It's like a misunderstanding—there's something inside of us that got . . . bent out of shape. So when something beautiful is in front of us, we see something ugly. Odo makes that go away. Beauty is everywhere, that's the truth. That's what *seeing* is."

"And how does Odo make you see?"

Joaquin slapped Faruq on the back. "You get hipped," he said.

By the time the sun set, Aeschylus had lit the firepit in the backyard, and the area, which had been carved out at the edge of a steep, high hill that swept out into the ocean at the bottom, was illuminated by the fire's glow and dozens of solar-powered string lights. No one told Faruq there would be a party, but he figured it out when the guests began arriving at the house, greeting Clover and Aeschylus and each other with daps, which seemed to change slightly depending on whose hands were involved. The dapping was reserved for fellow followers of the nameless; they greeted

Faruq like he was the person they treasured most in the world, holding his hands for too long, touching his face. Everyone knew his name.

Someone brought a guitar, and Aeschylus and Clover and their guests were gathered around as the guitarist played a song that was made up of long, wordless notes and the occasional lyric— *One world distorts the other; The cycle is a beautiful shackle.* They all seemed to know it. Even Faruq had to admit that the song was vaguely beautiful. Haunting. His phone buzzed in his pocket. He took it out and looked at the screen. Danish. Calling at what was a very late hour in New York. He looked around him, searching for some quiet corner.

"Hello, Faruq."

This was a young, freckled blond woman. She had *Instagram influencer* written all over her, from the carefully arranged waves of sun-bleached hair to the floaty white dress she was wearing, embellished with little white flowers she'd braided together and woven around the dress's straps. The girl had introduced herself earlier, but Faruq couldn't remember her name—something archaic that didn't suit her. Esther. Or Effie. Florence? His phone stopped ringing.

Danish did not leave a voicemail. "It's Fannie," she said.

Faruq smiled sheepishly. "Sorry. I'm terrible with names."

"There's nothing to be sorry about."

She settled herself, cross-legged, on the ground next to his chair. Though he now had to look down at her, it had the feel of a parent—one who wasn't his—squatting on their haunches to talk to their kid.

"You seem thoughtful," said Fannie.

"Just observing."

Fannie smiled up at him. She shook her head. "No, I don't think so. To observe is to evaluate, to study with attention. You're watching, but your mind is somewhere else."

Faruq was still not used to how guileless these people were, how frank. "Sounds like *you've* been observing *me*," he said.

"Yes. We do not turn our eyes away, but toward."

"That's very poetic."

She shrugged, and again, Faruq noticed how young she was. She couldn't be much older than twenty.

"I am a poet," she said. "I think it's very cool you're a journalist. I love your work. I really liked that feature you wrote on model minorities. Freedom is failure. Wow."

"Thanks," said Faruq, embarrassed. "That means a lot."

"I wish you hadn't held back, though. Those parts where you talked about your parents immigrating—I thought, *There's a lot more to the story here.*"

Again, Faruq was taken aback by the frankness. She delivered the criticism with no sharpness, no gentleness, no malice. It was as though it would never occur to her that he might be offended. And so, he found, he *wasn't* offended. "My parents and I had a complicated relationship." Even this statement was an oversimplification.

"Oh. How about now? Is it still complicated?"

"My mom passed when I was sixteen," he said. "And my dad died last year."

He had been wrong to expect her to react as most people would—with an apology and a change in subject. Instead, her pretty freckled face lit up in a smile.

"And has that made things more or less complicated for you?"

He didn't quite know what to say to that. He thought hard. The firelight gave everything a warm glow. Faruq realized he was buzzed. He hadn't been entirely surprised to discover that the followers of the nameless were fond of mind-altering substances—he knew that Aeschylus regularly microdosed with LSD, and someone had brought hashish to this party. Clover had explained that drugs were far from required, but they could help train the Other Sight. Tonight, Faruq planned to stick with beer, but at some point, someone had pressed a mason jar of something golden and fizzy into his hand and it most certainly had not been beer.

Fannie was waiting very patiently for Faruq to answer her question. He got the sense that his answer was important. The guitar playing had stopped, and though all eyes weren't on him, a few people had crept closer to him and Fannie; one man was resting his hand on the back of Faruq's chair.

"More or less complicated," Faruq said slowly. "I guess both, in a way."

Fannie leaned toward him, her eyes turned molten by the firelight. The man who'd had his hand on the back of Faruq's chair joined her on the ground, crossed his legs.

"What do you mean by that?" asked Fannie.

Faruq could picture his mother, the mischievous smile that brought her face to life, the way she grasped her hair when she laughed, like her happiness was very near madness, the sandalwood and rain smell of her, the long, skinny fingers with the bitten nails, the blank smile she wore while silently enduring one of his father's lectures, the purple bags under her eyes, her limpness as she sat, sometimes for hours, barely blinking, not even getting up to pray, the slackness of her body under his aunts' hands, their white gloved hands on her head as they stood above her, and her eyes squeezed shut tight, hands clenched, a single, slick tendril of hair escaping her hijab. And in him the overwhelming tide of helplessness, uselessness, rising, rising.

"Take my dad," he said, a bit too quickly. He slowed down, tried again. "Take my dad. He was—well, it's a long story."

"Time is infinite," said the man seated beside Fannie. He looked like a cross between an elf and an Abercrombie model.

There were more people now seated on the ground at Faruq's feet, and all of them were looking up into his face, trusting as children. He shifted uncomfortably. Fannie touched him with her fingertips—she'd wiggled them up under the ankle of his jeans until she found skin. They were soft, reassuring. Was it flirtatious? Nameless women were off-limits, as far as he was concerned. He was a professional, but still, the attempt gave him pause. Was it to make him more pliable, like he was being tenderized? Or was it genuine tenderness? Here, among the nameless, everything was layered.

Someone quickly replaced the mostly finished drink he held

with a mug of something warm. He looked down, sniffed, and took a sip. Mulled wine. Out of season, but still just right.

"My dad was really religious," he said. "And really strict."

Their faces were so kind and gentle, their attention so warm and unabashed. He didn't tell them everything, but he told them more than he expected to. He told them about how 9/11 had happened shortly after his mother died, how the horror of it propelled him through his grief too soon. He told them how his father refused to assimilate, even when someone spray-painted GO HOME TERRORIST on the side of his car. How his father's previously successful real estate business began to suffer, and soon the only clients he could get were fellow Pakistanis and the occasional Manhattanite Iranian. How Faruq's own faith began to fall away from him, gone entirely by the time he was seventeen. How he had to pretend, so he wouldn't break his father's heart. How the mimicry of devoutness was so close to the real thing that sometimes Faruq almost couldn't tell whether he was still a Muslim or not. How, in the end, he was afraid he managed to break his father's heart anyway. How, after the heart attack killed his father, Faruq felt something like relief, because he didn't have to pretend anymore.

That last, he didn't say out loud.

"I came home from work and found him, collapsed on the stairs. He'd fallen so hard his AirPods had been jerked right out of his ears, and they were sitting there on the stairs next to him. And his feet were . . . just limp as he was lying there. He was slumped over, but he was still breathing. Not for long."

He closed his eyes momentarily, remembering the sounds of sirens, the sick whiteness of the hospital room, coming home alone from the hospital, the AirPods glaring at him from where they'd landed.

The house still smelled like the sandalwood oil his father rubbed into his hair every morning. It took weeks for that smell to go. And even now, Faruq could still sometimes get a whiff of it. He was never truly free from the eyes of aunties and ghosts.

He'd been talking a long time. There were more followers listening now. Their attention never wavered; no one had interrupted him. In that moment, he could see how someone might be seduced by this. How the openness and indiscriminate friendliness might start to feel a lot like utopia. How, for this moment, you were made to feel loved, important, a bit more. Fannie's fingertips were still warm and steady on his ankle.

Half of him wanted to pull his leg away from her touch. But only half. Gradually, the other followers began turning away, returning to their own conversations, though Faruq noted that many of their heads were still cocked in his direction.

"You know," said Fannie, "I had to let my family go."

"Your family? You mean you don't talk to them anymore?"

"They were poison, distorted."

"Whoa—what do you mean by that?" Faruq asked.

"Well, Faruq, love shouldn't bind you. It should liberate you. That's something that Odo teaches us."

Faruq frowned. "Didn't Maya Angelou say that?"

Fannie squeezed his ankle, a little hard. "You interrupt a lot, Faruq."

"Sorry."

"I know my parents thought they loved me. They gave me the things I asked for, set me up with money. But they wanted to hold me close to them. So close I couldn't move. They wanted to control who I was. That's not love. It took me a long time to accept. I met a man—a beautiful man—who finally loved me the right way, the *real* way. He introduced me to the nameless."

"I'm sorry"—Faruq raised his hand like he was in a classroom—"what do you mean when you say this guy loved you the 'real' way?"

"I mean that he never took from me. He never asked me to hold still. I was free to move, to change, to be nice, to be mean. All without judgment."

"And are you still together?"

"Our time together was finite. A few months into our relationship, my father died." She held up a hand to stop Faruq's condolences in their tracks. "I felt this overwhelming shame, this remorse. I didn't understand it. I was paralyzed—literally; I was barely getting out of bed. Finally, my lover introduced me to Odo.

"Odo understood what I couldn't understand myself: My grief was a distortion, a remnant of the poison I was raised on. Once I realized that, I could be happy for my father. I could let him go. I could be free myself. Meeting Odo was the greatest gift. It was the first time someone really stopped to ask me who I was, and then really *see* me.

"Faruq, it only takes that much, you know? Someone caring enough to look into you, open you up. I gave everything my parents had tried to use as a shackle to the nameless—money, *things*. I didn't need any of it. I never did."

"Was that the price of entry? Giving away all your stuff?"

Fannie smiled wryly. "No, Faruq. I didn't want to be held anymore, that's all."

"But you *did* give everything up, didn't you? When? After you met Odo?"

"You're going to the Forbidden City, aren't you? You're being welcomed to stay there?"

"That's what they tell me," Faruq said.

"Well, has anyone asked you to give anything up? Has anyone asked you for a dime?"

"I suppose not," Faruq said, "although, I am not here to get hipped, I'm here to write a story."

Fannie smirked in response, and then continued. "I told Odo all about my family, how sad I was that I couldn't get them to *see* me. Odo kept telling me I was a weakling, that I was just as distorted as them if I couldn't do what needed to be done." She laughed to herself. "Every time I saw him, he'd yell at me: *Did you free yourself yet?* And when I couldn't say yes, he'd refuse to talk to me. Refuse to look at me."

"Sounds cruel," said Faruq.

She shrugged. "Imagine someone like that caring about you that much. Imagine *mattering* that much to someone like Odo. It's what gave me the courage. And it helped me grow my Other Sight."

Faruq's mouth opened as he tried to find a neutral way to ask more questions, hide how unsettled he was, but just then, Aeschylus leaned in close to Faruq's ear, his face floating down from behind Faruq's chair. His breath smelled like mulled wine and the astringent grassiness of hash as he said, "Gotta get *Gray's Anatomy* to the Forbidden City. We leave tomorrow."

And this small victory felt so fragile and hard-won that Faruq didn't question it.

He was slightly hungover the next morning, and his muscles ached for a run, but Clover and Aeschylus bustled him into their car for the over-five-hour journey to the Forbidden City early in the morning. They evaded most of his questions on the drive, except to explain that Odo had retreated into the redwoods under the orders of Vutu—a shortened form of Mow Vutu, what they called their god, who was nameless and singular, and whose pronoun was They, used insistently in the singular.

Odo had made this retreat with nothing, and his followers had built up the Forbidden City around him. With their enormous resources, they'd cleared the land, built houses, planted crops. An inarguably impressive feat, and a show of incomprehensible devotion. Clover and Aeschylus avoided Faruq's questions about why it was being called the Forbidden City. He watched out of his window as the vista transitioned from glittering blues and whites to wet greens and rusty browns until he fell asleep.

When Faruq woke for the first time during the ride, it was with sleep paralysis. He used to get it as a kid, on the infrequent car rides his parents took to upstate New York to visit his mother's family. Faruq thought he could see Aeschylus and Clover in the front of the car, could hear their music—more beautiful and strange nameless songs. But he couldn't move. He tried making some kind of noise—he just needed someone to shake him, wake his body up—but he remained mute, could barely keep his eyes open, if they were open at all. But if they weren't open, how could he see Clover reach over and put her hand on Aeschylus's thigh, squeezing and squeezing? How could he see her look back at him and smile his mother's smile?

When Faruq woke for the second time, Aeschylus was pulling into a rest stop. They were halfway there, just outside of Humboldt County, stopped at a mom-and-pop gas station. The sign above it read WEETHEARTS—Faruq presumed a missing *S* at the beginning of that word—and the green and tan building advertised live bait and a café. Aeschylus filled the tank and, reluctantly, Faruq followed him and Clover inside. One half of the interior was packed with typical gas station snacks, along with mismatched items like Drano, black bear keychains, and minnow buckets. The other half was a dimly lit café with four cramped tables and a bar.

All of the tables were taken, so he, Aeschylus, and Clover sat at the bar. Everyone stared at them. One man with a bald head, bright red nose, and wraparound sunglasses that seemed partially grown into his head crossed his arms while he stared; hostility came off him in waves. Faruq looked nervously to Clover and Aeschylus, but they didn't seem to notice. For a moment Faruq envied their carelessness, to be able to enter almost any space and not have to read it, not have to be wary and sensitive like a jackrabbit.

When Faruq started school at Brooklyn College, his father had made him continue to live at home for fear that college life would corrupt him. Faruq was still dutifully miming belief, performing the series of bows and prostrations and recitations of salah, next to his father, automatically but emptily, thinking not of God but of lyrics—Common, Talib Kweli, Mos Def, Nas, Lupe Fiasco, Lauryn Hill. Despite his charade, his father's possessiveness irritated him so badly he'd shorn off his beard in protest. But he had felt so intolerably exposed without it that he let it grow back and hadn't been barefaced since. Perhaps it was a ghost of faith, clinging to him. Now, he ran a palm against his beard self-consciously.

He drank a lemonade that had a faintly savory note, like the mason jar it was served in had once held chicken broth. The waitress doubled as the mechanic, and her fingernails were caked with grease. Someone had framed a child's drawing of the American flag, under which someone—not a child—had written I STAND FOR MY FLAG AND KNEEL FOR MY GOD. Faruq surreptitiously snapped a picture of it with his phone, careful to do it in such a way that the bald man, who was still staring, would think Faruq was just answering a text.

After they ate, Clover and Aeschylus wanted to browse the merchandise, but Faruq didn't want to linger here. He went back out to wait by the car, pausing only to take a picture of how the mountains rose up behind the place like a great wave. Aeschylus and Clover returned with a case of bottled water and an apparently self-published book about the black bears of Northern California. They were in high spirits, even giddy. Faruq was irritated at their obliviousness, their blinding privilege.

"Did you see that guy in there?" he asked.

Clover and Aeschylus looked at him, their eyebrows raised, faces full of kind and rapt interest.

"I don't think they see many people like me around here," said Faruq. "I don't think they care to, either."

Clover and Aeschylus glanced at each other, and then their eyes returned to Faruq.

Clover stepped forward and put her hand on his arm.

"Get stripped, Faruq," Aeschylus said, tenderly, like he was giving condolences.

Just over two hours of driving later, Aeschylus pulled off of US-101 and began winding through a series of roads that eventually stopped having names, and then stopped being paved. It was late in the afternoon; in San Francisco, the fog would've burned off by now, but not here. It clung to the trees like cobwebs. Aeschylus turned down a road of packed dirt, marked only by a post jammed into the ground at an angle. It led them deeper into the redwoods.

The followers of the nameless had bought this swath of undeveloped land for an untold, but no doubt incredible, sum. It was a 16,000-acre patch of Northern California, just larger than Manhattan, dense with ancient trees and bordered on one side by the Pacific.

They reached a seemingly random spot on the dirt road where three black-clad young men—teenagers, Faruq thought—stood as though waiting. They drove up to them and they peered inside the car, nodded, and waved them through.

"Who were they?" Faruq asked.

"That's just the Deep," said Aeschylus in a tone that was almost too nonchalant. "Odo assembled them after all that shit went down in Texas."

"Needed a little more protection," Clover added. "They're mostly for show."

The Forbidden City gradually came into view—narrow roads laid with bricks, whitewashed houses, communal gardens full of produce, early spring flowers. Theirs was the only car in sight. People—the majority of them dressed in sky blue—smiled and waved.

Aeschylus pulled up in front of a building that Faruq recognized as a house of the nameless—the golden outline of a square above the door was a dead giveaway. He got out of the car and stretched. Faruq inhaled—the Forbidden City was perfumed by the smell of the redwoods, a green, mossy scent with notes of charcoal and turpentine, and, distantly, the ocean. Followers were gathering around them. They greeted Clover and Aeschylus with complicated and varying daps, and eyed Faruq with open curiosity.

Watching followers greet Clover and Aeschylus, Faruq had the impression of ants clustering on a drop of something sugary. Before he knew it, he was watching the only two people he knew here get swept off by a wave of blue-clad followers. He stood dumbly by the car, one hand on the passenger door as though it were grounding him. He had a very early memory of his mother teaching him to swim; she rocked him gently in the water, and then, with no warning, her hands were gone from underneath him and he sank into a slow, quiet, chlorine-blue world.

He'd been staring up at the house of the nameless, and now someone was coming down out of it, descending the white steps. He was a tall man, pale and slender and slightly androgynous, like a couture model. It took Faruq awhile to realize that the man was walking toward him. The man approached him as one might an injured animal. There was something condescending about that, Faruq thought.

"I'm Adam," said the man.

Faruq took his offered hand, but instead of the handshake Faruq had been expecting, Adam gently curled Faruq's hand into a fist and then wrapped his long, pale fingers around it, squeezing lightly so that Faruq's fist was nestled into Adam's shockingly silky palm.

Faruq found himself strangely off-balance. First, because of his sudden abandonment by Aeschylus and Clover, and now, because Adam was still holding his fist, holding his gaze unflinchingly. Faruq specialized in a hybrid of gonzo journalism and immersionism; he'd built his career on confessional narratives told through the lens of absorbing, sometimes harrowing experiences—he'd once spent two weeks following the daily life of a neo-Nazi. Generally, he knew how to keep his cool.

But for the first time since he'd pitched this idea to Anita, he was concerned that he'd made a terrible mistake. Maybe this time he'd really gotten himself into something he couldn't get out of. He thought of Jonestown. Of Manson. Heaven's Gate. Morin-Heights, Waco, Colonia Dignidad.

Adam let go of his hand.

"I'll take you to your guesthouse, Faruq," Adam said.

With his duffel bag slung over his shoulder, Faruq followed Adam along a bricked path that led around the side of the house of the nameless.

"Were you one of the people who helped build this up?" Faruq asked Adam.

"Oh, yes, I was here."

"What was that like?"

"Faruq, you wouldn't believe how beautiful that time was. Everybody working together, using their expertise for the greater good."

"What was your expertise?"

"I'm an engineer." Adam sounded proud. He pointed at the whitewashed followers' houses around them. "Pacific lodges," he said. "You know why?"

"Why?"

"The slope of the roofs. Keeps the house cool in the summer, and rain and snow slide right off."

"Does it snow much out here?"

"No," Adam admitted. "But we get plenty of rain. Gray days. But these houses have tons of natural light. That was important to us. And they're pretty easy to build—just have to pay attention to the grading."

"What made you come out here?"

"I wanted to be a part of this new chapter in the nameless. And I wanted to be closer to Odo. I had been a follower for a couple years, but hadn't fully committed. It was time."

"What drew you to the nameless in the first place?"

Adam leaned in a bit. "If I'm honest with you, Faruq, it was the girls at first. Ever notice how gorgeous they all are?"

Faruq chuckled. "I'd have to be blind."

"I *was* blind," Adam said earnestly. "I wasn't confident. I sucked at talking to women. So when I met some of the women with the nameless, I was shocked by how easy they were to talk to. I was shocked that they'd want to talk to *me*."

"So you got a confidence boost?"

"At first. But then it was more than that. I started to understand that my bullshit was all distortion. I met Odo, and he's just so—well, you'll see. This place, it makes me feel needed. I'm important to this community."

"Not just about girls anymore, huh?"

Adam laughed loudly. "Odo's going to like you, Faruq."

Behind the house of the nameless was a row of white A-frame cabins, only slightly smaller than the Pacific lodges the followers lived in. The guesthouses stood like guardsmen in front of the dense

woods that seemed to be pressing against the edges of the Forbidden City like a child might press his nose up against the window of a bakery.

Adam led him to a guesthouse on the far end of the row. It, like
the others, was white, but the door was a vibrant lime green, and
fresh flowers were hung from the door handle as though in welcome. Adam pushed the door open and gestured for Faruq to go
in. Faruq hesitated only a little before entering. The inside was
minimalist, surprisingly modern. The decor stuck strictly to a
black and white motif.

"Are all the guesthouses decorated the same?" Faruq asked.

Adam only smiled at him and gestured, an offer to take his duffel bag.

Questions and actions that seemed entirely innocuous to Faruq
did not always appear to be so to followers, as if they came from
entirely incompatible cultures; like throwing a thumbs-up in the
Middle East.

Adam showed him the kitchenette, the bathroom, the dor-
mered bedroom loft at the top of the rustic stairs. There was a
shelf of eclectic books in the living room, which didn't have a
couch or a television, but instead a faux fur rug and several oversized cushions. It was like the entire place was trying to be the
kind of Instagrammable bohemian getaway that young people
flocked to. For the vibes.

"You're free to go anywhere you like," Adam was saying.
"This is your home for as long as you want, Faruq." He made as
though to leave.

"Wait," Faruq said.

Adam paused.

"Does Odo know I'm here? I'd really like to talk to him.
Soon." Again, Adam only smiled.

"Well, don't I at least need keys?"

"We don't need keys here because we don't need locks."

Faruq let out a breath, exasperated.

Adam's androgynous smile changed then. Before, it was warm

but polite, a cleric's smile. Now it was luminous, benevolent and knowing.

"I thought it was creepy here too, at first," he said. "Before, I used to be Jewish—ever been to a kibbutz? But this"—he shook his head—"this is something else. It's really beautiful. You'll see."

With that, Adam left, shutting the door on the way out, and Faruq noticed for the first time how quiet this place was. There was, of course, the racket of the woods—birdsong and, quieter, more subtle, treesong—but so long as his lockless front door was closed, Faruq could almost believe he was the only human for miles. He made his way upstairs and fell backward onto the bed. Sunlight struggled through the trees and lent a green cast to the ceiling.

All there was, was a low bed, a white wardrobe, a lamp atop a bedside table. There was nothing covering the window. Curious, Faruq rolled onto his side and opened the drawer of the bedside table, half expecting it to be empty. But it contained a booklet, hand-bound and hand-painted. It was beautiful—the artist had created texture with layers of paint, a swirling storm of color, an abstraction of the phases of the sky, sunrise to sunset. The booklet felt heavy and fragile in his hands. He opened it and read:

THE 18 UTTERANCES

1. There Is No God But The Nameless.
2. Odo Is The Messenger Of Mow Vutu.
3. All Suffering Is Distortion.
4. Strip Yourself Of Distortion.
5. Sacrifice.
6. Create Beauty.
7. Get Hipped To Oneness.
8. Love Freely.
9. Meditate To The Vibration Of Vutu And The World.
10. Pray Regularly.
11. See Only Beauty.

12. Do Not Despair At Death.
13. Train The Other Sight.
14. Hip All Beings To The Nameless.
15. Create Order In Chaos.
16. Correct Distortion.
17. Harness Gosah In Pursuit Of Wholeness.
18. Seek The Face Of Mow Vutu.

Those first two Utterances in particular stood out to him. The Shahada, imprinted permanently in his brain, said, *There is no god but God, and Muhammad is the Messenger of God.* And he was pretty sure the Bible contained a similar assertion. So Odo was following a familiar rhythm. Faruq couldn't be sure whether the booklet had been made and planted especially for him, or if all the guesthouses had them. He placed it back in its drawer. But part of him feared that the booklet might disappear, that it might not be in the bedside table if he looked for it again, so he took it back out and took a few pictures with his phone. Then he went downstairs, thinking to step outside into the sunlight, maybe explore on his own. But before he could reach the front door, it swung open, and there was the man himself.

"Hey, I've been looking for you, man," Odo said.

Faruq had seen images and footage of Odo while doing his research. And, of course, there was the documentary. In person, Odo was taller than Faruq expected, though lean. He was wearing a sky-blue sweater and jeans. Faruq wasn't sure exactly how old Odo was, but he couldn't be a young man. Yet he was very youthful—his warm brown skin was uncreased, except for the smile lines around his eyes, and his hair, shorn close, held only a smattering of gray. His eyes were old and when he smiled, Faruq could see that his teeth were stained, the bottom row crowded.

Faruq was taken aback by how normal Odo looked. He had been expecting a more sinister figure, someone who frightened him. A man capable of bullying a young woman into disowning her family, causing a scandal in a small Texas town. But instead, Odo seemed like he'd be a good guy to grab a beer with. His whole face had lit up when he'd seen Faruq. There was something purely vulnerable about that. Maybe, Faruq thought, Odo wasn't the one who held the power after all.

Odo was stepping into the guesthouse now as Faruq stepped back, and Odo held out a hand, which Faruq tried to shake, but Odo shook his head. "Like this," he said.

First, he interlaced his fingers with Faruq's and then pulled away, came back in with a fist bump, tapped his fist on one side of Faruq's and the other, and then opened his hand, fingers stretched wide, like the impact of their knuckles against each other had caused an explosion.

Faruq noticed two things: that this dap was yet again unique, something that Odo had invented on the spot, and that it felt *good* for Odo to have created a dap for him.

"Great to meet you," said Faruq.

"Likewise, man," Odo said. "Just the same. I heard you were here and couldn't wait to come see you. They shown you around this place yet?"

Faruq shook his head. He was a little taken aback by Odo's friendliness. He'd expected him to be aloof, pontifical, maybe even something like an apparition; he'd expected their meeting to come with more pomp and circumstance. That it would happen days or weeks in, not now, not immediately. Again he was off-balance. He followed Odo out into the sunlight. Odo's friendliness was not like that of his followers—it was earthier, it was *cool.*

There was a golf cart waiting for them outside—Faruq had noticed followers driving around in them instead of cars. It seemed that cars were communal here, largely reserved for voyages outside of the Forbidden City. They drove around the perimeter and Faruq was struck by how large this place was. Odo explained that they had only cleared what was necessary, leaving nature as intact as they could. Odo showed him the stables, the amphitheater, the dining halls, the greenhouses. There was a large park in the center— Faruq could tell the Forbidden City had been built out from the center, their most vital buildings first, like the house of the nameless. Followers all wearing sky blue milled about throughout it all, stopping to wave at Odo and Faruq, smiling.

"I'll take you out by the vineyard," Odo said, steering the golf cart deftly. "Real nice out there."

As they drove, they passed an outbreak of trees. Among them, Faruq spotted a group of followers, all dressed in black—the same uniforms as the trio that had met the car when he'd entered the Forbidden City with Clover and Aeschylus. They seemed to be in some kind of formation, with sticks held over their shoulders. One of them shouted, and they all stomped, crouched, perfectly in sync.

"The Deep?" Faruq asked.

Odo nodded. "Our young people can sign up to join them, and they'll get trained up. Survival skills, discipline, agility—that sort of thing."

"Clover and Aeschylus said they were security. But just for show."

Odo chuckled. "They offer some protection, yes. Just in case. Not taking no more chances."

"After Texas?"

Odo nodded briskly. Clearly, he wasn't ready to talk about Texas. So Faruq tried pushing from a different direction.

"They kind of sound like a paramilitary. Aren't those outlawed in like all fifty states?"

Odo laughed. "You got a funny way of asking questions and then answering them in your own head. I ain't interested in nobody's military, Faruq. Been there, done that. The Deep are more about structure. Creating order out of chaos."

"Why just your young people?" Faruq asked.

"They got the most energy."

Faruq snorted. "Sounds like the military to me."

"Trust me," Odo smirked, "when I was over in Vietnam, wasn't no order. War is a *breakdown,* you understand? An abomination. The Deep are our defense against that kind of distortion."

"Well, how does that work? How do they defend against . . . distortion?"

Odo blinked at him. "Order, Faruq. They oversee our rituals. They pray for us, as you might put it. They make sure there are no disrupters getting into our borders."

"Disrupters?"

"People who don't mean us no good."

"Are they armed?"

Odo looked at him sideways. "No need for any of that here. They're more like ascetics. They live *strictly* by the 18 Utterances."

The Deep shouted something in unison, raised their sticks above their heads like warriors. Their arms were still raised as Faruq and Odo drove past them. Before long, the Deep were out of sight.

Instagram Post # 379

@thenamelessmvmnt: A quaint white house with a bright green door, the doorknob hung with fresh, blush-colored flowers neatly tied together by the stems; at the edge of the frame, the blurry suggestion of a human form—a bent arm, a gesturing hand, an unfocused sliver of bare, pink flesh.

#welcomehome #springishere #sustainablyfarmed

26,787 likes | 246 comments

Nero

FADE IN:

INT. CWE NAVE—MED. SHOT—WILL ROY

            WILL ROY
      I was born and raised right here in Burning
      Hill.

CLOSEUP—WILL ROY'S FACE
Will Roy nods.

            WILL ROY
      Love it.

INSERT—IMAGE

B&W baby photo of Roy, c. 1955/56.*

            WILL ROY
      I was the eldest of four boys, so my poor
      mama had her hands full. (laughs)

                                    DISSOLVE TO:
B&W photo of four boys lined up tallest to shortest, in
matching striped shirts, arms slung around each other.

            WILL ROY
      No, but we were good kids, though. My old
      man was the pastor at Christ the Word.

                                    DISSOLVE TO:
Photo of CWE, c. 1914; a white clapboard in the
Carpenter Gothic style, a single, cross-topped belfry,
dark horse tied out front, blurry shape of a man
emerging from around back. SLOW ZOOM.

            WILL ROY
      My great-granddaddy built the church in
      1911. I grew up watching my father preach
      the Word, and I always knew it was what I
      wanted to do too.

BACK TO SCENE
_____

   * Music: Waltz Across Texas (Ernest Tubb)

CLOSEUP—WILL ROY'S FACE

Roy glances down, smiles, runs a hand across his neck.

> WILL ROY
> (chuckles) I got my calling early, I guess.

INSERT—IMAGE

Senior photo of Roy's wife, c. 1975; mottled brown background, Maggie in a red blouse, dirty blond hair parted in the middle and curling around her shoulders. SLOW ZOOM on Maggie's face.

> WILL ROY
> I met my wife, Maggie, when I was 20 years old; she was 18. I knew right away I wanted to marry her. But she said we were too young. (laughs)

> DISSOLVE TO:

Photo of Maggie and Will posing before cutting their wedding cake, Maggie in a veil and long-sleeved, Empire-waisted satin gown, and Roy in a gray 3-piece suit with a bow tie.

> WILL ROY
> She made me wait 2 years.

> DISSOLVE TO:

Photo c. 1990 of Maggie in a floral dress, in front of an expanded, brick-exteriored CWE, a toddler on her hip and 2 young children at her side. (2 eldest children not pictured)

> WILL ROY
> We got 5 kids, 6 grandkids. My older daughter's got another one coming too. I'd say we're a close family.
>
> All my kids are still right here in Burning Hill. Except for my second youngest son. He went to med school in Austin and now he's in Africa.

                                      DISSOLVE TO:
Photo of Will Roy, c. 1988, holding a baby aloft,
grinning.

          WILL ROY
     My youngest got called, just like me. He's
     the youth pastor now, but he'll take my
     place one day.

BACK TO SCENE

Will Roy crosses his arms.

          WILL ROY
     Burning Hill is a quiet place. We're about
     20 miles outside Austin, but this is a small
     town.

     I'd say I know everyone here.

Roy nods.

INSERT—IMAGE

Recent photo of CWE, now with 2 new wings and a large
cross sculpture out front. SLOW ZOOM.

          WILL ROY
     Our religion is important to us here. And
     I'm proud to say that. My great-granddaddy's
     church is a big part of this town. Most
     people here come to Christ the Word. I'm
     proud to say that too.

                                      DISSOLVE TO:
Photo of Maggie reading to a group of children who are
seated, cross-legged, on the floor.

          WILL ROY
     Maggie's been running the Sunday school a
     long time, and—well, we've watched a lot of
     the kids around here grow up.

BACK TO SCENE

                    WILL ROY
          We watched Sue Mills grow up.

Roy nods quickly, then slowly shakes his head, arms
crossed.*

INSERT—IMAGE

Photo of Roy in a 3-piece suit and cowboy hat, one hand
holding a Bible and the other on a congregant's shoulder.

                    WILL ROY
          The church is family, you understand.
          Everybody in that church, I consider one of
          my own.

BACK TO SCENE

                    WILL ROY
          So when Sue Mills up and disappears for
          weeks, it was like one of my own kids.

Roy uncrosses his arms to jab an index finger to his
right.†

                    WILL ROY
          And come to find out, she went and got sucked
          in by those *people*.

                                        FADE TO BLACK.‡

EXT. CROWDED HARLEM STREET, C. 1959—DAY (HOME VIDEO)

People, mostly African-American, mill about.

                    MINH-AN
          We don't know a lot about Odo's early life.
          We know he didn't grow up with much. And we
          know he was raised Baptist.

---

* Music: fade in, Resurrection Blues (Otis Taylor); begin
at 1:39
† Silence.
‡ Music: fade in, Oh What a Night (The Dells); 1969
version

CUT TO:

INT. GREENHOUSE—MED. SHOT—MINH-AN

> MINH-AN
> Ask him much more than that, and he'll tell
> you to *mind yo business*. (laughs)

> With love, of course.

INSERT—FOOTAGE

Footage of Malcolm X interview at Berkeley, 1963 (audio
removed).

> MINH-AN
> He would have basically grown up with the
> Civil Rights Movement.

CROSS CUT:
Footage of March on Washington, 1963 (audio removed).

> MINH-AN
> All that enlightenment, all that—*audacity;*
> it got imprinted on him. It had to.

CROSS CUT:
Footage of MLK Nobel Prize acceptance speech at
University of Oslo, 1964 (audio removed).

CROSS CUT:
Footage of African-American soldiers in Vietnam,
smoking and laughing; one's gaze meets the camera
directly, and he blows a plume of smoke at the viewer,
c. 1967 (audio removed).

> MINH-AN
> But his *hipping*—his enlightenment—begins in
> Vietnam.*

CROSS CUT:
Footage of First Battle of la Drang, Vietnam, 1965
(audio removed).

---

* Music: transition, A Change Is Gonna Come (Sam Cooke)

          MINH-AN
He got drafted—just a kid, really. And he'll
tell you: *I was too bone stupid to be
scared*. (laughs)

BACK TO SCENE

          MINH-AN
He comes out of Vietnam decorated—Purple
Heart, Bronze Star, a Commendation Medal, a—
whatsit—the Vietnam Service Medal.

But that's not the real story.

INSERT—IMAGE

Photo of Odo's face; he seems to be mid-laugh, his eyes
are cast down, lips parted, his right hand resting on
his left shoulder. SLOW ZOOM.

          MINH-AN
The real story is that he got to Vietnam,
young and blind, and his eyes opened. He
realized that the world wasn't the World,
that there was so much more beauty than he
ever knew how to see.

And then he heard the 18 Utterances.

BACK TO SCENE

          MINH-AN
The 18 Utterances are kind of like the 10
Commandments. Or the yamas and niyamas. But
we are not a religion. They're our
guidelines for living a beautiful life. *Love
freely; pray regularly; see only beauty*.
Like that.

Minh-An leans forward on her stool.

          MINH-AN
The nameless is about seeing beauty and
making beauty.

Minh-An settles back in her seat.

              MINH-AN
We do that mostly through art and good
works. We all try to see clearly. But Odo,
he just—he sees all this incredible beauty.
And he can make you see it too.

CLOSEUP—MINH-AN'S FACE

Minh-An smiles, shakes her head, her eyes glittering.

INT. CWE NAVE—MED. SHOT—WILL ROY

              WILL ROY
'False prophets will appear and perform
great signs and wonders to *deceive*.'

'Do not believe it. For as lightning in the
east is visible even in the west, so will be
the coming of the Son of Man.'

'Wherever there is a carcass, *there* the
vultures will gather.'

CLOSEUP—WILL ROY'S FACE

Roy's gaze, directed to the camera, is bright and
steady.

INSERT—B-ROLL OF BURNING HILL, TX

A wild field with several grazing horses; quaint main
street with Mom & Pop stores; a herd of Texas
longhorns, noses twitching, calves underfoot; Roy's
gleaming white church; the water tower.

              WILL ROY
I personally didn't think much of it when I
heard that little 30-acre plot where the old
plantation was got bought up.

BACK TO SCENE

          WILL ROY
I even thought that maybe someone'd come and
fix the place up, restore it, you know.
(guffaws)

But then people started coming to me talking
about some *nameless*. We were concerned, sure.
Like I said, our religion is important to us
out here and I don't feel bad saying it.

We were confused too. Why set up here in
Burning Hill? We're just a half hour from
Austin—why not there, where they have more
liberal, New Age-type things? Those people
didn't belong here. That *Odo* didn't belong
in a place like this.

But we were never unwelcoming. We may have
had a few community meetings over here in
the church, but there were *no* protests.

Roy shakes his head.

                              FADE TO BLACK

before: 1969

CRAZY HORSE DANCED behind a veil of Preach's cigarette smoke. He snapped his fingers and jerked his shoulders. He held his arms open, he kept his knees bent, he crossed one foot over the other and then spun around. His eyes were closed and his mouth open, jaw jutting forward and chin nodding up. Some of the white soldiers shook their heads, even laughed. Others glared, eyes narrowed and lips drawn tight. He had the volume up high—James Brown.

Preach lit a fresh cigarette and leaned over to Bigger.

He call this his war dance. *Fool.*

Bigger's body moved—the music had gotten into him. His knees bounced, his head bopped. He grinned.

I saw this on television. James Brown—on that *Playboy* show. He had all them white girls shimmying along, singing about being Black and proud.

Silk sat across from Bigger and Preach and watched them. The kid was a mess of nerves. Silk could see it. They'd just gotten word of a mission—in twenty-four hours, they'd be out in the bush. The kid could barely stand it and Silk was the only one seeing it. Crazy Horse was too busy ticking the rabbits off and Preach was too busy enjoying it. Silk sat down next to Bigger, making sure to smile at one of the grim-faced white soldiers on his way.

Hey there, cherry. You wait til we get in that jungle. Then you'll really see why they call him Crazy Horse.

Bigger stopped moving, concentrated on holding himself still. If he didn't he was sure he'd begin to shake. The only thing more terrifying to him than what awaited outside of the base's perimeter was letting on just how terrified he was.

Why's that?

Silk laughed.

Just you wait and see.

Crazy Horse was sweating now, no longer fully aware of his audience. There were only a few white soldiers left watching, and these were the ones who stood with arms crossed against something hot and painful, something that left a lump in their throats and murder in their hands; these were the ones who, when that smooth-talking preacher nigger finally got himself killed in Memphis last spring, felt a relief, an opening of the airways, a sense that, although they were surely in hell now, the real world was still something they'd recognize when they got back. If they got back. And that darkie with his dancing—didn't the other ones see it? Something animal, wild in it. Like a dog about to bite.

Things happen out there, in the bush.

Silk was smiling as he spoke, but a smile wasn't quite what he meant.

Things happen that ain't got no business happening outside a dream. Or a bad trip. Why, I remember one time . . .

Silk told Bigger a jungle story. He told him about how he'd earned his Purple Heart.

Until now, Bigger hadn't known about the Purple Heart, hadn't known that Silk had extended his tour. He worried at this information like a small stone. It meant something, that Silk had chosen to stay in Vietnam. But Bigger couldn't quite coax that meaning out into the light of his mind. Silk was too busy filling it up with his strange jungle story. He was taking up space.

There Silk was, jungle rot on his heel making him limp, the jungle close and hot and wet around him, and that heat a physical thing, like a hot tongue, pressing. His ears straining to hear what lay beneath the strange jungle noises. It was the middle of the day. A little later than that. It was the hottest part of the day and his C-rations were jangling around like river rocks in his gut. He swore you could hear them.

Pay attention now, because this part is important. The jungle, it kind of whistles. Between the birds and the bugs and the lizards and snakes and monkeys and vines and trees and the padded footsteps of predators—together, it is sound mud, a continuous warble of ambiguous pitch. But it pauses for battle. It is not the face of death the jungle recognizes.

Here Silk is, tired and nauseated and seeping. He is walking point. The jungle is whistling a song that is its own language, that transcends language. Silk closes his eyes to squeeze the sweat out of them, and when he opens them, he is looking up at canopy, late afternoon sun blinding. He was wearing his shades, but now they are gone. He is on his back, someone is pushing a molten blade into the center of his back. He can't make sense of it.

They never find the fucker who shot him—must be a sniper, they say. He'd twisted around as he fell without seeing a thing. Nobody else is hit. The medic runs over to Silk, turns him onto his side, and suddenly the birds begin to scream. Sharp, forceful chatter, clearly a reproach. It gets cold. At first, Silk thinks he must be dying, but he can see his breath. Then—and only just then—the jungle falls silent.

By now, Crazy Horse had finished his war dance, and here, he interrupted.

Nah, that ain't how it happened, man.

What you saying?

I'm saying it didn't happen like that. The jungle got quiet a spell, and *then* the birds started hollering.

How're you gonna tell me? I'm the one laid out. I tell you, you could hear the blood hitting the ground.

Nah, nah. Tell it right.

Silk jumped up.

I *am* telling it right. It got quiet and it didn't make a peep again until the bird came to get me.

Them birds were hollering so bad you could hardly hear the chopper coming. Ain't no use telling the cherry something that ain't wholly true.

Hold up now, man. It sounds like you calling me a liar.

I'm just saying you ought to tell it right. You got hit. The jungle got quiet and cold. The medic got to you, and *then* the birds started up.

Look. I'm the one that got hit. That means this story is mine. It's true the way I tell it.

I'm telling you, you got it *wrong*, brother.

Don't go calling me "brother" while you calling me a lie.

Then don't lie about the jungle.

What Silk wanted to say was that the cold and the quiet felt like his fault. That for a moment, amidst blood loss and agony, he was sure he'd found some ancient power within himself—an ancestral power—and that the silence was not just of the jungle, but of the world. And later, in the hospital, when they told him it was a miracle the bullet didn't hit any of his organs, it seemed to confirm that the power was real. He wanted Bigger to know that there was magic, something hidden, but that could be found again. That's what he wanted to say. But Bigger was shrugging.

What does it matter?

Silk threw up his hands.

You can't fucking *lie* about the jungle.

Preach stood, holding his hands out, palms forward.

Hold up, hold up. Call the Devil a lie, but not each other.

Bigger wanted to know why Silk came back, why he extended. But now Preach was starting up his thing.

Don't you know the Devil's got all the lying we need? My, my, my. Didn't you know that the Devil came to Brother Abe, calling himself Brother Morrow? Brother Abe, he say. I got a song'll make the meanest man you know cry. And Brother Abe, he just laugh.

Preach had a funny way of talking, Bigger thought. He wasn't theatrical, didn't raise his voice like the preachers Bigger knew. But he got people's attention just the same. Soldiers nearby had stopped what they were doing to listen. And yet Preach didn't seem to notice. Bigger wasn't sure if he was even talking to Silk or Crazy Horse in particular anymore.

This song'll make you rich, say Brother Morrow, and now

Brother Abe say All right, you better tell it to me then. And Brother Morrow sang a song like nothing you ever heard before. Whoa. After he done, Brother Abe tell him to sing it again, so he can memorize it right. But Brother Morrow say No, you got it in you now. And he up and disappear. My, my, my. Brother Abe think: That must be the Devil.

Preach was standing, his hands in his pockets, his head bare, his shades hanging from the collar of his shirt, sweat collecting on his temples, the bridge of his nose, his upper lip. In the bright light, he looked as smooth and black as volcanic glass. Looking at him now, you could easily forget he was barely twenty; he was as timeless and sibylline as an ancient idol.

Well, Brother Abe got to singing that song. And it sure did make the meanest man he knew cry—that was Big John. And it sure did make Brother Abe rich. He traveled all over singing. Married the nicest-looking woman he could find, had him a whole mess of children. Mmph. Then it come time for Brother Abe to die. And who do you think come to take him away? Why, the Devil himself, yes he did. All them riches up and evaporated— *poof*—and left his wife and kids with nothing at all. And not a soul could remember how that song went, neither.

Without fanfare, Preach sat back down and lit a cigarette. Silk and Crazy Horse, who seemed to be unconsciously mirroring Preach's movements, also sat. Silk took out two cigarettes and handed one to Crazy Horse. He lit his own. Crazy Horse placed his cigarette between his lips and brought his face close to Silk's, the ends of their cigarettes touching. They both inhaled.

Evening settled around them with a gasp of thick air. Their bellies full and the night hours stretching out long ahead of them, the men found things to do that would distract them from the morning. From the mission. Crazy Horse was showing Bigger his collection of feathers. Glistening black from magpies and carrion crows and blackbirds, long white plumes of silver pheasants, scarlet of crested bunting, chartreuse of green pigeon and mustached barbet. Whenever they went out on a mission, he liked to select new ones to tuck into his helmet strap.

You don't want to stick out too much. But you've got to have something that gives you power out there.

Bullwhip walked by them with a wry laugh.

Just as bad as the thieving white man.

Crazy Horse threw a feather at Bullwhip's back.

You don't own feathers. Think they ain't got birds in *my* motherland?

Just like a magpie. See something shiny and you take it. Feathers, languages, dead warriors . . . none of it belongs to you.

Hey, man, that last was *given* to me.

Preach watched silently as Crazy Horse continued instructing Bigger on what to carry out into the world beyond the parameters of base camp.

They'll give you whatever weapons you want. So you have to be careful. They'll give you a goddamned samurai sword if you ask for it. Don't weigh yourself down, now.

Crazy Horse, aside from weapons and ammunition and C-rations, and in addition to his feathers, always made sure to have a jar of Blue Magic. Preach knew a white soldier—a rube from Pennsylvania—who combed through the latest issue of *Playboy,* sent to him by his crippled older brother, and carefully selected a page to rip out and fold into his helmet strap, one side painted black so it wouldn't be a target. There was a brother from Louisiana who carried a little sack of chicken bones.

Bigger, who had been paying rapt attention to Crazy Horse, looked up warily when a white soldier entered and approached Preach. The rabbit grinned at Preach.

Say, Preach. How about it, brother?

Crazy Horse laughed and shook his head.

Here you go with that "brother" stuff. You sure are one confused cracker.

The rabbit smiled uncertainly, but Preach waved his hand dismissively at Crazy Horse.

Don't pay him no mind.

The white soldier shuffled closer to Preach.

How about it, brother?

Crazy Horse snorted.

Brother. Say that to the wrong brother, and you'll really have yourself something, *Brother* Ned.

What's he want?

Bigger did not address himself to the white soldier, though he was talking to him. Crazy Horse laughed again, though this time at Bigger.

Hey, Brother Ned, you meet Bigger here? Bigger, this is Brother Ned. A Georgia cracker who's convinced he's in love with Preach's Black-ass sister, all from a photo he saw.

I *am* in love with her. Preach is going to—pleased to meet you, Bigger—Preach is going to let me write her just as soon as I get the right words. So how about it, Preach? Will you let me carry a photograph?

Well, she *did* just send me a new one. I suppose I could let you have her graduation picture. You don't have anything untoward in mind, do you?

Gosh no. Nothing like that, I swear.

Preach pretended to think it over. In truth, he thought his sister might like Ned once she got over him being white. Soon, he'd be back in the real world, and he'd be able to get back to the business of making sure his mother and sister were all right. He thought his sister would be okay with Ned. They'd have to move up north, of course, and he figured that would be all right too.

Well, okay.

Ned clapped Preach on the shoulder.

Wow, *thank* you. I'll take good care of it, I swear.

Preach went and got the photograph and handed it to Ned. In it, his sister stood in her cap and gown, her hair freshly pressed, their mother's faux pearls—their mother's most expensive piece of jewelry, aside from her wedding ring—clasped on her ears. She is bright-smiled and apple-faced, her large doe eyes full of laughter and pride. Bigger watched Brother Ned handle the photograph as though it were dipped in the blood of Christ and marveled—he might really be in love after all.

Ned tucked the photograph carefully into his shirt pocket.

You're getting short now, aren't you, Preach? What're you going to do once you get back into the real world?

Preach closed his eyes.

I'm going to get some college on that G.I. Bill and go to seminary just like Dr. King. But first, I'm going to get some of Mama's chicken. Nothing like it in the world.

He could taste it—his mother's chicken and his sister's lemonade and pound cake. It was the rope he'd use to guide himself back. Just a little while longer. Weeks is what it came down to, when you thought about it.

Bigger bristled at Preach discussing chicken in front of this white man.

What do you carry with you, Preach? For power?

Just my soul.

This wasn't strictly true. He didn't carry his Bible, sure, but every time he was out in the bush or out in the jungle, he had a prayer in his thoughts like a song. A different one each time. Sometimes he made it up and sometimes he didn't. He believed in the Lord, he did. But what he didn't believe was that any amount of feathers or photographs or naked ladies or crucifixes or bones or girlfriends' stockings or Virgin Marys were going to keep you from dying out there.

He lit a cigarette.

It might not even be the Lord, he thought. It might just be luck.

They set out the next morning. For the first few hours of humping, Bigger was almost able to convince himself that it wasn't that bad. The elephant grass was waist-high, the *swish-clump* of their footsteps nearly the only sound. There was a soldier in front of him, and a soldier behind. The weight of his pack was an unexpected comfort—it kept him connected to the earth, which was reassuringly solid and firm beneath his boots. For the first time since he'd crossed into the underworld, he didn't feel afraid.

But then the quiet, the monotony, began to drag. It sagged, a heavier deadweight than his pack. When they paused, his water and his C-rations both tasted like tin. Soon he couldn't think of anything but the weight of his legs as he lifted one foot, and then the other. The soldier behind him—a blood and a giant of a man— began, quietly, to hum. It was an old, wordless Delta song, as old as the first Africans dragged by the Dutch into Mississippi, the only languages common among them grief and dread and this wordless song, a membrane between untold tribes, which, incongruously, communicated not despair but exaltation, hearts that loved to beat.

With each *swish-clump*, Preach lost his grip on his prayer. He'd been reciting in his head an invocation, one from his church back home. He could hear the blood's old, wordless song, and he knew it too, though the notes were different here and there. His mouth was dry, the saliva congealing at the back of his throat. He spat. *Trying to get back home.* That was in a song, Preach thought, though he couldn't remember which song. It had a melody not far off from the Delta song that the brother was humming. *Trying to get back home.* Lord, weren't they all? Men were always trying to crawl back home. Usually, they failed.

He *was* getting short, though it was impossible to imagine that home as he knew it existed somewhere. Not with the elephant grass clutching at him and the damp funk of this country in his nose, in his mouth. Home to a man is the home of his youth, which dies as soon as he leaves it. The home of Mama and heavy foods and the careful cushioning of his ego. A traumatized man will never get home. And the world excels at making trauma, making a hurt man. Or, men excel at being hurt. And then they are just hurting and hurt*ing*.

From far off, he heard the haunting call of a gibbon—a strange, siren-like howl that ended in high-pitched chatter. Preach wondered what the monkey was saying. Sounded like *Go home* to him. The elephant grass gave way to a paddy field, the murky water tepid and shin-deep. They were passing a village. The rice farmers looked up from their work, dark faces shadowed by their conical hats. A trio of children, the oldest no more than eight, stopped their capering to stare at the American soldiers, who looked to them like bloated and mutated ma đói. Brother Ned smiled and waved at the kids, and the youngest—a four-year-old girl—attempted to run away, but the oldest boy grabbed her and held her in place, slightly behind his back. His eyes did not leave Ned's.

An old man and his daughter stood together, watching the soldiers slosh like giants through their rice. Some of the soldiers looked at them and raised their hands in the air. The old man flinched each time they did—his daughter could feel it through her grip on his arm. She bowed with just her head at the soldiers, her face tight and dry as the skin of a drum. Her village was behind her, like a hand on her back, and the others were watching. Especially the ones the soldiers couldn't see.

Silk swore he saw streaks of iridescent orange darting around his shins in the water. He paused to wipe the sweat out of his eyes, take a swig of water. The old man and the woman were looking at him. He pressed his palms together in front of his chest and bowed. After a moment, the woman bowed back. He resumed humping. The water had soaked the bottom half of his pants, and now the wetness was creeping up his legs. Once they were out of the rice paddies, they stopped briefly to peel off leeches. Silk hated the things, their fat, black bodies like dark, raised scars against his skin.

In the damp air, the sun could not completely dry them, so even when they were miles away from the village and the paddies, the uniforms hung heavy on their suffering bodies. They had been going up a steady incline for at least a mile now, and when the air stirred, you could smell the jungle. It wasn't far away. Now it was getting dark. A flock of birds performed their swooping ballet high up. The birds looked black from this distance, though, really, they could have been any color at all.

Silk felt it coming, as did Preach and Crazy Horse. But Bigger sensed nothing at all until the first shots cracked and sputtered. And even when he saw the soldier several yards ahead of him get hit, it still didn't fully register. The man had been hit in the head. Bigger had always supposed that a man shot in the head would go down immediately, the blood spraying out like a flower in bloom. But the man was still standing—he seemed to hang suspended in space and time—and the blood arced out in a stream, like water from a drinking fountain, horribly corrupted. When he did go over, it was in slow motion, as though the strings holding him up were being carefully set down.

Something slammed into Bigger's back, knocking him down. For a moment, he thought he too was hit, and the first seeds of panic began to sprout.

Wake up, cherry. And get your fucking gun off your shoulder.

Silk was on his stomach, teeth gritted as he fired in the direction of the shots.

My God, they're really trying to *kill* us. Bigger was glad that he managed not to say this out loud. But all of a sudden, he felt like he had taken one of those pep pills; he was filled with hot blood and hot rage. He couldn't remember his fatigue. Or his terror. He fired his gun into the smoking bush. All he saw was blood and gunsmoke.

The medic was belly-crawling his way to the hit soldier. Silk covered him, though they both knew the man was dead. A blood— the one who'd been humming that Delta song—got hit as well. Shot once in the thigh and once in the ass. He could see the bullets leaving his gun, watched their mathematical trajectory, a geometry as old as his song, but felt nothing.

Airfire had been called in. Word traveled down the line: Puff the Magic Dragon was coming. Through the crackle of gunfire, you could hardly hear the groan of the AC-47 gunship, but when Puff began to breathe fire, the bush lit up with orange light and thunder. Silk grabbed Bigger by the collar and dragged him out of the range of fire. Bigger crouched, panting, as bullets pelted down like hail, hitting men he couldn't see, snuffing out lives he knew nothing about. When Puff was finished, for a few moments it was as though there was no more sound in the world.

Crazy Horse, light and slightly nauseated in the aftershock of battle, made his way over to the Delta brother. His shock was wearing off, and the medic needed help holding the giant of a man down as he pried the bullet from his ass. Crazy Horse splayed himself across the brother's back. The man's muscles writhed and jerked like furious pythons underneath Crazy Horse. Then, Crazy Horse looked over into the face of the soldier who'd been shot in the head and recognized it despite the slackness of death. It was as though the angry pythons from inside the brother beneath him had made their way up inside him instead. He hopped off the brother and knelt by the dead man. He gently tilted the face up and found it pale, warped. Empty.

Crazy Horse ran out into the bush toward the team that was dragging out bodies, trying to get a kill count. He ignored the men who called out his name. He dropped to his hands and knees, searching the ground. He wasn't sure exactly where Hansel had been standing when he'd been hit, but Crazy Horse knew he was in the right general area.

Hansel, the Aryan-looking rabbit from rural Pennsylvania, who'd never met a Black person before joining the army, and yet held no prejudice, or really any malice whatsoever. Who never wanted to be in this war, never wanted to kill anyone. Who wanted only to help his parents run their farm and take care of his crippled older brother. Who believed in the holiness of simplicity, the grace in hard work. Whose only indulgence was *Playboy*, which his brother sent to him regularly, first as a kind of joke, and then as a kind of religion.

Crazy Horse felt a hand on his shoulder and knew from the smell of tobacco that it was Preach.

Come on, now.

Crazy Horse shrugged the hand away.

He ought to have his page with him.

You'll never find it, man. Hey, it's okay—come on, get up.

But Crazy Horse's rage was a demon, and now it took full possession. From the row of Vietnamese bodies, he heard a choked, animal sound. One of them was still alive. A shrieking roar filled Crazy Horse's ears as he charged over to them. In the dimness, he could barely see their faces. All but one of them were blank and unseeing. Or maybe the injured man couldn't see either. Or per-

haps what he saw was something just beyond the gates of possibility, a kaleidoscopic amalgamation of his father's religion, his
village's superstitions, the mythologies of this land, all of which
he'd stopped believing in, until now.

Crazy Horse came to at the sound of a single shot. Silk was
lowering his gun, grim reproach writ on his face. Silk had shot the
Vietnamese soldier in the head. Crazy Horse had been mindlessly,
viciously mauling the man with his boots, gore rising up and
grasping at his ankles. He'd been stomping the man into the earth,
kicking him to hell. He staggered away. The demon had had its
fun, and now it clambered up his throat. He exorcised it into the
bushes.

today

AS HE VENTURED out of the guesthouse in a dark hour of the morning, Faruq had half expected someone to try to stop him. But no one did. He'd found a barely cleared trail that led into the woods, and the air was hung with green dampness. Faruq had never seen fog so thick—it seemed to swallow the sound of his footsteps, and it wrapped itself around the trees, partially hiding them so that his pounding steps seemed to float, disembodied.

Running through the redwoods felt endless in a way that a city run couldn't. Here, there were no traffic lights or slow pedestrians, no sidewalk debris or confounded dogs, nothing to interrupt his flight; only the trees bobbing in soft white fog, ancient root systems, and the trail, which began to lose its shape the farther Faruq ran. His muscles rejoiced in the burn of a long run, his first real run since touching down in California.

As he continued, gradually, there was more light, fewer trees, and the fog seemed to churn out ahead as the dirt turned into sand. Suddenly there was the ocean, the fog hovering just over the white waves. The beach seemed to materialize out of nothing. The air was heavier here, more substantial, like the touch of flesh. The waves reached languidly for him again and again—a ballet gesture—and behind him, the land swept up, the trees featureless spectators. Down the beach, dark boulders sat, nestled in fog, like the giant eggs of a mythical bird. If Faruq believed in gods, or spirits, or devils, or monsters, he'd easily believe this place was rife with them, abounding with the angelic and the terrible.

A quick glance at his phone told him he'd progressed about

five kilometers down the beach. Sand stuck in clumps to his ankles. The fog seemed thicker here. Faruq's face was wet, his beard encrusted with salt. He increased his pace—just over a four-minute mile; he'd slow down again once he reached his turnaround point.

This was his fastest pace—unless he was trying to break his personal record, he liked to start slow, push himself near the halfway point, and then slow way back down to the finish. If he had enough energy at the end, he might sprint the last kilometer or so. He doubted he'd have the energy today. It was easier in the city, when he could pop into any bodega for a quick bagel, a small bag of peanuts—anything to fuel him. But here, all he had was the little baggie of almonds. Running in sand was taking its toll.

Faruq had to keep jerking himself back into the moment. Staying present was always a little more challenging when he ran without music, but being left mostly to himself and his own thoughts over the past several weeks made it harder than usual to turn off. He wasn't sleeping very well, either. His body felt heavier, as though he'd put on weight, though he was sure he'd lost pounds since being here.

As he neared his turnaround point, he suddenly got the sense that he was no longer alone on the beach. He kept expecting to see other people appear out of the fog like spikes. But no one did. And then he began to spot patches of busy footprints—not human. Too compact, the spacing not right for a biped, though the wet sand and the fog and the waves softened their edges, blurred their shapes.

Before long, Faruq could actually hear the other presence; beneath the ocean's growl, beneath his own breath, its quiet, prodding steps. It was *following* him, he realized. Faruq's fear kindled—there was no one around, he had nothing on him to defend himself with. He stopped. Small muscle twitches traveled up his calves, and his lungs burned.

He waited. He heard the thing take a few more loping steps, slow down, stop. Then nothing. Faruq stayed still for several moments—long enough for his breathing to slow, for his muscles to begin to cramp. Tentatively, he began again, a jog at first, and then up to speed. It took awhile for him to hear it, but there it was again—the presence did not seem to be chasing him, but rather, keeping pace.

Faruq's heart thrummed almost painfully. He stopped again, panting. His hands shook.

He heard the presence trot past him and then stop. He waited, got the sense the thing was waiting too. He could feel it, the mass of its body somewhere in the fog, a kind of spectral heat; it was close to him. And then, in front of him, a shape emerged. Gray and nebulous at first, and then more and more solid, the details becoming clearer as it approached. Something tentative in its step. Faruq froze. Its appearance was more than a shock; it made it impossible that this was just his imagination, just a dream—it was too solid, the detail too fine. The slender legs, the plushness at the ears, the dark rings around the eyes.

The wolf stopped just a few yards away from Faruq. His vision jumped and then focused, adjustment of a lens. Despite the distance between them, Faruq could see the wolf in unsettling detail. They stared at each other. Faruq's muscles tensed painfully. But the wolf seemed at ease. It seemed to study him, almost curious. Its nose twitched, picking up Faruq's scent, making something of it, drawing its own inscrutable conclusions. It could probably smell his fear, Faruq knew. He tried not to be afraid.

He couldn't remember what you were supposed to do in this situation. Were you supposed to play dead? Try to look big? Throw something? Make a startling noise? Or would that just convince the wolf to attack? He did nothing. The wolf did nothing. It seemed not even to blink. Faruq could see the intelligence in its eyes, the snapping, leaping sentience. He was sure then that the wolf had only emerged from the fog because he *wanted* Faruq to see him.

They were communicating, then. The longer he stared, the more Faruq's eyes zoomed in on the fine details of the wolf—he was uncanny, beautiful in some raw, uninhibited way. Mottled gray fur pierced with whites, reds, and browns, shivering droplets of moisture at the tips of his ears, a snaking white line across his black nose, like a vein through marble—a scar?—and beneath it, the droll slant of his mouth, the teeth tucked away. His probing eyes were a hotly lit yellow. To Faruq's surprise, as they regarded each other within a timeless eternity, he began to feel an abstract understanding dawn. There was a languageless language between them.

Incredulously, he came to just *know* that the wolf did not intend to hurt him. He nearly laughed out loud at himself. It was ridiculous, imbecilic, that he, an indisputable city boy, should presume to know what this wild animal did or did not intend. Yet, beneath a topsoil of instinctive fear, what Faruq felt was a grotesque calm, a communion.

Experimentally, he performed the same slow blink that he often directed toward his cat, Muezza, not really expecting it to translate. To Muezza, Faruq believed it to mean something like *peace*. He wasn't sure that this was something a notoriously wary apex predator could understand. But after several taut moments, to Faruq's utter awe, the wolf returned the slow blink. Deliberately, Faruq thought. The equivalent of slowing down your speech for someone who doesn't speak your language well.

It took suddenly hearing the ocean again for Faruq to realize he'd somehow blocked out its sound. He didn't know how long he'd been deaf to it, how long he'd been crystallized in time with the wolf. He felt his body again too, all at once—it was cold, hot, cramping, trembling with adrenaline. Faruq took a careful step back. The wolf only watched. Another, and another. The wolf tilted his head but didn't move. Pulling from a well of bravery he didn't know he had, Faruq turned and began to walk away. He could hear that the wolf wasn't following. He glanced back and found the wolf's shape once again being obscured by the fog.

Little by little, he increased his pace. Now he was running back up the beach. His own gravity slammed back into him, time returning, maniacal. He was going too fast. There were the wolf's footsteps again; not chasing, but keeping pace. A shadow sound. A ghost sound. Faruq reached the trees again far too soon. Nausea rose up in him. The woods swam before his eyes.

But still, as he broke back into the damp redwoods, the ground firming up beneath his feet, he did not slow down. He ran through the cramping, the stitches, the twisting of his gut. He was limping now as he ran, his form breaking down, his stride skipping like a record. He hadn't noticed when he'd stopped hearing the wolf, wasn't sure that he really *wasn't* hearing him.

When he finally reached the woods at the edge of the Forbidden City, his legs gave out. He collapsed. The meager contents of his stomach splattered into the grass. His whole body shook so violently he barely had any control over it. He'd beat his personal record.

Odo appeared, as though from thin air, beside him as he slowly hobbled his way to the guesthouse, his stomach still aching from overtaxing himself. Faruq nodded in greeting, afraid he might vomit again if he tried speaking. For several moments, Odo simply walked beside him in silence. At first, this felt odd to Faruq, but as the quiet stretched on, Odo keeping Faruq's slow pace, it began to feel soft. Comforting. When they reached the guesthouse, Odo opened the door for Faruq and then followed in behind him.

"Better sit down, scholar," Odo said once they were inside. "You don't look well."

Faruq sat on the cushions. He could feel that he needed sleep. His body was heavy, more sore than usual and hard to move. Odo disappeared into the kitchenette and was gone long enough that Faruq thought he might have left. He rested back against the cushions, longing for a hot bath. One of the luxuries he missed from his father's Brooklyn brownstone. He let his eyes close for several minutes. Had Odo left? Was he alone? He felt alone. But then Odo was pressing a hot mug into his hands, and he wasn't sure if he'd fallen asleep or only just closed his eyes.

"Drink that," said Odo. "Just tea," he said, grinning, when he saw Faruq's hesitation.

Faruq took a sip and it was way too hot. He held the mug between his tired hands. Odo sat on the floor before him, watching.

"Lemme ask you something," Odo eventually said. "Where are you running to?"

Faruq closed his eyes again. The dark was nice. He could concentrate better without the noise of the seen world in front of him. "What do you mean?"

"Oh, I know the cliché is to ask what you're running *from*. But seems to me you're running toward something. *For* something. Where you tryna go, scholar?"

Faruq kept his eyes closed, though his brow furrowed. He answered without thinking too hard. "Forward."

"To what? What do you need?"

Faruq shook his heavy head. "I don't know."

"Nuh-uh. You know. You *know*, Faruq. Speak it."

He could still hear the waves, feel the presence of the wolf just outside of sight. The mug warmed his hands. "I need answers."

"To what? What're you asking?"

"I don't know—nothing new. The same thing everyone asks: Why? What's the meaning?"

"Nah, don't do that—stay inside yourself. What are *you* asking? What are you trying to get to?"

"The truth, I guess."

"What truth?"

"I don't know, general truth, truth of the world, of my life?"

"And what's the truth gonna do for you? Hold you down? Anchor you? Give you some promise that makes all the shit worth living through? Make you feel like what you've lost, you haven't lost in vain?" Odo chuckled. "You believe in Nothing, scholar. And I mean that with a capital *N*. But you ain't comfortable with it. Nah. You trying to fill all that Nothing with *truth*."

Faruq opened his eyes. The room seemed too bright. Odo's words were a shock of cold water. Uncomfortably close. There was a vacuum of silence left behind where his parents used to be, and there was no afterlife to offer him comfort. Only the truths of this world. But that's what he did, wasn't it? He glanced down at Odo—the man was watching him carefully, those dark eyes bright with focus. He was looking for a reaction, Faruq thought, looking to see if he'd hit gold.

Faruq smiled and sat up straight. "I'm a journalist. Truth is my job," he said.

Odo smiled back at him, a sly, knowing smile, like a child who'd been caught sneaking a cookie from the jar. Faruq took another sip of the tea. Just right this time.

They called themself Zephyr, though in a previous life, they had been known as Leslie Bowater, child of a Republican councilmember in North Carolina who had come under the ridicule of his most conservative constituents when Zephyr née Leslie had very publicly come out as nonbinary. Faruq had specifically requested to speak with someone who had perhaps tried to leave the nameless, but, as Zephyr was now explaining, they were not that person. He remained unable to find any *former* followers, and no one from Christ the Word Evangelical would speak to him. In fact, Faruq was beginning to wonder if the followers that lived in the Forbidden City ever left the redwoods at all.

"Okay," Faruq said, hitting the record button on his phone, "so just for my records, can you tell me when you first came to the Forbidden City?"

"About five years ago," Zephyr said, running a finger over a carefully manicured eyebrow.

"And you've been here ever since?"

"That's right." Zephyr smiled. Faruq noticed a jewel on one of their teeth and wondered if it was a permanent adornment.

"Do you *ever* leave?" he asked.

"I leave the Forbidden City on sweeps all the time," Zephyr told him, flashing another smile, this one a bit tart.

"What's a sweep?" asked Faruq, irritable.

"They're like mission trips. We go out and spread our philosophy to people who might need it."

Faruq raised an eyebrow. "I thought you all didn't proselytize."

Zephyr grinned and lit a joint. "We don't. We spread our philosophy. Whoever is drawn to it is ready to receive it."

Zephyr offered Faruq the joint and Faruq shook his head. He tried again. "Is that how you came to be part of the nameless?" he asked. "Through a sweep?"

"Yes, actually," Zephyr said. "Coming from a political family, I found the nameless philosophy . . . refreshing. I wanted to be a part of this thing." Zephyr sighed wistfully. "If our government adopted the wisdom that Odo gives us, honestly, the world would be a better place." They took a pull from the joint and smiled conspiratorially at Faruq. "But there's a new generation of nameless kids coming up. They'll change things. From the inside out."

"Are you talking about overthrowing the government? Something like that?"

Zephyr chuckled. "We're just trying to change the world."

"Okay," said Faruq. "And how will you do that?"

"By following the 18 Utterances. By creating beauty to combat distortion."

"I hear folks here talk about creating beauty a lot. What does that mean, exactly?"

"Basically, we all have certain gifts. Some of us are poets, some are painters, some are builders, thinkers . . . you get it. Our job is to share those gifts with our community, and with the world. And we make sure to support art and education, so more beauty can be made."

"That doesn't sound so bad."

Zephyr laughed. "It's *not* bad. Let me ask you a question, Faruq: Are you looking for something sinister here?"

Faruq shifted on his feet. "Well, no offense, from the outside looking in, this does look a bit like a cult."

Zephyr nodded, unsurprised. "No one is here by force. People can leave anytime they want."

"That's just it, though," Faruq said. "It doesn't seem like anyone actually leaves. Even today, I asked to speak with someone who's at least attempted to go, and they sent you."

Zephyr stubbed out their joint and tucked it behind their ear. "And so you're thinking it must be because we don't *let* anybody leave? Rather than, I don't know, maybe nobody *wants* to leave?"

Faruq took a breath. "The latter seems improbable."

"Oh, Faruq," Zephyr snorted. "Don't you think, if we were so terrible, we'd have a whistleblower or two out there by now? I mean, *besides* a crazy church of fascists."

Faruq cracked a smile at this.

Zephyr placed a hand on Faruq's shoulder. "You know the number one thing people complain about when they're new followers?"

"What?"

"Having to give up Christmas."

Faruq laughed. "Seriously? But you guys do have holidays, don't you?"

Zephyr nodded. "The 3 Rituals. Ewa is in May. We celebrate beauty, do big sweeps and mass strippings."

"Strippings? Is that the one where you walk through the streets naked?"

"No, no," Zephyr chuckled. "Getting stripped is basically getting ritually cleansed with coconut water."

"Hmm."

"And then we have Fall Day—July thirty-first. It commemorates the time of the original fall. It's also Odo's birthday. *That's* the one where we do the procession. Some people do it without clothes, yes."

"Why?" Faruq asked.

"It symbolizes vulnerability, surrender. Getting stripped."

"A bit on the nose, isn't it?"

"I guess it kinda is." Zehpyr shook their head, smiling. "Then the last one is Bacchanal, which happens during the winter solstice. We combat distortion wherever we see it."

"The protests," Faruq said.

"There have been protests, yes."

From what Faruq had seen online, those protests could be

quite controversial, like when some nameless followers had gotten arrested for incapacitating several construction vehicles in Washington, DC, in order to protest gentrification.

Another follower jogged up to Zephyr and whispered something that looked urgent into their ear. Zephyr nodded at them and then smiled apologetically at Faruq. "I've got to go, Faruq, I'm sorry."

"Everything okay?" Faruq asked.

"Everything is fine. Just a little logistical hiccup. It was so nice talking to you."

In the dimming of the day into early evening, Faruq wondered how the followers would react if he began to run, right now.

Freshly showered, Faruq ventured out and found Odo speaking in front of the house of the nameless. He was seated cross-legged on the ground, and he was talking as though to a couple of friends, rather than the growing crowd of followers, some of whom were recording him with their phones. He wasn't even raising his voice—his followers and Faruq had to pack in close to hear him.

"Life is a beautiful thing," Odo was saying. "That's right. Life is a beautiful thing. But if you're one of those that doesn't think that death is a beautiful thing too, then you got no idea how beautiful life is. Whoa."

The woman next to Faruq burst into tears. She wasn't the only one crying. Faruq took his phone out and began to record Odo.

"If you don't think death is beautiful, you got no business going around talking about life is beautiful. Don't come around me talking about no sanctity of life if you haven't got any respect for death. Well."

The woman next to Faruq, now sobbing, was being gently cradled by two other followers, both of them with Mother Mary smiles on their faces. Faruq wondered what she was hearing, what she thought Odo was saying to her. He moved forward, closer to Odo. People were packed more closely together here. He willed himself to relax in the press of warm limbs on either side of him.

"Life is a beautiful thing. Death is a beautiful thing. *Fear* is a beautiful thing." Odo looked directly at Faruq.

"Well, well, well. That's it—fear is a beautiful thing. Lemme ask you this: If you're walking through these old redwoods here, and you come across Mr. Gray Wolf, what is it that gives you the speed you need to get the hell out of his way?"

Odo's gaze never left Faruq; it was like Odo was talking directly to him. He even paused after posing his question, as though giving Faruq time to answer. Tension built between Faruq's shoulder blades. He held his phone and his eyes steady.

"That's fear. Now you try and tell me that fear is not a beautiful thing. See, most people don't understand beauty—*real* beauty. Wasn't so long ago you couldn't find Mr. Wolf around here at all. And why? Because most people only see distortion."

Faruq's eyes were burning. Odo didn't blink, and so he fought not to, either. Faruq, much to his annoyance, hadn't been able to get more than superficial conversation out of Odo since his first day in the Forbidden City, over a week ago. Now, in front of all these followers, Odo was singling him out. Odo leaned forward, hands clasped. Was he testing him? To tell him something? To humiliate him? Faruq drew neutrality over his features like a drape.

"I told you that fear is a beautiful thing. But when you're living distorted—well. Mr. Wolf was here long before you or I. Millions of wolves, living and loving. Wolves are complicated brothers, you know. They *understand*—they naturally have the Other Sight. If you show him some respect, if you see him, he'll see you. Oh yes. But when the Europeans came here, they couldn't see right. They were distorted, and so their actions were distorted. They killed up all the wolves, murdered the last one in California back in 1924. All of 'em killed that last wolf, even if they didn't pull the trigger. They all got that blood on their hands."

Odo held Faruq's eyes. Faruq felt his neck grow hot. Odo was sermonizing directly to Faruq, without so much as raising his voice. It was intimate, like being serenaded. Yet no one seemed to think Odo's steady attention on Faruq odd. Followers held their hands over their mouths, their hearts, their cheeks glittering with tears. And Odo's eyes glittered too, though not with tears—it was a light, either holy or infernal, but, either way, hungry.

"And what happened when they got rid of all the wolves? Too many deer, elk, and rabbits. All the shrubs and trees getting ate up. Erosion. Rivers changing course, drying up some areas, and soaking others. For almost one hundred years. Whoa.

"But then, Mr. Wolf came back. A wolf they called OR-7 came to California and made his family here. Now the wolves are back. Some people are still distorted about it, but if you see Mr. Wolf, he'll see you. Do you understand what I'm trying to say to you? When you see clearly, fear is a beautiful thing. You don't have to do anything about it. *No.* You don't have to *conquer* it. You don't have to take out what scares you. No. You just have to see without distortion."

Odo's face suddenly opened up into a wide grin.

"And me—even if you don't see me, I'll see you."

Laughter. Faruq didn't exactly get the joke. It sounded more like a threat. Faruq stopped recording and lowered his phone. Odo looked up to the sky—the signal that he was about to begin a prayer. Everyone but Faruq looked up to the sky as well.

"There is no good or evil; only beauty. All else is distortion."

This was the nameless call to prayer, recited by Odo in a tone that was somewhere in between calling and singing. Its proximity to the adhan got Faruq every time. Thorns grew from his spine—guilt, grief, anger, and, still, reverence. Odo's followers repeated after him in a monotone echo.

See the cycle of time—it's a great whirlpool hurling endlessly through birth and death. Outside of it waits Mow Vutu. Outside is the World, our shelter from the chaos of the universe, the end of distortion. Thank you, Vutu, for the World. Thank you, Vutu, for helping us break the cycle. Thank you, Vutu, for beauty. Thank you, Vutu, for fear.

The followers kept their eyes closed and their faces lifted for several moments after the recitation. Aeschylus and Clover—

who'd said their goodbyes to Faruq late the night before—had explained this to him: It was the silent part of prayer, where followers asked their nameless god for personal blessings. Though they weren't asking, really. They were visualizing the thing they wanted, trying to use all five senses, and thanking Vutu as though the thing were already theirs. Faruq looked around at their faces. At the edge of the crowd, a flash of black: the Deep. There were only a few of them, in a single line. Their hands were clasped behind their backs, their faces blank and facing the crowd, not the sky.

Someone brushed their fingertips against his palm, and he startled briefly. Zephyr smiled at him with an irking look of benevolent patience.

"Faruq, I'm leaving for another sweep soon. I wanted to say goodbye."

"Everything work out?"

Zephyr furrowed their brow in confusion.

"You know," Faruq said slowly, "with the logistical hiccup."

"Oh. Yeah. Everything is as it should be," Zephyr said. They dapped and Faruq watched Zephyr walk off amidst the dispersing crowd of followers. He lingered, hoping to get a few moments alone with Odo, but followers clung to him, eager to be near him, eager for his attention. He treated each one of them singularly, dapping them, touching them with familiarity as though he had nothing but time. He showed none of the micro-signals of fatigue that most people would when greeting and talking to person after person. No uncomfortable shifting, no wandering eyes, no increasingly distant smile; Odo didn't even rise from his seat at the base of the stairs until the last follower walked away and Faruq approached.

Odo smiled at him, his dark, largely unlined face glowing. Faruq was a tall man; he and Odo were about the same height, and yet Faruq got the impression that Odo was looking down at him paternalistically. They performed their dap, and briefly, Faruq wondered how he remembered them all, the variations he seemed to invent for each person he met.

"Do you have a minute?" Faruq asked.

"Always."

Odo began to walk, picking his long legs up and setting them down deliberately, as though walking through long grasses. Faruq followed, keeping pace at his side.

"I'm hoping to spend more time with you. I'm curious about the man beyond the lawsuit."

Something slipped in Odo's face very briefly—Faruq would have missed it if he weren't so practiced at being observant. Just a quick wavering of the mask and then it was gone. "That lawsuit— a bunch of distorted silliness. And Minh-An just *had* to do that documentary."

"Didn't you agree to it too? Wouldn't you have had to?"

Odo's smile was mischievous. "They all talked me into it. Minh-An, mostly. And then Vutu said *nuh-uh*, so I came out here and got real quiet."

"You don't strike me as the kind of man who can get 'talked into' anything."

Odo chuckled. "A scholar, sure enough."

"A scholar?" Odo stopped walking. They were standing in front of a fence, beyond which was a field, bordered by wild weeds and bushes. The field contained a large white barn, and, occasionally, Faruq knew, a few stallions whose flanks shone in the fog-blurred sunlight, and who, for the price of an apple, would condescend to saunter over and allow a couple of strokes on their muscular necks, though their expressions made it clear this was an immense favor. Without them, the field looked barren.

"A scholar. One of the ten Tintan." Odo placed his hands on the fence. "We all come from the ten original Tintan. Your father's religion would call them angels. Something like that."

Faruq was taken aback by Odo's casual mention of his father. Faruq had only spoken of his father's religion at Aeschylus and Clover's party. Maybe he should have anticipated it, but it was unsettling that someone had reported what he'd said to Odo.

"When the Tintan fell," Odo continued, "they fractured into

gosah, that spark that makes life. Whoa. And so, every living thing is a fragment of the ten original Tintan."

Faruq was listening hungrily. It sounded like nonsense, the kind of thing a child would dream up, but there had to be something in it that grabbed so many—people like him: young, progressive, creative.

"So, what, they're like archetypes now, because of this? Personality types?"

Odo chuckled again. "Something like that, scholar."

Odo looked out onto the field, seeing something, Faruq thought, other than the field. Odo's face was still as a mask. It was easy to forget, Faruq thought, observing Odo out the sides of his eyes, that Odo was an elderly man. He claimed to have been a soldier in the Vietnam War, which would put him in his seventies at least. Yet he was strong and spry, ageless in both appearance and presence. Right now, he looked as smooth and serene as the Sphinx.

For a while, Faruq didn't think Odo was going to speak again. But after a few silent moments Odo adjusted his grip on the fence and leaned forward.

"They balance each other out," he said. "Light and dark, yin and yang, masculine and feminine. Like that. Nothing good and nothing bad. Just Creator and Destroyer, Seeker and Absconder, Guru and Scholar, Savior and Adventurer, Reveler and Peacemaker."

Faruq played the list again and again like a song, committing it to memory. "And I'm a scholar. That makes you—the Guru?"

Odo only smiled. Faruq could feel him closing up like an oyster. He gritted his teeth, but then softened, inserted some joviality into his tone, hoping playfulness might encourage Odo to give him what he needed. "Come on, give me something," he cajoled. "Or am I being fucked with here? I'm here to observe, but I'm the one being observed, I think."

"Look into the void and the void looks back at you," Odo said.

"What does that *mean*?"

"Don't whine, scholar. Ain't you a man grown? Then you ought to know that you don't have the right to look without being looked at yourself."

Faruq wondered if Odo was *admitting* to the wolf lecture being somehow pointed. Somehow, someway, Odo knew about that wolf. Or maybe Faruq was going crazy already. "Well," he hedged, "I *did* have an interesting experience on my run earlier."

"Lots of things in them woods," said Odo vaguely.

"Like what?" Faruq didn't want to admit to seeing the wolf. He wanted to keep the extent of that experience private, if privacy was an option here. But he also wanted Odo to admit it if he was watching him, if he somehow *knew*.

"It's the woods, scholar." Odo shrugged.

"I don't know," Faruq said, "at times I felt like someone was watching me run."

"And how does that make you feel?" Odo asked, smirking.

"So someone *is* watching me?"

"I ain't say that. I'm asking you how you feel. You're in them woods, alone, and you feel eyes on you. Are you curious? Are you scared?"

"I guess both."

"And I bet that fear is doing something for you. I bet you're running harder than you ever were before, huh?"

"So someone is watching me . . . to scare me into being a better runner?"

Odo laughed. "Scholar, that feeling you're talking about is in your head. Don't make it any less useful, any less real."

Odo slapped Faruq on the back and stalked off, shaking his head. Chuckling to himself.

There was no reception in the guesthouse. He took his cell phone and walked into the middle of the Forbidden City where he'd been able to get a signal once before. But not today, apparently.

He couldn't even find one bar; if he wanted to use Wi-Fi, he'd have to go someplace less private. Right now, he needed to vent, and no one would understand his frustration like Anita.

He began to wander, waving his phone as though to stir a signal into existence. A week ago, this would have made him self-conscious, suspecting, as he did, that he was constantly being watched, and his actions reported back to Odo. But now, after Odo's pointed wolf sermon, Faruq had decided that his otherness was unavoidable.

"Looking for a signal?" Faruq turned. The woman who had spoken to him was tall, willowy, with features that, on their own, were too large, but together were striking. There was something wry in her smile, like she was gently making fun of him.

Faruq lowered his phone. There was a little self-consciousness left in him after all. "It's so spotty out here."

The woman nodded. She had long, dark hair that she parted in the middle, and Faruq noticed that she had large eyes, the kind that always looked watery.

"I know a hotspot," she said. "Come on."

She led him down the tree-surrounded path that ran more or less through the smattering of guesthouses. The followers called this path River Trail because it led, eventually, to the narrow Gosah River, which wound behind the school and into the woods. As they walked, the woman gave her name: Kaya. She already knew his. Faruq wondered idly if Kaya was her given name. Some followers seemed to adopt new names according to preference, according to who they would like to be as followers of the nameless. Odo didn't really make a practice of renaming anyone. Kaya, dark-haired and dark-eyed, was racially ambiguous enough that Faruq couldn't easily guess whether she was Kaya by design or by choice.

Once they reached the river, Faruq reluctantly followed Kaya as she gingerly walked into the water, toward a small mass of land surrounded by the river's sluggish waters. The water was shallow, the river rocks steady underneath their feet.

"We call this Ø Island," Kaya explained. "There's always reception here for some reason, and it's tucked away enough that
it's private."

She smiled at him, and Faruq, wondering if she'd leave him to
his phone call or if he'd have to come back later, alone, was about
to thank her when his phone began chiming in his pocket.

He took it out and looked at the screen. Because of the spotty
service, he hadn't been getting Danish's text messages, and now
they were coming through all at once.

Aunties are mobilizing lol

Theyre trying to come over . . . bro. Help.

The aunties want to meet with you asap. Think theyre trying to marry
you off.

Hey man where are u? Answer ur phone.

Aunties are threatening to call their ppl in CA.

Kaya, to Faruq's irritation, was looking over his shoulder.
"Family stuff?" she asked.

"Mm-hm," said Faruq.

He was distracted. Clearly, he was going to have to come back
later if he wanted to call Anita and Danish in private. It was unlike Danish to text him so insistently. But if something had happened, he would just say so. Faruq was starting to worry that
somehow the aunties had found out what Faruq was really doing
in California. He sent Danish a neutral text just to let him know
he was all right, just the victim of barely-there cell service, and
that they'd talk later.

"Sure you don't want to make a call?" Kaya asked. "I know
how families can be."

"Do you have an intrusive family too?" Faruq said this in a
mildly pointed tone.

"Oh, this is my family now," Kaya said, holding her arms out. "It's such a beautiful thing, being able to choose a family for yourself."

"What do you mean when you say 'choose a family for yourself'?" Faruq asked. "Is that how you think of the nameless? A family?"

"Sort of," Kaya laughed. "But not in the Manson way—don't worry. My old family," she continued, "the one I was born into—they taught me only distortion. They taught me to hate what I saw, to somehow still believe that I wasn't worthy of any of it, either."

"They taught you self-loathing? Distortion?"

"Religious zealots," Kaya said. "Everything was a sin."

Faruq nodded in understanding. They began walking back the way they'd come, back toward the center of everything.

"You can only teach what you know, and what they knew was to hate themselves and their own bathwater."

"So you escaped fundamentalism?"

"It took a few tries. When I was sixteen, I downed two full glasses of bleach. As it turns out, Clorox isn't nearly as toxic as you might think. You can't keep it down, really, and then you get force-fed milk and that's the end of it. While I was in the hospital, I tried to saw through my wrists with a plastic fork I had sharpened, but I couldn't get deep enough, fast enough—the nurses caught me."

She'd told him about her suicide attempts with such frankness, not a tear in sight. It was a relief, really, because the tears would have made this a performance; tears were so often expected, even demanded. But maybe the absence of tears was another kind of performance after all.

It was exhausting, not knowing what was sincerity and what was artifice.

Faruq rubbed his beard, wiped a thin sheen of sweat from his temple.

"They mucked my mind up with their medicine. I could barely even see, you know? I tried slitting my wrists again when I was twenty, and I tried overdosing on oxy when I was twenty-three. I just couldn't get it right. I figured there must be something I'm missing. Turns out, I was right. And it was *here*."

They had made it as far as Ewa Park, where trees stood like sentinels around a small pond, their reflections in the water as stern as the trees themselves.

"And how did you get here?" Faruq asked.

"I convinced my parents to let me go to college." She laughed. "I'd been homeschooled most of my life. But I got in, and I met a follower at a party. She took me to meet Odo. I was instantly floored. I dropped out."

The treetops hovered over them, seeming to dip down like eavesdroppers.

"You sure you don't want to call home?" Kaya asked. "I'll give you space—I'll stay here." She nodded, planting her feet in the ground as though to demonstrate her commitment to the spot she was standing in. "Go on. Go back and call your mother."

Faruq was suddenly quite cool. She had to know. Had to. The nameless was a great spider's web with Odo at the center—Faruq couldn't tell one of them something without the rest of them knowing. But as he looked at Kaya now—her face soft and bright and clear, albeit half masked by the shadows of tree limbs—he just couldn't imagine her being deliberately cruel.

"My mother is dead."

Something passed over Kaya's face, but it moved too quickly for Faruq to recognize it, and then she was smiling gently.

"That doesn't mean you can't reach her."

She held out a hand. It seemed to Faruq that she had no doubt at all that he would take it. There was something patronizing about the gesture. Or, if not patronizing, presumptuous? He was sure he was being manipulated. She seemed to take it for granted that he was attracted to her. And, of course he was—dark hair and dark eyes, almost black, smooth olive skin. It irritated him that she was right.

He met her almost halfway; he reached his hand out toward

hers without touching her. Just taking a careful temperature, like checking to see if the oil is hot in the pan. Let her be the one to take hold. She closed the distance and clasped two of his fingers in her warm hand, and squeezed. His fingers pressed into each other until he felt bone on bone. He felt the bite of her nails against his skin.

She began to pull, gently but firmly, and, in silence, Faruq followed. In silence, Faruq allowed himself to be led away from where they had come from and into the house of the nameless. He had already been inside, of course. It was a more rustic version of the flagship in Brooklyn. Wooden beams, clean white halls hung with original art. The hardwood floors were covered with expensive rugs.

Kaya gestured to him that he should remove his shoes. Obediently, instinctually, he crouched down and began untying his laces. Kaya simply kicked off her own shoes and held out her hand to help him back to his feet. She did not tell him he had to take off his bright red beanie, so he left it on; it offered a not wholly imaginary protection, especially against the maroon that everyone else seemed to be wearing in the Forbidden City today.

They settled down, cross-legged, on a rug in the middle of the room, facing each other. The light in the room was strange because of the whitewashing of the windows. On one wall, there was a huge portrait of Odo—Faruq recognized it from the nameless's Instagram profile. Only, instead of black and white, this version was in full color, and the dusty sunlight coming in through the whitewashed windows brushed up dully against it, creating shadow.

Kaya's face had gone serious, even somber, though no less warm. "Do you know the 18 Utterances by heart?" she asked.

He shook his head.

"I'll do the recitation for you, then. Close your eyes and breathe in and out of your nose as fast as you can."

Faruq nodded. An ex had once dragged him to a yoga class, and he remembered doing something like this—it felt like hyperventilating but it was supposed to be "cleansing." He began, and under the clamor of his own breathing he could just make out Kaya's voice, softly reciting the 18 Utterances.

> There is no god but the nameless Odo is the messenger of Mow Vutu All suffering is distortion Strip yourself of distortion Sacrifice Create Beauty Get hipped to Oneness Love freely Meditate to the vibration of Vutu and the World Pray regularly See only Beauty Do not despair at death Train the Other Sight Hip all beings to the nameless Create order in chaos Correct distortion Harness gosah in pursuit of Wholeness Seek the face of Mow Vutu . . .

He was lightheaded now, and so when he felt Kaya's fingertips on his shoulders, pushing, he fell back easily, landing softly on the plush rug, his legs unfolding like awoken pythons.

"Now just stop breathing, Faruq. Hold it for as long as you can."

He was surprised by how comfortable it was at first, how long it took for his lungs to begin to fight him.

"When you let it back in, just relax. Whatever comes, let it."

Faruq's last thought before giving in to his lungs was that this was stupid, exactly the kind of kombucha-chugging, crystal-hoarding, turmeric-snorting bullshit that had people believing you could cure pneumonia with sunlight and positive thinking.

See her face, he thought he heard Kaya whisper, though her voice sounded only half real, irritatingly indistinct.

The thing was, as the breath came rushing back in, his mother's face *did* appear, unbidden, spinning out of the darkness behind his eyelids. She seemed to be hurtling toward him; or else, toward the center of him. Eyes wide, lashes clinging to each other, mouth shut tight, both in defiance and protection against choking on water, against drowning, the vein throbbing at the temple, hijab clinging wetly, and the single escaped tendril of hair, black, shining, wet—*No not that.*

There was an impact, there but muted, as though he were

wearing armor; something hit him in the center of his chest, but from the inside—his mother colliding with his ribs? He jerked, a burst of neon green behind his eyes, intricate and creeping as moss, and then it was his mother's hand on his shoulder, soothing, the other pushing hair back from his forehead, the touch achingly familiar, remembered and well missed, a most tender, most cruel haunting. His eyes snapped open. It was not his mother touching him—of course it wasn't—but Kaya.

"Are you all right?" she was asking.

He sat up shakily. She watched him, nodding faintly.

"Do you need to scream?" she asked. "Or cry? It's okay—you're in exclamation now. You can do whatever you want."

Faruq was slightly out of breath. He brought a hand up to the middle of his chest, where he'd felt the hit. "What . . . the fuck?"

Kaya nodded some more. He noticed now that she had moved back a bit, away from him; she was being careful not to touch him, like he was a live wire. He felt like a live wire.

"What the fuck?" he repeated.

Kaya smiled, leaned in, still not touching him.

"Odo will make you see exactly what the fuck is." She raised an eyebrow. "Get stripped, Faruq."

Faruq thought he saw something moving outside of one of the white windows, the briefest flash of shadow. Maybe just a trick of dusty light. In a far corner, a man, finished with his meditation, began his own exclamation. Suddenly, the eerie wail of a loon. Or, a wolf's howl.

Instagram Post # 380

@thenamelessmvmnt: Odo's face, so close you can see the occasional gray hair in his 5 o'clock shadow. His head is bare and his ageless eyes meet yours, a faint and playful challenge; hint of mischievousness, hint of a smile, not showing teeth.

#Odo #nofilter #themostbeautiful

32,656 likes | 1,082 comments

Nero

FADE IN:

INT. GREENHOUSE—MED. SHOT—MINH-AN

Minh-An shakes her head, smiling wryly.[*]

INSERT—IMAGE

The Ecstasy of St. Teresa, by Gian Lorenzo Bernini.
SLOW ZOOM on Teresa's face.

> MINH-AN
> Teresa of Ávila,

CUT TO:

María de Jesús de Ágreda, anonymous painting on
copper.

> MINH-AN
> María de Jesús de Ágreda,

CUT TO:

Icon of St. Francis of Assisi and a dove.

> MINH-AN
> Francis of Assisi,

CUT TO:

Photo of St. Pio of Pietrelcina, c. 1910, arms crossed
to stigmata on hands.

> MINH-AN
> Pio of Pietrelcina . . .

BACK TO SCENE

> MINH-AN
> These are all people who claim to have
> experienced miracles. You know . . .
> stigmata, being in two places at once,
> visions.

---

[*] Music: fade in, Miserere Mei, Deus (Gregorio Allegri)

Teresa of Ávila, Francis of Assisi, and Pio
of Pietrelcina—they're all canonized. María
de Jesús is venerated.

Odo had a vision too.

Minh-An nods firmly.

> MINH-AN
> Lots of them. He's brought something so
> beautiful to us, to everyone who's ready to
> see. His followers—we love him for it.

Minh-An leans toward the camera.

> MINH-AN
> So let me ask you this: What's the
> difference?

How are you so sure this is a 'cult'?

Minh-An creates air quotes with her hands.

> MINH-AN
> What if it's the beginning of something more
> beautiful, more . . . *true* than Will Roy's
> Christianity?

Minh-An settles back.

INSERT—FOOTAGE

Silent footage of Columbia University's campus,
c. 1980–1984.
SUPER: "Columbia University in the City of New York"

> MINH-AN
> Around 1980, some guy starts showing up on
> Columbia's campus.*

BACK TO SCENE

---

* Music: fade in, Danse Macabre (Camille Saint-Saëns)

          MINH-AN
Odo.

And he's magnetic, he's—he's saying things
no one's ever heard before. People—they *want*
to see.

INSERT—FOOTAGE

Footage of students in front of Low Library, c. 1983;
focus on groups of students sitting together and
laughing (audio removed).

          MINH-AN
I mean, a Black man on campus—at the time,
this was still pretty rare, even in the
middle of Morningside Heights.

BACK TO SCENE

          MINH-AN
Just a few blocks from Harlem, but Columbia
at the time was still a little white oasis.
(laughs)

INSERT—FOOTAGE

Footage of CU students gathered, listening to someone
who is obscured by the crowd, c. 1983 (audio removed).
SLOW ZOOM.

          MINH-AN
So yeah, at first he's attractive because
he's novel. But then people begin listening
to what he's saying. And people begin
following him. Students, even professors.

In zooming past the people in the crowd, it is revealed
that it is Odo at the center talking; he is young and
lean, his hair a short afro under a powder blue newsboy
cap; he is wearing jeans and a black cabana shirt, and
he is talking, not shouting—as though to only one
person.

                    MINH-AN
          People are inviting him to live with them—
          it's an honor to have him staying in your
          apartment. He'd talk about the war, but not
          the way you normally heard about it, you
          know? It was a terrible thing, but he was
          thankful that it had given him his
          revelation.

INSERT—IMAGE

Photo, c. 1985: Odo seated in a living room strewn with
Persian rugs, people seated around him raptly listening.

                    MINH-AN
          Everyone's inviting him to their parties—
          from frat parties to house parties thrown by
          the trust fund kids, to professors' dinner
          parties.

                                              CUT TO:
Photo, c. 1987: Odo holding the hands of a young blond
woman—she is in jeans and a green and blue striped
shirt, and she is down on one knee, sobbing.

                    MINH-AN
          And he's hipping people wherever he goes.
          He's beloved everywhere he goes.

                                              CUT TO:
Photo, c. 1989: Odo standing on 5th Ave. next to a
well-known model, 2 collared doodles sitting at their
feet. The model is blowing a cloud of smoke toward the
camera, and Odo's gaze is direct, his expression
neutral.

                    MINH-AN
          He never asks for anything, you understand.
          But people recognize him for what he is, and
          they try to treat him like a king. One
          couple tried to buy him a Cadillac. Brand
          new. But he said no.

BACK TO SCENE

                    MINH-AN
      I can see the beauty, but I am not the
      beauty itself. Give everything to the beauty
      itself.

INSERT—FOOTAGE

Silent footage of the flagship house of the nameless in
Brooklyn, c. 1991.

                    MINH-AN
      In 1991, the first house of the nameless is
      established in Brooklyn. More and more
      followers come to the nameless.

The camera moves through the main entryway, past people
smiling and laughing in the hall, past a grand
stairway, and into a bright room with huge, whitewashed
windows.

                    MINH-AN
      People fly in—from Toronto, D.C., San
      Francisco, L.A., even outside America.

In the middle of the room, a group of young people, all
dressed in painter's coverups, dance together in a
circle, eyes closed.

                    MINH-AN
      Everyone's so hungry to see, to have their
      vision cleared. To finally find the beauty.

BACK TO SCENE

                    MINH-AN
      In 1998, I was 22 years old, and I was . . .
      fine.

INSERT—IMAGE

Photo, c. 1998, of a young Minh-An with long, loose
black hair, wearing a black unitard, sober-faced, arms
stretched out to the sides and one leg lifted up high,
knee bent at a 90°angle.

> MINH-AN

I had just graduated from Julliard with a
B.F.A. in Dance, and I was auditioning for
these really cool contemporary companies
around the city.

BACK TO SCENE

> MINH-AN

I was an artist, I was living on the Lower
East Side, I had this brooding Serbian
boyfriend—I thought I was happy. (laughs)

It was the end of July. I used to go for
these long walks because my studio didn't
have air-conditioning or proper ventilation.
There was this little park not far from my
apartment—just a few blocks away.

I could see that there were all these people
gathered there, chanting something. (laughs)

Yeah, I thought it was kinda creepy. But I
was curious, you know? So I just
listened . . .

Minh-An closes her eyes.

> MINH-AN

Beauty is not suffering. The beautiful are
free.

Minh-An opens her eyes. They are watering.

> MINH-AN

I don't know why. I—I just felt myself pulled
toward them. I was walking closer without
really knowing it. And as I got closer I saw
that their faces were just full of bliss.*

I walked into this crowd of beautiful
people. It was a hot, sweaty city day, but

---

* Cello drone in G (faint)

all of a sudden, I felt like I'd slipped
into cool spring water.*

Before I knew it, I was saying it with
them:†

Minh-An gestures with her hands, like she's conducting.

                MINH-AN
        Beauty is not suffering. The beautiful are
        free.

Minh-An rests her hands back in her lap.

                MINH-AN
        I was raised Catholic, and, by that point
        in my life, atheism seemed to fit my brand.
        So at first, they were just words. I
        could almost convince myself I was being
        ironic.

        But then something happened.‡

        It was bright out. I closed my eyes.

INSERT—B-ROLL

The sun glares in the camera, slowly turning everything
white, and then warming into a washed-out orange.

                MINH-AN
        I don't know how much time passed. Suddenly,
        it was like something hit me right in the
        gut. It didn't hurt, but I could . . . I
        could *taste* the color yellow. And there was
        this clarity: these words weren't nothing;
        they were speaking right to me.

BACK TO SCENE§

---

* Cello drone in A (slightly louder)
† Cello drone in B♭
‡ Silence.
§ Cello drone in E♭

                    MINH-AN
     I had bought into the fetish of the starving
     artist, this myth that creation must come
     from suffering. It was like a film had
     been removed from my vision: I was broke,
     directionless, I lived in a shithole, and
     my boyfriend didn't like me very much.
     (laughs)

INSERT—IMAGE

Photo of Odo, c. 1998, surrounded by followers, some of
whom are laughing, and some of whom are crying.[*]

                    MINH-AN
     And then I opened my eyes, and there was
     Odo. He was looking right at me. I'd never
     felt so seen.

     What I didn't know was that I'd walked right
     into Fall Day, our most important holiday.
     It's the day we commemorate the fall of the
     beings that are our origins, 9 billion years
     ago.

     I'd joined the recitation of that year's
     mantra. Once we'd repeated it 108 times, the
     procession began.[†]

INSERT—FOOTAGE

Footage of Fall Day, 1998: followers of the nameless
walk silently through the streets of New York;
gradually, some of the followers begin to strip off
their clothes, peeling off socks, shoes, pants,
shirts, and bras. The camera focuses on the stoic
faces of the followers, their toned bodies, the
bewildered, occasionally hostile expressions of
spectators.

BACK TO SCENE

---

     [*] Violin joins cello drone at A♭
     [†] Silence.

                    MINH-AN
Remember, I was raised Catholic. And I had
no idea that it's technically legal for
women to be topless in New York. (laughs)
But someone brushed me on my shoulder.

Minh-An gestures.

                    MINH-AN
Just the lightest, most tender touch—I never
saw who. And I wasn't afraid anymore. I got
stripped.

And I have never in my life felt so alive,
so free. So beautiful.

22 years later, and I'm just as in awe, just
as ecstatic.

And Odo hasn't aged a day. (laughs)

It wasn't even a question. I dropped
everything to follow Odo to L.A.

INSERT—IMAGE

Photo of L.A. house of the nameless, c. 2006.

                    MINH-AN
Odo has changed so many people's lives, and
some of them have been very powerful people.

                                      CUT TO:
Photo of Odo grinning beside a Hollywood heiress,
c. 2008.

BACK TO SCENE

Minh-An shrugs.

                    MINH-AN
We were able to build houses of the nameless
in San Francisco, San Diego, Beverly Hills.
And we were helping people really *see* every

step of the way. We built community art
gardens, performed at homes for the elderly,
bought books to stock school libraries.

Sure, some people thought we were odd—that's
just distortion—but nobody had a *problem*
with us.

Until we started putting out feelers to
expand into Texas.

Minh-An smiles.

          MINH-AN
We were getting all these new followers with
broken hearts. Some of them heard of us
through social media, some of them
encountered us for the first time in real
life. They were coming from these families
right in the middle of America—families with
wealth, privilege. Politicians, CEOs. The
type of families that should have been able
to make so much beauty.

But they weren't making beauty. They were
breaking their children's hearts. And so Odo
got the command to make beauty at the
source: we were to reach into the center of
America's heart. Texas was where we were
going to begin.

                        FADE TO BLACK.

INSERT—B-ROLL OF BURNING HILL, TX*

Long, flat country road, sun-gilded field with long grass
and wildflowers, occasional clusters of cedar elms.

          MINH-AN
One of the followers found out about this
empty piece of land in the Texas Hill

---

* Music: fade in, Make Me a Pallet on the Floor (Sam
Chatmon)

Country. Just 30 acres, and just 20 miles or
so outside of Austin.

In a dry stretch of land, an Ashe juniper tree spreads
up toward a bright, cloudless sky.

> MINH-AN
> Odo loved the idea of building a house of
> the nameless there. But unlike the other
> cities we had houses in, he felt here, in
> this great expanse, they needed not just a
> house of the nameless—a *community*, a place
> to be together.

Around the tree, the grass has turned brown, but the
grass shaded by its branches is bright green.

FADE IN:

INT. GREENHOUSE—MED. SHOT—MINH-AN

> MINH-AN
> And so Odo went out to Burning Hill. I went
> with him, and a few other followers too. It
> was absolutely beautiful out there—we bought
> those 30 acres, *cash*. And that's when things
> got ugly.

Minh-An holds up a small, thin piece of paper, a
clipping from the Bible.

> MINH-AN
> We had only been there maybe a couple weeks
> when we found this taped to the windshield
> of one of our cars. Genesis 9:20-27. The
> Curse of Ham.

Minh-An lets the clipping flutter to the ground.

CUT TO BLACK.

INT. GEORGETOWN OFFICE—MED. SHOT—FATHER SCHUYLER

Father Schuyler fidgets uncomfortably.

                    FATHER SCHUYLER
The Curse of Ham happens in the Book of
Genesis.

Noah has 3 sons: Ham, Shem, and Japheth.
What happens is that Noah becomes drunk off
the wine from his vineyard, and falls asleep
naked. Ham sees this and tells his brothers,
who go in and cover Noah.

But when Noah wakes up and realizes that Ham
saw him naked, he curses Ham's son, Canaan.

INSERT—IMAGE

Noah Damning Ham, by Ivan Stepanovich Ksenofontov[*]

                                    DISSOLVE TO:
The Redmption of Ham, by Modesto Brocos y Gómez[†]

                    FATHER SCHUYLER
The Curse of Ham has been thought to explain
the origin of Black skin, and was used to
justify slavery.

                                    DISSOLVE TO:

Cruelties of Slavery, engraving from the Anti-Slavery
Record, May 1835[‡]

BACK TO SCENE

                    FATHER SCHUYLER
Look, this story has been causing
debate for over 2,000 years. But the
fact is, skin color is never mentioned.
Unfortunately, some people still use the
Curse of Ham to support their belief that
people of African descent are naturally
corrupt, inferior.

---

[*] Single piano note, C4
[†] Single piano note, C4
[‡] Single piano note, C4

CLOSEUP—FATHER SCHUYLER'S FACE
Father Schuyler's gaze is steady, his eyes clear and
gray. Eventually, he looks down.

INT. GREENHOUSE—MED. SHOT—MINH-AN

                    MINH-AN
      These were not the first people we ever
      encountered who had a problem with a Black
      man as influential as Odo. Those lawmakers
      and representatives who spread their poison
      in America's politics and broke their
      children's hearts were often not too pleased
      to have those hearts repaired by someone
      like Odo. But this . . . vitriol. This was
      a new one.

Minh-An shakes her head.*

                    MINH-AN
      They put up signs all over Main Street that
      said we were trying to take over Burning
      Hill; they called us Satanists; people were
      yelling at us that this was a Christian
      country.

      They started picketing us—they were actually
      holding rallies where they'd stomp around
      with signs like: GO BACK TO L.A.; SAY NO TO
      ODO; NOTHING MORE BEAUTIFUL THAN MY GOD.

Minh-An smiles.

                    MINH-AN
      Of course, the irony is that it was at one
      of these rallies that we first met Sue Mills.
      (laughs)

                                    FADE TO BLACK.†

_____

* Music: fade in, Where Did You Sleep Last Night (Lead
Belly)
† Increase music to full volume until end of song.

before: 1969

PREACH SMOKED QUIETLY, using his hand to hide the glowing tip of his cigarette. Aside from the unpleasantly damp end of his smoke—moistened by the heavy jungle humidity, his own sweat, and spit—he was focused on Crazy Horse and his teeth, which seemed to flash continuously in the indigo night as he talked, even and square and white. Crazy Horse had awoken to the sick seep of tears from his eyes, and now words came out of him like a flinch; he'd gag on them if they poured out any slower.

. . . wasn't even the first guy I wasted. Nah, this was some skinny dude out in the field in the last village, only the sky was this hot green, man, like . . .

Somehow, Preach knew not to interrupt. Crazy Horse was going on in a manic whisper; his voice seemed to fit into the jungle nocturne. Preach also knew that Crazy Horse wasn't really talking to him, but to the cherry, though Bigger was wound up tight in his bedroll, fast asleep.

. . . first few times I reached around in myself to feel something about it, and I couldn't get nothing. They trying to kill you, the motherfuckers. And when they run . . .

Preach supposed Crazy Horse might've been trying to puncture Bigger's dreams, inject them with the truth, the real, jungle truth. All of them, those who had been there awhile, knew the force of jungle dreams. But Crazy Horse didn't really see Preach or the cherry. He saw the skinny man he'd shot from thirty yards away, how, up close . . .

. . . he wasn't that skinny, man. I mean, he had a gut. Couldn't tell how old he was. The spot where I hit him wasn't too messed up. Just a little blood. Looked like a flower, like a rose, like a . . .

Like a jewel, Preach thought. Something preciouser than diamonds. That's the kind of gift life must be, for the Lord to take it away so easily. He wanted to tell this to Crazy Horse, but Crazy Horse was gone, like a mirage, like a dream.

. . . I got to be dreaming, now. Because things in the jungle—well it's weird out here. Impossible, even. But I never saw no body just up and disappear like that, nobody but Jesus disappearing from his tomb.

And that was a miracle, really, Preach thought. That he'd made it this far. Preach didn't think himself any kind of killer, but apparently he *was* a survivor. And now he was getting short. It was nearly all over for him. Carefully, he lit another cigarette, burning his thumb a little, stinging pain.

The pain a hot bud. I look down—now *I* got that hole in my chest. I took his place, you dig? Nah—I was him all along. We're them and they're us. Ain't no difference. And I'm telling you, brother, I still feel dead now.

Preach heard a strange wonder in Crazy Horse's voice, a kind of exaltation, the pastor's vicarious euphoria when his congregation catches the Spirit. Made him wonder if Crazy Horse's secret tears weren't more like tears of reverence. Some complex joy. Preach hissed out a current of smoke, unsettled. Crazy Horse was silent now; there was a space for Preach to minister into.

The Lord said dreams and many words is meaningless. Fear God instead.

But I saw my own self die.

Crazy Horse's eyes were round and white in the darkness. To Preach, they looked like the sparrows' eggs he and his sister used to find behind their tenement building. Mama would never let them touch them, and so they held a kind of sanctity; fragile kernels of life.

"I am the resurrection and the life. The one who believes in me will live, even though he dies, and whoever lives and believes in me will never die."

The verse slipped right through Crazy Horse, thin and ghost-like as the paper it lived on. Or maybe he was the ghost. He couldn't feel the jungle lapping at him, couldn't feel the blade of war, couldn't feel his own body. If not electricity, if not blood, then this was the measure of true death—numbness. He'd not had a dream about dying; he'd had a dream that killed him.

Better'n getting shot.

What's that?

Crazy Horse didn't repeat himself. He wasn't in the mood for more of Preach's proselytizing. It made something stir up in him, something mutinous and hot. God was God. But this was the jungle. Crazy Horse turned on his side away from Preach, and Preach put his cigarette out in the damp earth.

The terror itself became monotonous, and this was the first mutilation Bigger underwent in the jungle. The hoofing, the heat, the damp, the horror—it all became as repetitive and droning as a chant. Above them, bloated monsoon clouds hung, dark and sodden, and when they burst, the rain was an onslaught. Soon that too became monotonous. But the banality did not make the terror dissipate. It only ingrained it, sunk it into the flesh like jungle rot.

And this was the second mutilation Bigger underwent in the jungle. It started as a hot patch of skin on his shin, and then the skin domed into a red knot, puckered, and now it was in the process of opening wetly—he could feel its moist complaint every time he took a step into the sodden, sucking earth. Silk said he was lucky, said he'd once seen a soldier get the rot on his heel so bad he cried the whole time they were hoofing.

Thing was, he didn't *feel* lucky. What he felt was something he'd never felt before, and therefore had no name for. It was something more irritable than boredom, more pathetic than rage.

Silk's word for it was "crazy." It was all right; the jungle, the bush—it all *made* you crazy. But still, Silk kept half an eye on the cherry. The kid was walking around like a raw wire. Silk could smell it. The sun was beginning to droop heavily up behind the bruised sky, its light turning canary yellow. They'd been hoofing uphill for most of the day, fighting the slip of mud, and the ground was finally beginning to level out.

Preach's lungs were complaining, his breath was rough. He longed for a cigarette but didn't have one ready behind his ear. He'd tucked his smokes away when the clouds ripped open to keep them safe, and now they weren't in easy reach. The rain would have ruined it, anyway. Bigger, a man behind Preach, saw how he kept reaching up to his ear reflexively. After a while, Bigger began to do it too.

Bigger never smoked—Mama'd told him it was dirty, though Granny couldn't hardly ever be found without a cigarette, had died with one in between her ashen lips. He'd been there—her breath rattled every time she took a feeble draw, until it didn't, and the cigarette hung limp, dully burning itself down. And even though it hadn't been so long ago, he was trying to remember the sound of her voice and couldn't.

Silk's Big Mama used to say that you couldn't conjure a fish in a desert. He didn't know why this had suddenly come to mind. It may have been because the cherry was looking more and more like a fish out of water—there was even a fishy floppiness to his hoofing now, probably due to exhaustion and the rot on his leg. Silk remembered the feeling, remembered his first time in the jungle, the strangeness, the airlessness. The shock of seeing a fellow soldier die.

All the same, though he wasn't the first to see it, Bigger was the first to *register* it. The rain had eased up, and over everything was a rotting, watery haze. The uniform drooped in the tree like a hanged man. Once he called attention to it, they halted. The men around him spoke overlappingly, their quiet voices merging into a hiss.

ARVN, no doubt.

The fuck's it doing up there?

Deserter?

Could be a booby trap.

Fuckin dinks.

What're we gawkin at it for? Leave it.

Maybe a booby trap.

Might trip something.

What's it doin up there, for God's sake?

Gotta be a warning.

Or a goddamned trap, more like.

Bigger had taken down his gun—several other men had too, and it seemed right. It was hot as fevered flesh in his hands. The uniform flapped in a barely felt breeze, splotchy camo seeming to shift, short sleeves like amputated arms. Somewhere in the distance, something in the jungle snapped. The sound licked through Bigger like a flame and he spun, pulling his gun up and firing in the direction of the noise.

Sound rises up all around him—crackle of gunfire as others begin to shoot, men shouting indistinctly. The air grows hazy with gunsmoke and sprays of jungle floor, sappy fragments of trees. He can't see or hear now. If the enemy is there, he is obscured. The command to cease barely penetrates the haze. Bigger's hands buzz as he lowers his gun. Someone is shouting, demanding to know who started firing.

That fuckin green nigger. Sneer like a lash.

I guess a spook'll spook easy, ain't that right?

Cool it, Mountain Dew.

Crazy Horse slipped an easy arm around Bigger's sharp shoulders.

Happens to the best of us.

Happens to the worst of us, too.

Silk was on Bigger's other side. He could swear the kid was sending a frantic thrum into the ground—he could feel it vibrating beneath his feet. He spat.

Crazy Horse dug his fingers into Bigger's shoulder until he felt the kid tense. Everyone got spooked, but it sure as shit wasn't a mistake you wanted to make twice. Sweat dripped into Bigger's eyes.

The L-T stomped over, face bright red and puckered, stopping inches from Bigger. He was a little shorter than the cherry, he noticed, so he casually backed up a few steps, as though to appraise the kid from a distance. He didn't want to be looking up at a negro. He glanced over at Crazy Horse, whose eyes had a way of having nothing in them, and that nothing was a challenge. They sure did look after their own. He respected that.

I thought I heard something.

The squad leader broke out into a grin. His front teeth were discolored, one of them chipped.

Need your jungle ears, is all, boy. Be able to tell a monkey's fart from a gook.

Silk didn't laugh. Only spat again. The L-T thought that, where Crazy Horse's eyes were blank, Silk's were full of everything, and just as impossible to read. All three of the negroes towered over him. He turned away, laughing again to cover his retreat. Bigger's face was burning; he shuffled his feet.

Didn't sound like no monkey fart to me.

Silk nodded at Bigger paternally.

Still. Better not let em all know just where we are.

An errant bullet had snapped the uniform further into the branches, so it looked like it was getting socked in the gut. Or like the tree was devouring it, had maybe devoured the man who'd worn it too.

Preach didn't really mind walking point. It became a ritual after a while, like the order in which you soaped your body during a shower. Aside from the constant feeling that something was crawling on him, he was at peace. The lieutenant liked to boast that Preach was his best point man; God gave him a whole new set of senses when he was pulling point. He could tell whether a twig had been broken by an animal or a boot, pick a punji stick out from a tangle of weeds. He and the other men walking point were focused as blades.

The monsoon rains had been pelting them for three days, and now the sky rested. They all exhaled, a bit lighter. Bourbon— a white boy from Kentucky who managed to stay fat even when the rest of them were swimming in their jungle fatigues—was following behind Preach.

Bourbon was shorter than him. He was in the last days of his tour. Just that morning, Bourbon had been taunting him—*Just five days and a wake-up and they'll put me right outta here. Won't even look back at your Black ass.* Every once in a while, Preach paused just long enough to wiggle his Black ass at Bourbon for posterity's sake.

For most of the morning, they'd been trudging through dense foliage, every now and then having to cut their way through with their machetes. But now the jungle was beginning to thin out. Before long, word traveled through the line that they were taking a break; Thumper, the veteran point man at the front of the line, had found a trail and was going ahead to check it out.

Every time they took a break, Preach liked to send up a prayer of thanks that he was still alive. When he was still green, shocked still by the breakdown of order over here, the prayer used to hit him with so much force it brought tears to his eyes. Man, he'd *made* it. Thank you, Father God. But now, the prayer had dulled some. Not that he was taking his survival for granted—you couldn't, in the jungle—but more that he didn't know for sure whether a prayer that pitiful could penetrate the thick canopy and make it up to God.

Pitiful—they all were. Starving and stinking and coiled like springs.

Thumper reported back—he'd found huts, but Charlie was gone; empty rice sacks, no livestock left, and the huts' roofs soggy and gaping with holes. They began to move again. They leaned forward as they walked, under the weight of their rucksacks. Mosquitoes, drawn to them because of their sweat, sucked at the exposed skin. Preach saw a bright green feather and snatched it up, thinking of Crazy Horse.

As the afternoon came upon them, the jungle began to thicken again, darkening the world around them. Vines clung to their ankles as though possessed of agency. Preach spotted a green snake resting blithely on a branch, watching them with sly black eyes. It would be easy to imagine the jungle as hostile to them—a simple, if clumsy, metaphor for their place in this war and in this country. But to Preach, the jungle seemed not hostile, but indifferent. Maybe that was more sinister.

The machetes reemerged as they began working to cut a trail. Their whole bodies ached as they hacked, and the heat threatened to smother them, but there was a rhythm to it that hypnotized them. Preach hummed to himself as he went, an old hymn his mother liked. The noise from the machetes covered his low song.

The men fanned out slightly, and Preach found himself working his way down a slight slope, mostly alone. Though Thumper didn't think Charlie was still around, he was moving them slightly off point, just to be safe. They were nearing a river; Preach could hear the moving water, smell its must. Slowly, through the foliage he decimated, the river became visible to him, brown and bloated with monsoon rains. As he got closer to the water, Preach paused to give his aching arm a rest.

He saw movement across the river and his whole body tightened like the string of a bow. Lord Jesus, he doesn't want a fight. But there is the enemy—just one man—emerging from the jungle across the way. Preach holds himself as still as a dead man. The soldier—Preach can only assume he's a man, though he's fairly androgynous, a word Preach does not know—falls to his knees at the river's edge and drinks muddy water desperately from cupped hands.

Preach's own hands are poised—one on the handle of his machete, though he really needs his gun, and the other over his radio. One move and the soldier will spot him, he's sure.

The soldier is very slight, even for a Vietnamese, and Preach can see that his hair brushes his shoulders, which reminds Preach of the girl, and it stirs up a nauseating combination of tenderness and guilt.

While humping on a previous mission, they were approached by a young village girl. This wasn't unusual—while traveling past the roadside villages, sometimes the villagers would approach, of-

fering water, jackfruit, cigarettes. This girl was offering her body.
She looked too young, though it was hard to guess the age of the
younger Vietnamese. Something in her face—maybe the shape of
her nose, maybe the baby roundness of her cheeks—reminded
Preach of his sister. And once he saw it, he couldn't stop himself
from imagining it *was* his sister offering herself to a bunch of un-
predictable, hulking soldiers.

They'd probably burned her village. Preach himself may have
set his Zippo to her family's home. He may as well have raped her.
He may as well have sold her himself. A few of his fellow grunts
were haggling her price, laughing through an argument over
who'd go first and who'd go last. Preach pulled down his gun.

Any one of you touches her, I'm shooting.

Say, Preach, what's the matter with you?

Preach approached the girl, careful to keep his gun pointed to
the ground. Still, there was a flinch in her, one she tried to hide
with a thrust of her small breasts. The girl smirked up at him flir-
tatiously, one hand on her hip, but Preach could see the posture
was practiced, inexpertly executed. He felt bound up, like he was
being squeezed by a boa constrictor. He couldn't save her, could
never make it right. Carefully, he put his gun down. He rummaged
through his rucksack, pulled out his cigarettes, his C-rations—his
peaches.

At first, the girl didn't take them, didn't understand what he
was offering. She nodded to a dense bamboo grove, wiggled her
little hips. But Preach shook his head, pressed his offering firmly
into her hands. He noticed a burn on the back of one of her spindly wrists. He dug into his rucksack again, and then, careful not
to let the other soldiers see, pressed his Zippo into her hands as
well. A veil slipped down in her dark eyes. She bowed to him and
then turned, hurried off.

It could never be enough, Lord forgive us all.

No other Vietnamese emerges to join the little man at the river.
Preach's muscles begin to cramp. It could almost *be* that girl.
Preach's mouth goes entirely dry. Though Preach doesn't move, the

soldier's head suddenly snaps up, and he looks right at Preach. The river seems to suck in, pulling them toward each other, both of them as still as prey. An eternity of stillness.

So slowly it hurts, Preach puts his machete down. He eases his hands together in front of his chest and bows, never taking his eyes off of the soldier. The other man stares for a long time. Then, without rising from his crouch at the river's edge, he brings one hand up, palm forward, and pushes it toward Preach, snapping it up and back at the last moment as though he's made contact with Preach's palm.

Preach grinned. They both edged away from the river, away from each other, gradually disappearing back into their respective sides of the indifferent jungle. Preach relaxed when the jungle once again obscured that swollen river. He wasn't by himself anymore—there was Bourbon, huffing and puffing with his machete tip-down in his hand. Preach wiggled his ass at him dutifully.

Getting short. Getting short.

today

FARUQ SAT HEAVILY alone. Solitude had always been a weakness of his, a wound inflicted by his mother's death and, finally, deepened by his father's.

Orphan.

He was sitting in the middle of the floor in the guesthouse, heart hammering. Maybe it was because he wasn't in the house of the nameless; maybe it was because he couldn't quite remember all 18 Utterances without peeking at the handmade booklet from his bedside table; maybe it was because Kaya wasn't with him. But he couldn't re-create his experience with the meditation, could not pull his mother's face back out of the void from which it had come spinning. And he had been trying for a week.

And maybe it was a good thing. The wet tendril, the animal-wide eyes, the terror, his own; the certainty of his father, his aunties, the ustad. His own.

Faruq stood. This was not the face of his mother he wanted. Kaya had explained to him that Vutu showed you what you needed to see during meditation—even if it was nothing—until you were ready to see Their face. And naturally, Odo was the only one to have ever achieved that. This, of course, was bullshit. It was only that something about the meditation had stirred up that old trauma. If he could re-create it, maybe he could, at least, understand it.

That's what I like about you, Zaidi, Anita sometimes told him. *You never look away, even when it ain't pretty.*

Frustrated, he shook out the cramps in his legs. His time here was fixedly unstructured. No one asked anything of him, there was nowhere he needed to be, no appointments to keep. When he tried to set his own schedule, it invariably collapsed. It should have been liberating, but instead it worked to isolate him, confine him—an effect Faruq supposed was intentional. The nameless, unlike him, were regimented, always busy. Everyone had a role, responsibilities, jobs to see to. Everyone got to feel vital. Except for him.

He found himself, more often than not, shadowing Kaya. He felt very much shepherded into this friendship. After he'd met her the first time, he saw her more and more frequently until seeing her on a daily basis became an expectation, part of his routine. Odo certainly wasn't making himself available. And Kaya wasn't just objectively pretty, she was Faruq's *type,* almost as though she'd been hand-selected. He recalled the early trickle of beautiful nameless women—and men—who'd gone out of their way to befriend him at first. They had all more or less disappeared now. Trial and error.

Once he left his guesthouse, it didn't take him very long to find Kaya. She was in the building at the head of Ewa Park that sat behind the amphitheater. It housed a midsize stage and artists' studios. Kaya was dressed in a turmeric-colored shift; Faruq noticed that followers had an eerie way of echoing Odo's dress—he seemed to change up his color palette on a weekly basis, and they all followed him with no comment. Faruq thought it might have something to do with their Instagram account, though he sometimes noticed followers changing their colors before a new post was up. But it was another way in which he was passive-aggressively othered in this place. He was either in jeans or running clothes while everyone else draped themselves in sunset colors.

Kaya smiled up at him as he walked over to the small table where she sat, white tulle billowing up like froth from the tabletop and spilling into her lap. She was painstakingly embroidering the fabric with tiny crystals.

"Wedding dress?" Faruq guessed.

"Costumes," she said.

"So, close."

Kaya laughed and Faruq joined her briefly. "What for?" he asked.

"Ewa. It's one of the 3 Rituals; our holy days, so to speak."

Faruq leaned down to take a closer look at Kaya's project. Crystals winked up at him. "What is Ewa about again?"

"Art," Kaya said. "Beauty. On Ewa we have shows, concerts, exhibits. Our ballet company is performing. I make costumes. Hence, the tulle." She clenched some of the cloudy fabric in a fist and let it spring free. "Come walk with me," she said. "I need a break."

Without seeming to think about it, Kaya held out a hand and without questioning it, Faruq took it, helping her to her feet. Together, they stepped out of the theater and into a bright, vaguely briny spring day. Ewa Park sat just north of the community's massive fruit, vegetable, and herb gardens, and was itself roughly a third of the size of Manhattan's Central Park. At the south end, just north of the amphitheater, was the oversized waterfowl pond. The park's landscaping was supposed to look wild, almost accidental, but Faruq wasn't fooled. From his own research and what Adam had told him when he first arrived, Faruq knew that the Forbidden City had come up under the labor of engineers, architects, contractors. None of it was random. He and Kaya walked along a stone path bordered—but never encroached upon—by unkempt marionberry bushes.

Kaya didn't speak, but her silence felt expectant, so Faruq filled it. "Tell me more about—what was it? Ewa?"

"Ewa, yes. It's a lot of fun—we exchange gifts, do good acts, and do strippings."

"Strippings—that's the coconut water baptism."

Kaya laughed. "That's one way to put it."

"Why coconut water?"

Kaya shrugged. "Something about Odo not having clean water for a while in Vietnam. It's not really important. Just symbolic, you know?"

The nameless were so open most of the time—Faruq was always caught off-balance when they dodged things.

"Symbolic of *what*?"

"Cleansing, I would think, Faruq."

"Yeah, but what are you symbolically cleansing?" he pushed. "Like, in Christianity, when you baptize, you're washing away sin, right?"

"Well then, we're washing away distortion. So we can defend against it."

"Defend? Is that where your paramilitary comes in? The Deep?" He was testing her now; Odo had already denied that the Deep were a militia.

"Oh Faruq," Kaya said, laughing a little. "I'm talking about spiritual defense. Not violence. That's your own distortion speaking."

"What if I don't believe I'm—'distorted'?"

Kaya shrugged.

"Okay, so, it's a day of shows, strippings, and presents?" Faruq asked.

"And sweeps," Kaya added. "You can think of those like missions—we spread the 18 Utterances."

Faruq nodded, having heard of this from Zephyr. "Recruitment missions," he said. "And how do you know who might be open?"

Abruptly, Kaya bent down and scooped something up from the ground just in front of Faruq's feet. She straightened and held her cupped hands up to his face. Nestled there was a little green frog. Its toes were spread wide, clinging moistly to Kaya's finger; black stripes ran across its eyes and down its sides. Faruq did not think he was afraid of frogs, but he'd never been this close to one.

"This guy's awfully far from the pond." She tucked her hands into her stomach, holding the frog, who was likely petrified, against her navel. She grinned over at Faruq. "There are four circles we try to target."

For a moment Faruq was confused.

"For the sweeping," she clarified. "First, the academics—your professionals, doctors, lawyers, architects, engineers. And then the intellectuals. You know, philosophers, politicians, teachers. Then, the creators—artists and patrons of the arts. And the found—the young, families, children."

Gently, Kaya placed the frog down on a nest of still-dewy grass. "You, my friend, are of the found, I think."

"Odo told me I was a scholar."

"*And,* not *or,* Faruq."

Another nameless slogan. "So, then, I'm being swept."

Kaya giggled. "Sweeping isn't the same as converting. It's just information. Isn't that what you came here for?"

So it was. And he was getting maddeningly little of it, despite Kaya's continued willingness to talk about nameless theology, beliefs, and rituals. He wanted to know more about what the nameless really wanted, why they were building what seemed to be their own state, like the Vatican, seemingly in response to everything that had happened in Texas. Odo himself was slippery, though Faruq often got glimpses of the man watching Kaya and him, perhaps listening to what she told him. By now, Faruq had been here a month, and Anita was starting to ask for pages. She was expecting him back in two weeks, but he was beginning to think he'd need to beg for more time.

Kaya began to hum while they walked. The tune meandered; Faruq got the sense that she was making it up as she went.

Anita *had* said she would give him six weeks. So he guessed there was time. He just didn't like being played with.

"What kind of music did you listen to growing up?" Kaya asked suddenly.

Faruq had to give this some thought. "Well," he started, "my father only really liked hamd singers—Islamic music, basically. But my mother loved old-school soul and R&B—Sam Cooke, Marvin Gaye, Donnie Hathaway. She'd play it when it was just the two of us."

Faruq could feel the warmth of those moments, his mother, hair loose, singing along and getting the words all wrong. A respite from the silence between his parents, which leaked all over the apartment, and only got worse after the accident, after she was dead.

"My father wouldn't allow music in the house after my mother died. I discovered rap when I was a teenager, but I'd have to sneak out to listen to it, even with headphones."

Kaya caught his eyes and didn't let them go. "What was her *favorite* song?"

"'Stairway to Heaven'—the O'Jays? She thought it was a religious song."

Kaya laughed.

Faruq remembered how she'd slow-dance with herself, singing out of tune and getting the lyrics wrong. Her eyes would be closed, her feet bare and face flushed. Sometimes she'd blindly reach out a hand and Faruq would take it, and she'd lead him around in slow circles. *The door is wide open for you / The door is open for me.* Why hadn't it been this version of his mother that'd slammed into him during meditation? Belatedly, he laughed with Kaya, if only to keep what was rising at bay.

Faruq was surprised by how happy he was to hear his cousin's voice.

"Where have you *been,* man?" Danish said.

"Sorry," said Faruq, smiling. "There's barely any reception out here."

He was at the hotspot Kaya had shown him, wrapped in a throw from the guesthouse bed. The morning was sunny but still held some crispness. Water whispered around him.

"Everyone's worried about you."

"I'm just working." Faruq's words were faint, blue-white apparitions in the chilly air.

"You know how the aunties are."

"You haven't told them where I am, have you?"

"Are you kidding? They'd be on the next flight, to save you from the kaffirs. And if they found out *I* knew?" Danish exhaled dramatically.

"They been pressing you for information?"

"Pretty soon they're gonna start waterboarding me, man."

Faruq laughed.

"Auntie Naila found your spare key again, by the way."

"Fucking hell," Faruq swore. "I *told* her I didn't want her just going into the house."

"She said she was just checking on the cat. Said you left the place a mess."

"Tell her I'm changing the goddamn locks again when I get back." His heart was racing. He thought of her touching the Air-Pods, *moving* them. "Tell her not to touch anything, please, Danish."

"Tell her yourself. I'm not getting cussed out." Danish chuckled. "You know they're always going to find a way to get in. They're your family."

"I don't need anyone—family or otherwise—telling me how to live. Don't I have a right to privacy?"

"No. Look, they think they're taking care of you. Ma wants to stock your fridge for when you come back, and clean up the place."

"And rummage through my shit." He tried to breathe through his nose. *Let it go,* he told himself. Nothing he could do about it now. Moving the AirPods, rearranging the clutter in the house wouldn't kill his father again, after all. Or bring him back. Still, he couldn't stand how violated he felt.

"Hey, Faruq," Danish said, seeming to sense his upset, "you know they love you, right?"

"They're intrusive."

"I know."

"And stubborn."

"Yep."

"And they have no respect for boundaries."

Danish laughed. "*Boundaries?* Boundaries are for white people."

Faruq snorted, a small portion of his tension easing up.

"Just last night, over dinner, Ma was asking when you're coming back, 'from wherever he is.'" The last part Danish delivered in a falsetto that was an unsettlingly good imitation of Auntie Qudrah's voice. "Apparently they've lined up a bunch of girls they want you to meet."

"For fuck's sake . . ."

"I know, I know."

"Can't they just leave my love life alone?"

"Come on, man—they're *aunties*. They think you have to honor your father by marrying a nice Muslim girl or some shit."

"Can't you stave them off?"

"I *have* been, Faruq. But to them, it's already been a year."

Faruq rolled his eyes. "It's been a year for me too."

"You know what I mean. They're worried about you—they think you need a woman to take care of you."

"They think I'm lost." *Lost, found*—if they only knew how similar their rhetoric was to that of the nameless.

"Well—"

"Well, *what*?"

"I mean, is it so bad, Faruq? It's not like you're meeting anybody on your own. If you got married, it would quiet them down, and you wouldn't have to be alone."

"I can't marry some good Muslim woman, D. I'm an atheist."

"Does that really matter?"

"Of course it fucking matters."

"What I mean is—well, couldn't you just pretend? Like you did with your father?"

The banal ritual of wudhu—the metallic tang of tap water from old pipes as he washed out his mouth; the threadbare prayer rug, his mother's; rote gesture and genuflection; and all of it empty for him, hollow as a tomb. Sometimes, after they'd finished, his father would have tears on his cheeks, and in those moments Faruq hated him a little.

"That was hell, Danish. You have no idea."

"But what if it didn't have to be all the time? What if you found a girl who was conservative in front of the family, but let you be you?"

"Danish—"

"You know I don't care, man. You don't have to be religious. *I'm* not even as devout as they'd like me to be. You just put up a front for them. It's easier, honestly."

Faruq hated to bring it up, but he didn't like how his cousin was pushing. "Remember my mother? How'd that work out for her?"

There was a long silence before Danish spoke again.

"It's different now." Danish's voice was subdued. "They misjudged the help Auntie Fatima needed. I think they understand that now—they're not unreasonable just because they're religious, man. I mean, Auntie Maryam's been in therapy for years, Faruq, you know that. And you know they didn't cause the accident."

"I know that."

"Good. Because thinking like that—it'd be as superstitious as they were back then."

"I *know*, D."

"Okay. You brought it up."

He had. And now Faruq wasn't sure how to get this conversation back on track. "Well," he said, "I kind of actually met someone. Kind of."

"What? Who? Not one of those people—oh no, Faruq. It'd go over better if you came out as gay."

"I said 'kind of,'" Faruq hedged. "Her name is Kaya."

Faruq felt guilty, like he was throwing Kaya under the bus, soiling their friendship with his lie. He was attracted to Kaya, sure. Even genuinely liked her. But deep down, he supposed he thought she had to be crazy.

"Well, I guess she could convert," said Danish. "Keep that kooky cult stuff under wraps."

Faruq laughed. "We're not getting married, D. Just—maybe you can tell everyone I've met someone."

"Seriously? They'll want to meet her parents, they'll want to know where they're from, her salary, her grades, if she can cook, her Social Security number . . ."

"I don't know—come up with *something*, D. I don't want them trying to set me up. I'm not even sure when I'll be back."

After Faruq hung up, his ears seemed to ring. Back home, it would be time for him to begin his commute into the office. The muscle memory of his morning routine was like a ghost limb; by now, he'd be just in from his morning run and the hot shower water would be like pinpricks on his charged skin. He'd rush through a bowl of microwaved oatmeal, check social media while hopping into his clothes, find his keys beneath whichever stack of papers he'd tossed them under. Jeweled clink of Muezza's cat food landing in his dish, rusted whine of the door's lock, sudden rush of city noise like heat escaping from an oven, asthmatic screech of the A train. And here, in nameless land, there was not technically silence—there were the people, the animals, and, in the distance, the sea. In some ways noisier than his life back home, the quiet itself full of meaning.

Odo was still keeping himself scarce, and Kaya was busy with preparations for Ewa, so after he got off the phone with Danish, Faruq took it upon himself to explore more of the Forbidden City. No one stopped him when he borrowed a golf cart from the communal garage. Followers waved at him jovially as he rode past them. He drove to the northwestern corner of the city, where they had set up a botanical garden, orchards, an apiary. There was a vineyard, a winery, a distillery. One of the followers he found working at the greenhouse adjacent to the botanical garden happily showed Faruq the more illicit substances they grew there—various strains of marijuana, psilocybin mushrooms, salvia, ayahuasca, and a few hallucinatory weeds Faruq was not familiar with.

The man gave Faruq a small cutting of one of these weeds, explaining that, while drug use was not required among the nameless, it might help him.

"Help me what?" Faruq had asked.

"You know," the man said with a sympathetic smile, "help you *understand*."

The man left him then, and Faruq took the time to wander around the botanical garden. The plants there were plump, lush. He touched the drooping leaves of a densely green plant he couldn't identify, and they felt as full and substantial as an earlobe. There was a patch of plants so colorful and unrecognizable that Faruq suspected they weren't at all native. He wondered if plants were like frogs—the more vibrant, the more poisonous. He opened his palm to look at the little weed the man had given him; he wondered if it'd make him hallucinate, and what he would see if he did. The thought scared him, though he stuffed the fear away, thinking it might be best if none of that fear showed.

Faruq rode away from the greenhouse with the plant tucked into his jeans pocket, where it felt as heavy as metal.

The water was a little salty, vaguely sulfuric—well water—but it was hot, the pressure strong. He brushed his hair wet, leaning over the bathroom sink. He always left his hairbrush on the vanity in the bathroom, as it was his habit to brush his hair fresh out of the shower. Or at least he *thought* he always left it there. Today he'd found it on his dresser. Things kept appearing out of order. But only slightly. The bristles of his toothbrush facing the mirror when he thought he'd placed it with the bristles facing out. The booklet with the 18 Utterances tucked slightly under the base of the lamp when he could've sworn he'd left it closer to the corner of the bedside table. Surely he was being paranoid. If someone *was* doing this, what would be the point?

Unbidden, he thought of the Manson family's "creepy crawling." Just a way of sowing unease. Psychological harassment. That's what cults did—destabilized you so that you ended up craving the structure of the cult. Its answers. At least, that's what *destructive* cults did. He remembered his notes from his research on cults, which he'd completed before he ever set foot in that house of the nameless in Brooklyn.

All cults were typified by a charismatic leader, devotion to a belief system outside of the norm, and control. However, not all cults had a theology or resulted in members poisoning themselves and others. There were religious cults, which people often thought of when they heard the word "cult"; doomsday cults, whose members predicted and prepared for the end of the world; com-

mercial cults, which harbored undue loyalty to a brand or prod-
uct; and political cults, which focused on social and political
ideology. Any of these types of cults could fall under the broader
umbrellas of *destructive* or *benign*. A benign cult did not ask its
followers to hurt anyone, though there was an argument to be
made for the inherent harmfulness of cult mentality. A destructive
cult led its followers to harm, to themselves or to others. Often
both. Faruq still wasn't sure that the nameless was destructive. It
was part of what he'd come here to find out.

That, and what answers, what peace, it offered its followers.

He stepped out into the bedroom, where the jeans he'd been
wearing yesterday were still slung at the foot of the bed, the little
weed still hidden in their pocket. Faruq had never been exactly
adventurous when it came to drugs, aside from weed and a couple
tentative experiments with Ritalin in college. But now, as he sat
alone back in the guesthouse, he wondered if the plant might return him to that first experience of meditation, return his mother's
face to him. Faruq did not think of himself as suggestible, so there
had to be some explanation for what he'd experienced in the
house of the nameless. Why couldn't he replicate it? Why the
burst of green? Why the physical sensation of impact? Why his
mother's face, and not his father's?

What would his father say, if he could see him now? Faruq
carefully slid the plant cutting out of his jeans pocket and studied
it. It was probably him misremembering, but he couldn't recall
seeing that pink streak down one of the leaves before. He imagined taking it, his vision filling up with psychedelic pink. Carefully, he stroked down that pink streak with a thumbnail, resenting
all the while his father's hold over him, even now. That hold, that
gravitational force, had kept Faruq from bringing friends home as
an adolescent, had forced him to agree to living at home through
college and grad school, kept him in the apartment in downtown
Brooklyn even now, the place still very much his father's, though
his father was dead.

The only thing Faruq's father had not been able to hold Faruq
to was his religion, a secret that Faruq had taken pains to keep

because he and his cousins all agreed that the truth would probably kill his father. Give him a heart attack. If there was a God after all, He did, as the saying went, have a sick sense of humor.

Faruq wondered if his father, too, had felt that startling impact at the center of his chest. Whose face had he seen in his final moments?

He remembered his father's suffocating will, his sensitivity, his fervor. He in no way thought of his father as a victim, but maybe it was at least unfortunate that he'd wound up with Fatima as a wife and Faruq for a son, the two of them both too much and too little. The two of them, with their secrets—maybe they'd weakened his heart after all. If it hurt, his father had never showed it. The only time his father let any kind of tender emotion show was during prayers.

It was about the right time now for Isha, the night prayer. Maybe it hadn't been the nameless meditation itself that had caused the experience. Maybe it just touched something that had been dormant in Faruq, an anguish long contained. The ritual of nameless meditation was not so different from the ritual of Islamic prayer. Setting an intention—*niyat* in Islam—gesture, recitation. The only major structural difference was that, in Islam, you had to be clean and in good clothes before coming to prayer.

Faruq was clean now. Just showered. He tucked the plant cutting into a drawer.

The old feeling of being a fraud, an imposter, returned to him as he took one of the throws, set it down on the floor facing his best guess at Qibla. Vaguely, it surprised him how easily it came back—his muscles had retained the memory of physical prayer, the positions of the hands, ruk'u, sujud. The words were there too—he only stumbled once through the recitation of the first chapter of the Quran, and the Tashahhud and Salawat slipped out of him as easily as breath. But it was like performing an equation; a series of rote steps that were meant to net him an answer he just wasn't getting. He remembered this feeling from high school.

Math had always been a struggle for him, but in his senior year, his father had forced him to take AP Calculus—he was still sure that Faruq was going to become an engineer. Faruq had drowned in that class. He'd felt out of place, a poser—everyone else seeming to rush effortlessly through the complicated math while Faruq floundered. He'd move through the same steps and wind up with a wildly different answer, never able to find where he'd messed up, where he'd gotten lost.

What he felt now was a dull ache in his knees from kneeling, an itch at the back of his head. His feet were cold. As a teenager, when the salat was finished, and he and his father knelt on their mats with their hands cupped to make *dua*—supplication—instead of speaking to Allah from his heart like he was supposed to, Faruq would silently recite rap lyrics, trying to think loudly enough to drown out his father's sniffling.

Now, Faruq waited, his hands cupped in front of his face. His fingers were shaking slightly and the warmth from his palms reached toward his face. Nothing came to him but a faint embarrassment, a sense of his own aloneness. He let his hands drop, and with them his shoulders, his brow, his mind. A return to Earth, his own body, its weight, its mass, cells, death, regeneration, degeneration, infinitesimal fireworks across the nervous system. Miracle enough.

What bothered him, really, was that Odo and his stupid meditation ritual had managed to take control of some process in Faruq that he had yet to get control over himself. In the end, it was really no more than some neurological process whose catalyst Faruq had yet to pinpoint.

Nothing more mystical than that. Faruq let it go for now.

He carefully laced up his running shoes, inserting a finger under the tongue as he tied the knot so they wouldn't be too tight. He'd first started running just after his mother died. He had no idea what he was doing—he'd just tear through Brooklyn in his school clothes and cheap canvas sneakers. After 9/11, it was safer for him to stick to the high school's track, where the track and field coach eventually noticed him.

As he began his stretches, he felt the little swell of adrenaline that always preceded a good, long run. He did a perfunctory scan of his body—stiffness in the right rhomboid, a little tightness in the groin, fascial soreness in the left foot. Nothing much. Cool air studded with moisture hit him when he stepped out of the guesthouse. He was wearing loose shorts and running tights, a fading, long-sleeved tee from a marathon he'd run a few years ago. He was going to warm up quickly. In the distance, he heard a haunting cry, several voices merged into one. He turned his head toward the sound. Flash of black through the trees. The Deep. They seemed to be doing a meditation. Or something. He turned from them, the cool air starting to get under his clothes.

The first strides always felt like audacity, like he was escaping prison. Like he was suddenly flying against nature. He carried nothing with him but his phone, a little plastic bag of almonds; when running in the city, he'd zip his keys and debit card into his pocket, but nameless doors had no locks, and there was nothing for him to buy here. Today, he hadn't even brought along his earbuds. He was in the mood to hear his own breath, his footsteps, the groaning and hissing of the redwoods. And, maybe, the subtle footfall of the wolf.

He headed west, toward the coast. Thick, damp trunks yawned past him in his peripheral vision. Twisting roots and forest detritus reached for him through the soles of his sneakers. Dew lapped at his ankles. He had to focus, in these first few kilometers, on pacing himself, not letting that initial hit of adrenaline trick him into unsustainable speed, even if his body wanted it, even if the body wanted to fly. As he got deeper into the woods, fog began to collect and grow thicker. It was as though Faruq was submerged, as though he'd entered another world.

The fog did something to the noise of the woods; everything wrapped in cotton, his footsteps muted, his breath seeming to echo. Breathing became an exercise in rhythm, in control, and so Faruq knew that he must be close to the sea. His body usually began to protest at about seven or eight kilometers in; he just had to push through it and then his runner's high would kick in somewhere around the 10k mark.

He heard the ocean before he saw it—a primordial roar, somehow both hushed and clamoring. And then the thing itself: white-caps swallowed by fog, the waves rumbling forward, biting at the shore. Wet sand jumped into Faruq's shoes, doing its best to wheedle its way into his socks. It was as though this land wanted his flesh. For the first time since leaving the guesthouse, he paused. He closed his eyes and it was as though there was a hand on him—on his cheek, his shoulder, his arm—though only one hand, his mother's.

He thought he'd learned how to live with his mother's absence a long time ago, but being here brought out that old longing as though it had only barely been scabbed over. It was odd. There was nothing of her here—not her scent, not her things, not her memory. Back home, those things that reminded him of her also reminded him of his want of her. But here, where those reminders were gone, he felt the empty space she'd left behind even more acutely. It burned. It hurt. A never-healing wound, which he often found himself exasperated with. It opened a hopelessness in him that he found excruciating. He opened his eyes.

The wolf was there, standing in salted fog, staring. Faruq froze, instinctual fear rising despite his curiosity, despite the fact that part of him had wanted this encounter even before he began his run. He hadn't really expected the wolf to show itself again. He doubted a photo would do any of this justice, but nevertheless, he took his phone out of his armband and paused the app he'd been using to track his pace and distance—he'd run eight kilometers, just under five miles. This was probably off by a bit, as cell phone service was spotty at best in the Forbidden City, and the app had probably been relying on slow GPS alone for a good portion of his run.

When he looked up again to aim his camera, the wolf was gone. He swore. Now that he'd stopped, his body began to tire. His legs shook, quads aching, and there was a familiar pain in his left ankle—an old injury that revisited him now and then. He swore again. It would take him forever to walk back, and there were no cabs out here, no Uber. He was going to have to run it, and he knew he was going to end up injuring himself. He set out.

By the time he reached the woods, every step sent shards of glass up his left leg.

When he reached the boundaries of the Forbidden City he stopped running, leaning now into the limp that had developed. All of the adrenaline from having seen the wolf again wore off, and he could feel the extent of the strain. He mentally scanned his body. Nothing too serious, he thought. A few days of bad soreness, and he'd recover. But he would have to lay off running. He'd have to wait to see the wolf again.

Faruq limped through the Forbidden City in search of Kaya. He tried not to think of how he'd committed a small act of treason against their friendship by telling Danish that she was something more. He tried not to think of how she sometimes got close enough to him that her black hair grazed him, and it was cool and heavy and smooth. He tried not to wonder what her bare breasts looked like, if they held their pert roundness when not contained by her clothing.

Because he had grown up in such a conservative household, Faruq still had the tendency to expect too much from sex. Part of him always expected women's bodies to be mystical, and was not disappointed but surprised when they were, in fact, as fleshly, as mortal, as his own body.

And then the sex itself was so fleeting, just that ephemeral moment of rapture.

He'd lost his virginity at fifteen, to a girlfriend he'd had to keep a secret from most of his family. He remembered being taken aback by her naked body; the darkness of her nipples, the subtle curve of her low belly, both things he couldn't have predicted from only having seen her clothed up to that point. He'd been fascinated by the stubble on her mons, the hairs short and pointed, glimmering slightly as though they'd been oiled. Years later, while on assignment in Ecuador, a fisherman had introduced him to blood clams, and the hair on their shells reminded him of her. The fisherman had pried one open for him, and its red blood oozed out, the meat inside like a clot—it made plain the violence of it, the murder.

He figured Kaya would still be working on costumes for Ewa, so he was headed toward the theater when a redheaded man Faruq had seen around but never spoken to approached.

"Hey Faruq, you all right?" the man asked, nodding toward Faruq's legs.

Faruq blinked, a bit unsettled. "Yeah, man," he said. "Just a hard run. Thanks."

The man smiled, looking directly into Faruq's eyes, and nodded. "Rest up." He patted Faruq's arm before walking away.

When Faruq reached the edge of Ewa Park, another follower Faruq didn't know—this time a very petite Indian woman—came up to him.

"Oh no," she said, her voice surprisingly deep. She too met Faruq's gaze head-on. "You're limping—what happened?"

Faruq chuckled uncomfortably. "It's fine. Just had a rough run. Hey, have you seen Kaya?"

"Kaya? No, I haven't. Feel better, though."

He thanked the woman and then awkwardly stepped around her. He thought he could still feel her gaze on him as he made his way to the theater. Inside, he didn't find Kaya in her usual spot, and so, feeling as though he might be breaking some rule, he made his way upstairs, where the artists' studios were. The studios were whitewashed, full of light and the smell of wet paint and pencil shavings.

The first studio Faruq poked his head into contained several canvases, all painted solid colors. Another held piles and piles of yellowing newspapers, a wooden table scattered with charcoals. The next room he looked into contained the dismembered components of some kind of installation piece. The sight snagged at Faruq, drew him further into the room.

Curved, tarnished metal, the suggestion of flames. A female torso, formed in classical style from black stone, arching unnaturally. Branches singed and tacked together, writhing limbs. And an incomplete head, fashioned from wire, the face humanoid, but barely so. Twisting horns, ragged holes for eyes, mouth stretched wide open. Teeth of bone, long, pointed. Teeth like scythes. Animal teeth.

"Hi, Faruq."

He turned. Not Kaya. A woman he hadn't met stood in the doorway. Pale and long-limbed like a model, a somewhat androgynous face framed by floating blond curls.

"Kaya isn't here," she said. "I think she's helping out at the Persian Garden. Flowers." She tilted her head. "Did you hurt yourself?"

"Pushed myself a little too hard on a run," he explained, the repetition beginning to chafe, though it didn't surprise him that she knew he was looking for Kaya. "This yours?" he asked, gesturing into the room.

The woman smiled. It softened her face, made her almost childlike. "Do you like it?" she asked, stepping around him and into the studio.

"It's—striking," Faruq said.

The woman stared directly into Faruq's eyes for a long while. "Why don't you tell the whole truth?" she eventually said.

Faruq laughed, discomforted. "Well, it's a little disturbing to me, if I'm honest."

The woman placed a hand on the feminine figure's granite hip. "Why do you think it disturbs you?"

Faruq thought. "I guess maybe because there's a violence to it. The way she's arching her back, that jagged metal, the teeth."

Again, the woman unflinchingly held Faruq's gaze. "Why does violence disturb you?"

He furrowed his brow. "Because people get hurt. People die."

The woman laughed, and Faruq was released from the hold of her eyes.

"We're all hurting, and we're all dying," she said. "Until we end the cycle. Your running—that's a kind of violence too. But it doesn't *disturb* you. You find beauty in it."

He noticed that she was a bit pigeon-toed, and stood with her shoulders slumped forward a bit. It imbued her with an endearing gawkiness. Faruq stood a little taller, stretching, hoping to alleviate the dull ache in his lower back. In the corner of his eye, sharp metal glinted.

"I guess I do," Faruq said, unsure of how else to respond. "I'm sorry—what was your name?"

Another childlike smile. "Thea."

"And I take it you already know who I am."

"Of course. There are no secrets among us."

"Yeah, so I've heard. Hey, what do you think you need to do to end the cycle, once and for all?"

"Well, Faruq, for that to happen, everyone would have to live according to the 18 Utterances."

"Everyone, as in everyone in the world?"

"Yes."

"That's a big ask."

"It is." She blinked, her gaze still unwavering.

"Well, what about people who don't live according to the 18 Utterances?"

She lifted a shoulder. "Maybe they just need a little more time."

"Do you find that frustrating? That not everyone sees what needs to be done to return to the World? To order?"

"No. That would be a distortion."

Faruq nodded thoughtfully. "I'd like to talk with you more about your art sometime, if that's okay. Now, the Persian Garden? Where's that?"

"Take a right out of here. You know where the post office and the dining hall are? It's behind there."

The Persian Garden was surrounded by a high stone wall, behind which Faruq had assumed there'd be one of the Forbidden City's pastures, perhaps livestock. But through a deeply set archway that Faruq hadn't seen on his previous trips to the dining hall, there sprawled a wide, geometrical garden complete with long pools, towering cypresses, and a bright pavilion.

He found Kaya squatting in the middle of a square of bare

earth with several other followers. They were tucking shrubby fistfuls of marigold into the dirt with their bare hands.

Faruq was a little self-conscious, approaching Kaya as she laughed, at ease with the other followers. But she smiled up at him, gracious and open as ever.

"Faruq," she said. "I heard you hurt your leg."

He frowned. "I don't think I'm going to get used to how fast word spreads here."

Kaya stood, wiping her hands on the front of her saffron-colored shift. "We're a family. There are no secrets here."

A few of the other followers grinned at Faruq as she said this, their lineless faces smeared with dirt, their eyes squinting and glowing in the sun.

"You'll have to stop running for a bit, I think," Kaya said. "Maybe this is your chance to try standing still."

Faruq's leg spasmed a bit, as though in protest to Kaya's suggestion, and he shifted on his feet. "It'll be better in a couple days," he said.

He wanted to tell Kaya about the wolf, but the other followers, though busy with their planting, were plainly listening. The experience with the wolf still sent tremors through Faruq. It felt private, fragile—if he shared it with too many people, it would stretch outward like a bubble and pop.

Instead, he gestured at the garden around them. "What is this place?" he asked.

"Isn't it beautiful?" Kaya said. "Huma—she's the one who designed it—came all the way from Iran to join us here. She didn't even speak English when she first heard Odo talk, but she recognized the truth anyway."

Faruq's journalist instincts perked up. He wanted to speak to a woman who'd heard something so compelling in a language she didn't understand that she'd fled her homeland for something radically different. "Is Huma here?" he asked.

"Huma returned to the World," said a voice behind Faruq.

Faruq hated the jolt of hyperawareness that crackled up his spine; it seemed to validate Odo's hubris without Faruq's consent.

He turned. Odo was approaching as though out of nowhere, an apparition. Faruq could find no smugness in his face, no matter how he searched for it.

"Not too long ago," Odo said. He stopped with a small distance between himself and Faruq, as though approaching a wounded dog. The followers all rose to their feet. In an interesting contrast to Odo's conduct, they all pressed in, so close that Faruq could feel Kaya's arm against his, hear the breaths of the man to his right.

"Returned to the world?" Faruq asked. "You mean she left the Forbidden City? The nameless?" Faruq was briefly hopeful—finally, maybe someone who'd left who'd be willing to talk to him, to tell him the truth.

But the followers crowding Faruq in laughed, making his body shake with theirs. Odo smiled patiently. "Returned to the *World,*" he said. "That's a capital *W.*"

"Oh. You mean she passed away."

More laughter. Faruq had a curdled memory of being pressed to some adult's chest, half asleep, their laughter an earthquake in their body and his.

"*Passed away,*" Odo repeated. "My, my, my. You make it sound like she was out for a walk and just—fell into a manhole."

Tittering.

"I don't believe you believe in those words, Faruq. *Passed away.* Tryna pretty-up something you think is ugly. But dying ain't ugly. Nah, Huma didn't *pass away.* She returned. To. The World."

The followers had inched closer to Odo, taking Faruq with them in the press of their bodies, a riptide. He was getting warm, uncomfortable. His words came with a little effort.

"But isn't that doing the same thing? Aren't you avoiding the word 'die' too?"

"Not avoiding," said Odo. "Just being more accurate. You die and then something else happens. The body falls and begins to rot; *you* return to the World, our shelter from the chaos of the universe."

"Like heaven?" Faruq asked.

More laughter, Odo joining in this time.

"You know," Odo said, "a Persian garden's got a certain geometry to it. A sacred geometry. It's a mortal version of the World, a kind of reflection in miniature. Can you see it from where you're standing?"

The followers were leaning in toward Odo, almost imperceptibly, but the cumulative effect was that Faruq was slightly off-balance. He glanced around at the garden. The neat squares where the marigold was being planted, the ruler-straight lines of shrubs, the tall, upright trunks of red alders through which he could see a glimmer of the pools, the high white wall.

"I can," Faruq said. "I mean, kind of." He sensed that Odo expected scrupulous honesty from him here, that it was, in fact, a test, his literalness a kind of passcode. "I can't see the whole thing at once. I don't have the perspective for that."

The corners of Odo's eyes crinkled. "*Perspective*. Now that's a word I dig." He tilted his head and examined Faruq, evaluating. "Yeah." He nodded. Deciding or approving. Maybe both. "Come to my spot for dinner tonight, scholar. I got something to show you."

Odo stepped forward, hand outstretched, and Faruq, slightly panicked, realized that he'd forgotten the complicated handshake Odo had created for him weeks ago. But Odo coolly taught it to him again, patient as a hunter, and Faruq thought the man must have an encyclopedia of his own choreography in his head.

When Odo left, walking unhurriedly in the direction of the garden's gazebo, the followers finally gave Faruq space, and he was suddenly on his own, supporting his own weight, his skin bleeding out the oppressive body heat of before. They were looking at him with something that resembled reverence. He shifted from one foot to the other, crossed his arms.

"Faruq," Kaya said, "this is going to be incredible. I'm so excited for you."

"I don't even know where he lives," Faruq said. "He didn't tell me."

"Your questioning is distorting your trust," one of the other followers said.

Faruq bit back a very sarcastic, very secular retort. Instead, he looked out at their faces. Beautiful, all, like their beauty was a uniform as much as their saffron-colored clothes. It made them like one organism, a segmented animal with minimally varied expression. Brush one of them and the whole thing quivers. It was genuine, Faruq realized. They really did feel what they said they felt.

But did Odo?

It wasn't until later that Faruq realized that not only had Odo not given him directions to his house, but he had also neglected to specify a time for dinner. Faruq dawdled for a long time in the guesthouse's bohemian living room, not knowing what to do with himself, before grabbing his laptop and scattered notes. If he was going to be in limbo, at least he could be productive.

Faruq's writing process was a lumbering, chaotic thing, improbably effective. The problem was his bottomless thirst for *information,* which invariably left him with the dilemma of how to organize all the information he'd collected. His notes on the nameless so far included everything from the broad rhythm of the Forbidden City—its rituals, its schedules—to what he'd cobbled together so far about nameless beliefs, to scraps of anecdote, stories he'd collected from individual followers, to observations about the weather, descriptions of the Forbidden City's layout, its pastures, its architecture, its crops and livestock, to his own musings about what he was feeling, what he was experiencing.

He always started with a rough skeleton, a patchwork of segments into which his haphazardly collected notes could be sorted. Later, he'd decide what he didn't need, what needed to be fleshed out. And after he'd learned all he could within the constraints of deadlines and people's willingness to open up to him, he'd add narrative, sewing it all together with an editorial thread.

Now he typed his notes into his outline, organizing them into a sketch of the piece they would eventually become. He cut here, expanded there, adding flesh to the skeleton, muscles, tendons, organs. It was unwieldy now, still unfocused, but he trusted himself to refine, to tame, when the time came. He tried not to edit now. Just release. The task was consuming, so that when he glanced up and saw Odo standing in the open front door, Faruq jumped.

Odo was standing with his hands clasped behind his back, his expression one of benevolent patience, as though he'd been waiting there a very long time and was perfectly content to indulge Faruq by waiting an eternity more.

"You scared me," Faruq blurted.

Odo grinned. "Nothing to be scared of, man. Just dinnertime. You ready?"

Faruq asked if he could record their dinner conversation and Odo agreed. By the time Faruq closed his laptop and made sure he had his cell phone, Odo was already outside, walking toward the dirt trail that meandered through the guesthouses. Faruq jogged to catch up, his legs complaining.

"I have to admit," he said, "I'm a little surprised you came to get me yourself."

"Expect me to send a henchman?" Odo asked, not looking at him, though there was humor in his voice.

"I feel special, is all."

Now, Odo did look at him. "I can hear the joke in your voice," he said without reproach. "That self-depreciating thing is a waste of your time, scholar."

He laughed, leaving Faruq slightly chagrined.

Odo walked fairly quickly, with long strides. Faruq's leg had begun to settle into evening stiffness, and it wasn't exactly easy for him to keep up. They were walking along the dirt trail that ran in front of the guesthouses, behind the house of the nameless. Faruq ran along this trail sometimes. It took him into the woods that opened, eventually, onto the ocean. But they were going in the opposite direction now, heading east.

To Faruq's surprise, they came to a stop in front of a whitewashed house not so different from Faruq's guesthouse. It was slightly larger, but in no way grandiose; it was nestled in a loose semicircle of trees. From the outside, there was nothing to suggest that the nameless's charismatic prophet lived there. It had only been a five-minute walk from Faruq's house to Odo's.

The front door to Odo's house opened, revealing a slender woman with jet-black hair that grazed her shoulders. It was a few moments before Faruq realized he recognized her face—Minh-An, from *Nero*.

Odo smiled at her as he moved toward his front door. "Minh-An pops in for dinner sometimes," he told Faruq.

When Faruq reached the door, he extended his hand and introduced himself. Minh-An took his hand loosely, but instead of shaking, she dapped him, almost absentmindedly. Her hand was bony and dry. Up close, Faruq could see that there were silver strands glittering in her black hair, her light tan skin stretched tight over her face. She had seemed tall in the documentary, but in real life she seemed shrunken; even with the layers of loose, bohemian clothes she wore, Faruq could tell that she was thin, sharp-boned, perhaps even fragile.

But her crescent-shaped eyes were backlit by something quick and knowing. Odo and Faruq followed her inside and Faruq hungrily looked around at Odo's home. Houseplants crowded the windows, threadbare carpets slouched on the floor, overlapping one another, and one wall was hidden entirely behind the meticulous stacks of books that reached all the way up to the ceiling. The walls in the dining room were encased in haphazardly hung art—everything from clumsy, amateur doodles to expensive reproductions of classics.

The impression Faruq got from it all was carefully curated chaos. Not really chaos at all, then. Just the painstakingly cultivated feeling of it. Somehow it didn't suit Odo, though Faruq couldn't have articulated why he felt that way. The dining table was already laden with food—sautéed greens and roasted vegetables, sweating slices of roasted chicken, half a loaf of that nameless bread—and in the background, music played so softly Faruq could barely hear it, though it had the feel of '60s soul.

Minh-An sat down, and then Odo. Faruq sat as well and placed his phone on the table, opened Voice Memos, and began to record. Then he paused, unsure of the etiquette here.

Odo laughed at him. "Just take what you want, scholar. We're not going to say an incantation over the food or anything. Eat."

Minh-An held up a hand. Faruq was surprised by both the assertiveness of the gesture and the transparency of the skin between her fingers. "Unless," she said, "*you* had something you wanted to say, Faruq."

He shook his head. Minh-An nodded and began piling roasted vegetables on her plate.

Odo looked on approvingly as Faruq followed suit.

"Well now," said Odo, grabbing a slice of chicken with his thumb and forefinger, "somebody tell me something. I've been doing all the telling all day today."

"I finally finished setting the ballet for Ewa," said Minh-An. "I think."

"You think?" Odo's tone was amused.

"Well, there's this bit in the middle—right before the last movement begins."

"And it's—what?" asked Odo.

"It's . . ." Minh-An could not find the words.

"It's . . . not perfect?" Odo supplied.

Minh-An laughed, self-consciously, Faruq thought. Though her plate was full of steaming vegetables leaking hot, amber oil, she hadn't eaten anything. Her fork was on her napkin, her hands tucked out of sight.

Odo swallowed a large hunk of bread before speaking again. "Perfectionism—it's just a symptom of distortion. You know that."

"I know," Minh-An agreed.

"You know? But here you are, bringing bullshit to my dinner table."

Faruq shifted uncomfortably, but Minh-An made no response.

"You want to twist yourself like you're blind again, I don't want to see it. Out."

Minh-An made as though to leave, but before she could fully stand, Odo held out a hand, laughing. "Come on, now. Sit down. Your problem is that you're looking at this thing with the wrong set of eyes. Try looking at it with your Other Sight."

Minh-An shook her head silently, as though in awe.

Faruq almost didn't want to interrupt, but he was fascinated, if unsettled, by this exchange. He had so many questions. "And this—*Other Sight*," he said. "It helps you see things more clearly?"

Odo laughed again and Minh-An looked at Faruq with what he thought was light disdain. "Can't forget about our scholar, now," Odo said. "Do you know that Minh-An here is a refugee of the Vietnam War? The very war I fought in. She was just a little old baby when Saigon fell, you know. But imagine that. Imagine how a thing like war would distort you if you were *born* into it."

Faruq nodded because he wasn't sure how else to respond.

Odo laughed so suddenly it scared Faruq. "Me and Minh-An got that in common—we was distorted by that war, fucked by white men. Wonder we ain't out for blood. But that would be a distorted way to go about things. And Minh-An here came up Buddhist." For a moment, he was thoughtful. "Why don't you tell me about the religion of your father, scholar?"

"My father?" said Faruq, caught off guard. "My father was Muslim. But I'm not—I mean, I'm an atheist."

Odo waved a hand dismissively. "I know all that. I asked about the religion of your *father*. Islam. Tell me about it."

"Well, I—hm. It's, um—I don't . . . ." Faruq stammered. "I don't know where to begin." He laughed. Odo and Minh-An waited patiently. "I guess Islam is . . . well, there's only one God—that's Allah. And Muhammad is the messenger of God." Now he was basically just translating the adhan.

"Yes, but what is Islam *about*?" Odo asked. "What does it want from you?"

Strangely embarrassed by his inability to explain the religion he was born into—his culture, really—Faruq poured himself a glass of unfiltered nameless wine from the bottle at the center of the table. What would his father say? He adjusted himself in his seat. "Muslims are supposed to submit to Allah, always. We—they have to believe in God, practice the teachings of the prophet, and defend their faith. This is all supposed to give them peace. Bliss."

"It never gave you any peace, did it." Odo stated this, rather than asking it.

"Just the opposite."

Odo nodded, satisfied. "Minh-An here came from Buddhism. I come from Christianity. And you, Islam. The religions of our fathers and mothers. And their fathers and mothers." He shook his head. "All those religions—Islam, Christianity, Judaism—they all say you have to believe or you'll be punished. Well, Vutu isn't like that; They doesn't care whether you believe in Them or not. You only hurt your own self if you don't try to break the cycle."

"The cycle of birth and rebirth?" Faruq asked.

"That's right," said Odo. "You see, we suffer because we're born with these two eyes that see ugly better than they see beauty. We get all bent out of shape—distorted. If you want peace, all you have to do is train the Other Sight. Then you start to realize that all that ugly is just a distortion. You're not going to see things right with those two eyes you were born with."

"So," Faruq said, "basically you're training yourself to see the beauty in everything?" Something was rubbing up against Faruq the wrong way, but he couldn't figure out what.

"You're starting to get it a little, scholar. Only it's not the beauty *in* everything. It's that everything is beautiful. That ugliness you see—it's a lie. A sickness." He gestured vaguely toward Minh-An. "That's the problem with this idea of *perfection*. All these religions are obsessed with it—get perfect so you're let into paradise. But *perfect* is a thing that exists only if *imperfect* does. That's just distortion, is all that is."

Something faceless still nagged at Faruq. He checked to ensure that his phone was still capturing the conversation. Minh-An had not touched her food. He was unsettled by the fact that Odo's philosophy made a kind of sense. That is, he could understand its appeal, could imagine the immense relief it must be to learn that all your negative experiences were just a symptom of something curable—a kind of misunderstanding.

"It's a habit," Minh-An said, looking distastefully at her vegetables. "Like smoking. I'm not trapped by the religion of my father anymore, but even now, after all this time with Odo, I sometimes slip into that distorted way of thinking."

"Nobody's perfect," Odo said with a grin. He and Minh-An burst into laughter.

Faruq adjusted himself in his seat. He felt like a schoolboy. He felt as he used to feel in Islamic weekend school in his father's masjid, sitting cross-legged on the dingy carpet with a bunch of other boys, listening to a pimply seventeen-year-old drone on about the Day of Judgment, the other boys nodding solemnly here and there, and him feeling none of it—none of it at all, and fidgeting until his cousin Danish slapped his sharp little knee with his sharp brown knuckles.

"Have some chicken," Odo said.

And because Faruq had briefly not been paying attention, he wasn't sure whether Odo was talking to him or Minh-An, so he added a slice of chicken to his plate. Minh-An's food remained untouched, her hands hidden. She was openly watching him now. Under her bright black gaze, chewing suddenly came with effort. He wondered what she was doing with those sharp, dry hands. Were they in her lap? Were they still or engaged in some reflexive dance?

"Why are you here?" she asked out of nowhere, staring directly into Faruq's eyes.

Somehow, he knew she didn't mean "here" as in Odo's table. Odo's house. "I'm writing about you," he said. "The nameless, I mean. I want to write the story the documentary didn't tell. I want—"

"That ain't it," interrupted Odo in between sips of wine. Minh-An's face softened into a half smile.

"That *is* it," protested Faruq, adjusting himself again.

Odo pointed his fork at him as though it were an extension of his finger. "You want the truth from me, then *I* want the truth from *you,* scholar."

Faruq felt exposed, uneasy. "I—I'm not sure what you want me to say."

Odo speared a lukewarm carrot from Minh-An's plate and dropped it onto his own. "Why don't you start here: Why do you run?"

Again, Faruq was stammering. "I've been—uh, well. I—it's good exercise. It's how *I* find peace."

Odo shook his head, chewing his pilfered carrot. "That ain't it either." His fork stabbed into Minh-An's plate again. A fingerling potato this time.

"I'm lost," Faruq confessed.

Odo snorted. "Oh, I know. You're out there in the fog, trying to make out shapes. But you're doing it with them two eyes."

A shiver ran through Faruq—a chilling suspicion that Odo somehow *knew* about the wolf on the beach. But that was impossible. He hadn't told anyone, didn't plan to. Odo couldn't know. Still, something snagged at Faruq. Something Odo had said, he was sure, but he couldn't pinpoint what. The conversation was twisting and morphing too quickly.

Odo reached out and placed his large hand over Faruq's. The hand was warm, even hot; discomfortingly familiar. It sent a kind of tremor through Faruq's nervous system.

"You're here to see," Odo said, his eyes boring into Faruq's. "That's what scholars do. They try to see."

Odo drew back his hand and ate Minh-An's potato. Faruq left his hand on the table, splayed out flat like an unconscious animal.

"I'm getting tired," said Minh-An.

"Try some bread," Odo told her. Then, to Faruq, "Minh-An's getting short."

"Cancer," she said, holding up a skinny arm as though to prove it.

Faruq was startled by their nonchalance, was oddly devastated, but he wanted to keep his face and voice neutral. Do not despair at death. Utterance 12. He struggled to come up with something to say, managed only "Ah."

Minh-An chuckled. "Nothing to worry about."

"Then it's not serious?" asked Faruq, confused.

"It's going to kill me," said Minh-An with a shrug, "which is what you're asking. But it's nothing to worry about."

Faruq frowned, disturbed again. "Is treatment not an option?"

"No, it is not." Odo answered for Minh-An. "Why should she let them pump her full of their poison?"

"Well, because it might save her," said Faruq. "Or prolong her life."

"And why do that? What's wrong with dying?"

Faruq stuttered, looking between Minh-An, whose face was serene, even slightly amused, and Odo. "Well, at the very least, isn't it her choice? I mean, you're speaking for her."

Again, that wavering of the mask, so quick Faruq could've missed it. The face Faruq glimpsed in that flash was cold, but Faruq had a feeling it was no less calculated than Odo's typical mask. He watched as Odo seemed to make the decision to put that other face away, keep himself genial, nonintimidating. He watched Odo's precise calculation take place, the iron control enacted.

"Well, she's right here, scholar," Odo said. "Yet you're not talking to her. Why don't you ask her yourself?"

Faruq looked to Minh-An and she shrugged, an eyebrow raised as though humoring a precocious child. "Everything is everything," she said.

"I don't know what that means," Faruq said.

"It means," said Minh-An with an air of strained patience, "that I'm ready to return to the World. I've made my peace, if it makes you more comfortable for me to put it that way."

He nodded, not wanting to pry more.

"Do you think," Minh-An said slowly, "that you're having a reaction right now out of a place of suffering?"

He scratched at his beard. "I think that's a safe guess."

"Well, what do you want to do about it?"

Faruq flashed her a wry smile. "I don't know. What would you want to do about it, if you were me?"

The skin around Minh-An's eyes crinkled. "I'd want to clear it out," she said. "I'd want to pluck it out by the root."

Faruq looked down at his plate: a few slick beets, a puckered sliver of chicken skin, a torn corner of bread. The food was good, but he couldn't eat any more of it. He'd once heard the Imam say to someone, "Life, eh?" And he didn't know what the Imam and the other person were talking about, but yes, that seemed to sum it up—*Life, eh?* Sadness like the thick, black roots of an ancient tree. And beneath that sadness, still, something unsettled. The niggling sense that something was off.

When Faruq lifted his eyes again, he watched Minh-An rip off a piece of the soft bread, roll it into a little ball, place it carefully into her mouth, and chew. It looked like it pained her. Faruq stopped the audio recording on his phone. He didn't stay much longer after that.

Faruq couldn't sleep. The thing that had been bothering him at Odo's house was only getting louder, but he still couldn't quite identify it. He took out the booklet, scanning the 18 Utterances as though they might contain a clue. They did not.

It had been something about Odo's condemnation of all religions but the one he had built. Maybe his strange insistence on that archaic-sounding turn of phrase—"the religion of your father." No, not that. Just the narcissism of it? The hubris? The hypocrisy? Not that either. He'd said something about Buddhism that didn't ring true—as far as Faruq knew, Buddhism didn't encourage perfectionism. That wasn't it, either. But—

With a sudden jolt of energy, he grabbed his laptop. He'd watched *Nero* at least four times, had even purchased the DVD. He loaded the movie into his external disc drive, pressed play, scrubbed forward. His heart thudded. There was Minh-An against that stark, black background—that minimalism trend that was sweeping through documentary filmmaking—her face pale in contrast, but glowing, a champagne moon. She looked younger, though the documentary was only about a year old. Her face was fuller, lit pink with blood. Had she known then, about the cancer?

Beauty is not suffering. The beautiful are free. Whine of a cello.

I was raised Catholic, and, by that point in my life, atheism seemed to fit my brand . . .

Faruq paused the movie, let out a gust of breath. He played it again.

. . . raised Catholic, and by that point, atheism . . .

He leaned in close to his computer screen. He *wasn't* going crazy. One more time.

. . . raised Catholic . . .

At dinner, Odo had said that Minh-An grew up Buddhist. He'd said it twice. Did he only assume that because she was Asian? Faruq doubted that. It seemed like something Odo would know about one of his closest followers. Faruq wasn't even a follower at all and Odo knew that he'd been raised Muslim. A mistake then? Why hadn't Minh-An corrected him? She'd been sitting there, content as a milk-drunk cat.

Twice—that was almost an insistence. Something more deliberate, then? A lie? But he couldn't think of why they'd lie about something so seemingly inconsequential. They had to know he'd seen the documentary. Hell, he'd *mentioned* the documentary. It seemed like such a silly thing to be hung up on, but still, the inconsistency made him dizzy. He pulled his mother's scarf out of his duffel bag. He knew firsthand how the lens through which you viewed the world could make it hard to see all the possibilities in front of you. Was his cynicism clouding his vision? Making him see malice where perhaps there was some other explanation? He didn't think so. He scrunched the scarf tightly in his fist.

On his computer screen, Minh-An's face glowed. Her mouth turned up at the corners in a lopsided smile, her black eyes were bright, her black hair shining in front of that stark black background, and just a small slip of white teeth.

Instagram Post #381

@thenamelessmvmnt: A circle of women, dancers, in gazelle-legged arabesques, extended legs reaching out and slender arms reaching into the circle's center, fingertips touching. Sinewy bodies sheathed in sparkling pink, tulle floating up toward a pale gold sun.

#divinedance #Ewa #beauty

82,752 likes | 2,066 comments

Nero

FADE IN:

INT. CWE NAVE—MED. SHOT—WILL ROY

Roy smiles, fidgets in his seat, crosses his arms.*

                    WILL ROY
          It's God's country, plain and simple.
          Everyone in our community is very welcoming.
          Southern hospitality, you know?

ZOOM—WILL ROY'S FACE

                    WILL ROY
          But then we started hearing things about
          this 'nameless,' this—*Odo*.

Roy shakes his head, lowers his eyes, sniffs, raises
his eyes again.

                    WILL ROY
          And the more we heard, the more we—well, my
          wife was gettin' scared, and I was gettin'
          pissed.

PAN OUT

                    WILL ROY
          It's right there in the Bible—all you gotta
          do is read: 'Every spirit that does not
          confess Jesus is not from God. This is the
          spirit of the antichrist, which you heard
          was coming and is now in the world already.'
          That's John. (scoffs)

Roy shakes his head.

                    WILL ROY
          Now I'm looking into this Odo and his
          nameless religion for myself, and *all* I see
          are signs of the antichrist.

_____

* Music: Nothin' (Townes Van Zandt)

INSERT—IMAGE

B&W photo, c. 1980s, of Odo walking down an NYC street, flanked by followers. SLOW PAN.

> WILL ROY
> He rose from obscurity, he speaks
> boastfully, he blasphemes my God and
> slanders His name.

                              DISSOLVE TO:
Photo of Fall Day procession, c. 2004; followers walk solemnly, in various states of undress, down a boulevard lined with palm trees. SLOW PAN.

> WILL ROY
> He doesn't answer to anyone, does just as he
> pleases, and he's trying to define a new era
> after himself. He's got no regard for the
> religion of his ancestors.

                              DISSOLVE TO:
Sepia-toned closeup photo of Odo, date unknown. ZOOM in to Odo's eyes.

> WILL ROY
> He's got all these people *worshipping him,*
> believing he can do all kinds of things—
> miracles, signs, and wonders.

BACK TO SCENE

Roy sits with his arms crossed, his face growing increasingly splotchy.

> WILL ROY
> 'Even Satan disguises himself as an angel of
> light.' Corinthians.
>
> These nameless folk, they go around talking
> about beauty and paradise, but really, all
> they're doing is trying to take over, trying
> to make the faithful question themselves.

'God is not a God of confusion, but of peace.' That's Corinthians again.

They came here looking to *corrupt*.

Roy slaps his knee for emphasis.

> WILL ROY
> This isn't a game, you know? We're God-fearing, and it is our *responsibility* to drive out the Devil. Now, they'll tell you we protested them.

Waves a hand dismissively.

> WILL ROY
> We didn't protest anything.

Roy shakes his head.

> WILL ROY
> Myself and some other members of the church got together to talk over our concerns and how we could use our faith to protect our community. And Odo and his *nameless* made that out to be some kind of attack. (scoffs)
>
> Of course, that's what the antichrist does. He sows chaos and confusion.

CLOSEUP—WILL ROY'S EYES

> WILL ROY
> He lies.

FADE TO BLACK.

INT. GEORGETOWN OFFICE—MED. SHOT—FATHER SCHUYLER

> FATHER SCHUYLER
> The relationship between Scripture and the concept of the antichrist is more complicated than people realize.

The basic tenet of apocalyptic ideology is
that all of human history is actually this
great cosmic battle between good and evil—
God and Satan.

The term 'antichrist' *only* appears in 1 and
2 John.

Father Schuyler holds up a finger.

            FATHER SCHUYLER
But these references *are not* to a single
embodiment of evil. These instances refer to
those who deny that Jesus Christ was the son
of God, that he was *in the flesh*.

He lowers his hand.

            FATHER SCHUYLER
Then we have the Book of Revelation.

INSERT—IMAGE

St. John Receives his Revelation, by Saint-Sever
Beatus. SLOW PAN.*

            FATHER SCHUYLER
First of all, the term 'antichrist' never
actually appears in the Book of Revelation.
The portents of heaven—the major vision in
the Book of Revelation—describes a great
cosmic battle between good and evil, with
Christians sort of stuck in the middle.

                              DISSOLVE TO:
Apocalypse 12, the Woman and the Dragon, by Beatus
d'Osma. SLOW PAN.

            FATHER SCHUYLER
It also tells us that Satan has two helpers,
two beasts—one from the sea, and one from
the land.

---

* Music: Concerto for Flute and Harp in C Major, KV 299
(Mozart)

DISSOLVE TO:

The Great Red Dragon and the Woman Clothed with the Sun
(Rev. 12:1-4), by William Blake. SLOW PAN.

> FATHER SCHUYLER
> The beast from the sea gets its power from
> Satan himself, and the beast from the land
> convinces people to worship the beast from
> the sea.

BACK TO SCENE

> FATHER SCHUYLER
> And to return to Revelation—if you examine
> everything *in context,* it becomes clear that
> the beast from the sea is a kind of metaphor
> for the Roman emperor. Probably Domitian. He
> ruled from 81 to 96 C.E.

Father Schuyler smirks.

> FATHER SCHUYLER
> And our beast from the land would most
> likely be the emperor's henchmen in Ephesus
> and Asia Minor. Deniers of Christ. *Not* Satan
> himself, embodied.

Father Schuyler holds up both hands and shrugs.

FADE TO BLACK.

FADE IN:

Photo of Sue Mills smiling and clutching a Bible to her
chest outside of Christ the Word Evangelical, c. 2014.
SLOW PAN.*

> WILL ROY
> Sue Mills is born and raised right here in
> Burning Hill. Her folks—that's Duncan and
> Heather—is good, God-fearing people, members
> of the church. Duncan's got a family business—
> insurance—right up there on Main Street.

---

* Music: fade in, For the Sake of the Song (Townes Van
Zandt)

                                        DISSOLVE TO:
Photo of Sue Mills with her arm slung around her
brother, her dark hair in stark contrast to his
white-blond hair, both of them freckled in bright
sunlight, c. 2011. SLOW PAN.

          WILL ROY
     Good girl, Sue; church every Sunday,
     graduated high school with honors. She was
     always taking good care of her younger
     brother, Eddie. (laughs)

                                        DISSOLVE TO:
Photo of Sue Mills in profile, seated in a pew in Christ
the Word Evangelical, face pensive, chin resting in
hand, elbow on knee, hair held away from her face with
a white headband, c. 2016. SLOW PAN.

          WILL ROY
     At the church barbecues, she'd fix her daddy
     a plate, then her little brother, and *then*
     herself. Good girl. Real close to Briana
     Joy, my youngest son's fiancée.

BACK TO SCENE

          WILL ROY
     Once she graduated high school, she started
     working as a receptionist at her daddy's
     company. She did well—hardworking,
     responsible.

     And then Odo and his nameless showed up in
     town.

Roy stares balefully into the camera for a few moments.

INSERT—B-ROLL

Sepia-toned footage of kids in Halloween costumes,
trees tipped with autumn leaves in the background.

          WILL ROY
     Every year, around Halloween time—Devil Day,
     we call it—God delivers me a special sermon

to put on the radio, and then the church'll
go all around town—door to door, if we have
to—and *beg* people to give glory to the Lord,
not demons.

So that's how I remember this was late
October, 2018.

BACK TO SCENE

                 WILL ROY
Heather Mills calls my wife early in the
morning. Well, we knew that was strange
because that early in the morning you're
supposed to be studying your Bible. As a
family.

That's something my granddaddy started in
the church and we still do it to this day.

CLOSEUP—WILL ROY'S FACE

                 WILL ROY
'Blessed is he whose delight is the Law of
the Lord, and on His law he meditates day
and night.'

Roy closes his eyes briefly and nods.

                 WILL ROY
Mrs. Mills is dang near hysterical on that
phone. Maggie can't understand a word she's
saying, so she hands the phone over to me.

CLOSEUP—WILL ROY'S HANDS

Roy gestures with his hands.

                 WILL ROY
Well, I got her calmed down. Told her God
didn't give us the spirit of fear. That's
just the Devil.

MED. SHOT—WILL ROY

                    WILL ROY
She tells me Sue ain't been home in 2
nights. She had called her mom on Thursday
to tell her don't wait up—she's going to
visit with Molly Kemper after work. They
were going to go see a film. When she never
came home, they figured she must've stayed
over at Molly's. But when Heather called
Molly, Molly said they never had plans.

Roy shakes his head.

                    WILL ROY
Well then we thought she might've gone
somewhere with Jeremy Lee Walker—they were
about to be engaged. Old Duncan Mills nearly
lost his religion over that, I'm sure you
can picture. (laughs)

But they called Jeremy Lee and he hadn't
seen her either. Matter of fact, he'd been
over there in Wimberley working for a couple
days and was looking forward to seeing her
when he got back. But he couldn't get ahold
of her either. Her father found her cell
phone in her desk at work.

Roy licks his lips, sniffs.

                    WILL ROY
Me and Maggie went over there to the Mills
house, and we called the police. They talked
to us for a while, but they said they can't
do nothing because she's nineteen and it
looks like she just—left. Didn't matter how
many ways we tried to tell them she ain't
that kind of girl.

Roy raises an eyebrow and shakes his head again,
disapprovingly.

                    WILL ROY
So I had the whole church praying for Sue
and her family. 'Whatever you ask in prayer

you will receive, if you have faith.' That's
Matthew.

He nods firmly.

> WILL ROY
> A few days go by. A week. 10 days. 2 weeks.
> The cops still ain't doing anything—they say
> they are, but then they keep telling Duncan
> and Heather they may need to accept she just
> ran off somewhere. She'll probably turn back
> up all her own, they're saying. (snorts)
>
> This whole time, that Odo and his nameless
> are starting work on that land they bought.

Roy fidgets in his chair, crosses and uncrosses his arms.

> WILL ROY
> They're pulling up trees, sleeping in tents.
> You couldn't take a walk through town
> without seeing them floating around.

Roy makes a fluttering gesture with a hand.

> WILL ROY
> Then Jeremy Lee finally spots her—Sue Mills
> is with *them*. He was over at the gas station
> and they came through in one of their fancy
> trucks. Sue was sittin' there in the back
> with a bunch of 'em.

Roy lifts both hands, spreads them, lowers them.

> WILL ROY
> Jeremy Lee called out to her, but she never
> even turned toward him, like Sue wasn't even
> her name.

He leans forward.

> WILL ROY
> Come to find out later, that Odo had her
> going by *Alethea*. (snorts)

Leans back again.

> **WILL ROY**
> Utter nonsense. Sue's a good name, and it's
> the name her *parents* gave her with the love
> of God in their hearts.

Roy crosses his arms.

> **WILL ROY**
> So I say we need to go and talk to these
> nameless folks. You don't go around dragging
> a good girl—a child of God—into your filth.
> Not on my watch. No sir.
>
> I was going to see them on my own, but her
> parents insisted on coming along. Can't
> blame them.

Roy shrugs.

> **WILL ROY**
> The first time we went to see them, they
> told us she and a few others had gone off
> to Austin. I didn't believe that for a
> minute—the Devil is a liar and so are his
> henchmen.
>
> The next time we went over there, this
> woman comes out to meet us, said her name
> was Horsefeather, or something ridiculous
> like that. She invited us to eat with
> them.

Roy crosses his arms again.

> **WILL ROY**
> But I didn't care to do that and I didn't
> mind telling her so.
>
> She tells us Sue is happy and doesn't want
> to see us.

Roy raises an eyebrow.

                    WILL ROY
Well, we went back to the police. I knew by
then it was useless, but Heather insisted.
And don't you know it, they told us she was
a grown adult who wasn't being forced to do
anything. Congratulated us on finding her
alive and well.

Congratulated us.

Roy slaps his knee.

                    WILL ROY
They had kidnapped her, brainwashed her to
where she wouldn't even see her own mama.

Closes his eyes.

                    WILL ROY
'This kind cannot be driven out by anything
but prayer.'

Hesitates a moment before reopening his eyes.

                    WILL ROY
So we prayed. When there's nothing in your
power to do, leave it to the power of the
Lord.

The frame of that nameless 'temple' was
going up, and I tell you, I couldn't even
drive by that land without the fire raging up
inside of me. Because I knew it was the work
of the antichrist.

Shakes his head.

                    WILL ROY
Why else build it here, in God's country?
They were mocking the Lord. But I had to be
patient and pray.

'One who is wise is cautious and turns away
from evil, but a fool is reckless and
careless.' Proverbs.

Heather managed to get Sue to see her. You
should've seen what all that was doing to
poor Heather. (tsks)

Well, Heather got in to see her, and she
said Sue was like a zombie. A *smiling*
zombie. Wouldn't answer unless she called
her *Alethea*. Just kept saying she was happy
there and didn't want to go home. There was
a follower in there with them the whole
time.

But Heather said she could still see the
Light deep down in Sue's eyes—they hadn't
put it all the way out. So when her
brother's birthday was coming up, Duncan and
Heather *begged* Sue to come home, just for a
bit. Just to celebrate with him. Sue was
always such a good sister. And hallelujah—
she agreed. (laughs)

CLOSEUP—WILL ROY'S FACE

> WILL ROY
> We knew we couldn't squander an opportunity
> like this. I made sure to be there, and I
> was full-up with power from the Lord.
>
> As soon as she got in that house, we had her
> in there with her parents and her brother
> and Jeremy Lee. And I was ministering that
> antichrist right out of her. I prayed over
> her, and I reminded her that she was one of
> God's Chosen, that He'd forgive her if she
> renounced the antichrist and begged.

Roy's eyes moisten.

> WILL ROY
> We were there probably 4, 5 hours—the Lord
> was working through me, so I never felt
> tired. Finally, the Light reawakened in her
> and she agreed to stay.

MED. SHOT—WILL ROY

           WILL ROY
Not a dry eye in the room.

I blessed her and cleansed her right there
in the kitchen sink.

Roy nods, smiles briefly.

           WILL ROY
Now, everyone was relieved to have Sue Mills
back in the fold, but—(sighs)—she just
wasn't the same. She was listless at home,
wouldn't go to work.

At church, people noticed she didn't seem to
remember the words to our praise songs. Which
is bizarre—I mean, she grew up singing 'em.

Jeremy Lee said she told him he'd better
forget about her, find him somebody else.

The nameless had hurt her spirit real bad.

Shakes his head sadly.

           WILL ROY
(tsks) I told her parents she needed to be
away from the evil. They sent her over to
Arkansas, to stay with her aunt and uncle.

Roy crosses his arms.

           WILL ROY
Now, that nameless had shown me everything I
needed to know. That Odo is the antichrist
just as sure as I'm a man. I couldn't let
them finish that Tower of Babel. 'Put on the
full armor of God so you can take your stand
against the Devil's schemes.'

                    FADE TO BLACK.

INT. GREENHOUSE—MED. SHOT—MINH-AN

Minh-An's head is thrown back in laughter, one hand on
her chest. She wipes her eyes and looks directly at the
camera.

          MINH-AN
We didn't 'bewitch' Sue Mills; she came
to *us*. She was *begging* to be hipped.
Odo doesn't have to force anyone to come
to him. When they're ready, they just
come.

Sue Mills was happy with us, happier than
she'd ever been. We didn't frighten her into
submission, didn't tell her she was a
sinner. (snickers)

And *just* when she was about ready to be
stripped, they snatch her away, trick
her, trap her. Send her off to fucking
Arkansas.

We weren't the ones who did the kidnapping.

In all of human history, people go to war
for two reasons.

Minh-An holds up 1 finger.

          MINH-AN
Rape,

Minh-An holds up 2 fingers.

          MINH-AN
and real estate.

Minh-An puts her hand down.

INT. CWE NAVE—MED. SHOT—WILL ROY

Roy sniffs, scowls.

WILL ROY

Word got back to Heather and Duncan from
Arkansas: Sue Mills was pregnant. That
antichrist had forced himself on her.

FADE TO BLACK.

before: 1969

FOR DAYS NOW the rain had been unrelenting, until finally the sky seemed to have emptied itself, the jungle panting wetly, the sun a vague light through the canopy, sweltering if muted. Unless you're humping through that sodden, stinking heat, with the constant noise of unseen beasts, of insects, of jungle boots and rough breath and private prayer, of squelching jungle-rot sores and dully jangling ammunition, and death and terror in every inch of every moment, you couldn't possibly understand.

Everyone's jungle fatigues were sagging damply from their bodies; they were all beginning to look like soggy scarecrows. And those purple moons under the eyes—white or colored, you got those purple hollows, and from deep inside them the eyes shone too bright, like a cat in the dark.

Every time Preach thought about how short he was, how close he was to getting back to the world, the whole inside of him lit up with a glow so bright he was afraid the Vietnamese might see it. So he tried not to think about it. Instead, he focused on the torturous monotony of the humping. One foot in front of the other. Glory be to God for every second something didn't kill you.

The jungle and its heat got so heavy by midday they usually had to pause for a rest. Today, one of the cherries up front—a beardless little white kid from Ohio—passed out before they took their break, wilted right out of the line. The line stopped, taking respite while the medic checked the cherry's pulse and dripped fluid into him. The kid's face was hot red; other soldiers laughed over him, calling him a pussy, a shrinking violet, a sweet little missus who got dizzy on her way to the market. Their jeering was medicine just as much as the solution being funneled into his veins. Sheer pride would keep the kid upright from now on. Until something forced him down.

Preach squatted on a mossy stump. It gave a little under his weight. The flint on the back of his box of army matches was damp by now, and there wasn't much here dry enough to strike on. He cursed as another of the flimsy matches went dead on him, his unlit cigarette dangling from a corner of his mouth.

Here.

Brother Ned held out a light and Preach gratefully leaned into it, taking a deep breath in. As Brother Ned settled down next to him, Preach saw that he still carried the photo of his sister.

Preach smiled.

You ever going to get around to writing my sister?

Brother Ned exhaled, dual streams of smoke jettying out from his nostrils.

Just as soon as I get the right words, brother.

Better hurry, *brother*. You ain't the only one whose attention she's got.

Brother Ned let his cigarette burn between his fingers for a few moments. Preach thought Ned's hands looked fine enough. They were gentle, long-fingered and pink-knuckled, the nails shiny and unbitten. Yes, they looked fine enough when they weren't killing. Brother Ned drew the back of his hand across his brow. It came back sweaty.

Say, I was thinking . . .

Thinking bout what?

I was thinking—well, you're getting real short, aren't you?

There went that glow—Preach wished Brother Ned hadn't brought it up.

Sure nuff.

I was thinking—maybe, when you get back, you ought to bring a picture of me. See if she likes me first.

Ned patted the pocket that held the photo. Preach chuckled.

You're not going shy, are you?

I just wanna see, you know, if she'd like somebody like me.

A white boy?

Brother Ned blushed. Preach had never even heard his sister talk about a white boy before, doubted if one had ever occurred to her. But she hadn't met many. And Preach didn't mind Brother Ned so much.

And just where am I supposed to get a picture of you?

Shyly, Brother Ned pulled another photo from his pocket. In it, he was freshly shaven, standing, wide-legged, in his khaki pants and white undershirt, smile wide open. Preach chuckled again and took the photo, tucked the picture into his own pocket, giving it a little pat to show Ned it was safe. Brother Ned took a relieved drag of his cigarette.

What's the first thing you'll do once you're back in the world?

Preach didn't want to talk about it, not here. He didn't want to think about it. He flicked ash onto the jungle floor.

Can't think that far ahead. Doesn't even feel like the real world is still there sometimes.

Brother Ned nodded.

Know what I'll do?

Marry my sister?

Brother Ned grinned.

Aside from that.

What, then?

First, I'll take a long, hot bath. Then I'll go to a diner—any diner—and get a warm apple pie with a slice of good American cheese on top.

With *cheese*?

You ain't living until you've had a slice of pie with cheese.

Man, you outta your mind.

Brother Ned laughed, slapped Preach on the back, dropped his cigarette to the ground.

Preach finished his smoke as Brother Ned meandered away. Then he picked up Ned's discarded roach—half of it was still left. Shaking his head, Preach put the still-smoking nub between his lips and pulled in.

. . .

Liking or not liking someone was too complicated out here, but Silk had decided he didn't quite trust Bigger. It was twilight now, and the kid was twitching at every bird's trill, every monkey's shriek, darting his pinprick eyes all around like a street dog. Back in the world, on the street where his mama still lived, drunk and alone now, the street dogs would slink around in the alleyways, all patchy fur and bone and open hunger.

He could never stand the sight of them, their petrified need, growling desperation. And what good would his Purple Heart do him there, on that street that smelled of old cooking oil and sun-baked trash and piss, and the dogs? And that little two-room apartment with its yellow windows and broken radiator, and Mama—who, more often than not, he just called Tia—in her chair, smoke dangling between her half-alive fingers, breath sour with drink, wig falling forward on her head.

At least here, dying or not dying meant a little something. So when his time had come after that first tour, he'd thought, Why not stay a little longer? Silk spat, his mouth foul-tasting, as it nearly always was here. What a damn fool. He couldn't even re-member what it was like to be as revved up as that kid was right now. Crazy Horse swooped down beside Silk, plucked a slender fern leaf to chew. The leaf was cloyingly bitter, a taste Crazy Horse had come to crave. Silk nudged him with an elbow, nodded at Big-ger.

Unlike Silk, Crazy Horse felt a certain affection toward the kid, but was clueless about how to handle such a thing. Most of his relationships—friends, girls—came rolling right up to him like marbles down a sloped floor. He either picked them or he didn't. He didn't know how to do the rolling.

There was a flutter of unseen wings from somewhere in the dark canopy above them, and Bigger's hands jumped like leaves disturbed by a sudden gust. Crazy Horse smirked, the fern drop-ping from between his teeth, and swaggered over to the kid.

Bigger nearly left his body when Crazy Horse touched his shoulder. Crazy Horse held up his hands in mock surrender.

Whoa there. If I didn't know any better, I'd think you took one of them pep pills.

Bigger shrugged self-consciously. Crazy Horse laid a hand on his shoulder—cautiously this time—and leaned in close.

Now, you remember what happened last time you got all worked up, don't you?

Crazy Horse pulled a joint from his pocket and waved it in front of Bigger's nose.

Wanna get mellow?

Bigger shook his head.

Don't know if that'll make it better or worse.

Crazy Horse's expression was benign but otherwise unreadable. Bigger was surprised when Crazy Horse tucked the joint away instead of lighting it up for himself. He drew a hand across his mouth. His palm came back slick with sweat.

I've never felt this fuckin tired before. And I got this funny feeling. All the time, I got this funny feeling.

Crazy Horse nodded.

You need your Blue Magic. Nah, don't laugh. A charm, a ritual—*somethin* to keep your head on out here.

Bigger looked down at his boots. They were filthy, the green uppers stained muddy brown, the toes thickly caked in jungle muck. Beneath them, the ground seemed to vibrate. Or it was him vibrating. A strange combination of being so tired but unable to relax, ever, left him full of this baffling, buzzing energy that threw everything into such hyperfocus that he could hardly see anything clearly at all. That he'd come here just because he and his mother had run out of money, just because it was so important that he finish college, seemed nauseatingly ridiculous now, gut-wrenchingly misguided. Better to just drop out. Better to sell dope. Better to run to Canada and scrape by. Better anything than this.

The vibrating shimmied up from his feet, climbing up his ankles, wrapping around his calves, pulsing into his veins and reach-

ing for the muscles of his thighs. The mind is a powerful thing. He
felt like he could fall right through the ground, right through the
middle of the Earth. He barely registered the chatter from the men
around him.

Shit, you feel that?

The fuck *is* that?

The men dropped their cigarettes, their joints, ground out the
lights. The command travels among them in a hiss.

Quiet. Nobody fuckin fire.

Crazy Horse's hand, which had never left Bigger's shoulder,
now tightens painfully, a warning, a restraint.

The jungle *was* trembling. Then came the call: something between a roar and a scream. It starts low, a growl more felt than
heard. A few guttural chuffs. Then something deep and wholly
primal, thunderous, and ending in an angry shriek. Each sound
closer than the last.

Without realizing what he's doing, Bigger leans into Crazy
Horse, into that painful grip. He can feel Crazy Horse's nails
through his jacket.

Without realizing what he's doing, Silk inches closer to Bigger
and Crazy Horse, until he can feel the tense heat from their bodies.

As awesome and terrible as a giant whale breaking the surface
of the ocean, the tiger bursts forth from the dark tangle of jungle
foliage, yellow eyes wide and phosphorescent in the low light,
stained teeth bared, ears pinned back, tail whipping wildly, its
body a wonderous work of deadly muscle. It weaves its way
through the humans who eagerly dive out of its path. The ground
rumbles so strongly now the trees quake.

Again, that grotesque, growling shriek, still closer.

Crazy Horse, Silk, and Bigger are pressed tightly into each
other now. Preach not three meters away, crouched down and
quietly praying.

Nobody fuckin fire goddamnit. Get outta the way.

Shit, we're gonna get trampled.

A secret, shameful trickle of urine makes its way down Bigger's
leg.

The quaking jungle echoes with the booming sounds of snapped branches, breaking trees. With infernal power, the elephants charge after the tiger—there are three of them—heads lowered, tusks the same vicious, stained ivory of the tiger's teeth, ears flapping like wings. Men dive, tuck, roll out of the elephants' way. The elephants are blind to the men, blind with rage. The command comes, hissed, again to hold fire, but no one is thinking of firing. And not because the bullets might anger the beasts or draw the enemy. But because this war, this war of nature, of beasts, is bigger, older than their own. Their bullets don't mean a damn thing. Crazy Horse uses his grip on Bigger's shoulder, and his other on Silk's pants, to pull them both back. They tumble closer to Preach. The elephant at the head of the charge sounds another blood-blackening trumpet. Their bodies are impossibly large, unthinkably heavy. They should not be able to move so fast. Mountains should flatten beneath their dry, gray feet.

They should not be able to simply vanish back into the jungle, but they do, following the path the tiger took. Their thundering footsteps gradually fade, and it takes awhile, but the ground stills. There is a waiting silence before anyone has the nerve to move again. And then they all exhale at the same time. Tiger probably tried to snatch one of them elephant babies, someone said. In the afterglow, men began to joke.

Guess that'll teach him.

Man, that tiger sure was a pussy.

Think you could take three elephants?

Sure he could—have you seen his wife?

Crazy Horse relinquished his grip on Bigger and Silk. He'd been clenching Bigger's shoulder so hard that now, the blood rushing back into the area hurt worse than the grip itself.

Silk dusted himself off and scooted closer to Preach, who looked unbothered but for the sweat dripping down his face and wetting the cigarette he was trying to light.

Bigger figured he already stunk to high heaven enough that no one would know he'd pissed himself, but the very next time they came across a body of water, be it mud puddle or leech-infested

stream, he was going to find a way to surreptitiously rinse himself off. Crazy Horse stood close, dusting himself off like Silk had.
He felt wild inside. Exhilarated, even. He laughed, met Bigger's
eyes.

What'd I tell you? Things happen out here. Shit that shouldn't
happen outside a dream.

Bigger could only hold Crazy Horse's gaze for a moment. He
was still too keyed up, and Crazy Horse had something wet and
green stuck to the corner of his mouth—Bigger found it unsettling. He remembered Silk's jungle story bout getting shot and the
jungle going quiet.

Hadn't it been Silk who'd said that about dreams? He couldn't
remember—his thoughts were sluggish, unfocused. It probably
didn't matter. He *did* feel like he was in some psychotic dream.

Nobody back home is going to believe this.

Crazy Horse laughed again.

Nobody back in the world would understand a damn thing
about it, believe it or not.

Bigger nodded.

Crazy Horse took a deep breath, took in the green-smelling air,
the scent of rot and sweat and piss. *Lions and tigers and bears—oh
my.* He *was* wild inside. He closed his eyes, threw his head back,
baring his throat.

From high above the canopy, you'd see nothing but draped green,
like fur, with rounded peaks and valleys, the shimmer of fog,
maybe the occasional darting of birds. Zoom in a little closer, and
you'd begin to notice the subtle movements of the trees, how they
seemed to breathe, the variations in the shapes of their leaves,
their greenness. Closer still and you'd make out the current of
movement just under the trees—the frantic flights of insects, lan-
guorous dancing of camouflaged beasts, the long line of men dis-
tinguishable because of its movement, as undulous as the snakes
that hide among the branches.

Though this line of men is one animal, each man is in his own private world, spun from semiconscious thought and somatic suffering and fear made dull by its own pervasiveness. Word travels through them like electricity rippling through a wire: They're nearing their objective. Just a few more kilometers uphill and they'll reach the spot where they've been commanded to clear an LZ. The endless humping is nearing its end.

The news pumps vigor into the line so that it seems to pulse with newfound energy. It inches ever forward, ever uphill. The closer it gets to the top of the hill, the more the jungle begins to clear; trees are farther apart, elephant grass begins to crop up and grows denser and denser.

Bamboo joins the elephant grass eventually—together they tower as high as the tallest man in the line. The point man at the head of the line sends down word of a trail—doesn't look like it's been used in a while, he reports. The line gets the command to hold still and silent while the point man sneaks ahead to check things out. Just one hundred and fifty meters or so, and there's a little charred O in the ground where a fire used to be, stalks of bamboo hacked down, the wounds dry and browned, and here and there bald patches in the elephant grass. All signs that someone has been here, if not necessarily recently.

The point man sends word back to the L-T, who calls in gunships. In just twenty minutes, the men are listening to the cacophony of the birds dropping their terror down on the area. Silk hates the sound, he really does. Cowardly, is what it is. He doesn't like the idea of killing up men he can't even see. Feels like something is being taken from him.

Preach is praying, though no one can tell. On the outside he's just another grunt waiting for the ugly business of death to be over, cigarette balanced at the corner of his mouth. But really he's asking God for those birds to be firing down onto nothing, for Charlie to be long gone.

Now the canopy is lace above their heads, ripped full of holes. The point man sees no movement after the onslaught. The men move forward. Everything reeks of burnt foliage and smoke and hot metal. Things are too quiet, Silk thinks, and Preach thinks nearly the same thing: It's too still. Even in the echoes left behind by the birds, the jungle has gone quiet.

The first booming shot is a desecration; the shots that follow, a war song.

At first, no one can tell where the enemy is. They just let their training take over. Crazy Horse finds a bush and dives onto his belly, firing in the direction he thinks the enemy fire is coming from. Bigger wildly checks the nearby trees, letting the occasional bullet fly off to seek an unseen mark. Silk and Preach are crouched down next to each other, covering a trio of soldiers dragging off a blood who's been hit in the arm.

It's Brother Ned who spots the small group of Vietnamese crouched in a patch of dark foliage with sawed-off M60s. He shouts to alert everyone else and fires at them, hitting one in the shoulder right away.

Bigger catches a fleshy brown flash in the lower branches of a nearby tree and, without thinking, fires. He misses, but the two Vietnamese hiding there announce their presence by jumping down, their guns flashing fire. Brother Ned takes one of them down and another soldier gets the other one.

Preach swings his head around and spots Crazy Horse, who is still on his belly firing. He gets one Vietnamese in the leg and someone else finishes the man off. Preach can see what Crazy Horse can't: a Vietnamese soldier crawling up behind him, knife poised—he'd either run out of ammo or somehow lost his gun. Preach shouts a warning, but Crazy Horse doesn't hear him. Preach begins running at the same time that the Vietnamese soldier springs and jumps.

Strangely enough, Crazy Horse's first reaction when the man lands on his back is to laugh. He does not particularly excel at hand-to-hand combat, so it is pure animal reflex that catches the man's slender hand as it moves to slash the knife across his throat. Crazy Horse can feel that he is larger than this man, but the soldier is surprisingly strong. Crazy Horse can't buck him off, and he has to let go of his gun so both hands are free to keep that knife out of him.

Preach reaches him and kicks Crazy Horse's gun out of the Vietnamese soldier's reach. With a split second to carefully aim at his tussling target, he slams the butt of his gun into the side of the soldier's head. The man slackens enough that Crazy Horse is able to toss him off. Crazy Horse rolls onto his back, but the soldier springs right up. Before Preach can shoot, the soldier is crouching low and shooting out a foot, sweeping Preach's leg out from under him.

Preach curses on the way down, his shot flying up into the wrecked canopy above. Now the soldier is on him, coming in with a preloaded punch, which Preach takes to the gut, hard. A carnivorous blossom of pain bites into his core. Even as he sputters, he manages to bring his knee up into the man's crotch. It doesn't disarm him as much as Preach had hoped, but it slows him down enough that Preach is able to shove the man off. Moving with visceral swiftness, Preach rolls onto his side and fires.

Now the man is still. Familiar nausea rises up in Preach, but he shoves it back down along with the staggering pain from the man's punch. All the Vietnamese are apparently dead now—seven of them in total. Crazy Horse reaches down and pulls Preach to his feet. Crazy Horse softly claps Preach between the shoulder blades and they both know.

Silk comes over, shaking his head.

Holy shit. Either of you need the medic?

The medic is occupied with the soldier who got hit in the arm. Just a flesh wound, as it turns out, but they'll need to stave off infection. Both Preach and Crazy Horse shake their heads.

We lose anyone?

Nah.

Preach pulls out a cigarette and lights it, but when he tries to pull in, his entire abdomen spasms in dense agony. He pinches the cigarette out and tucks it behind his ear for later. Silk looks him up and down carefully.

You sure that sumnabitch didn't get you with that knife?

Preach runs a hand over his front. His jungle fatigues are untorn, unbloodied but for a small spray of the soldier's blood on his wrist and near his shoulder.

I'm sure. But Christ, he socked me good. Can't even stand up straight yet.

Silk laughs. Crazy Horse lights a joint.

Little fucker had a lotta fight in him. It's almost a shame.

Silk's smile fades. Preach doesn't want them to stop talking. He is taking little breaths, each a little deeper than the last, working against the pain.

Hey, maybe I'll get a Purple Heart before I'm outta here after all.

Silk chuckles, but his smile doesn't reappear.

Always tryna be like me.

Man, please. You oughta be more like me.

Bigger joins them now, eyes still lit up from battle.

You see me get them two gooks in the trees?

Preach shakes his head a little. Silk sucks his teeth. He nods toward the bodies being lined up.

It may be "gooks" over here, but it's still "niggers" back in the world. Best leave that kind of talk to the white boys.

Bigger widens his eyes.

Aren't they trying to kill us?

Aren't we trying to kill them?

Bigger goes silent. They're all silent now. Is the jungle silent too? When they tell their stories to those who weren't there, sometimes it will be, and sometimes it won't.

The elephant grass up there was so tough, so unused to the destructive touch of man, that the grunts had to hack away at it with their machetes to clear it, and that's not to speak of the bamboo. It was easily going to take them hours to clear the landing zone.

Both Silk and Crazy Horse worked topless, their shirts draped over their heads to shield from the sun, which poured moltenly through the wrecked canopy. Bigger worked alongside Preach, who, he couldn't help but notice, was working slowly, wincingly. But when Bigger asked if he was hurting, Preach just muttered something about the Lord's strength, and paused to light a cigarette.

The cigarette just hung from between Preach's lips, slowly burning itself down. By the time it had shrunk down to a roach, Preach was squatting with his arms wrapped around his middle, face turned inward and eyes closed. The roach fell, still smoking, from his parted lips. Bigger squatted down beside him.

Say, Preach, you need the medic, brother.

Preach breathed thinly. His short puffs of breath steamed briefly as he released them.

Naw. Just sore. Helluva punch, is all.

But the L-T had noticed him by now. Anyone else, he thought, and he'd get in the man's face for being a useless pussy, but Preach—he never slacked, never complained, kept relative peace between the whites and the Negroes. Preach was no dramatic, no pill beggar, no slouch. The L-T walked up and looked Preach over. The man was just about gray—the L-T had never seen the like of it, not in a negro. He called the medic over. Preach protested.

Don't need no medic. Just need a break.

Crazy Horse and Silk came over now. Silk tested Preach's forehead.

Christ, brother, you feel like a cold bowl of sticky rice.

How you know it's my head and not your hand?

Preach tried to laugh, but it sparked a spasm of pain that radiated from behind his belly button around to his back. Silk pursed his lips and patted Preach gently on the biceps. It was with some effort that Preach peeled one of his arms away from his stomach so that the medic could check his pulse. The medic put two fingers to the inside of Preach's wrist and pressed. Preach watched little crescent moons appear at the top of the medic's nail beds, his fingertips going from pink to yellow-white. His hands were too soft for a soldier, Preach thought. The medic's brow furrowed and he raised his hand to take Preach's carotid pulse.

You're palpitating. Lemme check your temperature.

Brother Ned came over now, still holding his machete, his eyebrows drawn toward one another. The medic shone a light into Preach's eyes, found them dilated. He pulled the thermometer from Preach's mouth.

One-hundred-and-one point one. Looks like heat exhaustion to me. Can you stand? Let's get you in the shade.

Silk and Bigger helped Preach stand, supported him as the medic led them to a shady bamboo grove. Brother Ned and Crazy Horse cleared the ground as Bigger and Silk helped lay Preach down, and the medic lifted Preach's feet up to rest, elevated, on his pack. Brother Ned gave Preach his water flask, and the medic arranged a damp cloth on Preach's forehead.

Now, you just take a rest and you'll be yourself again.

Reluctantly, Silk, Bigger, Crazy Horse, and Brother Ned returned to their work clearing the LZ. Preach let his eyes close. It did feel good to be out of the sun, yes Lord. Even if the pain in his abdomen was pulsing, reaching around his sides and up his back. His mind began to wander, and eventually he drifted into something blanker, stiller than sleep. Occasionally, he'd float back up to consciousness a little at the sensation of the medic running a cool cloth along his arms, his neck. In time, there was that feeling of falling we all get sometimes at the onset of sleep, only this time, the fall was interrupted by something blindingly strong pulling him up, up, up up up up up. Up.

The medic noticed the cold stillness of Preach's body and began chest compressions, the cloth still in hand, his body heating as Preach's cooled. He threw himself into the compressions, even as he saw that they were doing nothing, could do nothing. Cursing, he hurled the damp cloth to the ground. He pinched the bridge of his nose, felt the grit of sweatsalt and dirt on his face. He studied Preach's shuttered face. Already, enough muscles had slackened in death that the man didn't look quite right, quite like himself. It was always like this. Each man had something unnameable in them, and they took it with them when they left. The medic sat back on his haunches. He'd missed something. He felt like throwing up. Heat exhaustion didn't cut it. He had to report it, of course, but not just yet. It was just him and Preach in this bamboo cathedral. He didn't quite believe in God anymore, but still, in the mottled shade, he began to pray.

today

HE KNEW IT was her even though her face was half formed, an unfocused impression of her features, a mismatch of what he could remember. Recognizable still, always. The field was flat and bright, the grass tipped in gold.

She was here to heal him.

Lurching forward, he fell at her feet. There was a copper bowl full of water nestled in the sharp grass next to her. He anticipated the coolness of the water pouring over him, the relief as it cleansed him. But she seized him, her fingers pressing into his arms, pressing toward bone.

Ganday jin, she spat in a voice that was and was not the voice he remembered, though he couldn't say how it was different, couldn't pick out the notes that were not his mother. *There are demons inside you. You got them from me, my son,* she cried. *I will take them out.*

Something was wrong with her, he thought. He wanted to embrace her, to shake her, but her grip on his arms was too tight. The agony of fresh grief choked him.

She opened her mouth and he saw that there were guava seeds on her tongue. Swiftly, she pressed her lips against his, spit the seeds into his mouth. He wanted to recoil, but still, she held him immobile. He felt the dryness of her lips, the quick, nauseous slick of her tongue as it pushed the seeds in, the sour aftertaste of fruit.

She released him and he crumpled, breathless and anguished and repulsed, the seeds tumbling down his throat.

What is your name? she demanded.

He wanted to tell her he would not play this sick, vile game. But instead, in horror, he felt his mouth open wide, wider, too wide—his jaw ached with the strain—and out of it, something like a scream, something like a howl, genderless, wretched, full of rage, impossible; it came up out of him like bile.

He was not in control.

The howl went on for far longer than his lungs could sustain— even when he ran out of air and his face grew wet with tears it continued, his chest clenching in agony. It changed pitch, volume, one moment deep and guttural, and the next shrill and poly-phonic. When at last it was done, he could almost *feel* the thing inside him, its fury, its bitterness, its primal desperation.

I command you out of my son.

He began to retch. He knew he was vomiting up the seeds, but they were engorged; they got stuck in his throat. He choked, panic clogging his gut, his throat bulging. He clawed at his mother's bare feet. Her skin came up in chunks at the raking of his nails. It was bloodless, like clay. She stood impassive, a pillar. His vision blurred with tears.

With one last tortured heave, the mass finally came shooting out—not guava, but the oblong disc of a mango seed, blackened as though burned.

He sat straight up, his grief and terror a heavy blanket. He threw off the covers, his body sluggish and sweating. The air out-side of his blankets was uncomfortably cold against his skin. His heart was still beating rapidly. He realized he was scared. He hadn't felt this lingering post-nightmare fear since he was a child. Part of him was still in that dream.

He checked his cell phone. Its glow threw faint shadows into motion. Just after one in the morning. He crawled out of bed and made his way into the bathroom to splash cold water on his face. His reflection in the vanity mirror seemed slightly off to him, like he was looking at more than just himself. *There are demons inside you.*

He shook his head firmly, reminding himself that he didn't

believe in any of that shit. Still, he startled a bit when he thought he heard a knock on the front door. He turned the water off and stood still and tense, listening. After a few silent moments, the knock came again—three assertive raps, not exactly soft, but not hard either. If he hadn't been awake already he might not have heard them.

Opening the door revealed a black-clad Minh-An, like a magic trick. She looked even more gaunt in the cast of late-night shadow. Her mouth stayed in a thin, straight line even as Faruq, befuddled, greeted her.

"We need you in the stables," she said without preamble.

"Is something wrong?"

"Nothing's wrong." Minh-An sounded slightly exasperated. "But it *is* urgent." She looked Faruq up and down. "You'll want to be dressed warmer than that."

Faruq looked down at himself—he was in boxers and an undershirt. He blushed a little, but Minh-An's gaze was clinical. He invited Minh-An in and then dashed into the bedroom to throw on track pants, a hoodie, his sneakers. He got the sense that he was expected to hurry. He nearly forgot to drop his cell phone in his pocket.

"Where are we going?" he asked Minh-An, who had not come in, when he returned to the front door.

"To the stables," Minh-An said with an air of strained patience.

"Right."

For someone who appeared so frail, Minh-An moved at a New Yorker's brisk pace. The stables were a bit of a hike, down in the southwest quadrant of the Forbidden City, behind the sprawling market. Faruq wanted to ask Minh-An if it was okay for her to exert herself like this, but he didn't think she would welcome that kind of attentiveness.

"So, what's the emergency?" he asked instead.

"No emergency."

"You said it was urgent."

"Yes. Urgent. Not an emergency."

Faruq let out a short breath. "Are you not going to tell me what we're doing? Is it a surprise?"

Minh-An paused her brisk walk and turned to look at him, slowly rolling her eyes. "Odo would like you to help us with something in the stables. He thinks you need something to shake up your routine."

As it turned out, they only walked as far as Ewa Park before they hopped into a golf cart that had been waiting there.

There were, Faruq learned, two horse pastures and two stables, one situated behind the other. Minh-An took him to the further stable, the one he hadn't known about. The stable was huge, heated, and smelled of fresh lumber, hay, and manure. It was mostly empty.

"We keep the pregnant mares in here," she explained. "It's foaling season."

Before Faruq could ask what that had to do with him, a nameless follower—a Raphaelesque cherub of a man—emerged from one of the stalls and approached them.

The man smiled at Faruq. "Welcome," he said. "I'm Gabe."

"Has her water broken yet?" Minh-An cut in.

"Not yet," said Gabe. "But she's sweating and pawing. Should be soon now, I'd guess."

"I'm sorry," Faruq interrupted, "but I'm getting the sinking feeling you want me to help deliver a horse."

Gabe chuckled, but Minh-An did not so much as crack a smile. "That's right," she said.

Faruq sputtered. "But—You—I don't think I've ever *touched* a real horse before. I'm a liability, if anything."

Minh-An laid a small hand on his arm, squeezing assertively. It was surprisingly stabilizing. "You'll be fine," she said. "The horse is going to do most of the work."

"But—" He gestured beseechingly at Gabe. "You said her water hasn't even broken yet. This could take hours, right? At least let's come back in the morning."

"Horses tend to foal at night," Minh-An said matter-of-factly.

"Their labor is nowhere near as long as a human's," said Gabe.

"Why does Odo want me doing this again?" Faruq asked.

He saw Minh-An and Gabe glance at each other but couldn't decipher the look between them. "You'd have to ask him that yourself," Minh-An said. She tugged on his arm. "Let's go meet her."

Gabe led them into the stall he'd emerged from. It was huge, the floor scattered with straw, and in it, a large, chestnut brown mare, her belly noticeably distended, paced restlessly.

"This is Hattie," said Gabe.

Hattie snorted, her tail swishing maniacally, her top lip curling back to reveal strong, blunt teeth. Gabe made a soft cooing sound.

"Oh, she's close," said Minh-An. She turned to Faruq. "We need to wrap her tail."

Faruq gaped. "She is very large. And apparently, she is having contractions. I'm pretty sure that if I even think about touching her tail, she's going to kick the shit out of me."

Minh-An tsked. "Your fear is not doing a thing for you, Faruq." She gestured at him. "Let go and trust."

Gabe chuckled under his breath. "City folk."

Minh-An retrieved a wide length of clean muslin and a comb. Hattie snorted again, tossed her mane, and lay down. Faruq winced. He'd never seen a horse actually lie down before—Hattie bent her front legs, bringing her chest low, and then seemed to collapse the rest of the way down before rolling onto her side. Neither Gabe nor Minh-An seemed alarmed by this. Faruq took a deep breath, trying to calm down. He remembered reading some- thing about horses being sensitive to people's emotions.

At Minh-An's gestured direction, Faruq offered his hand for Hattie to smell. She gave him a few perfunctory sniffs and then allowed him to stroke her face. Her fur was surprisingly rough, short bristles against the tender skin of his palm. She blinked her liquid black eyes at him. She was much calmer than he was, he realized. Faruq took another deep breath.

"See how her milk has come in?" Minh-An said, speaking softly. Hattie's swollen teats were steadily leaking white fluid.

They moved around to Hattie's sweating flank. Wordlessly,

Minh-An showed Faruq how to gently move the wide-toothed comb through her tail, pausing for flicks. Minh-An then wrapped the muslin from the base of Hattie's tail down. To keep it clean, she explained. Hattie looked back at them, sniffed, and then, yawning, rested her head in the hay on the floor. Faruq saw a strange, quivering ripple move along her flank.

"That's the foal," said Minh-An.

It was then Faruq noticed that Gabe was no longer in the stall with them. He hadn't noticed him slip out. He and Minh-An stood and backed away as Hattie labored to her feet. She held her wrapped tail aloft, shining lines of sweat trailing down her back legs. She paced to a corner of the stall, shat, and then walked over to nose Minh-An.

"You'll want to shovel that out of here," she said. Exasperated, Faruq did as he was told.

Hattie lifted one hind leg and then the other. She lowered her front legs to lie down again, only this time, with her rump still in the air, a surge of yellowish liquid came gushing out of her. Faruq would have mistaken it for pee, except that it was followed by the protrusion of a white sac.

"Is that—?" asked Faruq, speaking just above a whisper like Minh-An.

She nodded. "Won't be long now."

Hattie looked back at herself, and Faruq thought he recognized bewilderment on her face. The sac protruded even more and, to his astonishment, Faruq could see the foal's slender legs inside.

"Those are the front legs," Minh-An said. "That's good."

"What do we do now?" Faruq asked.

"We bear witness."

Minh-An sat cross-legged in the straw and Faruq reluctantly followed suit. Hattie sighed and rolled onto her side. More of the foal's skinny little legs came out, and the sac deflated, liquid fountaining out. Faruq didn't have a weak stomach, but the last time he'd watched anyone give birth was in the seventh grade. His father had gotten him exempted from sex ed—*Everything you need to know is in the Quran, beta*—but his friends had filled him in, in graphic detail. And later, in a dark corner of the library, he'd found *The Miracle of Birth* on YouTube. He'd been horrified, sick to his stomach. But he couldn't look away.

This was not as bad as he remembered that being. One of the foal's wet legs flexed weakly as Hattie stood, the foal still mostly inside her. Faruq tensed as she came over to snuffle at the straw right in front of him—you don't really accurately picture how huge a horse is until you meet one in person—but then she paced in a circle and lay back down. There was an unsettling squelching noise as she collapsed back onto her side. She rocked back and forth for a bit and then her whole body tensed as she began to push.

Faruq would have expected her to make more noise—he'd been sure he was in for a night of shrill horse cries. But Hattie was largely quiet but for a sigh here, a snort there, and some soft grunting. Were it not for the live feed supplied by the cameras Faruq spotted on the ceiling, one might simply wake up to a damp new foal at Hattie's side.

The foal's muzzle was visible now, slick and coated in pearlescent membrane. Hattie seemed more uncomfortable now than before. She kept switching from lying on her side to lying on her stomach, letting out a kind of grunting sigh each time she moved. Her whole body jerked with the force of her pushes.

The foal's head was out, its eyes closed, its body passive and limp. Alarmed, Faruq looked to Minh-An, but her expression was placid. Hattie seemed to consider standing but then collapsed back onto her side. One of the foal's front legs was straight, free from the sac, and the other was still curled inside it. Were human babies this quiet and still as they emerged, Faruq wondered? He was the only one concerned—not Minh-An, and not the horse.

Hattie pushed even more urgently now and shat again. Without being told, Faruq went to go clean it up. He got a good look at the foal, who was nearly halfway out now. The poor thing twitched jerkily each time its mother pushed. Faruq thought there might be a very good reason why one doesn't remember being born. With a spasmodic push, the foal was free but for its hind legs. Its passivity evaporated, and it began waving its head around, one wet eye struggling open a sliver.

Hattie looked back at her half-born child and watched with interest. Her urgency was gone now that only the foal's back feet remained inside her. Faruq wondered what she must be feeling now. Was she overwhelmed by maternal love? Was she afraid? Was she as astonished as Faruq was? What had his own mother felt when he'd emerged, howling and covered in gore? Had she loved him right away, or did she have to learn?

The foal's eyes were liquid black like its mother's. Faruq saw them regard each other. There was something fully cognizant, fascinatingly universal there. The foal began to nibble on straw. In another minute or two, its back legs slipped fully free and it squirmed closer to its mother, who began to lick and nibble, cleaning it. The foal's movements were like that of a poorly controlled puppet. It threw itself into its mother's side, shook its head like a wet dog.

Faruq checked his phone. They'd been here for less than twenty-five minutes. He glanced at Minh-An. "Is that it?" he asked.

Minh-An's expression was still placid. "We need to wait for the placenta," she said. "And the foal needs to stand."

The foal did, in fact, appear to be trying to get to its feet. It waved its legs around on the floor, stuck one back leg straight out. When that didn't work, it tried curling its front legs underneath itself, sticking its butt up into the air, short, scrappy tail windmilling. From this angle, Faruq was able to see that this was a baby girl—a filly, he thought they were called.

The filly got her legs under her and rose haltingly to standing. Hattie stood too, the tattered remains of the sac hanging out of her. She licked along her baby's back as the filly tried to find balance on those four long legs. She lurched into Hattie's side and nosed her, in search of a teat, Faruq guessed. Having found one, she suckled briefly and then stumbled over to investigate Faruq. He tensed, watching for signs of defensiveness from Hattie, but she only dipped her head to nibble at hay from over the side of the stall.

The filly tickled Faruq's hands with her wet nose, and then returned to her mother to suckle again. Hattie allowed this for a minute or two, and then began a rather irritated dance of lying down and then getting back up, which the filly tried her best to copy. On her awkward legs, though, the dance soon grew too tiring, and she lurched off to examine a corner of the stall. After Hattie stood for the sixth or seventh time, she seemed to bear down, and the placenta plopped out of her. The filly came over and nuzzled her flank. Only then did Minh-An stand.

"Let's go," she said, stretching.

"We don't need to do anything else?"

Minh-An was already leaving the stall. "Gabe will examine the placenta, make sure it's intact, and then clean the place up," she said. "Our part is done. They'll be okay."

Faruq hurried to keep up with her, closing the stall door behind him. "And if they hadn't been?"

"Then we would have borne witness."

After the heated stable, the cool, late-night air was sharp and clear.

"That's all?" Faruq said. "We wouldn't have helped? Tried to save the baby's life?"

Minh-An stopped and looked up at him. "You know what Odo has to say about death. Why are you so resistant?"

"I don't know, maybe I just love life?"

"No you don't." Minh-An began walking toward the golf cart again. "You can't love life and hate death."

Minh-An's certainty irked him, but he didn't want to argue about death with her when she was dying. "Well," he said, rubbing his eyes, "that was a once-in-a-lifetime experience. But why was it so important that I be there?"

"Odo wanted you there," said Minh-An. "He wants you at dinner again tomorrow night. Or tonight." She shook her head, sighed, and then continued. "You know the way now—he doesn't need to come get you."

"What time?" asked Faruq.

"It doesn't matter, Faruq," Minh-An said tiredly. "Come when you come."

They got into the cart and began the ride back to the guest-houses. Faruq wondered why Odo had decided he needed to see a horse giving birth. Was there some lesson in that? Some admonishment? Some warning? He had the unpleasant sensation of being toyed with without understanding how or why.

"Hey," he said to Minh-An. He tried to keep his tone light, conversational. He could tell that she was tired, and though he wanted to know what she knew, he didn't want to spook her. Or irritate her. "What do you make of all that stuff that happened back in Texas?"

She laughed derisively. "Which part?"

"Well, all of it. The harassment, Sue Mills, the trial."

"Racism and intolerance, all of it," she said shortly.

"But do you really think that was all there was to it?" Faruq asked. "All that ire—what, because Odo is Black?"

She shrugged with one sharp shoulder. "Can't underestimate the homogeny of small-town America."

Faruq decided to push a little harder. "People have been using the word 'cult.'"

She glanced at him. "And if we are one, Faruq? What does it matter? What are we doing to you?"

"People might say that cults take advantage of their members. At best."

"The people who come to us are not at risk of being taken advantage of." She shook her head. "They're at risk of being liberated. If anyone's vulnerable to getting taken advantage of, it's Odo."

"Odo? How? He doesn't seem particularly vulnerable. In fact, he seems savvy."

"He's wide open, Faruq. Imagine walking around with an open mouth all the time. You'll catch the goodness of the world, the sweetness. But you'll also catch the flies and the spiders and the dirt."

"Is that why you're so protective of him?"

"He would let anyone near him, do you know that? *Anyone.* Back when I first started following him, I'd watch him let attention-seekers and narcissists sit at his feet, drinking up all his energy for themselves."

"And shouldn't he do that? Isn't what he's preaching for everyone? Even the narcissists?"

Minh-An's mouth stretched into a thin line. "They're not ready," she said firmly. The cart sped up. Her foot had grown heavy on the gas.

"Doesn't Odo get them ready? By hipping them?"

She took in a breath and slowed her driving. "Some people," she said slowly, "are stuck in distortion. And they have a few more cycles of life and death before they're strong enough to get out. And sometimes those people are so distorted they get really good at pretending."

"And they can fool even Odo?"

Minh-An snorted. "Not for long. But I don't like them getting near him in the first place."

Faruq let that be for a while, let Minh-An calm herself down. Then, as he saw they were nearing the guesthouses, he ventured, "Do *you* think you're a cult?"

"No, scholar. We're no cult. We're the truth."

"Then, Odo truly *believes* everything he's saying?"

She stopped the cart and looked at him. "Odo *is* everything he's saying."

Minh-An walked him to his front door. "Five more of our mares are pregnant," she said, before turning to leave him alone.

Faruq didn't realize how tired he was until he reached the bedroom, saw his inviting, unmade bed. He barely had the energy to wash up. When he crawled under the covers the image returned to him: his mother's brown feet, as giving as wet clay. He pushed the thought away.

From the corner of his eye he saw the pamphlet with the 18 Utterances on the bedside table. He thought he'd put it in the drawer, but he was so tired he couldn't remember. He closed his eyes.

. . .

Faruq stretched outside in the drizzle. He tried to position himself in the overhang of the cabin's roof, but water dripped down onto his head, breaking his concentration. His left calf was tight, sending out a twinge of pain as he flexed his foot up. He took a deep breath, closed his eyes, leaned further into the stretch.

"Morning."

The voice seemed to come out of nowhere, and jolted him. His eyes popped open.

"Zephyr," he said, disoriented. "What are you doing here?"

Zephyr blinked. They seemed completely unbothered by the rain, seemed to not even notice it. "Time for prayer," they said, looking into Faruq's eyes.

"You—want me to come to prayer?"

"Only if you want to, Faruq. Thought I'd come say hello and see if you wanted to join me."

"I was just going to go for a run," Faruq said, gesturing down at his running clothes. "Wait, when did you get back?"

"Late last night," said Zephyr. "I'm not back for long. I wanted to see you before I left again. You sure you don't want to join me?"

"Maybe another time," said Faruq.

Zephyr smiled and patted Faruq on the shoulder. He could feel their eyes on him as he began jogging toward the tree line.

Rain made the forest around him strange. Distorted its noise, changed the shape of its echoes. As he ran, Faruq kept thinking he heard running footsteps nearby, keeping pace with him. He kept looking around and saw no one. But he felt the wolf. The more he tried to push away this line of thinking, the more he thought he could sense that animal presence just out of sight.

It had been like this on every run since he'd seen the wolf. He'd hear a noise, something that sounded like paws on leaves; he'd see movement from the corner of his eye but find only hulking redwoods when he looked; he'd spot paw prints on the forest floor, dew gathering in the wells made by roughened toes. He didn't *think* it was all in his head. But if it wasn't, then a wild animal—a *wolf*—was following him? Habitually?

Rain mixed with Faruq's sweat, drove it into his eyes. He blinked the salt away. There was a dull ache in his left hamstring that lit up every time his left foot hit the ground. It wasn't sharp enough to worry him but he sorely missed his foam roller. He remembered what the artist, Thea, had said to him in her studio of teeth and metal—his running was a kind of violence. It disturbed him when those nameless folks were right. He heard a twig snap, the rustle of something moving through foliage. He thought he heard a lupine grunt like distant thunder. He lassoed his fear, drove it into the run.

His father had loved animals. *They praise Allah too, beta,* he'd say. He told the story of Joseph, whose brothers were so envious of him they'd thrown him into a well, and then told their father a wolf had eaten him. *That's why the wolves in this country are all gone,* he told Faruq.

Men hide their own evil in wolf's furs. Then you think it's a wolf. But Allah sees the truth, Subhanahu wa-ta'ala. That was the day they'd found TERRORIST scrawled across the side of the car. They were still pulling bodies out of the rubble of the towers. His mother had been pulled out of the East River six weeks before.

Faruq shook his head viciously. Water and sweat flew off him in a pinwheel. When he'd first started running, grief and rage had propelled him. But he was not that child anymore. Again, the ghost of footfall, the padding of paws; the rain made it into a kind of whisper sound that echoed up into the treetops. Faruq turned around, about half a kilometer short of the foggy beach. He ran back to the Forbidden City.

"How much more time are we talking, Zaidi?"

The rain had calmed to a needling mist. Anita sounded far away, like they were talking on a landline. He was in the hotspot Kaya had shown him, and he'd just finished telling Anita about the disorganized deluge of information he'd collected thus far.

"I don't know," he said. "Maybe another week? Two? I just feel like I'm barely scratching the surface here."

She took a pause before speaking again. "Six weeks was a lot of time to be over there as it is."

"Trust me, I know, Anita. It's just—things are *weird* here. I'm pretty sure I'm getting fucked with. I want to know what the game is. And Odo—he's so . . . I don't know if 'interesting' is the right word. Fascinating, maybe. But in a fucked-up way."

"Look, Faruq, you're not getting caught up in their web, are you? I'm worried about you."

"No, no."

"Jesus, I *know* you're vulnerable right now. What the fuck was I thinking, sending you out into a cult?"

"Anita. I'm all right. I swear."

"You swear?"

"They're not getting to me. At least, not like that. Just, please, more time."

He heard Anita sigh. "All right, Zaidi. I'm trusting you here. But you *have* to come back, understand?"

"Thanks. I'll be back, promise."

"You know, I think I know what your problem is."

"What's that?" Faruq asked, pulling his hood tighter around his face.

"It's your father," said Anita.

Faruq rolled his eyes, which, bafflingly, Anita seemed to sense.

"No, really," she said. "You haven't dealt with it, Zaidi, so it's coming out on its own."

"Okay, Dr. Phil." They both chuckled. Then, Faruq scratched at his beard. "I don't know, Anita. Maybe this is bigger."

"Bigger than an article, you mean?"

"Maybe. I don't know."

"Have you considered that you're no longer writing an article, but a book?"

This gave Faruq pause. Anita continued on into his silence.

"I know you, Zaidi. There's a story in you that you've been holding prisoner for a long time. Being out there with those people—for better or worse, it's unlocked something. I think you're on the verge of telling it now."

Faruq let out a huff of laughter. Anita knew a lot, but she didn't know everything. "Look, you'll give me my article. I know you will because you always do. I'm giving you more time. If something else is coming out, I think you should let it."

After hanging up with his boss, Faruq texted Danish: wyd? It was about noon back in New York—time for the Dhuhr prayer. After five minutes Danish still hadn't responded. Faruq tucked his cell phone into his pocket and headed back for dinner. On his way back, he paused to watch a man painting a mural on the side of one of the buildings. The man paused to wave at him briefly before returning to his work. Something dizzying, large, spreading across the white wall like an oil spill. Faruq had the sense he was being watched as he was watching, but a glance around showed only a few followers milling about, walking, going about their days. He left the man to his art and continued his walk to Odo's house.

Odo was waiting outside when Faruq arrived. "I'm not late, am I?" asked Faruq.

In response, Odo only laughed, shaking his head, and gestured for Faruq to follow him inside.

This time, Faruq was not surprised to find Minh-An there. They nodded to each other in greeting. Minh-An was wearing a billowing kind of jumpsuit that hid how skeletal she was. The dining table was set with the nameless constants—grainy bread and unfiltered wine—along with roasted leeks, whole trout, and a serving bowl full of couscous. Faruq settled into the same seat he'd taken last time, noting that both Odo and Minh-An seemed to have their set places, and put his phone on the table, recording. Minh-An slathered a corner of bread with butter and then looked down at it with an expression Faruq had more than once seen her direct toward him.

Faruq thought Odo might say something about the mare and

her foal, why Faruq had been summoned to watch the birth, but instead he grinned and said, "You ever been fishing, scholar?"

One of the trout seemed to be waiting for Faruq's answer with dead eyes. He spooned couscous onto his plate. "Once or twice, when I was a kid. I never caught anything. My cousin Danish caught a porgy once, but we let it go." Faruq's uncle had insisted it was a garbage fish. It wasn't until many years later that Faruq had tried one, and found it delicious.

"Two main ways to fish," Odo said. "Angling and gathering. With angling, you bait a hook, lure the fish to its own death. Sacrifice the worm for the fish, and then the fish for yourself." He plopped a trout onto his plate. "But with gathering, there is no lure, no sacrifice. You just take what you can catch in your net. Or with your bare hands."

Faruq watched as Odo deftly cut behind the trout's gills, brought its white meat to his mouth with a fork. "Is this a metaphor?" he asked.

"I don't know about any fancy metaphors," Odo said. "That's what you scholars are for. But everything in life's got something else underneath it, like a soul. Everything that happens and everything that is—it's all manifestation. Possession."

Minh-An let out an awed gasp, barely audible.

Faruq felt suddenly queasy. "*Possession?*"

"Well, not literally, scholar," Odo said.

"Another metaphor, then," Faruq said, nodding. "Or whatever you want to call it. Is that what the horse thing is? A big metaphor?"

Odo laughed. "When else would you have the opportunity to help a horse give birth, scholar?"

Faruq looked down at his plate for a long time. The couscous had wet ropes of cooked spinach in it, slivered almonds like clipped fingernails. The dream was still there, trying to force a metamorphosis into memory. Faruq could still feel the unhinging of his jaw, that inhuman cry crawling out of his throat. He looked back up at Odo. "What about spearfishing?"

Odo laughed, but Faruq could see Minh-An's glare from the corner of his eye. "You're all right, scholar," Odo said. "Tell me, what is it that Islam says about reincarnation?"

Faruq chewed on a piece of bread. "I'm pretty sure the Quran says we only get one chance at redemption. So, one life. Any so-called evidence of reincarnation—say, déjà vu—is supposed to be the work of the jinn." He tore off another piece of bread. "Of course, *I* don't believe that. Or in reincarnation."

"You're beginning to sound like a broken record," scoffed Minh-An.

"We all know your beliefs, scholar," Odo said. "Or lack thereof. What's got you anxious?"

Faruq shrugged and thought about it. "Not really anxious. I guess I'm just wondering why you keep asking about my father's religion instead of telling me about yours."

"The nameless is not a *religion*," began Minh-An, but Odo held up a hand.

"I'm curious," Odo said, as though he were making a confession. "Some parents leave their children with scars. I think you're a scarred man."

Easy enough to guess, Faruq reassured himself. This is what men like Odo did—they threw shit at a wall. Inevitably, some of it stuck. Faruq carefully moved one of the trout to his plate, gingerly separating meat from diaphanous bone. The fish was good—fresh and savory. He chewed it down into nothing.

"My father was . . . extremely devout. After my mother died and 9/11 happened, I lost all my faith. But he—I could never tell him. I had to hide it from him until he passed."

Odo nodded. He already knew this. Faruq had told this pared-down truth before. He ate some more of the fish. Minh-An took a mouselike bite out of her buttered bread.

"Can I ask you a question?" Faruq said to Odo.

"Naturally."

"So you have your vision, right? Your revelation. Why not just let it change the way *you* live? Why preach it at all? Why amass followers? Why build a *city*?" He gestured vaguely around with his fork. "Why all this?"

Odo snickered. "You're putting a lot of things on me that I ain't actually ask for, scholar," he said. "I didn't ask for people to follow me, or even listen to me—they just do. And *they* built this city. Nah, the real question here—the *important* one—is why did I share my 'revelation,' as you call it. And the answer to that, scholar, is simple." He shrugged. "We only break the cycle if we all get hipped."

"This is the cycle of life and death," Faruq said. "Reincarnation?"

"Yes."

"And why do you think it was you, out of everybody else in the world, who received that revelation?"

Odo smirked and put down his fork. "You ever seen a man just come back from war? Look like their eyes been blown wide open. Like they're full of this crazy light most of us don't see." He shrugged. "I don't know. Maybe my eyes got blown wide open in just the right way."

Faruq tried to help clear the dishes after dinner, but Odo waved him off. "Leave it. They'll come clean it up for us."

Faruq asked, "They?"

"The ones who brought it over in the first place." Odo stood and regarded Faruq for a moment, hands on hips. "Will you be back tomorrow?"

Faruq confirmed that he would, hearing the unspoken dismissal. He and Minh-An made their way to the door. Odo dapped Faruq goodbye. Odo dapped Minh-An as well, but after they were done, he held both of her hands in his for a long while. Eventually, he leaned down to touch his forehead to hers before letting her go.

"I'll walk part of the way back with you," Minh-An said, once Odo's door closed behind them.

"What was that?" Faruq asked as they began walking.

"What was what?"

"That thing back there, with Odo. Are you two . . . together?"

Minh-An scoffed. "Right, because he must be fucking all his followers."

Faruq stayed silent.

"We liberate people to explore the kinds of relationships that work for them. Without judgment. But that doesn't mean we're all jumping into orgies with each other." She paused. "As far as I know, Odo's celibate."

Faruq could hear how winded Minh-An sounded, so he stopped walking for a moment. "But you love him. Even I can see that."

Minh-An smiled faintly up at him. "Odo and I are soulmates. It's something deeper than romantic love. Or do you not believe in something like that?"

"You could explain it to me," Faruq said, holding up his phone.

Minh-An nodded shortly and began walking again. Faruq hit record and followed.

"After the Fall, the Tintan shattered, like glass. We all have fragments of the ten original Tintan in us—they're called gosah. Sometimes we find people whose gosah fit together with ours, like when you're gluing a vase back together. That's a soulmate. It means that you and that person—you used to be part of the same being."

"So, then, can a person have more than one 'soulmate'?"

"Oh yes," said Minh-An. "But it's rare to find more than one or two of them in one lifetime. The world's too big and too broken."

"And these—gosah-mates, they're not always a romantic partner?"

"They're not even always human."

Minh-An smiled. As they walked past a row of nameless homes, he spotted the Deep, arranged in a circle, sticks held by their sides. He was becoming desensitized to the sight of them. He wasn't startled by their presence anymore. He wasn't sure what to think about that. Was Anita right to be worried about him? He didn't *think* so. Before long, they had reached Faruq's guesthouse without him noticing.

He reached out and touched Minh-An's frail arm. "You seem so independent," he said, following an impulse. "Tell me—what is it about Odo? What makes you want to follow him when you could be following yourself?"

Minh-An narrowed her eyes at him, and for a moment he feared he'd made a mistake. But then her face relaxed. "Faruq, I feel such empathy for you. Until I met Odo, I had never been loved like I needed to be loved. And, like you, I didn't even know it."

Faruq furrowed his brow, resisted the urge to correct her, tell her that he did have people who loved him, and whom he loved in return.

"I see your defensiveness," she said, smirking. "I understand it. Like I said, before Odo, I was you. I was constantly contorting myself to be acceptable to my family, my friends, my lovers. After a while, I didn't even know what my true shape was anymore. The contortion, that discomfort, became more recognizable to me than my own true face. But Odo, he—*untangled* me. He recognized me, and then I could recognize myself again too."

"How did he untangle you?"

"He got to the bottom of what I really wanted."

"And what did you really want?"

She closed her eyes briefly. When she opened them again, her gaze was firm. "Order out of chaos."

"Sounds familiar," said Faruq.

She chuckled. "Good night, scholar," she said, and turned to walk to her own home.

Faruq was tired, but he didn't feel like being alone in his guesthouse yet, in the whitewashed bedroom where that dream had come. He began to walk, no particular destination in mind. The Forbidden City was a twinkling chorus at night. There wasn't much lighting—he had to use his phone's flashlight in some of the less populated areas. But all around him floated the sounds of laughter, of music and singing, of instruments, low conversations, doors opening and closing, silverware clinking, water running, amorous sighs, the bells of children's voices. And, under it all, the soft night noises of the woods and the animals that lived there.

Once he realized that he wanted to go to the stables, he borrowed one of the golf carts and made his way to the stable where he'd watched Hattie giving birth to her foal. Gabe was there. He seemed genuinely happy, if not surprised, to see Faruq.

"We decided to name the little filly Cora," Gabe said, leading Faruq to their stall.

"How are they doing?" asked Faruq.

"Happy and healthy both."

Gabe left Faruq alone in the stall. Inside, Hattie was languidly chewing hay while Cora stood under her and nursed. Hattie regarded Faruq from the corner of her eye.

"Hey, big girl," Faruq said, holding up his hands. "Remember me?"

Cora stopped nursing to curiously swing her head toward him, and Hattie took the opportunity to settle down onto the ground with a huff. The filly copied her mother, curling into Hattie's side. Hattie watched Faruq. He gave her the slow blink he often gave to Muezza, that he had given to the wolf. She continued to stare for a moment before blinking back at him with her long-lashed eyes. Faruq smiled, blinked again. This time, Hattie's answering blink came sooner.

Carefully, Faruq inched forward, watching Hattie for any sign of fear or protectiveness. When he saw none, he crouched down next to mother and child. Hattie leaned forward to nose him briefly, and then turned her head away, snuffling at the straw on the ground. Cora timidly stretched her head forward to sniff Faruq's outstretched hand.

"Hey there, girl," he said, moving his hand up slowly to see if she liked being scratched behind the ears. She leaned into him. "You don't really look like a Cora. It's an old lady name."

Cora half got up to then sprawl across Faruq's lap. He was

surprised by the clumsy weight of her—only her head and shoulders fit on him.

"You are sweet." He stroked her neck and her tail flicked contentedly. "You should have a sweet name."

Hattie looked over at them, unconcerned, and then rolled over onto her side as if to sleep. This touched Faruq more than he might have guessed.

"My mother would sometimes call me *shakkar*. That's Urdu for 'sugar.'" He paused his stroking and Cora complained with a gentle toss of her head. "Of course, it can also mean 'shit.'"

He resumed petting Cora's coarse neck. He was tired enough now that his eyes burned, every other breath a yawn. But he wanted to stay here in this warm, quiet stall with mother and baby. Just a little while longer.

Part of Faruq wanted to skip his run this morning, but he got up and got dressed despite it. Lightweight tee and running tights under loose shorts. He tended to run hot—even in the New York City winter, he seldom wore more than a long-sleeved tech shirt, a headband thick enough to cover his ears, and three-dollar Duane Reade gloves he could toss aside if his hands got hot.

He glanced at his reflection in the mirror. He'd always been lean, but he'd lost weight since staying in the Forbidden City. Now he was Spartan—all shadow and angles and muscle coiled around bone. He'd never had any luck trying to bulk up, and it was an especially lost cause here. He laced up his sneakers and made to head out the door, but upon opening it, found Odo.

Odo looked him up and down. "Good morning, scholar. Today, you try walking, instead of running."

Odo led them into the redwoods, onto the same path Faruq so often ran. They walked in silence for a long while. Odo walked with long strides so that even Faruq, who normally walked with a New Yorker's brisk pace, had to make some effort to keep up. At about half a mile deep, Odo stepped off the trail, heading sharply north. He seemed to know exactly where he was going, even as the trees crowded in closer, making one stretch of forest all but indistinguishable from another. If not for Odo, Faruq would be lost.

"Where are we going?"

"Dangerous animals out here," Odo said instead of answering. "Black bears, wolves. Even elk."

Faruq flinched internally when Odo mentioned wolves. He'd begun to think of the wolf as a kind of guardian. But Odo was right—it was a predator.

"But all these dangerous animals," Odo continued, "are also *beautiful* animals. In nature, beauty *means* danger." Odo paused long enough to tilt his head up, take a deep breath in. "Danger is beautiful, then."

"I'm not sure I follow," said Faruq.

Odo paused long enough to collect a fallen branch. He snapped off its remaining leaves with practiced hands and then jabbed one end against a curl of hardened roots pushing up from the ground, blunting it. Chips of bark and branch ricocheted off the roots. Odo's teeth were bared and he struck the ground with jarring violence. For a moment, Faruq felt more unsettled at being in the woods alone with Odo than he did at being alone with the wolf following him. But then Odo began to walk again, as though everything were perfectly normal, using the branch as a walking stick.

"You like animals, scholar?" he asked.

"Sure. I mean, I grew up with cats. My dad's cats, really. According to the Prophet, Muslims are supposed to protect animals and treat them with respect in life and death. That's what my parents taught me." He shrugged.

"Tell me about these cats."

"Allama Iqbal and Muezza, who's still alive. Muezza is named after Muhammad's favorite cat. Allama Iqbal was named after this Pakistani poet and philosopher. Some people think of Iqbal as, like, a saint, basically, and some people say he was a nationalist." Faruq shrugged. "I don't know. Praising Mussolini, which Iqbal did do, is not a great look. But my father adored that guy, and my mother loved that cat."

This was only part of the truth. His mother had loved Allama Iqbal, yes, but, more than that, she had *needed* that cat. On the days when she went dark, Allama Iqbal would stay curled up into her belly, forgoing even food, until, eventually, she came back to the surface. Even on the days when she wasn't gone dark, he'd follow her around like a lovestruck kitten. When the cat died, two years after his mother, it broke his father's heart all over again. And Faruq's too.

Odo had been quiet for a while. Faruq was surprised when the woods abruptly opened up onto a circular little bay, where blue-silver ocean water churned quietly. The sand here was crowded with a breakout of rough rocks. Odo led them right up to the water, where the sand was smooth and wet. Faruq could feel it sticking like a paste to the bottoms of his sneakers.

"I didn't realize there was a beach this close," he told Odo. Odo nodded sagely. "This land is full of secret places."

"I bet," said Faruq. "It's beautiful here."

"A well-fed cat will still kill."

"Huh?"

"They're not like other predators. Their drive to hunt isn't only because of hunger. They *like* to kill. Most common pet in the world." He let out a little laugh. "*That's* what I mean when I say danger is beautiful."

"But cats aren't really dangerous to *us*."

Odo reached forward and took Faruq's forearm in his large hand. "Let go, scholar," he chuckled. "You're blinding yourself, man." He gave Faruq's arm a squeeze. "Do you know what humping is?"

Faruq wanted to pull his arm away but resisted the urge. Odo's grip was firm. No, a vise. Nearly bruising. But he would not pull away. Odo was toying with him, somehow. Or this was one of his little tests. He didn't want to show weakness.

Odo laughed and let go of Faruq. "In the war," he said,

"'humping' meant walking. And oh, us grunts were humping *all* the time, man."

"And what was that like?" asked Faruq, probing gently, sensing that Odo might be on the brink of telling him something real.

Odo turned to look out over the water with its muted waves. "Like the curtain had been lifted and the illusion revealed. The world as we know it—we don't know it. It's not safe; the safety is a lie. It lifted the curtain up on that great lie and I could see. And now me and men like me know not to trust anything. It could be thunder you're hearing or it could just as soon be death. Because the curtain is gone—it can't be unseen. We were made to see. What the fuck you supposed to do with that, man?" A snort. "Couldn't walk around scared shitless for the rest of my life."

Faruq's pulse quickened. Odo was going to let him in. This was the most honest Odo had been with him. He'd perhaps been more honest than he'd meant to be. Faruq had to tread carefully.

"You were scared," he said.

"Terrified. I didn't have the Other Sight then that I have now." He turned to face Faruq again. "But even those who haven't been hipped yet have moments of true vision, you know."

He held Faruq's eyes for a long moment before continuing. "This once, we'd been humping through the jungle. Felt like forever we'd been humping. Got to the point where we were just like zombies—you didn't think, you didn't tell your body to move. It just kept moving forward. And that jungle—just like any wilderness, it was full of secrets. Some of them could eat you alive.

"Well. We were resting. Having a smoke, eating C-rations, tending to the jungle rot. Whatever. And the ground started to shake, like an earthquake. Most of us were just holding still, listening. Then—*crash*—the trees nearly split open, and then out ran three elephants. Their ears were flapping, and their breath was steaming. You could see the whites of their eyes.

"And then, right on their heels, a tiger. He was snapping those yellow old teeth. The thing is, a tripped-out elephant can kill a man, easy. Not to mention a *tiger*. But not a one of them was paying any attention to us. It didn't concern us, you see. So none of us hollered and none of us shot. In a split second, the elephants and the tiger disappeared back into the jungle." He shrugged.

"And then what happened?" asked Faruq after it seemed Odo wasn't going to continue.

"Then we went on about our business."

"That's it?"

"That's what I'm trying to tell you, scholar. Even in the un-hipped, the Other Sight will sometimes shine through."

"Was this before or after you, uh, received the 18 Utterances?"

"Before. The nameless god was speaking to me already, though. As They speaks to all of us."

"In the documentary, Minh-An says the 18 Utterances are like the Ten Commandments. But they remind me of the Shahada: *There is no god but God.* There is no god but the Nameless. *Muhammad is the messenger of God.* Odo is the messenger of Mow Vutu. Is that where you got your inspiration?" Faruq thought he was being generous by using the word "inspiration." It was "appropriation" that really came to mind.

Odo shook his head. "Wasn't about inspiration. It came from Vutu theyself, scholar."

"But *how* did they—Vutu—communicate the 18 Utterances to you, exactly? Was it a vision? A dream?"

"Nothing like that. It was—a dawn."

"A dawn? What do you mean by that?" Faruq was hungry now—ravenous for answers. But Odo only smiled slyly. "You've seen the sun rise before, haven't you?"

"I—guess so?"

"Hey, scholar, what's it like running through here, early in the morning? You must see some incredible things."

Faruq licked his lips. He could tell Odo about the wolf. He wondered if that was what Odo was asking for. "It's surprisingly boring," he said. "Nothing but trees and mist."

Odo made no response. Faruq had the unsettling feeling that Odo saw right through him.

Odo suddenly jammed his walking stick into the sand, and dug it in, pushing back wet sand in glops until he revealed the oblong shell of a razor clam. The clam's siphon protruded, wet and thick like a slug. With a long, thin knife Faruq hadn't realized he had, Odo pried the shell open. The white meat inside undulated almost imperceptibly. With a wolfish grin, Odo popped the meat out of the shell and into his mouth. He chewed it raw, and, disgusted, Faruq could almost taste it in his own mouth: the briny, slick flesh, the leathery chew of the siphon, the mud of its stomach. The metallic finish of its death.

Instagram Post #382

@thenamelessmvmnt: Young blond man wearing tan cargo shorts and a yellow plaid button-down with short sleeves. He stands in skate sneakers, he is crowned with a backward trucker hat, his back is to the camera. He is spray-painting onto a whitewashed wall, an intricate yellow design that fans out like spread wings. From the corner of the photo, hint of an olive-skinned, bearded man, watching.

#createbeauty #art #bliss

92,698 likes | 465 comments

Nero

INT. GREENHOUSE—MED. SHOT—MINH-AN

Minh-An grimaces, rolls her eyes.

                    MINH-AN
          A white woman making a false accusation of
          rape against a Black man—how original.

                              FADE TO BLACK.

INT. CWE NAVE—MED. SHOT—WILL ROY*

                    WILL ROY
          Sue Mills herself told us that Odo had raped
          her. She described—in detail, mind you—the
          giant tattoo Odo has on his back. A great
          big dragon. Beast of the land.

CLOSEUP—WILL ROY'S FACE

Roy nods, smirks.

                    WILL ROY
          We had that sumgun arrested right away.

                              DISSOLVE TO:
Cell phone footage of Odo being led out of a white
building in handcuffs, followers looking on, many of
them in tears. Odo is smiling reassuringly and nodding
as he passes his followers, until he is placed inside a
police cruiser (audio removed).

                    MINH-AN
          Well, you know, we have a legal team. You
          have to these days. And I knew who would be
          just right for this job.

                              FADE IN:

INT. LOS ANGELES OFFICE—MED. SHOT—OWN RYKER

_____

  * Music: The Planets, Op. 32: I. Mars, the Bringer of War
(Gustav Holst)

Owen Ryker reclines in an ergonomic chair behind a
glass-topped desk that is scrupulously clean and
organized.
SUPER: "Owen Ryker, JD, Attorney for the Nameless"

             OWEN RYKER
        There was never any question. That I'd do
        anything I could to help Odo and this
        beautiful movement. I'd do anything for Odo
        and the nameless.

Ryker nods.

INSERT—IMAGE*

Photo of Owen Ryker, c. 1978, naked in a kiddie pool,
smiling up at the camera.

             OWEN RYKER
        I grew up in the '80s, which I always say
        was one of the best times to be a kid.
        Idyllic childhood. My parents were upper-
        middle-class. My father was a dentist, and
        my mother, a kindergarten teacher. They
        worked hard, both of them.

                                      DISSOLVE TO:
Photo of Owen Ryker, c. 1983, in a blue T-shirt with
his hands on his hips, his mouth open as though
speaking, a yellow tricycle on its side to his left.

             OWEN RYKER
        I was a happy kid, sure. I had friends, I
        played sports, I even *liked* my kid sister.
        (laughs)

                                      DISSOLVE TO:
Home footage of Owen Ryker, c. 1987, at a kitchen table
with his younger sister, both of them singing and
laughing as they pick Cheerios out of their cereal
bowls with their hands (audio removed).

---

* Music: Just Like Honey (The Jesus and Mary Chain)

OWEN RYKER

But I always felt different, like I didn't really belong anywhere, and I didn't know why. When you're that young and you feel different, it's really easy to conclude that something's wrong with you. Kids are great at that.

DISSOLVE TO:

School photo of Ryker, c. 1990; Ryker poses, grinning with braces-covered teeth, against a mottled gray backdrop.

OWEN RYKER

By the time I was a teenager, I was seriously depressed. My parents took me to a psychiatrist, and he put me on meds, and they *did* help me. But they didn't *fix* me.

DISSOLVE TO:

Photo of Ryker, c. 1996, seated at a wooden desk in a college dorm room with an open textbook in front of him, grimacing up at the camera.

OWEN RYKER

Education was really important to my parents—they always stressed to us, you work hard, you go to college, you get a degree. Lucky for them, I wanted to be a lawyer. (laughs)

DISSOLVE TO:

Home footage of Ryker, c. 2002, in blue Columbia graduation robes with 3 black stripes on each arm, royal purple sash, and black cap, smiling and waving with one arm, the other arm slung around the shoulders of 2 identically dressed graduates, one a bespeckled man, and the other a tall, redheaded woman (audio removed).

OWEN RYKER

I went to Columbia Law. You'd hear about the nameless—they threw great parties off-

campus. Me and my friends would go, mostly
for the girls. (laughs)

Everyone knew nameless women were beautiful.
But I never met Odo.

                                    DISSOLVE TO:
Photo of Ryker, c. 2009, at a fundraiser, seated at a
table full of celebrities.

          OWEN RYKER
          I really threw myself into my career. As it
          turned out, I made a good attorney. I won a
          few high-profile cases, and all of a sudden,
          I was one of the hottest attorneys in New
          York City.

                                    DISSOLVE TO:
Footage of Ryker, c. 2010, laughing and gesturing
emphatically while talking to a laughing couple, both
of them politicians (audio removed).

          OWEN RYKER
          Celebrity clients, just, *crazy* retainers—
          I mean, I was making *money*.

                                    DISSOLVE TO:
Photo of Ryker, c. 2012, shaking hands with Vice
President Joe Biden.

          OWEN RYKER
          But I wasn't happy. Finally, one of
          my clients told me, 'You know, I think
          this guy Odo can really help you.'
          And just like that, my life changed.
          I changed.

BACK TO SCENE

          OWEN RYKER
          The first time I ever met him, Odo had me
          bawling my eyes out within 5 minutes. The
          next time, it only took him 2.

PRODUCER (O.S.)
What did he say to you?

Ryker's eyebrows draw toward each other, he shakes his
head.

OWEN RYKER
He told me I was beautiful. No one had ever
said anything like that to me before. Smart?
Yeah. Accomplished? Sure. But the idea that
I could just . . . *be*? And I'd still be
valuable? Beautiful?

Ryker closes his eyes briefly, blinks back tears,
chuckles.

OWEN RYKER
It got to the point where I'd just *look* at
him and . . . Niagara Falls.

Ryker waves a hand over his face.

OWEN RYKER
He really *listened* to me. I've never felt so
seen. He heard past all my bullshit, all my
corporate talk, all my veneer, you know? He
asked me what I wanted, and I said I wanted
to be loved. And he said, *Why?*

No one had ever asked me anything like that
before. I had to think about it. And he just
listened to me. I could be totally honest,
totally myself. I was releasing something,
that thing that had me so sad no matter what
I did. When it was finally all out of me, I
was so *light*.

That's the thing about the nameless that I
wish more people understood. This is a
community where you truly feel unconditional
love, unconditional acceptance,
unconditional understanding. And it starts
with Odo. Odo teaches us how.

So I told Odo, 'Look. I'll leave it all
behind. I don't need any of it. Let me give
myself over to this movement.' And Odo just
put his hand on my shoulder. And he said,
'As you like it, savior.'

Ryker shakes his head and smiles reverently.

> OWEN RYKER
> Odo is the most beautiful of men. And that's
> really not hyperbole. He's trying to save us
> all.

Ryker closes his eyes.

> OWEN RYKER
> When he looks at you—I don't know—it's like
> he's looking *into* you. Like you're naked.
> And it's not something to be ashamed of or
> anything like that. You feel free. You feel
> fresh as a baby. Reborn. Everything is ahead
> of you again. Odo is like a master key. He
> is so, so good.

He opens them.

> OWEN RYKER
> So when I heard about what was going on in
> Texas, how these racist fanatics were trying
> to smear him, I was furious. And I knew I
> needed to be a warrior for the nameless in
> the legal battlefield.

>   FADE TO BLACK.

Will Roy speaks fiercely.

> WILL ROY
> We had powerful people on our side too.*

INSERT—IMAGE

Portrait of Preston Wade in a black suit, his arms
crossed and his expression cloudy. SLOW PAN.

---

* Music: Piano Sonata in B Minor (Liszt)

                    WILL ROY
Preston Wade was a big-time lawyer over
there in Dallas. Well, he was accustomed to
dealing with corporations. But he was born
and raised right here in Burning Hill, and
he was one of ours.

                                   DISSOLVE TO:
Photo, c. 2016, of Preston Wade and Will Roy standing
next to each other at a ranch, both of them wearing
jeans and cowboy hats. SLOW PAN.

                    WILL ROY
Me and Preston as good as grew up together.
His daddy and my daddy was friends. He
might've been a big shot—(laughs)—but he
never forgot where he came from.

                                   DISSOLVE TO:

INT. CWE NAVE—MED. SHOT—WILL ROY

                    WILL ROY
When I called him up and told him what was
going on, he dropped everything to come out
here.

Roy nods, sniffs.

                    WILL ROY
The good Lord provides for the faithful.

                                   FADE TO BLACK.

before: 1969

A BIRD CAME to lift away Preach's body, and the LZ was fully cleared in a day and a half. It should've been sooner, but the sudden loss of Preach slowed everyone down. Bigger was surprised to see men openly crying. Now, the men were waiting, but no one could say what exactly for. News of what killed Preach spread from the radio out, faceless as a whisper: *abdominal aortic aneurism. Ain't that what got that cat Houdini? Nah, that's what wasted Einstein. Bro-ther.*

Silk kept repeating the words to himself under his breath, not believing them. They couldn't be true. Something like that couldn't be all there was to killing someone like Preach. Besides, didn't an aneurism happen in the head? Preach had been so close to going home, so close. And alive, at that. Silk had been here long enough to know that things happened just like that sometimes. You survive malaria twice, have a Vietnamese bullet miss your heart by a hair, and then you go off to take a piss and trip a Bouncing Betty. You could make it through two tours and earn a Bronze Star, only to get got on your very last day in country.

But not Preach. Silk had bent over the body for a few moments, not believing its stillness. *Abdominal aortic aneurism.*

Bigger and Crazy Horse lay side by side in the trench, their helmets tilted over their sweat-slick faces for shade. Crazy Horse was crying, was not trying to hide that he was crying, but was behaving as though he didn't even feel the wetness on his cheeks.

Hey man, you think a thing like this was always going to happen? Even if it wasn't for the war?

Bigger closed his eyes against the stinking darkness inside his helmet.

You mean was it his time?

I don't know. Maybe.

Bigger shrugged.

Shit. This would've been a question for Preach.

Don't I know it. Huh. We need him here to explain this shit cause I sure don't get it. Was he sick all along? Did being here make him sick?

Would he have had a few more months if he'd just gotten back to the world? Would he have lived to be an old man if he'd never come here?

Right. It's like if a brother got shot or blown up, you *know* he probably would've been better off at home. Didn't realize that was a comfort. Until now.

Abdominal aortic aneurism.

Silk jumped up from where he'd been sitting.

Why don't the two of you shut the hell up? Talkin nonsense. What's the use in speculating? Preach ain't here. That's what's real.

Crazy Horse and Bigger exchanged looks as Silk stalked off. They found themselves holding back laughter. Crazy Horse moved his helmet to his sweaty chest and closed his eyes against the sun. He only opened them again when Brother Ned came over and threw his large shadow over him and Bigger.

Hey, brothers.

Crazy Horse rolled his eyes.

What you want?

I wanted to ask Bigger here a favor. Hey, Bigger, I wondered if you would help me write a letter. To Preach's sister. You see, he said I could write her, before—uh. And now the words have got to be just right. And, well, you've had a little college.

Crazy Horse jumped up all of a sudden and snatched Brother Ned by the collar, shaking him.

You leave Preach's sister alone, you sumvabitch. You hear?

Motherfuckin cracker. Leave that girl alone or I'll knock you *see-through*, whitey.

Brother Ned was holding up his hands, not holding back.

C'mon, you know I don't mean her no harm. I just want it to be right.

Bigger stood and grabbed hold of Crazy Horse's arm, found the muscles there live as a wire.

I'll do it. *Hey.* I said I'll help. Let him go, Crazy, he ain't done nothing wrong.

Crazy Horse glared as he loosened his grip enough for Brother Ned to step out of it. Brother Ned grinned big, clapping Bigger on the shoulder.

I've got a notepad; I'll copy it out neat later, but I want to get the words down now, if that's all right.

Bigger nodded. He and Brother Ned went off to put into words the languageless, the unspeakable.

Silk had gotten those senseless words—*abdominal aortic aneurism*—to stop flaring in his mind, was cooling himself off—as much as one could in this heat—by a snatch of bamboo they'd left unchopped near the perimeter of the LZ. From here, now that the hilltop was cleared, you could look out over the steaming jungle, the nappy-headed parts of it they hadn't touched, and the parts they'd beaten ragged with their feet, and their E-tools, their bullets, their fire, their rage.

Silk squinted. Below, he thought he saw foliage moving in a manner not influenced by wind. He strained his eyes to see, and then glanced around, searching for a slightly higher vantage point. There wasn't one—the hilltop was largely flat. He pulled out his binoculars. Probably just an animal, he thought—or was it a wish? He looked through binoculars and adjusted the lens.

Nearby, a trio of white soldiers sat eating syrupy canned peaches. No use saving them now. Rumor was they were getting lifted out of here soon. The blond one elbowed the other blond one and nodded toward Silk. They shook their heads. Whatever you felt about Preach, they'd all lost friends by now.

But the dark-haired one—the oldest of the three—narrowed his eyes, slowly set down his can. They called him James, which wasn't even close to his first, middle, or last name, but somehow suited him better than all three. James stood, dusting off his pants, and was still for a moment with his hands on his hips, observing Silk. Then the two blonds watched as he walked over to join the Negro.

Silk could never get these goddamn binoculars to focus right, so the zoomed-in jungle appeared to him slightly blurred. He searched for moving foliage, expecting to see a flash of an animal. Too low to the ground to be elephants. Maybe monkeys, then. Or another tiger. He caught a flash of what was unmistakably flesh. Brown flesh. In an instant, his whole body froze cold. He didn't know how it was possible. There'd been some confounding mistake. Some kind of miracle. That was Preach out there.

James had taken out his binoculars as well, and so he too saw that flash of dark flesh. But his eyes did not see that flesh as the recently fallen blood.

Shit, that's Charlie.

James did not think Silk could really hear him, so, cursing, he got word to the L-T. Then he grabbed Silk's shoulder and shook it hard.

Pull yourself together, boy. The VC.

The entire LZ went dead quiet. Multiple eyes were on the jungle below now. Grunts crept into position. The Viet Cong were moving uphill, toward the LZ; their movements didn't suggest they realized they were being watched. A couple of point men ran out to check for signs of an L-shaped ambush. They reported back that they saw none. It was hard to tell exactly how many Viet Cong there were—eight or ten, James estimated, and most trusted his word.

From the angle he'd positioned himself in, Bigger could clearly see the wave of movement creeping closer uphill, if not the men behind that movement. The Vietnamese were close enough that he thought he could hear them breathing if he listened carefully, but far enough away that they might not even know the hilltop was cleared. Not long after the word spread that this was probably not an ambush, the first of the snipers' bullets cracked out. Answering fire crackled back.

Now the Vietnamese were running up the hill. You could see it in the ripple of foliage, the quick strobe of skin. Adrenaline seemed to sharpen Bigger's vision. As he peered into the foliage, he felt he could see the thoughts of the Vietnamese as well as he could see their movements. He saw how he could end this firefight. He had two grenades. He could just blast them and end it. He must end it.

He unpinned the first grenade and threw, yelling for his fellow soldiers to take cover. The blast came a split second later than he thought it would, and it was shocking, horrible. A column of yellowed smoke shot up. He unpinned the second grenade and threw again, harder this time, shouting again, but not in words. Then he waited. Crazy Horse waited and Silk waited. Brother Ned waited. James waited. Everyone waited. Bloods and rabbits.

The jungle below was wrecked now, smoke swallowing steam. But it was still. A few men went down to confirm the kills. A single shot rang out and, in the distance, a flock of birds fled their tree. Word came back up the hill: six Vietnamese, all dead now. They'd found one clinging torturously to life—the single bullet had been for him. It was a mercy, really, to grease him. A few more men went down to help drag the bodies up.

Now that the kill count had been confirmed, soldiers began congratulating Bigger.

All right, cherry.

Bout time you got your shit together.

You a cold motherfucker, ain't you?

Greased them dinks good.

Bigger reached down deep for whatever it was he was supposed to feel, whether it be pride, shame, guilt, disgust, power. He got nothing. All he felt was his ache to go home. God, he wanted to go home. He wanted to go home even if it meant he'd never get the money to finish college. Being nothing back in the world was better than being nothing over here.

When they got the bodies to the top of the hill—or most of

what was left of them—both Silk and Bigger went over to have a look. Silk because he wanted to make sure it really wasn't Preach the kid had just blown to smithereens, and Bigger because he wanted to see if he'd still come up empty. There were indeed six, in various states of wholeness. But right away, the two bodies on the far right caught Bigger's eye.

In the direct sun their skin was a kind of muddy gold, not bronze. They were slender, boys—Bigger thought they looked younger than him. They were wearing Ho Chi Minh sandals, though one of them had had his foot blasted off. The other had strangely high arches, like a woman, like a ballerina. And one of his eyes was slightly open, the white dimming to gray.

Silk saw Bigger studying the dead Vietnamese and sighed. The kid unnerved him and he didn't know why. Maybe he was too wide open. Silk stalked off.

One was taller than the other, the one with the foot blasted off. Bigger could see shards of skull like spikes in his hair; the back of his head was gone. The other, the one with the ballerina feet, was out a chunk of shoulder, and the front of his uniform was so red it looked like it'd been issued that way. His jaw was slack, the inside of his mouth was coated in dark blood. And his eyes were closed, but his eyelashes were a scar crusted with dried blood.

Crazy Horse came to stand beside Bigger, not touching him, not saying anything. A grim vigil. In time, they'd read the news of this kill in the *Stripes,* they'd hear it over the radio. The *Stripes* would report that they'd killed ten Viet Cong, or maybe an even bigger lie. Crazy Horse and Bigger stood together in silence for a long time, and then Bigger, swiping sweat from his brow, went to continue helping Brother Ned with his letter. Crazy Horse lit a joint. Silk continued to watch the perimeter, hoping not to see Preach. Preach was dead. If he saw his ghost, it meant there really was a hell and they were already rotting in it.

The hill had been captured. They'd be flown out of here soon. None of it meant a goddamn thing to any of them anymore.

today

AS HE COMPLETED his stretching, he thought about how monotonous his days had become. Some of it, he'd brought on himself—distance running, by nature, was monotonous—but there was something hypnotic about repetition. It was part of why chanting, mantras, moving meditation seemed to work; monotony could settle you into thoughtlessness. Something easy for the wrong person to use against you.

He hopped up and down a few times before beginning to run, his body falling into the familiar task. He listened to the rhythmic hiss of his breath, in and out, in and out, the pace and intensity increasing little by little. As he passed into the tree line, his peripheral vision snagged on something pink and moving. All adrenaline, he jumped back. It took a moment for his brain to process what his eyes were seeing.

The couple were not in the least disturbed by him, didn't even startle when he jumped. They just continued fucking, their bodies goosebumped and flushed. He didn't know these two followers, and perhaps, he thought, that was why he was having trouble looking away. He was disturbed—they seemed to have been placed *for* him to see, to bear witness.

He also felt the unsettling tinge of longing. It had been awhile since he'd had sex, and now he felt the delicious burn of blood flowing into his crotch, filling him, hardening him. With the erection came shame. He looked away and ran.

. . .

It came as a surprise to Faruq how happy he was to see Kaya again. It had been a couple weeks—he'd been beginning to suspect she was being deliberately kept away for some reason. His mind flitted, inconveniently, to the couple, and he had to admit to himself that he had a little crush on Kaya, despite himself. He wrenched his thoughts away from that glimpse of pink flesh in the woods, the rush of tingling warmth into his groin.

Kaya was in the house of the nameless, which he'd visited because Odo had given him permission to snap some photos of the interior. He came equipped with his refurbished camera, and was getting several shots of the meditation room when Kaya walked in. Thea was with her, light blond curls dancing to their own music as she walked.

Together, the two of them looked like something from a magazine. They had their arms slung around each other's narrow waists, and they were wearing similar yellow dresses, which cascaded down their willowy bodies so that he could see a hint of their forms underneath. They were smiling at each other, fresh off a laugh. When they saw him their focus brightened, but they stopped in their tracks as though wary of getting too close to him.

"Hi, Faruq," they said in unison, and then burst into a fit of laughter.

"Ladies," Faruq said awkwardly.

"How are you, Faruq?" Kaya said, unwinding her arm from around Thea and stepping forward.

"It's been awhile. Both of you." He gestured toward Thea, who stepped forward slightly in response.

"Crazy busy," Kaya said, nodding.

"I heard you're Odo's de facto dinner guest now," said Thea. "That's really beautiful, Faruq."

Faruq nodded. "It's been—enlightening."

"You have his eye," said Kaya. "He can see that you're special."

"Not everyone gets so lucky," said Thea.

"Oh, I don't know about that," Faruq mumbled. "You know,"

he said, "I came across the strangest thing this morning. I saw a couple just in the woods—they were . . ."

Thea and Kaya looked at each other, giggled. "What's strange about that?" Thea asked.

"Well, they were out in the open."

"Sometimes the mood strikes when the mood strikes," Kaya said.

"In public, though?"

"*Public, private*—those are distortions, Faruq. Here, we're free. Some people practice abstinence, some people are all free love. There's no shame in any of it here."

"And there are no secrets among the nameless," Thea added.

"It's just—not something I'm used to," Faruq said.

"Did you find it exciting?" Kaya asked, looking directly into his eyes with that unsettling nameless stare. Her tone was matter-of-fact, but the question, Faruq felt, was meant to be provocative.

Still, he felt shame because of his physical reaction to the sight—both the initial startle and the arousal. He could admit one aloud but not the other. "It was—jarring," he said.

Kaya and Thea giggled at each other again.

"Hey," he said, happy to shift the topic to something else, "Odo said it was okay to get some photos." Interestingly enough, he'd noticed, the Deep were nowhere to be found whenever his camera was out. "Would you guys mind?"

"Not at all," said Kaya.

She and Thea slung their arms around each other again and smiled model smiles for Faruq's camera. He showed them the results once he'd taken several shots.

"They're all beautiful," said Thea.

He chuckled. "Yeah. You know, Thea, I'd love to get some shots of you in your studio, if that's all right."

"Sure thing, scholar."

Before Faruq could fully react to someone besides Odo calling him "scholar," Kaya said, "Have you tried meditation since the last time we were here together?"

Faruq hesitated. He was generally unsure of the wisdom of being completely honest with these people, but it always felt like they were asking him ten questions underneath the one they actually voiced.

"Honestly," he said, "I *have* tried it. But I don't think I'm doing it right."

Both Kaya and Thea tilted their heads questioningly.

"Look, can I be real with you guys?"

"Please," said Thea.

"Like, no disrespect to what you guys are doing here or anything, but you know—I'm not a believer."

Kaya nodded for him to go on.

"Anyway. When you told me to try your meditation, I didn't really think anything special would happen. Again, no disrespect. It's just—I've tried meditation before, you know? But something happened."

"What happened?" Thea asked, stepping closer. Both she and Kaya were staring directly into his eyes. It was unnerving.

He told them everything. He hoped that by reliving it, he might be able to understand it. Maybe honesty, candor, was the key to finding that moment again. His mother's face, the sensation of impact at his chest, the burst of neon green, the vivid memory of how his mother's hands felt on his head, brushing his hair back. They both listened raptly, seeming not to blink.

"Faruq," said Kaya when he was done, "that's so incredible."

"And you haven't been able to replicate it?" asked Thea.

"No, nothing like it."

"I think we should try again," said Kaya decisively.

"Right now?" said Faruq.

Kaya shrugged. "Why not?"

"We'll help you," said Thea.

The women sat down. Faruq put his camera down and followed suit, settling cross-legged onto a rug. Kaya told him to close his eyes and he obliged. In unison, they recited the 18 Utterances. Faruq was disturbed to realize that by now, he almost knew them by heart. Then he felt Kaya's and Thea's hands on him, gently pushing him back.

"Stop breathing," said who he thought was Kaya—the women's voices were quite similar. "Just relax." Maybe Thea.

"When the time is right, let the breath back in."

He waited until his lungs were burning to breathe again, and when the air finally came flooding back in . . . nothing. He stayed there, breathing deeply, for several minutes. But nothing came. If anything, he began to feel how tired he really was. Sleep pulled at him. Before it could fully sink him, he opened his eyes. Thea and Kaya weren't there anymore. Odo stood over him. For a crazy second he thought he really had slipped into a dream.

Dumbly, he said, "Oh. Hey."

"Hey there, scholar. Trying to meditate?"

"Yeah." Faruq chuckled self-consciously. "It's not really working for me."

He was uncomfortable with the man standing over his prone body, but he tried not to show it, tried not to fidget.

Odo held out a hand. "C'mon. I want to show you something."

Odo pulled Faruq to his feet—again, Faruq was struck by how strong Odo was, given he had to be at least in his late sixties. Faruq glanced around, looking for Kaya and Thea. He saw no sign of them. Odo led them out of the house of the nameless. He was surprised to see a Jeep Wrangler idling in wait for them. They hopped in, and Odo began to drive. There wasn't much conversation as they drove—most of Faruq's questions were met with one-word answers, so he focused on the scenery as they rode into the forest. What there was of a road was narrow and so rough Faruq's head frequently met the roof. Then the road abruptly stopped. Odo put the Jeep in park.

"We'll have to hoof it from here."

Faruq wished he'd known they were going for a hike—his cheap tennis shoes weren't really up to the task. He felt every rock, every hardened root, through his soles. After about fifteen minutes of stumbling after Odo, they reached a wonderland of waste. The corpses of burnt trees stood ragged and black, and patches of scorched earth still showed. New grass shot up like a pathetic teenaged beard.

"Wildfire?" he asked.

Odo nodded. "This part of the forest has been in recovery for a couple years, though. I like to call it the secret garden."

"The 'secret garden'?"

Odo smirked. "So you see only the devastation?" He shook his head. "Open your eyes, scholar. In a place like this, the cycle is right in front of you. That's what makes it beautiful. Look."

He pointed to the remains of a tree that had fallen over. It lay on its side, covered in moss.

Around it, new grass and stalky flowers grew. Faruq stepped closer. When he looked more carefully, it *was* beautiful. It was like the sarcophagus at the center of a tomb, the sunlight hitting the felled tree dramatically, so that it nearly had a glow, one stub of a branch reaching up, frozen in the middle of its growth, the moss encrusted with jewel-colored beetles. And the birdsong echoed as though in a cathedral.

"That there," said Odo, pointing, "is wart-stemmed California lilac. And over there, that's the Pacific bleeding heart. These shoots are wild ginger. Oh—and my, my, my. We've got baneberry over here. This stuff'll cure a snakebite. If it doesn't kill you itself." He grinned. "Poisonous."

"How do you know so much about plants?"

"I know a little about a lot, scholar. Let's sit."

Reluctantly, Faruq sat down on the rough ground with Odo. The new flora wasn't soft or giving. It poked into his skin.

"Let's try that meditation thing again, scholar."

"Oh—yeah?"

"Yes. Maybe you just need something a little different. Close your eyes."

Faruq did, but Odo was quiet for so long that he was tempted to open them again to make sure Odo hadn't abandoned him. Just as he was about to give in to that temptation, Odo spoke.

"You got to trust, scholar." Odo's voice was different now; deeper, soothing. "If you don't tell yourself the truth, you'll lie to everyone else. I asked you why you're here. It sure ain't for the nameless. It's not for me. It's not for any *article* or *book*."

Faruq had to consciously stop himself from fidgeting. Odo *couldn't* know about his conversation with Anita, couldn't know she'd gotten him thinking about writing a book.

"All suffering is distortion. Strip yourself of distortion. Do not despair at death." Utterances, Faruq recognized.

"Faruq Zaidi. You're here for your father."

Suddenly, Odo pushed his hands against Faruq's chest with something that was close to violence. Faruq fell back, rendered off-balance by Odo's last statement. He gained control of his fall just in time to prevent the back of his head from smacking against the hard ground.

"*Open* your eyes, scholar."

Faruq blinked up at the redwood canopy. Something about those scarred treetops against cloudless, livid blue made it seem like the sky was pressing down on top of him, pushing him, like Odo's hands, into the earth. It felt like, were he to try to sit up, his back would cling to the ground like gum. He was overtired, he reasoned. Even now, it was becoming difficult to keep his eyes open.

"Keep those eyes open," Odo said. "Now I want you to breathe. In. Out. Quicker. *Quicker*."

Odo had him panting now, rapid breaths that beat in and out of him like percussion. He felt stupid and he wanted to stop, but that desire was overridden by his curiosity. So he kept going for what seemed like a very long time, trying to keep his eyes fixed on the treetops, the sky. His eyes and chest burned. He was dizzy.

"Hold it. That's right. Now let it all out, scholar."

Faruq's vision slipped slightly out of focus as he began breathing normally again. His eyes watered. Only, no, it wasn't that. *Shit.* He was crying. He lifted a hand to wipe at his face, but Odo pushed it back down.

"No. Stay with it, scholar."

Faruq didn't even really feel *sad*. It was something baffling and huge. The tears were seeping up from some undiscovered well. He was a beetle on its back. He was full of beetles. He crossed his arms over his stomach. Odo was speaking in a comforting tone, but what he was saying didn't even make sense.

"Good, Faruq. That's all right. Hey, there's no choice to be made. Love is love is beauty. You don't have to choose. You hear? It's not the rose *or* the snowflake."

Faruq closed his eyes, willing the tears to stop. He wasn't a crier, didn't like to cry in front of people. When the sniffling stopped, he sat up and wiped his eyes. Odo was still sitting across from him. He smiled benevolently.

"You drive back, scholar. I'll tell you the way."

When they got back to the Forbidden City, Odo announced that he was tired and retreated to his house, leaving Faruq alone. Faruq took the opportunity to retire to the guesthouse for a nap. He awoke blessedly refreshed. He went to the artists' studios hoping to find Thea. She was studiously twisting wire into tight coils. She put down her work when she saw him standing in the doorway.

"Is it time for my close-up?"

"If it's still okay," said Faruq. "Hey, where did you guys go earlier? It was like you guys disappeared."

Thea put down her coiled wire, lifted a shoulder. "You needed Odo, not us. So I just came up here."

Thea posed among the sharp teeth and twisted metal flames she'd created. She'd changed out of her flowing yellow dress and into a pair of loose jeans and a man's button-down that was un-buttoned just enough to make plain she wasn't wearing anything underneath. She posed unselfconsciously, staring directly into the lens with a Mona Lisa smile, or turning her head to show off the classical lines of her profile. It was like he was photographing a professional model, not an artist in a cult.

"Show me your other pictures," she said once they'd finished and she'd again approved 100 percent of his shots.

He handed her the camera and let her scan through the digital images. He occupied himself by looking at the magazine pages she had pinned to the walls. Ads, mostly. Even the wordy ones for prescription drugs and cosmetic procedures.

"You have an eye for composition, you know," she said, handing the camera back.

He shrugged. "I know the basics." Thea seemed to be full of artistic sense. Sage, almost. He thought back to Odo's words. "Hey," he said, "do you know what it means to choose between a rose and a snowflake? Or really, to *not* have to choose between a rose and a snowflake?"

Thea looked over at him with a raised eyebrow. "That some kind of riddle?"

"Odo said it to me."

Faruq thought he saw a faint blush as Thea paused before answering. "Oh. That's—beautiful, actually."

"So you know what it means?" he asked.

"If Odo said it to *you*, Faruq, then I can't do the work for you."

He raised an eyebrow. She was full of shit. "I see," he said.

Thea hadn't let go of the camera after he'd taken it from her, and now she was standing too close. She fixed him with a hard look that gradually morphed into something more like curiosity. Determination. Faruq knew what was coming, knew he should step back. He stood stiff and still. Thea rose up onto the balls of her feet and brought her face close to his, pausing there. A pause for consent. Faruq gave it by not backing away.

She brought her lips to his.

The kiss was stilted somehow, calculated, even when they parted their lips and tasted the soft insides of each other's mouths. Faruq could feel the delicate breath from Thea's nose against his mustache. Warm, wet. He could do this, he thought. It meant nothing. But it could satisfy a need. He hadn't had sex since before traveling out here, before meeting up with Clover and Aeschylus. He and Thea—they could be this for each other.

But they couldn't.

He couldn't. He knew he was being manipulated. Thea was conducting an experiment—he could feel it in the way she kept changing the tone of the kiss, trying to find what he liked. And maybe he too was conducting an experiment of sorts. Hadn't he been curious about these ubiquitously beautiful nameless women? Hadn't he been titillated by the glimpse of Thea's bare sternum in that button-down? He let the kiss end naturally, but then, finally, stepped away. Thea laughed, like they were two kids experimenting.

"What's next?" she asked, all harmless mirth.

"Uh—well," Faruq chuckled uncomfortably. "I was actually going to try and shoot the school before I lose the light."

"I'll join you," she said. "I could use a break."

She went over to a closet at the back of the room and took off her shirt and pulled the yellow dress back on. Her back was to him, so all he saw was the plane of it, all sharp bone and shadow. She reached up under the dress to grab the waist of the jeans and shimmied out of them. When she turned and saw Faruq's face, she burst out laughing.

"Get stripped, scholar." Her voice contained a teasing note.

The school was a kind of A-frame longhouse, whitewashed like almost every other building in the Forbidden City. He and Thea made their way around it so he could get shots from multiple angles. Then they went in. The inside was not so different from any other school except for two things: the main hall contained a giant decal of Odo on one wall, and there was a breezeway that led to a modular addition, which Thea informed Faruq was the school library.

"I can show it to you, if you want."

Faruq followed Thea into the library, which was full of late afternoon sunshine thanks to three large skylights. But there were no windows. The walls were packed with books, and there were rows of bookshelves in the center of the room.

"We're really proud of this library," said Thea. "It took a lot of donations."

Faruq ran his hand along a shelf. The books weren't arranged according to any system he could discern. They weren't in alphabetical order by title, publisher, or author's name, and any given shelf could contain genres ranging from cookbooks and field guides to philosophy and poetry to textbooks and children's stories.

"How does anyone find anything in here?" he asked.

"What you need will come to you," said Thea. She was plucking books from the shelves at random.

"They're books," said Faruq. "They aren't sentient. Or mobile."

"You're funny, Faruq."

He stopped when he caught sight of a very old copy of *Native Son*. He took it down from the shelf and carefully opened the cover. As he suspected, it was a first edition. He nearly gasped aloud. This had to be worth a lot of money.

"Thea," he said, "this is the *children's* library? Some of these books are really valuable." She chuckled. "Our children know to treat art with respect—it's sacred. The 5 Ewas." She began walking away but Faruq stayed in place, looking down at the book skeptically.

"You've seen us celebrate Ewa, been to Ewa Park," she continued. "*Ewa* is a Yoruba word—it means beauty. You can think of the 5 Ewas as the five arts—literature, music, dance; the two-dimensional arts, like painting and photography; and the three-dimensional arts, like sculpture and architecture. We believe that art is sacred. Utterance number 6: Create beauty."

"Still. I don't know if I'd trust kids around books like this."

He'd been clutching *Native Son* to his chest protectively without even thinking about it. "Why don't you hold on to that for a while?" she said, nodding toward the book.

"What, really?"

"Yeah. And here"—she shoved the stack of books she'd been collecting into his arms "—these are for you too."

"Wow. Don't I—do I need to check them out or something? Do you guys do library cards?"

"Relax, scholar. If Odo trusts you then I do too. We all do."

Did Odo trust him? It didn't exactly seem to Faruq that he did. Odo may be curious about him, even amused by him, but trust? Faruq wasn't sure about that.

"I have to get back to work," said Thea. "Walk me?"

They left the school, and Faruq half expected someone to stop him once they saw what he was carrying, but he and Thea were met with the same open and friendly faces as always.

"We're working on building a Hall of the Ewas," Thea told him. "It'll be like a temple of the arts—libraries, galleries, theaters. Just full of beauty."

"Where will the art come from? Are you going to have to hire curators or something?" Faruq asked.

Thea shook her head. "We believe that art is not owned. Our followers donate their collections to us, their estates. Sometimes we send people to buy for us with the communal fund—auctions and estate sales and rare book dealers and the like. But for the most part, the art that you'll find here symbolizes an act of devotion."

They'd reached the theater that held the artists' studios. For the second time that day, Thea laughed at the expression on Faruq's face.

"I know how it sounds." She stepped in so close to him he could feel her breath on his face as she spoke. "You're not alone, you know? I first came to the nameless because they were offering grants and studio space. I didn't believe in any woo-woo shit. I thought Odo was fucking crazy. At best." Her eyes seemed suddenly to light from within. "But then, I started to really listen. I think you're beginning to listen a little too. It's okay. We don't bite."

She smiled softly at him for a moment. He thought she might try to kiss him again, and he wondered if he'd let her this time. But then, quickly, she snapped at him, her teeth clicking together about an inch from his nose. He flinched back in surprise and then laughed. Thea tapped his nose with a finger and all but skipped off into the theater.

. . .

Later that night, Faruq sat in bed with the stack of books Thea had given him. Most had no one author and were instead credited to "the nameless." They were on nameless theology—explaining the 18 Utterances in detail, discussing the nameless god and the World, a collection of Odo's sermons. But she'd also given him a thick volume of fairy tales, which contained sections dedicated to the Brothers Grimm, Charles Perrault, Joseph Jacobs, and Hans Christian Andersen.

Perplexed, Faruq thumbed through the book, wondering why Thea would give it to him. Even though his parents never read fairy tales to him—his father forbade them—most of these titles were familiar: "Hansel and Gretel," "The Sleeping Beauty," "Cinderella," "The Little Mermaid," "Goldilocks and the Three Bears." He was surprised how well he knew these stories despite growing up in a household devoid of them. His father wouldn't even let him watch Disney movies. But pop culture finds a way.

He turned a few pages and narrowed his eyes. "The Snow Queen." Odo's words about snowflakes rang in his head and he began to read. The story began with the Devil making a magic mirror that made everything it reflected look hideous. Some trolls take it for laughs and end up breaking it into a million pieces. These shards get into people's eyes and make them see the bad in everything.

Years later, a shard gets into this little boy named Kai's eye, and he destroys his best friend Gerda's rose garden, which was particularly cruel because Gerda's love for the roses is equal to her love for Kai. The only thing Kai can see beauty in are the snowflakes he studies through his magnifying glass. So the Snow Queen takes him to her palace and makes him forget everything and everyone he once loved. But Gerda goes looking for him, and after a long, meandering journey, finds him. When she hugs him, her tears wash the shard from his eye, and he's himself again.

The snowflake. The rose. It was too much to be a coincidence—

had Odo been referencing this story? And Thea—she'd seemed to be picking out books randomly, but maybe she wasn't. Which would mean she wasn't being entirely truthful when she'd acted confused by Faruq's question about the snowflake and the rose. And that kiss—misdirection, distraction. But why? He cursed. It was all a big game of chess. No—backgammon, which he'd always found incomprehensible. This kind of deliberate mind-fucking made him want to go home. But his curiosity was stronger.

Faruq couldn't ignore the fact that the fairy tale was oddly similar to the nameless cosmology, their narrative of what they called the Fall—the ten original Tintan becoming distorted, seeing only ugliness, falling and shattering, and every living thing containing their shards, their distortion. But why would Odo allude to this story? What did it mean that he didn't have to choose between the rose and the snowflake?

And why didn't Thea just admit she'd understood the reference? Why lie and then lead him right to the tale? She'd given him this book of fairy tales along with a bunch of nameless literature. It was like she *wanted* him to make the connection. Irritated, he reached for his camera. Thea's face was serene among that twisted metal, the hellscape of her own creation.

Faruq frowned as he clicked back through his shots. He'd taken a series of photos of the horses, especially the mothers with their foals. Those pictures should have appeared before the images of Thea posing amongst metal and teeth, but he couldn't find them. He squinted down at the camera's monitor, clicking back until he got to the first photos he took at the Forbidden City, and then forward again. Gone. His horses were gone.

Faruq brushed a hot hand through his hair. His camera had been with him all day today—it was crazy to think that someone would have managed to steal it off him, delete those photos only, and then put it back where it belonged. More than likely, it was some strange glitch with the camera itself. It was a professional camera, but he had bought it refurbished, not new. Anita had been getting on him for months to get something nicer, but the camera had always worked just fine. Until now.

Or maybe it *wasn't* the camera. Faruq chided himself—he wasn't thinking logically. What would one's motive be for deleting those pictures? And *how* would they have done it without him noticing until now? It didn't make sense. None of it made sense, actually. Something in his chest squirmed. Occam's razor—it was far more likely that the refurbished camera had failed in some way. And he could reshoot the horses.

Faruq swept all the books off the bed—*Native Son* was tucked safely in the bedside table's drawer. He turned off the light. The last conscious thought he had before sleep was of Thea's teeth snapping together, her warm, mossy breath in his nose. His body twitched, a quick spasm as his muscles relaxed.

Days passed with no sight of Odo. Faruq focused on taking more photos of the Forbidden City and its residents, and hammering out copy. He ate his meals with Kaya and Thea if he could find them, or else at a friendly table of followers in the dining hall. He called Danish to reassure him he was still alive and still unbrainwashed. *My mind is as dirty as ever,* he joked to his cousin. He didn't tell Danish about the kiss. He and Thea never mentioned it. Soon it became insubstantial, as inconsequential as a dream.

The wolf had been following him a little more closely each run. Faruq couldn't see him but he wasn't afraid anymore. Maybe that was foolish, but he only wondered if it was going to show itself again. On the beach, the sand was riddled with indistinct animal markings, but he didn't hear anything. He sat, not caring that sand was going to stick to his ass, his sweaty legs. He waited. Nothing emerged from the woods. For reasons he didn't understand, *this* frightened him more than the thought of the wolf trotting out. He looked down at the sand. There were little holes forming on its surface.

His brow furrowed, he plunged a finger into one of the holes, wiggled it around to widen it. Then his whole hand. He tore clumps of wet sand away, opening up the earth. When he peered inside, he saw a razor clam furiously tunneling its way down. Ignoring his own squeamishness, he reached in and grabbed it. He held the clam up to his face. Its shell was a muddy gray, slit open a little. Did these things have eyes? Were he and it regarding each other? He thought of Odo eating one of these things raw. Eating it alive. He dropped the razor clam back into its hole.

Faruq awoke to the far-off sound of knocking. It took him awhile to understand that someone actually *was* knocking. And on his door. He checked his phone for the time. Nearly three in the morning. Groaning, he got out of bed. Minh-An was outside.

"I've been knocking *forever*."

"Well, I was asleep," he said with a yawn. "Is it another foal?"

"Let's go."

They took the electric golf cart down to the stables. Minh-An was looking worse for wear.

Her dark eyes were nearly swallowed by shadow.

Gabe greeted them at the entrance, chipper as ever. He was not by himself this time—beside him was a pale, dark-haired teenaged girl. Faruq frowned. Or boy. The kid was pretty androgynous.

"Liam here already wrapped her tail for you," he said. He looked at Faruq. "This one is Winnie."

"Are all your horses 1920s housewives?" Faruq asked.

Minh-An rolled her eyes, but Gabe let out a sincere guffaw, and even Liam, who looked beyond bored, allowed himself a half smile. Gabe led them into the birthing stall, where he left them, like last time. Faruq squatted on the floor next to Minh-An while Winnie paced restlessly. Winnie was nearly all white, aside from her black face and rump. She seemed a little more agitated than Hattie had been. In only a few minutes, she stood, let out a shuddering sigh, and her water broke in a great gush. It splattered as it hit the floor and Faruq shrunk back a little. Minh-An didn't move an inch.

Winnie struggled down onto the ground and on her side. Her body seized with contractions. Twice, she shat, and Faruq scurried over to remove it. The foal in its membrane was protruding more and more with each contraction, making a sound occasionally like the stuttering expulsion of air as you squeeze lotion out of a bottle. Winnie grunted. The membrane covering the foal wasn't tearing as easily as Hattie's had, but he could see the foal's spindly legs, its sleek head encased inside.

Winnie surprised him by letting out a plaintive neigh. Her back legs flexed and the rest of the foal came slipping out, slick and flaccid as a fish. Right away, Faruq could see that something was wrong. Winnie was on her side, panting, but the foal wasn't moving at all.

"Minh-An," he said, standing. "I don't think it's breathing."

Minh-An did not move, and she didn't answer him right away. When she spoke, her voice was soft, distant. "We are here to bear witness, scholar. It is up to you—will you let it be, or will you bring it back?"

"Okay, how do I do that? How do I save it?"

"Do not despair at death."

"Goddamn it."

He rushed over to the foal and ripped the membrane open, pulling it off. Winnie stayed on her side, sniffing at the air as though she could smell the wrongness. The foal's eyes were closed, its little rib cage unmoving.

"Shit."

Faruq pulled out his phone. He Googled the necessary steps, processed the information in barely comprehensible shreds. *Heartbeat . . . can't breathe through their mouths . . . breathe into the nostril.* Faruq plugged one of the foal's nostrils with a thumb, and placed his mouth over the other. Its nose was wet, tasted of salt and metal. He blew. The foal's rib cage didn't expand.

Winnie was sitting up now, looking over her shoulder at them and chuffing almost inaudibly. Faruq blew harder. He blew as hard as he could. He blew until he was dizzy. He didn't know how long he'd been giving the foal CPR before he felt Minh-An's brittle hand on his shoulder.

He shook her off. "I can't let this horse die, Minh-An. I don't care what your Utterances say."

"Look," said Minh-An.

The foal's rib cage and belly were shivering with breath, its dark eyes open a slit. Winnie began to work her way up to her feet. Faruq collapsed back into sitting. He was trembling. The foal's breaths became stronger, more regular. It sluggishly blinked its eyes up at Faruq. It was a colt, black legs and head, and a black patch on his belly, but pure, impossible white everywhere else. Faruq's face flushed.

"Fuck."

Minh-An handed him a blanket. "For the foal," she said.

Right. The article he'd skimmed in his panic said to rub the foal vigorously. He draped the blanket over the foal and rubbed. The colt's eyes opened more fully and his legs began to move around inexpertly. With a great heaving breath, Winnie pushed out the placenta. Minh-An didn't have a secure hold on it, so it slipped from her hands to the floor, landing wetly. This time Faruq didn't flinch.

The colt decided he'd had enough of Faruq's attentions and struggled shakily to his feet.

Winnie lowered her head to lick at her newborn, but he stumbled stubbornly to her teat. Once he began to suckle, Minh-An signaled that it was time to go.

She seemed to need all her meager energy to drive the golf cart. Faruq looked down at his hands. He'd wiped them on a towel, but they were still sticky. His mouth tasted like offal. He needed a shower. He needed a drink.

"What the fuck was that?" he asked her.

"Life," she said. "Death."

"That was cruel, Minh-An."

She glanced at him. "How?"

"You would've let that poor thing die. A *baby*. Maybe you all are cavalier about death, but what about that foal's mother? What about *me*?"

"What about you?"

"That shit was traumatizing, Minh-An." Faruq realized that he was raising his voice a bit. He took a deep breath.

"Scholar, I would encourage you to think about *why* you're attached to the distortion that is trauma. I've told you before that I'm a refugee. Losing a foal doesn't have anything on what happened to the country I had to flee as an infant. If I were distorted, I'd be traumatized. If I were distorted, both Odo and I—we'd be full of *wrath*."

"And you're not?"

"We're full, scholar," she said, sounding exhausted. "But not with wrath."

When they pulled up to the guesthouse, Odo was standing on the front steps, his hands clasped behind his back.

"Welcome back," he said. He nodded at Minh-An and she smiled back tiredly before driving off. "Well, scholar. You're something more than a guest now, aren't you? Gather your things tomorrow. If it's all right with you, I'd like you to stay with me."

"O-okay," Faruq stammered.

Odo left him there, the earliest risers among the birds calling into the dark.

Faruq was too tired to run the next morning. Even getting up by eight—usually the latest he could sleep in—was a struggle. He didn't have much stuff to gather—his notes, the books he'd borrowed, his laptop, his camera, a small duffel bag full of clothes and toiletries, two pairs of shoes. He'd always traveled light. Nevertheless, Odo sent a team of four followers to move him and he followed behind them, carrying nothing but his phone, as they walked in a procession to Odo's house.

Odo was not at home. No one claimed to know where he was. The room Faruq was escorted to was a guest suite on the first floor, full of light and overgrown plants. He put his clothes away in the closet, lined his toiletries up on the bathroom sink, closed his notes and laptop away in a drawer. Faruq felt strange in the house by himself. He pulled out his phone to scroll through the nameless's TikTok. There was a new video—a very short clip of Odo seated with a plate piled high with some kind of red meat.

The song that accompanied the video was America's "A Horse with No Name."

Something in him sank. He knew people ate horse, but surely—but he *could* see Odo ordering one of those horses butchered. To punish him. Because he'd seen Odo's mask slip a couple times now, and no matter what Minh-An said, the man was full of rage. Faruq was sure of it. He borrowed one of the many bikes strewn around the city for anybody to use and went down to the horse stables. Gabe greeted him as enthusiastically as ever.

"We named the colt Asher," he said, leading Faruq to a fenced-off grassy area. "It means 'blessing.'"

"And the others?"

"The others?" Gabe asked.

"The other horses," Faruq said impatiently. "I saw a video on TikTok. It made it seem like Odo was eating horsemeat. I want to see the other horses."

Gabe let out a shocked laughed. "The horses aren't for *eating,* Faruq."

But still, he led Faruq through the stables, and Faruq was reassured to see that all the horses were accounted for. "Then what was that meat in the video?" he asked himself aloud.

"*What* video?" Gabe asked.

Faruq pulled out his phone and navigated to the TikTok page. But he couldn't find the video. He scrolled up and down. It had been a new video, so it should've been at the top. But instead, there was only a video of a couple followers doing a silly TikTok dance in the Forbidden City's orchard.

"It was just here," he said. "I just saw it."

"Are you sure it was our TikTok account?" Gabe asked.

"*Yes,* I'm sure. This is ridiculous. I'm not fucking crazy."

"Hey," Gabe said. He placed a hand on Faruq's shoulder, squeezed. "It's all good. Whatever you saw, I can promise you it wasn't one of our horses, okay? Why don't I take you to visit Asher? It'll be grounding."

It may not have been horsemeat after all, but Faruq knew what he'd seen: The video was there and had disappeared just as quickly.

Winnie nibbled on grass while Asher nursed. When he was done he bolted away from her playfully, and, seeing Faruq, trotted curiously over to him. Asher rubbed his nose into Faruq's shirt and then ran away with his unpracticed gait. Faruq looked at this creature, which was perfectly formed, a masterpiece of muscle and exactly tuned instinct. Life really was a miracle. All the more so if there was no design behind it. Asher was perfect, and it was all but an accident of science, evolution's trial and error. The truest blessing. And he'd breathed life back into that masterpiece.

Instagram Post #383

@thenamelessmvmnt: Odo in profile, laughing, bright yellow sunlight making a shadow of his face. Two women flank him, both lean and tall, one a brunette holding a basket full of something unseen and the other a blonde with light curls wisping, weightless, around her head. They are laughing too, their arms easy around him, each other.

#purejoy #solstice #rayoflight

89,492 likes | 2,850 comments

Nero

FADE IN:

INT. LOS ANGELES OFFICE—MED. SHOT—OWEN RYKER

                    OWEN RYKER
          This country has a long, ugly history of
          African-Americans being victims of violence
          due to false allegations from a white
          person.

          So this accusation was particularly ugly.
          And (voice cracks) we knew it wasn't true.
          We *knew* Odo did not do this.

Owen Ryker wipes his eyes, leans back in his chair,
fingers interlaced.

                    OWEN RYKER
          Sue Mills would not testify. So this entire
          case was built around her ability to
          describe what Odo looked like without his
          clothes on—you know, the *huge* dragon tattoo
          all across his back. (chuckles)

INT. CWE NAVE—MED. SHOT—WILL ROY

                    WILL ROY
          That poor girl was traumatized. No one was
          going to make her get up there in a
          courtroom. Her testimony was enough. And we
          had her medical records—she *was* pregnant.

                                             FADE IN:*
Footage of Odo standing over a female follower who is
crouched, planting flowers. Odo places his hand on the
follower's shoulder and she smiles up at him. SLOW ZOOM
on Odo's back (audio removed).

                    WILL ROY
          It was a big ol' dragon, yellow eyes,
          snarling with bloody teeth. She said he
          turned around to take off his shirt and

————————————————
* Music: Last Kind Words Blues (Geeshie Wiley)

that's when—that's when she saw it. Said it
was like looking at the Devil himself. Said
she thought that dragon was gonna eat her
alive, swallow up her soul and spit it out
at Satan's feet.

Roy shakes his head.

                                    DISSOLVE TO:
Footage of Odo smiling wordlessly at the camera, his
face soft, almost beatific.

          MINH-AN
     You know, an inexperienced liar will shoot
     themselves in the foot by giving too much
     detail. (chuckles)

     It's a rookie mistake.

                                    FADE IN:

INT. LOS ANGELES OFFICE—MED. SHOT—OWEN RYKER

Owen Ryker smiles.

          OWEN RYKER
     They didn't even need me for this part.
     (laughs)

     The tattoo Sue Mills described doesn't
     exist. Odo does have a tattoo—but a small,
     maybe medium-sized one, on his shoulder.

     Of a tiger.

CU of Ryker's eyes, which crinkle at their corners.

          OWEN RYKER
     I believe he got it to cover a scar,
     something he got over in Vietnam. The tiger
     isn't even snarling, like they said the
     dragon is supposed to be—it's simply
     staring. In black and white. (laughs)

I mean, it's like Ms. Mills *wanted* to be easily proven wrong. The charges were dropped. And Ms. Mills recanted the whole thing.

INT. CWE NAVE—MED. SHOT—WILL ROY

> WILL ROY
> Nonsense. Utter nonsense. The shoulder may as well be the back. And dragon? Tiger? If you're scared senseless it don't make a fair bit of difference. (scoffs)

Will Roy flicks a hand in the air, scowling.

> WILL ROY
> Ought to be ashamed of themselves, all of 'em. No justice for that poor girl. They obviously got to her, intimidated her. I mean, it's *obvious*.

> FADE TO BLACK.

BLACK SCREEN:

SUPER: Sue Mills and her family declined to participate in this documentary. Attempts at communication went unanswered.

> FADE IN:

SUPER: Until we received a strange email with no subject line. It contained only an attachment.

INSERT—IMAGE

Photo of Sue Mills, date unknown, sitting on a picnic blanket and nuzzling the white-blond head of a small, pale child, who looks to be no more than a year old. (censor bar over the child's eyes) SLOW PAN.

INT. GREENHOUSE—MED. SHOT—MINH-AN

Minh-An throws up her hands.

                    MINH-AN
I don't *know* who the father of Sue Mills's
baby is. I doubt *she* does. From what I hear,
she very much thrived in our non-judgmental
culture and practiced a little free love.

Minh-An raises an eyebrow.

                    MINH-AN
That's what happens when you're repressed.

What Christ the Word Evangelical tried to do
was very serious. It could have cost us
everything.

When Odo was released from jail, we were all
there, full of joy, waiting to receive him,
welcome him back. But Will Roy's
congregation was there too.

                                    DISSOLVE TO:
Cell phone footage of Odo stepping out of Burning
Hill's jail. Followers and congregants yell at each
other. A red-faced young woman can be seen throwing
something indiscernible toward Odo. Someone jogs into
the frame, jostling the person holding the cell phone.
(audio garbled)

                    MINH-AN
They spit slurs at him, they threatened us,
they threw things—rotten food, crumpled-up
paper towels . . . their trash, basically.
It was a race riot.

INT. CWE NAVE—MED. SHOT—WILL ROY

                    WILL ROY
Weren't no *race riot*.

Roy rolls his eyes, crosses his arms.

We'd just had enough. This whole thing was
unfair. That poor family. We. Had. Had.
Enough.

I didn't hear nobody on our side say
anything unchristian. And the only people I
saw gettin' physical was *them*.

                              DISSOLVE TO:

Cell phone footage of Odo speaking to a group of
followers who are huddled around him. His arm is around
one of the followers, a young woman who is standing
with a lowered head, one hand clutching her arm.

                    ODO
          My, my, my. Violence is a distortion, yes it
          is. It was a distorted man who threw the
          broken bottle that injured Macy here. We
          should feel sorry for him. But sorry ain't
          everything. We ain't got no book telling us
          to turn the other cheek. Naw. They don't
          follow that old book anyway. Just look at
          'em. Look at Macy. Sometimes you have to be
          a mirror. Sometimes you have to *force* people
          to see.

                              DISSOLVE TO: .

INT. GREENHOUSE—MED. SHOT—MINH-AN

Minh-An sighs, crosses one leg over the other.

                    MINH-AN
          You know, Will Roy's god punishes sinners.

Minh-An nods grimly.

          We—the nameless—combat those who make
          distortion.

Minh-An nods again.

                              FADE TO BLACK.

before: 1969

THEY FILLED THEMSELVES with bounty. Roast turkey with cornbread stuffing, glazed sweet potatoes, buttered carrots, cranberry sauce, hot butter biscuits, fruitcake, pumpkin pie with real whipped cream. A stunning indulgence after weeks of C-rations. It was Christmas Day, two days into a three-day stand-down, and for some of the men, returning to the base for the holiday cease-fire felt a little like it used to feel to go home, and it tore secret holes in them, which they tried to fill with food and determined cheer, but which, really, would never fully heal.

There was a Christmas show, but Crazy Horse preferred to blast his jungle music. The Isley Brothers, "It's Your Thing." The music drew the other brothers, coaxed them into that stomp, that jerk in the hips, that bend in the elbows and knees, that snap in the fingers, the snap in the neck. Even Bullwhip joined in, putting his hands on his hips and stomping his feet. Crazy Horse and Bigger were trying to do the Philadelphia two-step—forward, two, three, four, and *bop,* and out. A spin for Crazy Horse. A spin for Bigger. The other cherries laughed, snapped on them even as they began to pair up and join in.

Silk laughed at the two-steppers, but he was in the middle of an unspoken dance competition himself. He and some other grunts—including some of the more with-it white boys—were in a loose semicircle, taking turns showing off their stuff. One of the white boys did some cowboy-looking line dance shit, and laughed good-naturedly when he got jeered. Bo Weevil, a big old country Negro from Mississippi, could really move, dropping his thing all the way down and then zipping back up into an impeccable grape-vine.

Brother Ned stepped into the center next. Some of the cherries snickered, but Silk happened to know that Ned wasn't any kind of slouch. The record slipped into "Give the Women What They Want" and Brother Ned's face changed. He furrowed his brow, his eyes squinting and his eyebrows drawing in toward each other, and he pursed his lips into a pucker, like he'd just finished sucking the marrow out of a rib bone. Then he clapped his hands, spun, and began to dance like James Brown. He tucked his hands behind his back and let his feet do the talking, and sometimes it was both feet and sometimes it was just one. He jerked his chest around, nodding his head. He spun like a top on ice. He fixed an imaginary tie and dropped into a split.

The brothers lost it. They were jumping, tumbling into each other with shock and delight. Brother Ned was pink and sweaty now. A few of the other white soldiers tried to imitate him, but they didn't have it. But Silk did. He squared up with Brother Ned, grinning, and began to mirror him. Before long, they fell into their game: Brother Ned did something and Silk copied and added a little something more, and then Brother Ned did the whole thing and added a little something of his own, and so on. The two of them grooving and sweating and thinking of Preach and the world and their mothers.

Mail call interrupted them. Everyone huddled together, waiting to hear their names called. They delighted in each other's Christmas care packages, the magazines and hometown newspapers, the tins of homemade cookies and candies. More than one of them received a synthetic Christmas tree. One medic got a pair of underwear from his mother as a kind of joke and he bawled. Brother Ned stood holding an unopened letter as though it were porcelain, his face, splotchy from dance only moments ago, gone white as milk. Silk frowned at him.

What's the matter?

Others were beginning to notice Brother Ned. They all still had the aftertaste of Preach's death in their mouths, so they all understood what Brother Ned was going to say before he said it.

It's her. She wrote me back.

Crazy Horse felt a hot branch of fresh grief piston through him like lightning.

Well? Go on, man, open it.

Brother Ned opened the letter with clammy hands.

She sent a *picture*.

He held it close to his face, inhaling. The other men jostled, asking for a look. Brother Ned passed the photo around, and the others handled it carefully, reverently. In the photo, Preach's sister was sitting on a flowered couch, a shy smile on her round face. Her hair was slicked down and gathered into a puff on top of her head. Her big eyes were liquid and dark—they had changed since the last photo she'd sent over, that one to Preach. She was wearing a light sweater and a dark vest, a skirt that revealed her smooth calves as she sat.

Read the letter.

Yeah, what'd she say?

Brother Ned began to read.

Dear Mr. Ned,

Thank you for your lovely letter. Grieving my brother has been so tiring, but your letter gave me a little spot of strength. I was afraid that going to war would change my brother, but from your letter I now know that he was himself even in Viet Nam, and that is a comfort.

I have been trying to keep busy. I started work as a Secretary, but I hope to become a Nurse one day. It has been bitter cold here, colder than I can ever remember it being. I saw a little yellow kitten on my way home from work and I felt so bad for him (he was shaking in all that cold, and thin!) that I took him home. I named him Preach, like you all used to call my brother. I think he would've liked that.

I have to admit, Mr. Ned, that my brother wrote a little about you, and I was happy to see your name on that stripped envelope. Please take care of yourself. I hope you will write again real soon.

Merry Christmas & God Bless You,
Melissa (Missy)

The men who had gathered around to hear hooted, clapping a furiously blushing Brother Ned on his back. But a trio of good-ol-boys sneered, one of them draped in the Confederate flag he'd received in his Christmas care package. He spit something brown into the dirt.

I'll tell you what: Ain't nothing worse than a nigger lover.

Bo Weevil, who was nearby, felt the words curdle in him immediately. He was usually a peaceful man, and, being from the Deep South, he was used to people like the good-ol-boys and the kinds of things they said. He was used to getting along under the burning white rage of men like that, was even proud of it. He wasn't no sensitive Northerner, no troublemaker. But Preach's death still hurt. And the trouble with getting along was that more often than not, it kept you moving in place until you died. So without thinking about it, and with no warning whatsoever, even to himself, Bo Weevil swept up his E-tool by the mean end and brought the handle across the good-ol-boy's face. The good-ol-boy's friends started howling immediately, and it covered the sharp crack of his nose breaking.

The good-ol-boy's flag slipped off his shoulders at the blow, and lay in the dirt where he'd spit. His face was streaked in tears and blood and snot, and he was cursing like he was speaking tongues. The good-ol-boys charged and the brothers charged back. Three bloods pulled Bo Weevil away, though he wasn't making a fuss anymore, didn't really want to fight. These melees, Silk knew, never led to anything worth the fight. So he jumped in the middle, held his hands out to the sides.

Now hold up, everybody cool it.

But no one was listening to him. Those who heard him could

not make sense of his words. Bloods jostled by him to get to the good-ol-boys, nearly knocking him down. Crazy Horse saw it and thought, oddly, of that little kids' movie, *The Jungle Book*. There was a scene where Bagheera, regal and wise and a little self-satisfied, is on his way to help Baloo, and Baloo accidentally screams in his face, startling the black panther. And as Baloo's yell echoes, Bagheera falls back on his ass, loses all composure, all his carefully cultivated dignity. Impotent. *Humiliating,* Crazy Horse thought.

Now, just what in the hell is all this?

An NCO stomped into the middle of the group of men, hands on his hips. He took one look at the good-ol-boy with the broken nose and just about snarled.

I wanna know who started this shit and I wanna know *now*.

That fuckin nigger, sir, that fuckin *nigger*.

The good-ol-boy's face was beginning to swell, so his words came out like chewed-up food, mucusy and unrecognizable. But he was pointing right at Bo Weevil, and one of his friends, hurriedly, explained what had happened, conveniently leaving out his friend's insult. The NCO turned his fiery gaze on Bo Weevil.

You outta your goddamn mind, boy?

The fists were all lowered now; it was the time for words. Silk was back in his element. He stepped forward.

Aw, sir, now you know we all still hurt because of our friend. You never had no trouble from Bo Weevil here before.

The NCO jabbed a finger in Bo Weevil's direction.

He hit that man upside the head with his *E-tool*. Coulda killed him.

Some of the brothers—and a few rabbits—were smothering chuckles, but Silk held a straight face.

Well, sir, he *coulda* smacked him with his Ka-Bar.

The chuckles were less contained now. *I know that's right,* they mumbled. *Least his nose is still attached to his face.* The NCO's scowl had gone soft around the edges. Crazy Horse was used to this skill of Silk's, but Bigger was fascinated. What was it about him? Anyone else talking like that to their NCO would be in deep shit.

Silk gestured at the good-ol-boy.

Really, you should be thanking Bo Weevil here. They won't let you back in the bush with that. Merry Christmas, cracker.

Now there was raucous laughter. Even the NCO's mouth quivered. He pointed a stern finger at Bo Weevil.

Look. Any more trouble with you and I'll have you court-martialed quicker'n you can hop over that Mandingo, you hear me?

Sir, yes sir.

The good-ol-boy shuffled off to the medic with his friends. One of them picked up the flag, did his best to shake off the dirt, and then slung it over his shoulder like a fallen grunt. Bigger approached Silk, shaking his head.

Man, how do you *do* that?

Silk gave him a sly grin.

I'm just like a snake charmer.

He walked off to open his mail in private. Crazy Horse poked Bigger in the side.

You know what a snake charmer's secret is, don't you?

Bigger shook his head.

Make yourself immune to the venom.

Both Silk and Crazy Horse were overdue for their R&R. They'd both selected Bangkok, and so they were flown over together. Whereas Vietnam was a stinking mirage, shimmering with heat, Bangkok emerged from a yellowish haze with its stalagmite buildings, studded with the honking of car horns, and the Chao Phraya like a slit. At night, it lit up like Times Square.

Neither Silk nor Crazy Horse felt like they were in the real world. The war certainly didn't feel like it, and their respite from it didn't either. But without the structure of being back at base, without the monotony of jumping through the jungle, they were little boys in a dream that all the time had a little something of a nightmare in it. And so they clung to each other, neither one of them admitting to the clinging. They shared a room, alternating each night who slept on the floor and who on the narrow bed. Their first night, Crazy Horse got drunk at a nightclub and took a combat nurse from Hawaii back to their hotel room. Silk waited outside the door until he heard the silence of sleep, and then crept in to go to bed.

The next morning, as they stepped out into the haze of the day, both of them thought that their five days—four remaining now— were too much, too vast. Neither of them would articulate this thought to the other. They were supposed to be happy to be here. This was supposed to be the great breath of relief. But really what they wanted was to go home. They found a restaurant that boasted that it was under European management, but when they asked to be seated, the host claimed they were fully booked. Crazy Horse was too hungover to ask the man to explain the dining room full of empty tables, and Silk decided it wasn't worth it.

Instead, they found a Chinese restaurant whose main attributes, according to the sidewalk sign, were air-conditioning and a live ocelot. The air-conditioning, they found out upon entering, was not working, but the ocelot prowled a mossy concrete patio that they could see through large, filmy windows. The restaurant was dim and humid, but there were good smells coming from the kitchen. Silk and Crazy Horse went to sit where they could see the ocelot, who stretched out on her side next to a small fan.

The table next to the one they chose was full of marines, all brothers. Before Silk and Crazy Horse sat down, one of the marines lifted up a jug of beer with one hand and waved them over with another.

My brothers. Come on over here—we family, ain't we?

So Crazy Horse and Silk sat down with the marines and introduced themselves. The marines introduced themselves in turn—Big Joe, Kwame, Akeem, and Miles. Akeem, quite possibly the blackest brother Crazy Horse had ever seen, seemed to be the leader of this little group. Or at least the one who did most of the talking.

Well, brothers? How do you find ol Bangkok?

Silk smirked.

Ain't too different from anywhere else.

He was thinking of the restaurant they'd just been turned away from.

Akeem chuckled.

That right, brother?

Crazy Horse was not thinking of the restaurant anymore, but of the ocelot, who had risen again to pace the courtyard, her body a work of bone and frustrated muscle. Crazy Horse looked away from her.

Just tired. Tired, tired.

Big Joe poured them both a mug of beer.

You tired because they got us fightin in the wrong war.

Silk narrowed his eyes.

What's the right war, then?

Akeem wiped a line of beer foam from his mustache.

The United States is at war with Black folk. *Our* war's back home, my brothers. Don't you know the United States declared war on Black folk when they took the first of us out of Africa?

Crazy Horse's gaze was drawn, almost involuntarily, back to the ocelot, but Silk rolled his eyes at Akeem.

I guess that's one way to put it.

Uh-uh, brother. Chairman Mao said that politics is war without bloodshed, but war is politics *with* bloodshed. When the pigs shot up Brother Huey Newton and threw him in jail, that was an act of *war*, you dig?

Silk took a swig of his beer.

I believe Brother Huey was framed, sure. But you cats march around with guns talkin bout killin pigs—you're causing *trouble*.

Kwame grinned, revealing a large gap between his front teeth.

A panther don't attack, brotherman. It just defends.

Crazy Horse took out a pack of smokes and handed one to Silk, who only tucked it behind his ear. Crazy Horse plucked out a little of the tobacco from his own cigarette and sprinkled it on the floor. For Preach.

Lemme tell you somethin. I can't *wait* to get the hell outta here and never hold a gun again. Don't care if that makes me a pussy. There's other ways to get freedom.

Akeem sneered.

Freedom. Ain't we here to fight for *freedom*? What this war really is, is an armed uprising of a colonized people. And they got us over here dying to support the colonizers. Do you feel free, brother? Nah. Freedom is having the power to control your own destiny. To do that, you got to *take* that control out of the white man's hands. You think he'll just hand it over to you?

Silk leaned forward.

That's what you Panthers never get. Even if you kill a white man with a gun, you've made another white man rich by using his bullets. You've made another white man rich by using his steel. You've made another white man rich by paying for his registration. That's three white men you've paid for the death of one. Nuh-uh, brother. We got to be smarter. We got to outwit them.

Miles smiled.

Hey, that's beautiful, brother.

Akeem nodded emphatically.

And education is part of our program. We go into the community, into people's homes, and teach folk about our real history, about politics and the law, and about things that's goin on in Africa and all over the world.

Silk threw up his hands.

Aw, y'all don't know nothin. Can't nothin last long in your brains—bunch a hotheads.

The table laughed. Crazy Horse blew smoke toward the ocelot as two waiters piled dish after dish in front of them.

The nightclub was foggy with cigarette smoke, heavy with drumbeat. On stage, six women performed traditional Thai dance, their feet aching, their minds tired, their breasts heavy with the gazes of men. Three days ago, a drunk marine had scrambled on stage, hooked his arm around the waist of the youngest dancer, and tried to run off with her. The five other women had sprung into action, beating the marine on his back, shoulders, and head until, laughing, he'd let the youngest dancer go. All six of them had been severely reprimanded for the whole ordeal. When the traditional dance was over, the dancers gave a bow with their hands pressed together in front of their chests, and the band began to play a warbling kind of jazz that Crazy Horse hated.

Man, I'm gonna go see if there's anybody here who can really dance.

Alone, Silk went up to the bar to get himself a whiskey. He was thinking of leaving after his drink, but then he caught sight of a sister in a tight pink dress. He smiled at her. She smiled back. She was rail-thin, her hair cut into one of those fashionable short styles, her dark eyes rimmed in black. Silk bought her a whiskey too and went over to join her.

Evening.

How are you?

Silk was shocked by her accent. Not a sister at all, then. He could see it now. Probably Cambodian. He didn't let this trip him up for long.

You speak English?

Uh-huh.

She nodded proudly.

Well, what's a pretty lady like you doing out alone?

She laughed, unsure. Silk realized she couldn't really understand him. He tried speaking more slowly.

What's. Your. Name?

Kong. Ke. Ah. Kong Kea.

He pointed to himself.

Silk.

Kong Kea giggled. His name was strange on her ears, soft like a woman.

Silk gestured toward the band.

Wanna dance?

Uh-huh.

Silk led her onto the dance floor, pressed her body into his.

They swayed to that warbling jazz, moving easily together. Silk tried at conversation, but Kong Kea could understand little beyond the basics, so they just danced. She was light, followed him easily, so Silk kept upping the ante, improvising more complicated steps, more movement in between the beats. Each time he did this, she laughed, delighted, and easily kept up with him.

If there's one thing I like, it's a woman that can *dance*.

Uh-huh.

Silk lost count of how many songs they'd danced through, but he was sweating, thirsty. Even Kong Kea had a little glimmer of sweat at her temples. Silk led her back to the bar, ordered them both more whiskey. He downed half of his in one gulp, and then Kong Kea grabbed his wrist.

Wanna go my place?

Silk let her lead him out of the club. Once outside, Kong Kea pulled out two cigarettes. Silk tucked his behind his ear and lit hers. She took a long drag, blowing the smoke up as Silk studied the smooth line of her throat. She grinned up at him.

Not too far.

Silk followed her like a kid entranced by the pied piper. There was a little switch in her hips as she walked. Smoke streamed out behind her like a cape. Silk breathed it in. Her apartment building was gray with tight little windows that couldn't let in much light. It was one in a row of nearly identical buildings, all narrow and pressed together like strangers in a subway car. The stairway was lit only by the light that shone underneath doors and smelled strongly of sweat, cigarette smoke, and cooking oil.

Kong Kea opened the door. The apartment was dim, close. There was a kitchenette and a little table at which sat another young Cambodian woman in a pink housedress, her hair done up in curlers. She was smoking a cigarette and reading what looked like a Thai newspaper. Kong Kea and her roommate had a not overly friendly conversation in Khmer. Then the roommate put out her cigarette on the table, gathered her newspaper, and left the apartment. Kong Kea looked up at Silk.

I tell her sleep roof.

She's sleeping on the roof? You sure she'll be all right?

Uh-huh.

Kong Kea undressed efficiently, without fanfare. Her body was spare, though with unexpected softness. Her breasts were plump with dark brown nipples, and there was a nice roundness at her hips and upper thighs. When Silk stood naked before her, she advanced toward him, determined and hungry. He'd been expecting submissiveness and got none. She ground herself into him hard until she jolted as though electrocuted and collapsed on top of him, panting. Only then was he allowed to take over.

When they were done, Silk sprawled on his stomach. Kong Kea fingered the scar left by the bullet in his back.

Got hit in the jungle. Didn't even see who did it. The birds screamed. I thought I was dying. And then—like *that*—everything went quiet.

Uh-huh.

Silk sighed, closed his eyes.

I love you.

Uh-huh.

He said it because he knew she wouldn't understand. But then he thought it might be true in some small, strange way. Finite and irreplaceable.

The next morning, neither Kong Kea nor her roommate were in the flat—Silk was alone. He could tell by what little pastel light crept in through the window that it was quite early. He'd kicked the thin sheet off in his sleep. He was sweating—the apartment had no fan that he could see. He got dressed and made his way down the dark stairwell, out onto the anonymous street, back to the hotel room, where he found Crazy Horse already up, sitting in the little chair by the window with his feet propped on the bed, smoking a joint.

Well, if it isn't Romeo himself. Saw you leave with that Cambodian number. How'd you do?

Silk laughed, reached for Crazy Horse's joint, and took a puff.

Girl didn't speak a lick of English, but she sure could screw.

How much you out?

Silk blinked.

Huh?

Man, how much did she *charge* you?

Nothing—she wasn't a prostitute.

Crazy Horse rocked back in his chair and cackled.

Brother, *that* was a prostitute. Didn't she say anything to you before you left?

She wasn't there when I left. I woke up to her gone.

Crazy Horse laughed again, tears in his eyes.

Then you were supposed to leave the money on the dresser.

Silk was sheepish.

There wasn't any dresser.

Crazy Horse put out his joint on the windowsill, holding his stomach.

You a fool, man. Cmon, bumpkin. Let's find us some coffee and chow. And none of that bland shit they make for the crackers and the French.

It took them a good hour of wandering, several confused conversations with locals, sometimes made up entirely of gestures, but they eventually found themselves floating down a khlong in a canoe manned by a stringy Thai teenager who didn't speak any English. They disembarked at a ghetto where the streets were narrow and unpaved, and children chased chickens, laughing, and women sat together peeling vegetables and nursing babies and chatting. The restaurant the teenager led them to did not look like a restaurant, but a two-story house with a thatched roof and laundry hanging from a carved wood balcony.

An old woman appeared in the doorway. She and the boy had a quick conversation in Thai, and then she beckoned to Crazy Horse and Silk.

My grandson. Very stupid boy.

She sat them in a room scattered with woven mats and wooden pallets that served as tables. Crazy Horse was mildly surprised to see they weren't alone—there was a young French couple that nodded at them in greeting, and an old Thai man who was slurping up some kind of soup, acknowledging no one. The old woman disappeared into the kitchen, which was concealed by a tattered hanging cloth, and then hobbled back out with two chipped mugs of coffee, which she set in front of Crazy Horse and Silk.

The coffee was strong, aggressively toasted, and sweetened to cloyingness. They both drank it greedily. The old woman set out a platter of mango seasoned with chili flakes.

You boys in army?

Silk nodded.

Yes, ma'am.

The old woman nodded too.

Eat a lot. Army boys always hungry.

The mango was sweet and tender, and the chili hot. Crazy Horse closed his eyes in pleasure as he chewed. Silk took a large gulp of coffee, singeing his tongue.

Just two more days aboveground before we head back to hell.

Oh, shut up, why don't you?

Silk chuckled.

Oh, come on, man. We're on the brink of a new decade. Lighten up.

The old woman returned with two plates of food for them— fried omelets, sticky rice, minced meat, garlic, green onions, and sweet chili paste. The old woman grinned as they began to eat, revealing crooked teeth and graying gums.

Eat a lot. You boys like Thai food?

Crazy Horse answered with a mouth full of rice.

Keep feeding us like this, and we may not want to leave.

The old woman laughed heartily.

Then why you go back for?

Don't got no choice.

The old woman shook her head.

My grandson, he stupid. He think Viet Cong is Mara army. You understand? Devil army. He want to fight with American.

The French couple was listening now, their expressions faintly amused. Silk shrugged.

Ain't no devils. No angels, either.

The old woman nodded in agreement.

Chai. Like I say, stupid boy. But you boys—you stupid too? Why you fight war over there?

Crazy Horse smirked.

Well, we were drafted.

The old woman clicked her tongue.

No, no. I mean why you fight? What the point?

Crazy Horse's thoughts snapped right away to Preach, and the sticky rice went dry in his mouth. Silk's mind went, strangely, to Kong Kea's roommate curled up on the pitch-black concrete roof in her pink housedress and curlers. It was probably too hot for her to sleep up there. She probably had to use her newspaper as a pillow, her sweat melting its pages away. She probably had to open up that housedress, baring herself to the hot stain of night and whoever else may come. Neither of them had an answer for the old woman, so she eventually just patted them on their backs, a little rough and a little tender.

today

LIVING WITH ODO was not what Faruq expected. That is, it quickly began to feel normal. Faruq seldom saw Odo before dinner, which a reverent crew of followers brought to the house and laid out on the table every evening. There were always leftovers in the fridge, which Faruq foraged and repurposed for breakfast and lunch. By all appearances, Odo only ate once a day.

Per his daily ritual, Faruq got up at the crack of dawn for his run. When he returned on this dusty yellow morning, sweaty and wolf-haunted, he found Odo waiting for him. He laughed upon seeing Faruq and drew him into a hug. And given how drenched in sweat he was, Faruq found himself touched by the gesture.

"I've got a free morning, scholar. I can give you that time you've been asking for."

"Oh great," said Faruq. "Just let me go grab a quick shower."

When Faruq reemerged, washed and in fresh clothes, Odo was waiting for him in the dining room with a steaming pot of tea and a bowl piled high with fruit. Faruq waved his phone at him and Odo nodded. Faruq set the phone down on the table, tapped the red record button, and pulled his chair up close to the table. Odo watched him with an air of patience.

"So," said Faruq, "I guess, could you start from the beginning?"

"The beginning?" asked Odo.

"Yes. Like, the *story* of the nameless—your story."

"And when might the beginning of that story be?"

Faruq tried not to grit his teeth in frustration. "I was hoping you'd tell me."

Odo laughed. "I'm not trying to be difficult, scholar. I just don't know what you're asking." He paused. "Do *you* know what you're asking?"

"Yes. I— Okay, let's try this: Tell me about yourself. How did you get to be where you are now?"

Odo smiled and poured himself a cup of tea. "I was born on July first, 1950. Grew up poor and Black at a time when being either was, more than today, likely to get you dead early. I got sent to Vietnam just about the second I turned eighteen. I lost some friends and earned some medals. But the best thing that ever happened to me happened over there—Vutu revealed Their 18 Utterances to me." He spread his hands as though to say *voilà*.

"So you got drafted?" Faruq asked.

Odo nodded.

"What was that like? Did you *want* to go? You were only eighteen—were you ready to fight in a war?"

"Didn't think of it like that. I had no choice. Soon as I got drafted, I knew where I was headed. If you were Black and you got drafted, you were headed to Vietnam."

"I would have been scared shitless," Faruq said.

"Don't know that I had the good sense to be scared. Not at first."

"When did you—receive—the 18 Utterances?"

"Right before I got out. I lost my last friend. I was despairing at death there, in the rain. And then something—Vutu—came into me and tell me, *Do not despair at death*."

"Was it like a voice? A feeling? Did you actually hear those words?"

"I *was* those words, scholar."

Faruq was furiously scribbling notes. He preferred to have his written notes in addition to the recorded conversation, to ensure he didn't miss anything. "So you only got the one Utterance that first time? When did you receive the others?"

"Naw, scholar, I got them all at once, in a flash. It was a moment that revealed the distortion that is time—I was suspended in a blank space, nothing but my own consciousness and the voice of Vutu. I was there for just a moment, for forever. But when I opened my eyes—and I didn't know I had closed them, scholar, you understand?—it was only seconds that had gone by. Just like that, I was changed. I saw. I had all 18 Utterances inside me."

"Were you on the battlefield when this happened?"

Odo nodded. "I'd nearly died. My last friend *was* dead. He was lying on the soaked ground next to me."

"So you were injured."

"That's right, scholar. I'd been shot."

"And your friend—he had been shot too? What was his name?"

Odo smiled an odd smile. "Name was Rufus. But we never called him that."

"What did you call him?"

"We all had different names, out there. Jungle names. War names."

"What was your war name?" Faruq asked.

Odo shook his head. "It's a deadname, scholar."

Faruq felt Odo's resistance and moved on, resolving to return to this question later if necessary. "Okay, so you'd been shot. You'd received the 18 Utterances in a flash. What did you do next?"

Odo closed his eyes, as if replaying the memory in his own darkness. "The medic came to see me. I don't remember much then—I think I must have passed out. I'd been shot in a few places, but it was the hit to the gut that did it. I woke up in a hospital, confused as all hell. I was so stiff I could barely sit up, and I could hear someone hollering in pain, but I couldn't see who it was. But still, I had that echo of Vutu's voice twisted up in me like a snake. I wasn't the same. Couldn't go on acting like I was. They were going to send me home. And I knew that's when my work would begin."

"What was the first thing you did when you returned home from war?"

"Well, I went home to my mama. For a while I didn't want to do anything at all. But Vutu wouldn't let me sleep. Every time I closed my eyes, the 18 Utterances would flash on the back of my eyelids, brighter than everything. I didn't sleep for a year. Then, my mama returned to the World."

Faruq was about to offer condolences, but stopped himself, remembering Odo's relationship with death.

"I won't lie to you, scholar—that hurt me. She was the only family I had. But the night she died, Vutu finally let me fall asleep. I dreamed of Vutu and the World, the ten original Tintan, their fall. I could see the ten Tintan, giant streaks of light in colors you ain't even seen before, scholar. I saw them fall, I saw them shatter, and I felt the shards of them hit my eyes, not blinding me but awakening me. I felt them burrow into me like worms. When I woke up, I was Odo. I began hipping people, I made friends. My friends began hipping people too. And so on. Like the nameless god, our movement never had a name, and so we are called the nameless."

"Why did you change your name to Odo?" Because of his research into the court case, Faruq knew Odo's given name, but he was careful never to deadname him.

"I didn't. I was reborn as Odo. I told you, I woke and knew that I was Odo and Odo meant me. The old name, it's dead, scholar. No use resurrecting it. Had nothing to do with me, anyway."

"I can't help but notice that your birthday coincides with one of the 3 Rituals."

Odo nodded, sipped his tea. "Fall Day. That's coming up soon, scholar. It's the most auspicious of our holidays, and not because it happens to be the anniversary of this lifetime's birth."

"Then why?"

"Because it's the day when, nine billion years ago, the ten original Tintan fell."

"How do you know that?"

Odo cocked his head. "How else? Vutu told me."

"When did Vutu tell you that?"

Odo sighed, getting exasperated. "You don't get it, scholar.

With Vutu, there is no *when*. That's all distortion. If it makes you feel better, you could say it was when Vutu gave me the 18 Utterances."

"So it wasn't just the Utterances you received?"

"It was everything."

"All right. So, Fall Day is the one with the naked march, right?"

Odo laughed. "Well that sure gets folks' attention, but the procession is really the least of it. The night before Fall Day, Vutu always reveals a powerful mantra to me. Then, we start Fall Day by repeating that mantra one hundred and eight times."

"One hundred and eight—that's an auspicious number in Buddhism, isn't it?"

"And Hinduism. And Jainism. It's also an Achilles number, the number of suitors Penelope had in the *Odyssey*, the exact internal temperature that would make your organs start to fail. Coincidence? Naw. We say the mantra one hundred and eight times because it is an auspicious number however you want to look at it. And then we begin our silent procession. We fast and abstain from labor all day—some people like to go on vision quests or gather in lodges. And then, at midnight, we feast. It's the beginning of our new year."

"Sounds . . . somber."

"That's one way of thinking about it. Actually, scholar, you've been asking about the Hall of the Ewas—we hope to have it finished by Fall Day next year. Then that will be my new home."

"You're going to live there? What will happen to this place?"

"Someone else will take it." Odo laughed again. "What, you think because I live here now this is holy ground or something? That's what I keep trying to tell you, scholar—it's *all* holy. It's all ours." He thought for a moment. "The truth about a black panther, scholar, is that, really, he's either a leopard or a jaguar. So he's either a shape-shifter, or he doesn't exist at all."

Faruq had no idea what that was supposed to mean, but when he asked, Odo only stood, said it would all come to him when the time was right, and took his mug into the kitchen. Faruq stopped the recording and tucked his notes away, wondering whether Odo was the shape-shifter or the specter.

Faruq was not really surprised to open his bedroom door at three in the morning and find Minh-An there.

"Baby duty?" he asked.

Minh-An simply led him out the front door. When they got to what Faruq had begun to think of as the foaling stable, Gabe took them to Ursula, an imposing tricolor mare whose water broke within ten minutes of their arrival. Ursula exuded a preternatural calm as her foal's legs protruded from her backside. Like her mother, the filly had white legs, a black tail and mane, and a white spot across her back. Robust and full of life, she stumbled up onto her legs and found her mother's teat within only a few minutes. Gabe came in just as Minh-An was inspecting Ursula's placenta. This time he was accompanied by the same pale, androgynous kid Faruq had met before—Liam—who looked half awake.

"Maeve is up and pacing," Gabe said. "Looks like we're getting two tonight."

Maeve, a sleek piebald who was in the stall next to Ursula's, was restless, but nevertheless took her time. Faruq fought to keep his eyes open as she paced her stall, nibbled hay, and alternated between standing and lying down. Her water finally broke after she agitatedly rolled from her side to her stomach and back again, and she groaned through her pushes, looking bewildered and a little indignant when her colt emerged, black with a bright white blotch that spread all along his back, his rump, and most of his neck. He was tall, gangly, notably bigger than Ursula's filly.

Faruq was so tired he could've curled up right there in that stall, but Minh-An was waiting for him in the golf cart, and so together they rode through the dark Forbidden City. Ever since the incident with the TikTok video that had mysteriously vanished, Faruq had, more than ever, begun to feel like the protector of these horses and their offspring. But he also recognized that it tied him to this place, tricked him into being invested in something to do with the nameless.

"Tell me," he said to Minh-An, "if I weren't here, who would be helping you with the horses?"

Minh-An shrugged. "You *are* here."

"I won't always be here. And I haven't always been here."

"There'd be someone else," Minh-An admitted. "Everyone has a place."

When he crawled into bed, his body hurtled so hard toward sleep that his last conscious sensation was the dizziness of a fall.

Faruq went searching for Odo at home, but no one else was there. The house was empty, so Faruq resolved to try to find Thea or Kaya at the theater. They were there, along with a slew of other followers who were all crowded around Odo. He was sermonizing in his strange, intimately conversational way. Faruq drew closer, feeling like he was intruding on a private discussion. Kaya shot him a smile when she saw him, and then turned her attention fully back over to Odo.

"Look now. What I'm saying is, nobody *wants* to be miserable. Nuh-uh. They just lack the Other Sight to relieve their misery. When you hip somebody, you're curing the blind. When you do a sweep, you're curing a *pandemic*. Oh yes.

"A whole lotta the world is diseased. *Deceived*. My, my, my. But y'all are building paradise out here. Yeah. The World in *this* world. Look around you. Look at each *other*. Matter fact, touch each other, go on. Grab the person next to you."

The followers tittered and did as Odo said, seizing each other in tight hugs. Faruq stiffened as he too was embraced by two followers, their arms warm and firm.

"Now stay there," said Odo. "Stay. That person you're holding *is* you. Yes, that's beautiful."

The followers obediently continued to embrace each other in silence. Faruq's face was pressed into the shoulder of a thin man whose stick arms had more strength than Faruq would've guessed on sight. Faruq held back laughter. The two followers holding him were so earnest, but without their foundation of faith, this whole exercise was ridiculous to Faruq. New hands settled on his shoulders. With effort, he turned to look. Odo. The followers released him and Odo pulled him out of their arms like he was saving him from quicksand.

"Well, scholar," he said, looking into Faruq's eyes, keeping hands on him. For a long moment, he didn't say anything more. Then, "I think you ought to join the procession. For Fall Day. Yeah. How 'bout it, scholar?"

Faruq was taken aback. In many ways, because Fall Day was such an important holiday, this invitation was even more intimate than Odo asking Faruq to stay with him. "Oh—wow. Honestly, I don't know if I'd be up to getting naked in front of, well, everyone."

Odo only smiled, his eyes crinkling at the corners. "You don't *have* to strip. Think about it, scholar." And he walked off, leaving the theater.

Faruq was a bit off-balance, like his blood sugar was low. He closed his eyes for a moment. When he opened them again, it was to Kaya and Thea.

"Faruq," Kaya said in a near whisper, "Odo asked you to be in the Fall Day procession? That's a crazy honor."

"Only the most beautiful," Thea agreed.

"Yeah," said Faruq. "I'm not sure. I guess I'll think about it."

Kaya nodded. "He sees something in you," she said. "That's a special thing."

Faruq shrugged, uncomfortable. "Hey," he said, "that whole bit about this being the World, *in* the world—why not just have the entire following live here? Is it some kind of privilege to get to the Forbidden City? What happens when people leave?"

"It's a choice," said Thea. "The Forbidden City is a powerful place, but no one *has* to live here."

"I see. And what about what happens when people leave the nameless?"

Kaya and Thea looked at each other and burst into laughter. "Who would leave?"

Odo instructed Minh-An to take Faruq to see the collection that was being curated for the Hall of the Ewas, and so the next morning, after Faruq had completed a mediocre run, he followed Minh-An into the gallery off Ewa Park, where there was a cellar full of treasure—original paintings, priceless antiques, stacks upon stacks of rare books in innumerable languages.

He'd been expecting Minh-An to act as a tour guide, or at least a kind of docent, but instead she left him there with the archivist, an older man who introduced himself to Faruq as Chol. Like the children's library, there seemed to be no real order to the collection—bland landscapes mixed in among works he recognized, which must be worth thousands.

"This is really something," said Faruq. "What's the plan, exactly? Will this be open to the public?"

Chol nodded. "It'll be like a museum. Without all the stuffiness." He laughed.

"What's that?" Faruq asked, pointing to what looked like the door to a vault.

"That's the fridge," said Chol. "That's where we keep the super old and fragile stuff. Wanna see?"

"Definitely."

Chol let Faruq in. It wasn't really a refrigerator, but a chilled room containing only a long table, upon which acid-free boxes were strewn, and a sink. The walls were lined with glass-covered shelves.

"Don't we need gloves or something?" Faruq asked.

"Nope—we just need to wash our hands."

After they'd done so—Faruq was mildly surprised to see they were using Dial soap, instead of something made by the nameless—Chol unlocked one of the glass shelves and carefully took down a pile of old books for Faruq to look through. He was almost afraid to touch them.

"So," he said, "have you always been an archivist?"

Chol sat down at the long table and spread his fingers across the lid of one of the boxes. "I was an art appraiser, once upon a time. Hated the art world. Full of pretentious snakes. But now," he spread an arm out to the side, "I get to use my so-called expertise for something much more beautiful."

Faruq joined Chol at the table. "What brought you to the nameless?"

"Odo did." Chol smiled. "Odo found me because I met the love of my life."

"Do you mind if I record you?" Faruq asked.

Chol waved a hand permissively and then began to tell his story. "I grew up a good little Jewish boy in Brooklyn. Got good grades, went to the college my parents told me to go to. But I made sure to never date. Because I knew I'd never be able to make myself marry the nice Jewish girl my parents wanted for me.

"Then I met Jacob. Met him at a work thing and I fell. Hard. We moved in together two months after we met. My parents disowned me. But we were crazy happy. We'd throw these big parties. We had all these loud, beautiful friends. This was the eighties.

"Our friends started getting sick. You heard about it first, and it seemed so far away. Terrible, but young people never expect tragedy to spread to them. But then it started getting people close to us, and it was like this terrible tsunami from hell. You know, something unstoppable and brutally swift, something that would reshape landscapes.

"These *young*, beautiful friends of ours were dying, emaciated and covered in sores. Sometimes their families wouldn't let us in to say goodbye. Sometimes their families wouldn't come at all.

"Well, Jacob and I were always monogamous. It was weird to a lot of our friends, but we knew it was what would keep us safe. I looked at Jacob one morning and knew—I told him I wanted to spend the rest of my life with him.

"Of course, we couldn't actually get married. Not then. But Jacob had been going to these parties, and he kept talking about this guy named Odo. He wanted me to meet him, said he could get rid of all our pain. So we went. And I met the second greatest love of my life. I wasn't going to get sick, but all that grief might've killed me. Until I met Odo.

"We devoted ourselves to him. He moved into our brownstone. He met our friends and showed them true beauty, unblinded them. In '88, Odo married me and Jacob himself. All our friends, and a big group of followers, were there. It was huge. I'd follow Odo anywhere. Absolutely anywhere."

"What about Jacob?" Faruq searched for the band on Chol's left finger. "Is he here too?"

"Oh, yes," said Chol. "He's one of the collectors—travels a lot. But our home is here."

Faruq nodded. "That's amazing. I have to say, your longevity is inspiring."

Chol chuckled. "Well, we're lucky. In so many ways."

"So you've been with the nameless for a really long time. How has the—movement—changed over the years?"

"Well, Odo hasn't aged a day," Chol laughed. Then he thought for a long moment. "Well, it's certainly larger. We're reaching more people than ever, which is beautiful. And Odo has always been great at maintaining the youthfulness of the movement without alienating his older followers—he keeps us all young. But the main thing is that our mission in service of beauty has expanded—not just art, but advocacy, conservation, charity, you know?"

"All that in the name of creating and preserving beauty?"

"That's right. Utterance number 6."

Faruq gingerly looked through the pile of books Chol had pulled down. Most Faruq had never heard of, or were in languages he didn't understand. But then he froze. A brittle first edition of Allama Iqbal's *Persian Psalms* in the original Urdu. He drew a finger across the cover and looked up to study Chol's face.

"This was my father's favorite poet," he said. "Not many people know him, not here."

Chol's face showed no guile, only unfiltered delight. "Will you look at that."

Faruq drew his mouth into a line, his brow furrowing. The fridge's chill air was beginning to creep under his clothes.

It took him a long time to lose the chill from the archive's fridge after his conversation with Chol, so when Faruq returned to Odo's house in time for dinner, he made his way to his room to change into a warmer sweatshirt. But in a way that was more undeniable than it ever had been, things were not as he'd left them. On the floor by the dresser, his DVD of *Nero* was broken in pieces. His laptop, which had been closed on the dresser, and on top of which he'd put *Nero* this morning, was open. An iridescent crack ran down the center of the screen.

He came forward woodenly. The shards of the DVD shone on the floor, like quicksilver. He swirled a finger on the laptop's touchpad and the screen lit up brightly. The crack shined like a strand of hair in sunlight, and little rainbow lines sprouted from it here and there like buds on a branch.

Faruq found Odo already in the dining room with Minh-An, the two of them seeming to be waiting patiently for him. This infuriated Faruq even more.

"What the hell happened in there?"

"In where, scholar?"

Faruq tried to suck in a deep breath but it ended up being more of a hiss. "In my room? The room *you* invited me to stay in. What the hell happened to my *things*? You're destroying my property now? Are you fucking kidding me?"

Minh-An frowned in disapproval and Odo raised a hand. "Now hold on. If you're going to accuse me of something in my own house, I think you ought to tell me what exactly you're saying I did."

"My laptop is broken," Faruq bit out. "The screen is all fucked up. I found my goddamn DVD of *Nero* on the floor, in *pieces*. If it wasn't you, then I want to know *who* is fucking with my shit, who is trying to fuck with my article, who—"

"Faruq," Odo interrupted. "I didn't touch your things. I haven't been home all day."

"That doesn't quite answer my whole question, does it? Who did it?" Faruq nearly growled.

"Now I wouldn't know that, scholar. But I don't see why anyone would've done that to hurt you. Sounds like an accident. People come through and clean the house every day when I'm not in—could be one of them made a mistake."

"A *mistake*? Someone went out of their way to open my laptop and crack the screen. I don't know about you, but I've never accidentally snapped a DVD into pieces. I don't see how there's been a *mistake* here."

"You really need to calm down," said Minh-An.

"Faruq," said Odo, cutting Minh-An off, "we'll get you a new computer. That's nothing but a thing."

"A new compu—" Faruq scoffed in disbelief. "I don't want a new computer. I want to know who fucked with my *property*."

Minh-An rolled her eyes, but before Faruq could say anything to her, Odo spoke up again. "And what are you going to do? Punish them? Break some of their—*property*?"

Faruq looked up at the ceiling, laughed. He put his hands on his hips like he sometimes did after finishing a particularly strenuous run. He brought his gaze back down to Odo. Blood swarmed in his fingertips as he pointed. "You. You do not fool me. You are a dangerous man."

Odo sat back in his chair, something cold falling down like a stage curtain behind his eyes. Ah yes, Faruq had seen glimpses of this Odo before. But he believed this was a mask like all the others. It did not scare him. It would not.

"Dangerous, am I? Nah, scholar, *you* are the one who's dangerous. Why? Because you don't know what the fuck you are. Ain't nothing scarier than a man who ain't got any idea of himself. That computer ain't you. That—*DVD*—ain't you. But here you are, eyeing me like someone done broke *you* into pieces. Get ahold of yourself, boy. Storming in here like you think you about to slay a dragon. I'm not afraid of you. I used to *be* you."

"Can you accept the possibility that it really was just an accident?" Minh-An asked.

"Explain to me how this could be accidental. If it were an accident, wouldn't somebody have confessed? Fucking apologized? Or is that one of your fucking Utterances?"

Faruq didn't take his eyes off Odo as he addressed Minh-An. How much of this bridge did he want to burn? Was he ready to leave the Forbidden City right now? He hated to admit it to himself, but no, he wasn't. There was still more he wanted to learn.

And Odo saw it. Faruq saw him see it. "Come on and sit down, scholar," Odo said. "We'll find out what happened. Don't go feral on me. Have something to eat."

But Faruq didn't break his stare. It took him several breaths, but he calmed his angrily beating heart. He had to remember that he was here for the story. Maybe he'd gotten too attached, too immersed. He'd lost his distance—he had to remember that he was the outsider. They were testing him. He'd been tested before. He couldn't let it get to him. Carefully, he coaxed the tension out of his face, out of his shoulders.

He turned his attention to Minh-An, watched as she forced a forkful of succotash into her mouth. He felt her revulsion as though it were his own. He wondered if she was in pain, how she managed it. Drugs, pharmaceutical and otherwise, were openly available in the Forbidden City, and yet Minh-An seemed to be opting out. He hadn't so much as seen her smoke a joint. Something like guilt arose. He'd lost his composure and forgotten that, despite the masks they gave themselves, he was talking to an aging narcissist and a woman dying of cancer who was so caught up in zealotry that she wouldn't even ease her own pain. If there was anyone in control here, it was Faruq.

He took a deep breath, trying to settle his own anger. He left dinner without having eaten a bite.

. . .

Faruq made his way down to the stables to check on the foals the next morning. He was tired, in need of grounding. He'd become invested in these horses, felt not only responsible for the stalky newborns, but somehow reassured by them. They were a refuge to him. The foals and their mothers were all together, the mothers snuffling through the grass, tails switching, and the foals playing with each other.

Gabe was out there with them, overseeing everything while eating a banana. He nodded amiably at Faruq.

"Hello, Asher," Faruq said, holding his hand out to the black-headed colt.

"Oh no," said Gabe with his mouth full. "That's Enzo. Maeve's baby. Asher is over there." Gabe pointed to the other black-headed colt.

Faruq narrowed his eyes. "You sure? This one's bigger. Wouldn't Asher be the bigger one, since he's older?"

Gabe laughed indulgently. "Asher is taking a little longer to come up to size. He was born a little weaker—you remember."

Of course he remembered. How could he forget? He had forced his own breath into that black nostril. Asher was white with black patches. The younger colt—Enzo—was black with a large, reaching white blotch. Faruq wasn't quite sure how he could tell the difference, but he could. The colt currently trying to nibble at the hair on his legs was Asher, not Enzo.

"Are you sure?" he asked again. "I'm positive this is Asher. They look similar, but I can tell the difference."

Gabe offered the rest of his banana to Winnie, who ate it peel and all. "You're not seeing straight, Faruq. Don't worry about it—I used to get confused too."

Faruq narrowed his eyes. "What do you mean, I'm not seeing straight?"

Gabe shrugged. "Foals," he chuckled. "They all kinda look alike, right?"

Faruq thought of the photos that had disappeared from his camera. Maybe not the malfunction he'd convinced himself to believe it was.

"I don't think I'm confused, Gabe." Nothing else had disappeared from that camera. Not since the horses. "Hey, you ever touch my camera?"

Gabe drew his eyebrows toward each other, all concern and innocence. "I'm not sure what you mean, Faruq." He smiled congenially. "Why don't you try some of that stuff you got from the greenhouse? You know? Maybe it'll help you relax, see things straight."

It should have alarmed Faruq that Gabe knew about the plant, but it only annoyed him. No secrets among the nameless. Irritated anew, Faruq left the stables on his bike. On the ride, he caught a quick glimpse of the Deep in some circular formation. He biked all the way back to Odo's house, thinking he might actually crawl back into bed for a while. But Odo was home, the dining table laden with food—eggs, bacon, sautéed vegetables, fruit, freshly baked breakfast pastries. Minh-An was there as well, along with, Faruq was shocked to see, Aeschylus and Clover. They grinned wide, each of them pulling Faruq into a tight embrace.

"Hello there, beautiful stranger," said Clover.

"I wasn't sure if I'd see you guys again," said Faruq. He was relieved to see them. Immensely happy, actually.

"Couldn't miss Fall Day," said Aeschylus.

"Are you going to join in, Faruq?" asked Clover.

Faruq smiled. He was the one with the control, he reminded himself. "I will, actually," he said, watching Odo from the corner of his eye. Odo's mask was firmly in place—he didn't react. "I'll do the meditation with everyone, and the fast. I'll even stay up for the feast. But I'll leave the procession to you guys."

"As you like it, scholar," Odo said, and Clover and Aeschylus nodded.

"Where have you been all morning, scholar? I thought you were sleeping, but then I went to get you to surprise you with these two, and you were gone."

"I went down to the stables," said Faruq, raising an eyebrow. He had no doubt Odo already knew how his time at the stables had gone. "I was saying hello to that little colt I revived, and Gabe absolutely *insisted* it was another colt."

Aeschylus chuckled, shaking his head.

Odo waved a hand. "It's both, it's neither. What's it matter?"

"Well, I don't like feeling crazy."

"Get stripped, Faruq," intoned Clover.

He gritted his teeth and looked to Odo. "You ever find out what happened to my computer?"

Odo waved a hand in the air again. "Ah, yeah. Like I said, it was just an accident. They were just trying to clean and dropped your laptop. Opened it to see if it was okay, and the CD slipped off."

Faruq narrowed his eyes. "Who is 'they'?"

"Liam. Good kid. Didn't mean to do it. I talked to him about being more careful."

"Liam," said Faruq. Not a particularly sinister figure. "Think he'd mind talking to me about it?"

"Sure, sure. Now, scholar, eat up. We begin fasting at midnight."

"Well, I've had my hands all over mysterious, identity-swapping horses," he said archly. "Let me go freshen up."

Faruq retreated to his suite, closed the door behind him. He went into the bathroom and washed his hands, splashed cool water onto his face. He braced his hands against the sink and closed his eyes, let the water drip from his nose and beard, breathed deep. When he emerged from the bathroom, he noticed that there was something on the dresser. He drew close. The Allama Iqbal book. And beneath it, the drawer slightly open, when he was sure he'd shut it. A glimpse of turquoise silk inside when he was sure he'd left that scarf in his bag.

The urge to take the book and hurl it across the room, to scream, to leave the Forbidden City and scrap the whole article, the whole book, was so strong, he had to ward it off with motion. He shook his hands as though trying to shake water off of them.

He took another deep breath. And another. He'd learned from his parents—losing it in the face of gaslighting never worked. He remembered his mother, throwing things at his father while his father stood seething, the two of them unable to understand each other. And in the end, it had been all too easy to say his mother was crazy. That she was possessed. He couldn't let them drive him crazy. He went out to join breakfast. But Odo was standing in the dining room, looking serene as Aeschylus and Clover watched him with nauseating wonder in their eyes.

"Scholar," he said. "Vutu has given me the mantra."

Both Aeschylus and Clover gasped.

"*Nothing is lost, only returned.*" Odo smiled serenely. "You folks'll have to excuse me. I need to retire until tonight, prepare."

He left them all in the dining room. Clover and Aeschylus were holding hands, real tears in their eyes. Faruq sat, lips tight. Furiously, he began to shovel food into his mouth, not bothering with the plate set before him. He was alone with Aeschylus and Clover at the table, Odo having slipped, once again, out of his grip.

Faruq was sweating. The house of the nameless was full of bodies, full of noise. People screamed, moaned, sang, cried—all exclamation. Faruq was himself silent, though he had joined in on the mantra. *Nothing is lost, only returned.* Having said it all 108 times, Faruq's mouth was uncomfortably dry. Part of him envied the trance it seemed to send the followers into; he felt only tired, hungry, foolish. Bodies pressed in on either side of him. It was a relief to step outside. The air was warm, but not close, as it had been inside the house of the nameless. And there was silence now as the procession began.

Faruq followed the direction of the crowd as people began to move. They were walking south, down toward the main road out of the Forbidden City. Everyone's footsteps on the ground made a soft, rolling thunder. People began to strip; a man in front of Faruq unbuckled his pants, a woman right next to him took off her shirt, baring her breasts. Faruq stuffed his hands into his pockets.

The pace was slow, the mood somber. Other followers watched wordlessly from the sidelines, from their yards and front porches. From the sides of his eyes, Faruq could see more and more flesh. There was no way in hell he was getting naked, but being clothed was beginning to make him feel out of place, awkwardly visible. He scanned the crowd for anyone who might be remaining clothed, like him. Odo had told him that the nudity was entirely voluntary. But everyone was in some state of undress. He caught sight of Thea, who was fully naked now. He looked away.

There were beautiful bodies on display everywhere. But it was strangely asexual; Faruq felt off-balance, like he was on the brink of stumbling, and only the bare bodies marching next to him protected him from a fall. He'd sworn he wouldn't join the procession, but he had simply been swept into it, and now it felt as though the crowd was moving him along whether he wanted it or not. Robbed of his own agency. It was eerie. No one had told him where they were walking to, or how long the procession would last. By his estimate, they'd been walking for about ninety minutes before they reached the fruit, vegetable, and herb gardens, where they stopped, the followers standing close together. In silent unison, they all looked up, staring for several silent breaths. Faruq looked up too. Nothing but blank sky.

Instagram Post #384

@thenamelessmvmnt: A procession of yellow-clad follow-ers, reverence on their healthily glowing faces. They are mostly ambiguous—racially, sexually. They have begun to disrobe—a sculpted arm, chiseled abs, hint of a breast—all beautiful, young, highlighted in golden summer sun.

#FallDay #stripping #barethesoul

107,898 likes | 4,382 comments

Nero

FADE IN:*

Footage of Will Roy preaching to his congregation,
gesturing emphatically from his pulpit; he pauses every
once in a while to dab sweat from his face with a white
cloth.

CROSS CUT:

Footage of the nameless Bacchanal ritual; followers are
gathered together, their faces uniformly solemn.

CROSS CUT:

Roy steps down from his pulpit and begins to walk
through the pews, congregants crying and nodding along
with his words, reaching out to clasp his hands in
theirs.

CROSS CUT:

The camera whip-pans to reveal Odo, who is speaking to
his followers and holding up both hands. He gestures to
something out of frame, and one of the followers
nearest him raises his hands up.

CROSS CUT:

Roy places his fingertips on a congregant's forehead,
closes his eyes, and bows his head. The congregant
begins to sob.

CROSS CUT:

The followers of the nameless are brandishing homemade
signs: BANISH DISTORTION; OPEN YOUR EYES AND SEE; KEEP THIS
WORLD BEAUTIFUL.

CROSS CUT:

Roy brandishing his Bible and shouting in the midst of
his congregation.

CROSS CUT:

The camera whip-pans to Odo, and then zooms in on him
as he smiles directly at the camera.

FADE TO BLACK.

---

* Music: Hymn of the Cherubim (Tchaikovsky)

INT. GREENHOUSE—MED. SHOT—MINH-AN*

              MINH-AN
Things took an uglier turn after the race
riot. Odo was hurt. He couldn't even be angry
anymore. He just—stopped talking about it for
a while. This man fought a pointless war for
this country, a war that tore *my* home country
apart. And these people falsely accuse him of
something twisted and distorted. (snorts)

We turned to our rituals, our guidelines for
making the world more beautiful. Bacchanal,
like pretty much all of our 3 Rituals—our
high holidays—is misunderstood.

December 21st. It's a day for confronting
and fighting against distortion, things that
obstruct our ability to see beauty. That
year, it was more important than ever to
fight the distortion around us.

Typically, for Bacchanal, we do sweeps,
where we try to hip people to Odo and our
philosophy, we give to the needy, and we
protest anything that promotes distortion. A
lot of us use it as an opportunity for
activism. Think protesting unethical
conglomerates that are polluting local
rivers and lakes. Things like that.

              PRODUCER (O.S.)
But some of these Bacchanal protests have
been controversial, haven't they?

              MINH-AN
(scoffs) Controversial to who?

Minh-An shrugs.

              PRODUCER (O.S.)
Well, in 2011 your followers picketed
several vigils being held for the deadly

———————————
* Silence.

Philippine tsunami because, quote, 'mourning
death is distortion.'

Same thing with Hurricane Palmer in 2012.
Then there are your protests of certain
megachurches and prominent religious figures
that, again, quote, 'promote an agenda of
distortion.'

Minh-An shifts in her seat, scratches her nose.

> MINH-AN
> (laughs) Are you asking Will Roy about his
> church's terrorizing Planned Parenthood
> locations across Texas? How about them
> chanting 'God's wrath is glorious' at vigils
> for the Baton Rouge nightclub shooting in
> 2016? Calling Black Lives Matter a terrorist
> organization made up of thugs?

Shakes her head.

> MINH-AN
> Look, what individual followers decide to
> confront for Bacchanal is *their*
> responsibility, not Odo's, or mine, or
> anybody else's. They're exercising their
> right to freedom of speech. A lot of our
> Bacchanal confrontations have actually led
> to real positive change, like that time we
> stopped some greedy corporation from eating
> up a historic block in Harlem.
>
> Honestly, what people get most hung
> up on for Bacchanal is the fact that it
> ends in 'sacrifice.' People think we're
> setting virgins on fire or something.
> (laughs)
>
> It's not all that different from the kinds
> of sacrifices Catholics make for Lent. Some
> people give up chocolate, some people
> practice mortification. Nobody's hurting
> anybody else.

The year that all that stuff with Sue Mills
happened, a group of followers in Burning
Hill decided to protest this local oil and
gas company for Bacchanal.[*]

INSERT—IMAGE

Photo of the Buchanan Oil & Gas office building,
c. 2019. SLOW PAN.

      MINH-AN
Turns out, the company had ties to a new
pipeline out in Houston, and had
infrastructure in place to dump their toxic
shit in Black and brown communities. Might
have even been Sue who told us about it.

BACK TO SCENE

Minh-An smirks.

      MINH-AN
As it happened, the owner of that company
was one of Will Roy's people.

Will Roy and his church took it personally.

                        FADE TO BLACK.

INT. CWE NAVE—MED. SHOT—WILL ROY

      WILL ROY
'Let no man deceive you, for the day will
not come unless the rebellion comes first,
and the man of lawlessness is revealed, the
son of perdition.' Thessalonians.

CLOSEUP—WILL ROY'S EYES

Roy's gaze is unwavering.

---

  * Music: fade in, Pièces Froides—Airs à Faire Fuir
(Satie)

                    WILL ROY
        It's plain as day: Odo *is* the antichrist.

MED. SHOT—WILL ROY

                    WILL ROY
        These people are dangerous. Not only
        will they lead your soul straight to hell,
        but they got the audacity to be bragging
        about human sacrifice.

        No one was listening to us, not even
        after what they did to Sue Mills and her
        family. Protesting Abe Buchanan's business,
        which he built up from nothing, was a
        cakewalk next to what these people were
        trying to do.

        It was clear the law wasn't going to help
        us. We did what needed to be done to protect
        our own.

INSERT—IMAGE*

Photo of a nameless trailer with SATAN LOVERS spray-
painted on the side. SLOW PAN.

                    MINH-AN
        Will Roy and his church started a campaign
        of harassment. Very Christian of them.
        (sardonic laugh)

                                        DISSOLVE TO:
Photo of broken glass outside a motel room occupied by
followers of the nameless. SLOW PAN.

                    MINH-AN
        It started with harassing phone calls. We'd
        pick up and there'd be no one there. Or
        someone would scream *'devil worshippers'* as
        loud as they could and hang up.

_____

* Music: Me and the Devil Blues (Robert Johnson)

DISSOLVE TO:

Photo of Odo holding up a flyer next to his face. The flyer
features a closeup of his face, over which someone has
drawn devil's horns and written, ANTICHRIST. SLOW PAN.

> MINH-AN
> They'd scrawl things on our cars, break
> windows, dump trash on our property, you
> name it. All this over a little protest
> that lasted a day. A lot of it was barely
> concealed racism. 'Forsake the Black One';
> 'Cursed be Canaan.'

DISSOLVE TO:

Photo of the side of a building, which has been
plastered with the same flyer featuring the photo of
Odo. SLOW PAN.

> MINH-AN
> It was annoying, but it could mostly be
> ignored. I mean, they were accusing us of
> downright crazy stuff—no one's doing any *live*
> sacrifices. And Christians self-flagellate all
> the time. Whatever. But then the church began
> using its ties in the community to stonewall
> our attempts to expand.

DISSOLVE TO:

Photo of Odo, arms crossed and unsmiling. SLOW PAN.

> MINH-AN
> And then there was the billboard.

DISSOLVE TO:

Photo of Burning Hill billboard, which features an
extreme closeup of Odo's eyes and red block text, which
reads: Are you going to Heaven or Hell? No man can
serve 2 masters! Do not be deceived by the Antichrist!
Rebuke the Dark One—Your only salvation is in JESUS!
ZOOM.*

FADE TO BLACK.

---

* Zoom in until song ends.

INT. GREENHOUSE—MED. SHOT—MINH-AN

>   MINH-AN
> Something had to be done.

Minh-An holds up a newspaper. Heading: "The Herald
Angel"; Subheading: "Christ the Word Evangelical."

>   MINH-AN
> (reading from newspaper) 'The leader
> of this cult, who calls himself "Odo,"
> claims that he only wants to spread beauty
> in this world. But like his false name,
> almost everything about this dangerous cult
> leader is a lie. His cult promotes death
> and depravity, encouraging its members to
> participate in orgies and other sexual
> abominations, sabotage small businesses,
> self-mutilate, and commit sacrifices.
> Perhaps the most offensive of Odo's lies is
> his claim to have served this country in
> the Vietnam War, going so far as to suggest
> he earned a Bronze Star and a Purple
> Heart . . . He favors wealthy followers
> so that he can embezzle their donations
> and estates, and harasses and stalks those
> that question his authority or leave his
> cult. His rule is totalitarian and
> satanic.'

Minh-An lets the newspaper fall to the floor, looks
directly into the camera.

>   PRODUCER (O.S.)
> And what was Odo's response to all this?

>   MINH-AN
> (mirthless laugh)

INSERT—FOOTAGE

Cell phone footage of Odo talking emphatically,
angrily, surrounded by rapt followers.

              ODO (FROM FOOTAGE)
. . . worshippers of little old words
written by little old men. If that's not
distortion, well, I don't know *what* is.
Distortion makes the world ugly. And Vutu
don't like ugly. My, my, my. Distortion is
the most vile sin. The *only* sin.

                                  CROSS CUT:*

Cell phone footage of nameless followers picketing
outside Christ the Word Evangelical. Signs read: CORRECT
DISTORTION; NO TO INTOLERANCE & RACISM; JESUS WOULDN'T
LIBEL; DEFAMATION IS DISTORTION; IF THY EYE DISTORT THEE,
PLUCK IT OUT.

                                  CROSS CUT:

Footage of nameless followers walking down Burning
Hill's Main Street, holding hands, laughing and
singing.

                                  CROSS CUT:

Footage of several Black followers of the nameless
outside of Christ the Word Evangelical, their heads
bowed and fists raised.

              MINH-AN
You *don't* want to get on his bad side.

                                  DISSOLVE TO:

INT. CWE NAVE—MED. SHOT—WILL ROY

Roy crosses his arms, rolls his eyes, sighs.

              WILL ROY
Look, as the leader of a flock and a servant
of God, I can't just stay still in the face
of the antichrist. It's my job to get a rise
out of Satan—the Devil can only hide his
horns for so long. And when he's good and
agitated . . . well.

---

* Music: Evil (Howlin' Wolf)

                                    DISSOLVE TO:

INT. GREENHOUSE—MED. SHOT—MINH-AN

                    MINH-AN
          Will Roy and his sheep underestimated us. We
          have 1.6 *million* followers on Instagram. 850
          thousand followers on TikTok. Not to mention
          our presence on Twitter and YouTube.

          We started by posting our truth about Will
          Roy and his church's intolerance,
          fanaticism, racism, and corruption. The
          false allegations. People were outraged. It
          went viral. Even non-followers were talking
          about it.

          But then, we started learning that the roots
          were even more rotten than we thought. The
          difference between what Will Roy did and
          what we did? Everything *we* said was the
          truth.

INSERT—IMAGE

Blog post: "Guns, Conversion Therapy & Arranged
Marriages: The Secret Sins of Christ the Word
Evangelical."

                                    DISSOLVE TO:
Twitter post: "Yall Christ the Word calling everyone a
cult is the pot calling the kettle black, I grew up in
Burning Hill and everyone there knows they run like the
mob. A THREAD . . ."

                                    DISSOLVE TO:
YouTube video: "I was a teenage bride in Christ the
Word Evangelical."

                                    DISSOLVE TO:
Slate article: "I Was a Member of Christ the Word
Evangelical. Here's Why I Left."

                                        DISSOLVE TO:

Austin American-Statesman article: "Christ the Word
Evangelical Leadership Accused of Infidelity, Greed &
Cover-Ups."

                                        DISSOLVE TO:

Houston Chronicle article: "Ernest Roy, Founder of
Christ the Word Evangelical, Tried to Resurrect Slavery
in 1905."

                                        DISSOLVE TO:

Los Angeles Times article: "Three Women Allege Sexual
Misconduct from Christ the Word Evangelical Elders."

                                        DISSOLVE TO:

The Washington Post article: "Troubled Waters: Christ
the Word Evangelical Tries to Quell a Tidal Wave of
Dirty Laundry."

                                        DISSOLVE TO:

New York Times article: "Roy's Last Stand:
Controversial Pastor Squares Off with Nameless
Movement."

                                        FADE TO BLACK.

                                        FADE IN:

INSERT—FOOTAGE

Nameless aerial footage of the plot of land in Burning
Hill, TX.[*]

                ODO (NAMELESS AUDIO RECORDING)
            Vutu *commands* us to correct distortion.
            That's right. Utterance 16.[†]

            Beauty is not rare. But it *is* precious. It
            is abundant and it is sacred. It's there for
            the seeing. Oh yes, it's there for the

   _____

   *   Cello drone in G
   †   Cello drone in A

living. Don't you think you ought to live in
beauty? Answer me.

The crowd murmurs in agreement.*

       ODO (NAMELESS AUDIO RECORDING)
Then you got to be free of distortion. Open
your eyes. You have got to be free.

                    FADE TO BLACK.†

                         FADE IN:‡

INT. CWE NAVE—MED. SHOT—WILL ROY

Roy's arms are crossed, his expression defiant.§

       WILL ROY
It was 2:30 in the afternoon when I got
served. I remember that because the missus
and I had just sat down to a big family
lunch with the kids and the grandkids.

Knew the boy doing the serving too. He
apologized to me as he handed over them
papers. I tell him, 'It's all right. Don't
worry.'

I wasn't surprised. The Lord told me to
expect as much. And I was ready for it. The
battle between good and evil can happen
anywhere, even a courtroom.

1 John 3:4. 'He who makes a practice of
sinning also practices lawlessness.'

                    FADE TO BLACK.

---

* Cello drone in B♭ (soft)
† Cello drone in E♭ (soft)
‡ Violin joins cello at A♭
§ Silence.

before: 1970

TO SOME OF the soldiers, returning to the bush after the holiday stand-down was a demented relief. But to others, it scorched the indignities of this lost year into them even more hotly. The latter group burned as they humped; their footsteps left brands on the earth, not seen, but felt, sowed.

They were humping, and none of them knew exactly what for. This was, they were told, friendly territory. A village squatted alongside the rice paddies and its inhabitants waved as the soldiers passed, their hands dead and their eyes full of something with teeth. They waved as though cursed to do so.

Most of the soldiers waved back at the villagers as a matter of reflex, but one man, a man on fire, felt bile rise at the sight of their dead fish hands, their eyes with fangs.

. . . ought to blast em all, fuckin gooks, ought to smoke each and every one of em right fuckin here torch this shithole, torch this whole fuckin country, ought to blast em like we did the Japs for all I fuckin care, smoke all these stinkin motherfuckers . . .

This started as a madman's mumble and then grew into a fevered monologue that pulsed out waves of tension. The air shimmered with barely repressed violence. It made you hot, made your pack heavier, made your jungle rot weep.

. . . every goddamn one of em don't give a fuck just look at em motherfuckin creeps every one I don't see why we don't just smoke all these dinks and be done with it . . .

Silk could take the man's rant for a while, but then it began to irritate a new thing in him. He had never been much of a religious man. He had never really felt what the sweating women and the shouting men in his mother's church had felt, and that had always been all right with him. But ever since Preach died, God—or something—had gotten into him. He felt he was looking at the world the way Preach saw things now, as though a little corner of Preach's spirit had burrowed into him as he'd laid hands on his friend's irrevocably still body. Yeah. Now he felt it, this God.

. . . kill em before they kill us, that's what I say just be done with it be done with the whole fuckin thing I know I've had it, *had* it motherfuckers . . .

Silk grabbed the mumbling man by the scruff of the neck and jerked him into his body as though about to invoke the Holy Spirit into him.

Cut it out, you hear me? Shut up before I really give you something to bitch about.

Silk shook the man a little and then pushed him down into the murky water of the rice paddies. When Silk pulled the soldier back up, the man was gasping and silent. Re-created. He didn't speak again. The villagers stopped their waving and only watched, still as gravestones.

No one would say it aloud, but they'd all found the friendly village eerie, and when it was behind them, they were glad. Bigger, however, was infected with a terror so potent it was making him ill. His blood was so hot it threw a heated film over his vision. When they were allowed to rest, about a mile or so outside the village, Bigger squatted unsteadily, opting not to reach for his C-rations because he was sure anything he tried to hold in his hands would fall from them immediately.

Crazy Horse came over to plop down next to him and Silk followed. Crazy Horse took out a smoke, pinched some of the tobacco out of it, and sprinkled it onto the ground.

For Preach.

Silk declined Crazy Horse's offer of a smoke, smiled a secret, knowing smile.

Preach is still with us.

Bigger thought he felt a tremor in the ground, but realized it was coming from him. His exhausted muscles thrummed as he sat. He tried to blink the heat out of his eyes, shifted.

I've been dreaming about him. Preach. Been having some crazy dreams.

Crazy Horse expelled bitter smoke. He smirked at Bigger.

That right, brother?

Yeah. Had one where Preach was watching me sleep, and then I was above my own body, watching me sleep too. And then I could see all of you sleeping, and I wasn't myself anymore. I was a tiger. And I was hungry.

Silk, who had taken on some of Preach's affection for the kid, nodded at Bigger. Silk didn't know if he could help the kid, but he knew he could listen to him.

What'd you do?

That's just the thing. I woke up and my stomach was going on like I haven't eaten in a week.

Silk looked Bigger up and down.

Have you eaten in a week? You looking peaked, man.

Before Bigger could reply, Brother Ned came over and joined them. Despite the ever-present heat and all the humping, he looked fresh-faced. Nearly jovial. Crazy Horse narrowed his eyes at him.

What's got you all pepped up, cracker?

Brother Ned grinned in the face of Crazy Horse's hostility. At this point, they all knew it was vestigial.

Well, well, well. Know what it looks like? Looks like I'm the shortest man here, that's what it looks like. I'm going to see my Missy *real* soon.

Silk smirked.

Your Missy?

Yessir. My Missy. I'm going to get that girl to marry me.

Crazy Horse put out his cigarette and spat.

Brother gets *one* picture and thinks he's nabbed her. Damn whitey.

You called me *brother*, brother. And anyway, you'll see. Bet we'll be married by the time you get back.

Bigger's muscles were still thrumming, and now, so was his

head. He had the most time left out of any of these men. What was he going to do when he was the last one here, being poisoned by his own terror? He swallowed, and his throat seemed to stick to itself.

And how do you expect to do that? Marry a Black girl?

Brother Ned looked thoughtful for a minute and then smiled.

We'll go to Philly. I've got some family in Philadelphia. I think we'll be all right there.

Just a few yards away, the good-ol-boy overheard Brother Ned's conversation and grimaced. His injury, as it turned out, wasn't enough to keep him out of the bushes—the tip of his nose was bulbous, and the bruises branching out to underneath his eyes were only just fading into washed-out brown. Aside from whistling in his sleep, he could breathe, and it didn't hurt so much anymore to bend over or touch his nose. Even still, he didn't feel like baiting the darkies and that race traitor. Not out here. He stood up and walked out toward the trees to take a piss. He hummed as he went—*Walkin in the sunshine, sing a little sunshine song; Put a smile upon your face as if there's nothing wrong.*

The Bouncing Betty clicked under his boot, and he closed his eyes, hoping not to feel much. He thought of Mama, of his sister and the twins. He thought of Shirlene, little Junior, who had yet to see his face. He thought of how he hadn't had enough time to fix the world up right, make sure everything was okay, so that Junior never had to feel afraid, could always feel like a man. All this shot through him in the space of a second and by the time he opened his eyes, he still wasn't dead. He blinked.

Everyone had heard the click. It had been as loud as a gunshot. And when the explosion they'd all been bracing themselves for didn't come, it was somehow even more terrible. They were as quiet as stalking tigers. Quiet as the rabbit who senses death.

It was Bo Weevil who saw it, figured it out first. The good-ol-boy's foot had tripped the Bouncing Betty partially, but his weight was holding the igniter in place, keeping it from fully activating. Bo Weevil stepped carefully forward, scanning the ground, holding his hands out in front of him.

Don't. Move. A. Muscle.

He glanced indeterminately over his shoulder.

I think I can get him out of this. Don't you move.

The good-ol-boy pressed his lips into a thin line to show he understood. His vision swirled. He fought to breathe slowly through his half-healed nose.

For Bigger, time has stopped. Two futures roll out before him like carpets—one in which the good-ol-boy lives, and one in which he dies. If Bigger moves, his foot might touch the corner of one of these carpets, and he'd select that path. He too must not move a muscle. His vision is filmed in red. He does not blink.

Bo Weevil searches delicately for something heavy, anything that can replace the pressure of the good-ol-boy's foot. He ordered the good-ol-boy not to move, and everyone is obeying, watching. But Crazy Horse can't let a brother work alone. He'd been admiring the good-ol-boy's motionlessness, but now he silently, cautiously, joins Bo Weevil's hunt.

Bigger's eyes water and spill over. He still won't move. He won't blink. It burns.

Bo Weevil finds a large rock near the trees. Crazy Horse prepares to help him lift it, but Bo Weevil waves him back and he retreats back over to Silk and Bigger and Brother Ned. Silk is praying. Brother Ned looks like he may either hurl or scream. Bigger's face is streaked with tears.

Bo Weevil hefts up the large rock and picks his way over to the good-ol-boy, praying himself.

Okay now, don't move. I think we can get you out of this.

The good-ol-boy doesn't answer—to talk is to move.

Bo Weevil squats down, sweating. This close, he can smell the good-ol-boy's urine, but he barely registers it. The trick is to keep the pressure on the igniter as he replaces the soldier's foot with the heavy rock. To do this, the rock and foot must move at exactly the same time. He slides the rock to the toe of the good-ol-boy's boot, and slowly, slowly, begins to push the soldier's foot back with it.

They both feel the minute shift of the igniter, and Bo Weevil immediately freezes. He licks his lips to wet his dry tongue with the sweat gathered there. He swears, but softly, lest the force of the word set off the bomb. He thinks, trying to work it out. The problem is that the rock is irregularly shaped, so there is a slip of a gap between it and the soldier's toe. It's causing uneven pressure. But it's all they've got. Blinking sweat out of his eyes, Bo Weevil slowly, slowly, rotates the rock, trying to get it more flush with the good-ol-boy's boot. When he's got it the best he can get it, slowly, slowly, he begins to push again.

But the igniter is sensitive now, jumpy like a prey animal. The minute differences in size and shape between the good-ol-boy's boot and the rock are enough to agitate it, make it go off. Bo Weevil can't remove the rock at this point. The good-ol-boy still can't move. And Bo Weevil is pressing down on the rock a little, to maintain the pressure, so if he steps off to try to find a new rock, it's both their asses.

There is a moment when, at the same time, Bo Weevil and the good-ol-boy realize that it isn't going to work, that they've reached a point of no return. Now it's only a matter of choosing the action that will kill them—should they step off together? Should Bo Weevil let go of the rock? Should they jump? How is it that they should let go? Now they can see right into each other's minds, hear each other clear as day. Too late now. We've done all we can. They look right into each other's eyes. Nothing for it, they say. Maybe it won't be so bad. In their eyes there is a helpless kind of calm.

Everyone sees that look between them. Everyone can see them letting go. Silk stops praying. Crazy Horse presses a hand to the side of his face. Bigger closes his eyes so he doesn't have to see the two bodies thrown up into the air. And then that blast hits them all in the heart, killing two, and leaving all the rest of them.

They trekked back the mile and set that village ablaze.

today

EVERY TIME FARUQ went to the stables to ask for Liam, Gabe told him he wasn't there. Odo said that Liam was no longer on cleaning duty. Finally, Gabe admitted that Liam had been assigned to work outside of the Forbidden City. Faruq did not see the kid again.

In the meantime, Odo had begun making himself less scarce around the house. Each morning, after Faruq had returned from his run and showered, Odo would sit for an interview. But Odo always asked something of Faruq before the interview could begin. A tithe, he called it. Sometimes he'd just ask Faruq to answer a question about himself, sometimes he wanted Faruq's opinion on something, sometimes he wanted a song.

This morning, Odo wanted Faruq to translate an Allama Iqbal poem for him. Odo and Faruq had not directly discussed the book, and Faruq sensed Odo was baiting him now. So instead of getting the book, as he was sure Odo expected, he recited a portion of his father's favorite poem from memory, translating clunkily as he went.

> From the page of the world, who erased falsehood?
> Who freed humanity from slavery?
> Who, with their foreheads, established my Ka'bah?
> Who pressed my Quran to their breast?
> Certainly, they were your fathers. But what are you?
> With folded hands, you only wait for a new day.

Odo smiled, nodded to indicate the interview could proceed.

But Faruq was emboldened. He remembered his father's baritone voice reciting the poem in its original Urdu, his eyes closed, and his face full of feeling Faruq couldn't access.

"It's way too generous," Faruq said. "The book."

Odo shook his head impatiently. "Scholar, nothing is everything and everything is nothing."

"What does that mean?"

"It means it doesn't *matter*."

"It matters to me. I'm not going to take it."

"As you like it, scholar."

"You know," Faruq said, "sometimes I really wonder what your motives are."

"The feeling is mutual."

"No, really," Faruq pressed on. "What do you want? Are you trying to change the world? Are you trying to save people? Do you want power?"

Odo released a harsh laugh. "The world changes all on its own, scholar. Doesn't need me. And it's not up to me to save people. Otherwise, I'd save *you*. But you've got agency. You and everybody else. There's no pied piper, no siren song. No one's singing 'O sinners' and leading people down to the river. I don't have any *power* you don't have yourself." He tapped the table firmly with one finger, his voice a bit rabid. "Order out of chaos. That's what I want."

Faruq could see then the quivering rage at the core of Odo, like a writhing mass of something awful, poisonous. He saw Odo yank it viciously back under control.

Odo leaned back in his chair. "Nobody's here that doesn't want to be here. Including you."

Odo had a way of sounding right while telling something that must surely be an incomplete truth. Faruq thought about Odo's words for a long moment. "But when you tell people they're blind and you've got the key to sight, and you surround them with beautiful things and tell them they know something most people don't, and they give you their money and their heirlooms, isn't that manipulation?"

Odo laughed again, but not harshly this time. "Nobody *has* to give anything, scholar. They just do. It's a community. You're the only one tithing."

"Which you asked me to do. And why's that? Why only me?"

"Because you're a capitalist. I mean spiritually. It makes sense to you. Otherwise you'd accept that book."

Now Faruq laughed. "A spiritual capitalist," he repeated slowly. "That's a new one. And I guess that makes you a spiritual socialist?"

"Sure, scholar, sure," Odo chuckled.

That afternoon, while Faruq typed away feverishly at the dining room table, he was surprised when he glanced up and found not Odo before him, but Aeschylus. His gray-streaked hippie hair was pulled back, a wooden mug was in his hands, and he was wearing a kind of periwinkle kurta pajama set. His face was awash with unabashed curiosity.

"When Clover and I left you here, we weren't sure we'd see you again. And now I find you living at the feet of the master." He narrowed his eyes, though he was smiling. "Why?"

Faruq shrugged. "Is that how you think of Odo? As your master?"

"We know he's not God, if that's what you're asking. But he is the deepest of men."

"Deep." Faruq nodded slowly. "Have you ever heard the saying, 'When you look into the abyss, it looks back at you'?"

"Nietzsche," said Aeschylus, sitting down at the other end of the table. "Of course."

"Maybe Odo has taken a bit of an interest in me because I'm interested in him."

Aeschylus chuckled. "I don't think that's quite what Nietzsche meant." He set down his wooden mug. "You're changed."

"Am I?"

"Aren't you? Tell me, what is it you're writing so . . . fervidly?"

Faruq felt exposed. After weeks of feeling aimless, like he had nothing worth reading to say, something was beginning to take shape amid the chaos. Ever since Fall Day, when he sat down with his laptop, words came out of him like that mango seed from his dream. Like that howl. He wrote about the things he was learning here, in the Forbidden City. He wrote about his childhood, about his father. He was forming a theory about the distinction—or lack thereof—between a cult and a religion in its nascency. He wrote about his fall away from Islam. He wrote, little by little, about his mother.

This deluge of words wasn't constrained to the page. At dinner with Odo and Minh-An and Aeschylus and Clover, he spoke about growing up under his father's stifling religiosity, about hiding his godlessness, about his terror in the face of the world after 9/11, without his mother, and appearing to all to belong to a religion he did not love, and that so many had come to violently hate. Aeschylus was right. Something *was* different. Something had been wrenched open.

"Well," he started, "just now, I was writing about a fight I got into with my father. It was stupid. He had a few ads around Brooklyn. After 9/11, people vandalized them, tore them down. He was going to take on the expense of replacing them all. I told him they'd just get vandalized again. No one was going to want a Muslim realtor."

"Did they get vandalized again?"

"Some of them did. He just kept replacing them." Faruq paused. "The thing is, when I look back now, I wasn't really against it because I was afraid for his safety. I was embarrassed. That's fucked up, right?"

Aeschylus spread his hands in a noncommittal gesture. "How do you feel about it now?"

Faruq thought for a moment. "I wish I understood my father better. All three of us—my parents and me—we were each so different from each other. I wish we had understood each other better."

Aeschylus nodded. "A rotten tree will fall."

"What's that supposed to mean?"

Aeschylus smiled. "That if your foundation is unstable, everything you put atop it will be unstable too." He shrugged. "It will fall."

Faruq sighed. "Where's Clover today?" he asked.

Aeschylus took a sip from his mug. "Doing some planning work at the library for the Hall of the Ewas. We're flying out early tomorrow morning." Aeschylus walked out, leaving Faruq to his work.

Danish reported that the aunties had made a visit to Faruq's apartment, and now they had even more questions about where he was and what he was doing.

"It's getting hard to keep them at bay, man. When *are* you coming back?"

"A few more weeks, I think. I know—hang in there."

"Faruq, it's been *months*. What kind of story is this?"

Faruq grimaced. Danish was right. He'd come out here thinking this was a six-week story, but then six weeks became ten, and then weeks stretched into months. Anita had been gracious for three months now, but Faruq knew he was pushing it. Both with Anita and with Danish and his concerned family.

"Does this have anything to do with that girl you told me about?" Danish asked. "Kara?"

"Kaya," Faruq said guiltily. "And no, that's nothing. But— I think I'm writing something . . . more. I think I'm writing a book."

"About that cult?"

"Not just that. I'm writing about myself too. About my father. And Mom."

Danish was silent for several breaths. "You really want to bring all that shit up?"

"I think I have to, D."

Danish let out a whoosh of air. "And *publish* it?"

"Yeah. I mean, maybe."

"You're gonna get in *trou-ble*." Danish drew out the word "trouble" in a singsong voice like they used to do when they were kids.

"I know," Faruq said. "The family's not going to like it. But my father's dead, D. I don't think I can play good little Muslim boy anymore." He sighed. "Just tell me you have my back."

Danish tsked. "You know I always do. Just bring an umbrella. Cause it's gonna be a shit storm."

After hanging up with his cousin, Faruq searched for Kaya, perhaps in penance for their fictional breakup. He found her at the Waterfowl Pond in the south of Ewa Park. She, like many of the nameless women lately, was wearing a pastel purple jumpsuit that billowed out at the legs. She was standing with her hands on her narrow hips, watching a family of ducks sun themselves. She gestured for him to come over and join her, and they sat together on the knotty ground, grass poking at Faruq's bare legs.

"Word is," she said, "you've got a *book* coming together, Faruq. That's impressive."

Faruq smirked. "There really is no privacy here, is there?"

"What you do at Odo's dining room table, you do at all our dining room tables."

They both laughed.

"Tell me the truth," he said. "Aren't you ever worried that people will see all this"—he gestured around them—"as a dangerous cult? Especially after what happened in Texas."

"What do you mean?"

"Well, it's just that you guys don't really try *not* to look like a cult. At the very least, doesn't that put you in danger?"

"Of what?"

"Oh, I don't know. Bad press? Losing followers? Fear? Scrutiny?"

Kaya pursed her lips. "A tiger will take down an elephant if he's hungry enough. But an elephant can make the whole jungle quake."

"Wait, what? Where did you hear that?"

She shrugged. "It's something my father used to say."

. . .

Gwendolyn gave birth at the crack of dawn. Her colt came out a lustrous black, knobby-kneed and rapacious. After they'd watched him stand and latch onto his mother's teat, holding on until the placenta plopped out into Faruq's arms, Minh-An was too weak and tired to drive Faruq back to Odo's house as she usually did. So Faruq drove her to the house of the nameless as she asked, and then trudged on alone to Odo's house, exhausted, waving at the early-rising followers who called out to him as he passed them. When he got back, Odo was already up, and waiting.

Faruq checked his phone. It was just after six-thirty. "You're up early," he said.

"I wanted to show you something, scholar."

"And I wanted to *ask* you something." Faruq was tired. Too tired for censure. "That story you told me, about being in the jungle in Vietnam and seeing a tiger chase a bunch of elephants— was it true?"

Odo nodded. "That was a true story."

"Then how come Kaya referenced that same thing yesterday, only *she* said it was something her father used to say to her?"

"She told the same story?"

"Well—no. But what she said, it was suspiciously similar."

"Similar, but not the same." Odo shrugged. "Sounds like I'm not the only man to have ever seen tigers and elephants. I have never lied to you, scholar."

Faruq scoffed. "Yeah? You ever notice how similar your story of the ten Tintan and their fall is to 'The Snow Queen'?"

"'The Snow Queen'?"

"It's a fairy tale. Coincidentally, one that was in your children's library."

Odo nodded as though this sounded familiar. "Maybe that's a true story too," he said.

Faruq snorted in exasperation. "So it's a coincidence? Awful lot of that around here."

"I wouldn't call it coincidence, scholar. You ever notice the similarities between Loki and Anansi? In the Book of Job and 'Cinderella'? Ever talk about something that happened to you and have someone gasp and say, *Wow, the same thing happened to me*? Stories are patterns. Order in chaos."

"And which Utterance is that again?" Faruq was being snide.

"Fifteen. What exactly are you accusing me of, Faruq?"

"Playing games. Making shit up. I don't even know if *you* believe the fucked-up web of fairy tales and other religions and pure bullshit you're weaving together anymore."

Odo smiled paternally, his eyes folding like tissue paper at the corners. "Faruq," he wheedled. "You're tired."

"Oh for fuck's sake," Faruq hissed. "I am not *tired*. I won't let you manipulate me."

And Odo's face changed. This, Faruq thought. This was no mask. Odo's face did not twist so much as it melted into something new; something, finally, honest. Odo's eyes were wide and bright, too bright, and too big, dilated like he'd just done a line of coke. And his jaw was full of hot tension, brown mouth drawn wide and firm, pulled so tight over his teeth that Faruq was sure he could see their impressions against his lips.

"You," Odo growled, "are as free as anyone ought to be. *I* know about bondage. And that father you're so mad at knew about bondage too. What it's like to smile through the spit in your eye because that's what it takes to *survive*. Even if inside you are writhing. Fire. *That* is what manipulation feels like. I cannot manipulate a free man." Odo pointed one of his long fingers at Faruq. "If you think I'm manipulating you, you must not think you're free. And that's a hell of a lot of nerve. Because I *died* for your freedom. Your father *died* for you to be free."

Faruq couldn't come up with a retort for this. Odo's rant was confusing. And, though Faruq hated to admit it to himself, this fury was intimidating. He was playing with fire. And Odo's anger burned hotter than his own. Was he ready to burn this bridge and leave? Or was his curiosity still ravenous, unsatisfied? Odo knew the answer to that question just as surely as Faruq did. Faruq saw him cool, like a lump of coal going from red to black. Odo was back in control of himself, back to only showing what he wanted to be seen.

"Come on, now, scholar," Odo said as though trying to tame a snake, make it dance. "I wanted to show you what you've been wanting to see. I wanted to show you the truth."

Too tired to resist anymore, Faruq let Odo lead him upstairs, into his room. Faruq had not been in here before—the room was neat, masculine; gray walls and black beams, a cherrywood wardrobe, cowhide rug, immaculately made bed. There was a low coffee table flanked by two leather chairs. Odo motioned for Faruq to sit in one of the chairs, and then went over to the closet, pulled out a long glass case. He brought it over to the coffee table and sat in the unoccupied chair.

Faruq leaned in close. The case was seamless, did not appear to open at all, and inside, on a dark green cushion, lay five medals. The medals were nestled in a row on the cushion, slightly dulled with age. Odo pointed to each one in turn, naming them.

"Vietnam Service Medal. Combat Infantryman Badge. Army Commendation Medal. Bronze Star. Purple Heart."

Faruq stared down at the medals. "So it's true."

"That I fought in Vietnam? Of course it's true. I haven't lied to you, scholar. Even with all that bad business out in Texas, that still got to me. That they said I was lying about being a veteran of that war. Not because I'm particularly proud of it, you understand. War is one of the gravest symptoms of distortion. But because that was where I got hipped. Just when I thought I'd never recognize beauty again. *All* my friends died, scholar."

Odo was quiet and still a long time before speaking again. "*I* died in that war."

Faruq waited for Odo to continue. When he didn't, Faruq asked, "What do you mean?"

Odo let out a slow sigh, rested his hand on the case before answering. "You know, for a little while, I tried staying with this guy I fought with, Ned. He'd just married my friend's little sister. My friend was dead. I didn't fit in their little house with them. I'd seen the face of Vutu, scholar. And now I was carrying it wherever

I went. My body wasn't only *my* body. Somebody'd call me by the name my mother gave me and I wouldn't know to answer."

"Melvin," Faruq murmured experimentally.

Odo shook his head, but not in a reprimand. "At the end of your story, scholar, 'The Snow Queen,' the boy and girl, they go home and realize they've become adults while they were away. Nothing's the same."

Faruq's focus snapped like a rubber band and he stared hard at Odo.

"It was the same for me," Odo continued. "Only it wasn't that I was grown. I was . . . resurrected. Reshaped." He turned to Faruq. "So you see, I guess it is a true story after all."

"So in the woods, when you said I didn't have to choose between the rose and the snowflake—"

"Snow is beautiful. Roses are beautiful. One kills the other. But it's not a betrayal to love them both. Do you understand me?"

With a disorienting feeling in his chest, Faruq thought he did understand. But that couldn't be it. There were things about his parents that Odo could've looked up. But there were things he'd never spoken of to anyone. Things he hadn't even brought himself to write yet.

Odo nodded. "You're starting to see patterns everywhere. Connections. That's good. That's a sign of the Other Sight. Don't be afraid. Get some sleep."

Faruq shuffled downstairs to his room. He wasn't afraid, exactly. He was disquieted. Uncannily exposed. In an untold, shadow part of himself, Faruq held his father responsible for his mother's death. It soured his love for his father, made him feel guilty for it. He'd never so much as uttered that aloud. But Odo seemed to know it all the same.

Instagram Post #385

@thenamelessmvmnt: Lavender, a vibrant purple, its stalks a fuzzy muted green. A field; lavender fills the frame so that it appears to go on forever, infinite floral sea.

#lavenderfields #naturalbeauty #livefree

113,708 likes | 1,832 comments

Nero

FADE IN:

INT. LOS ANGELES OFFICE—MED. SHOT—OWEN RYKER

              OWEN RYKER
    (laughs) Were we being petty? Absolutely.
    But Will Roy should have to pay for what
    he'd tried to do to Odo.

    I had to be really thoughtful in assembling
    my legal team. I mean, they had Preston
    Wade. (chuckles)

    I'd had some successes, but I'm some guy in
    his forties. Preston Wade had that many
    years of a career behind him already—they
    basically pulled this guy out of retirement.

INSERT—IMAGE

Courtroom photo of Preston Wade in a black suit and
silver bow tie; he is mid-sentence, with one finger
pointing up toward the ceiling. SLOW PAN.

              OWEN RYKER
    He wasn't someone to be taken lightly. He
    was experienced, and he had a reputation—
    Preston Wade played dirty.

                             DISSOLVE TO:

INT. CWE NAVE—MED. SHOT—WILL ROY

              WILL ROY
    Look, I wasn't surprised that the news media
    didn't treat all this fairly. The righteous are
    always persecuted in the eye of the public.

Roy crosses his arms over his chest.

              WILL ROY
    Preston Wade is a God-fearing family man,
    and a damn good attorney, and you can take a
    look at his résumé if you don't believe me.

But the news media painted Ryker out to be
young, hip—*progressive*. And they painted
Wade out to be some kind of stick-in-the-mud
racist.

Roy shakes his head derisively.

>   WILL ROY
> The media was biased right from the
> beginning. Unfair. But I wouldn't expect
> anything less from the antichrist.

>   CROSS CUT:

INT. LOS ANGELES OFFICE—MED. SHOT—OWEN RYKER

>   OWEN RYKER
> In my mind, I'm standing up for Odo, and I'm
> standing up for the nameless movement. So
> that was my priority.
>
> I really wasn't surprised that there was a
> lot of media coverage. I mean, it's a sexy
> story—the nameless's enigmatic leader goes
> toe to toe with a fundamentalist, racist
> church. (laughs)
>
> Defamation cases are notoriously difficult to
> win. Especially for a public figure. You have
> to prove that the defamatory statements were
> made with actual malice, uh, and that they
> have caused you real harm. *Tons* of fact-
> finding.
>
> But you know, the real drama here wasn't
> really what happened in the courtroom. It
> was what happened in Burning Hill as a
> result of all this madness.

>   DISSOLVE TO:
Footage of a diner in Burning Hill, TX. A server from
the diner stands in the open door, barring entry. She
is arguing with the person holding the camera. She
holds up a hand to prevent them from entering.

                    MINH-AN
Businesses closed their doors to us. In
town, restaurants, bars, stores—they
wouldn't serve us. They said they had the
right to refuse business. One guy said this
old man pulled a *gun* on him when he used his
driveway to turn his car around.

                              CROSS CUT:
Footage of a man standing in a Burning Hill pasture
with the sheriff. Both have their hands on their hips
as they look out over the empty grasses.

                    WILL ROY
Few folks had their cattle go missing. Wilma
Barry lost one of her mares.

                    PRODUCER (O.S.)
How do you lose a horse?

                              CROSS CUT:

INT. CWE NAVE—MED. SHOT—WILL ROY

                    WILL ROY
You don't. (chuckles)

It was them. Johnny Hughes down the road saw
a couple of them leading the old gal away.
Couldn't do nothing because there wasn't any
proof.

They searched all their properties.

Roy shrugs.

                    WILL ROY
No horse.

Things were real nasty in town. Made me sad
to see it. It was never like that before
they got here. This is *my home*. I have every
right to defend it.

Roy points his finger toward the camera.

          WILL ROY
In this country, we have something called
the *First Amendment*. That means I—and
anybody else—have the *right* to speak my
mind.

Roy lowers his hand.

          WILL ROY
We also have something called the separation
of church and state. And *that* means the
government is not allowed to persecute me
for what I believe.

Roy nods.

                    CROSS CUT:

INT. GREENHOUSE—MED. SHOT—MINH-AN

Minh-An lets out a long laugh.

          MINH-AN
It's just hilarious to me, you know? Roy and
his church talking about freedom of
religion. They could have just left us
alone, and this whole thing wouldn't've
happened.

They *countersued* us for intimidation.
(snorts)

We weren't *intimidating* them. They were just
intimidated. There's a difference.

                    FADE TO BLACK.

INSERT—IMAGE*

Houston Chronicle article: "Legal Battle Rages Between
Christ the Word Evangelical and Nameless Guru."

---

* Music: Raymonda, Op. 57, Act III, Variation IV (Victor
Fedotov)

DISSOLVE TO:

Twitter post: "Make no mistake, the feud between Christ the Word & the nameless is about race & power."

DISSOLVE TO:

New York Magazine article: "Taking the Pastor to Court."

DISSOLVE TO:

Los Angeles Times article: "Op-Ed: Why We Should All Be Watching Burning Hill, Texas."

DISSOLVE TO:

Twitter post: "Yall really tryna argue that calling a BLACK MAN satan is a constitutional right BYE [laughing emoji][laughing emoji]"

DISSOLVE TO:

New Yorker article: "The Man Who Got Sued by the Antichrist."

DISSOLVE TO:

Vice article: "Is the Apocalypse Playing Out in a Texas Courtroom?"

DISSOLVE TO:

Twitter post: "People will defend constitutional rights until it's about POC accessing them smdh."

DISSOLVE TO:

Slate article: "Is It Freedom of Religion, or Freedom of *Acceptable* Religion?"

FADE IN:

INT. CWE NAVE—MED. SHOT—WILL ROY

       WILL ROY
    Odo shows up wearing some kind of—light green sweater and these . . . almost *riding* breeches. To make a spectacle of himself or something, you know? It was disrespectful.

And he had this cocky expression on his face
the whole time. Arrogant. Like it was all a
big joke to him.

Anytime somebody'd ask him a question, he'd
answer real low. Like he was just talking to
one person, and not a whole courtroom full
of people. (sniffs)

I didn't care for his attitude, no. And if
it were me up in that judge's chair, I'd
have let him know too. (snickers)

But I had my ways of getting under his skin.
Because of the trial, we learned his real
name—*Melvin Blackwell.*

Roy smirks.

> WILL ROY
> Well, I didn't call him *Odo* not once after I
> learned that. I'd say the whole name every
> time. *Melvin. Blackwell.*

                              CROSS CUT:

INT. LOS ANGELES OFFICE—MED. SHOT—OWEN RYKER

> OWEN RYKER
> Roy's behavior in the courtroom was very
> antagonistic. The judge had to remind him
> more than once not to speak out of turn. The
> impression I got was that he was very, very
> angry, an angry man.
>
> And, to be honest with you, Preston Wade
> wasn't much better. He's a—a bulldog.
> (chuckles)
>
> His primary strategy seemed to be throwing
> up objections to any and everything.

Ryker shrugs.

INSERT—FOOTAGE

News footage of Preston Wade addressing the press
outside the courtroom.

> PRESTON WADE (FROM FOOTAGE)
> Well, now, this is about 2 things. In
> America, we have the right to believe in
> what we believe in. A lot of fine men—
> and women—died for that right. So whatever
> Will Roy and his church believe about
> good and evil, and what the Bible says
> about the antichrist—well, that's their
> right to believe it. That's the first
> thing. The second thing is Freedom of
> Speech. We're entitled to that in
> America, and we're entitled to live
> without fear of persecution, censor, or
> intimidation. And folks, that's all I've
> got to say.

Reporters yell overlapping questions.

                                        CROSS CUT:
News footage of Owen Ryker addressing the press outside
of the courthouse.

> OWEN RYKER (FROM FOOTAGE)
> Look, I'll keep this brief. This case *is*
> about religious freedom, yes. But it's
> about more than that. What's happened here
> in Burning Hill, Texas, is a *paradigm* of
> systemic racism. And with the whole country
> watching, we cannot stand for the selective
> application of constitutional rights. And
> as an ally myself, I really need to fight
> for what's right here. Men like Mr. Roy
> will be on the wrong side of history. Thank
> you.

Reporters yell overlapping questions.

                                   FADE TO BLACK.

FADE IN:

INT. CWE NAVE—MED. SHOT—WILL ROY

Roy is looking down at his hands, which are clasped in
his lap. He is silent a long time.

Roy sighs. He looks up, his gaze meeting the camera.

> WILL ROY
> You know, well . . . the laws of man just
> ain't enough to fight the antichrist.

Roy sits in silence for a while, not breaking his eye
contact with the camera.

DISSOLVE TO:

INT. LOS ANGELES OFFICE—MED. SHOT—OWEN RYKER

Ryker smiles.

> OWEN RYKER
> It's complicated, isn't it? (titters softly)

> PRODUCER (O.S.)
> Could you, like, summarize? The SparkNotes
> version.

> OWEN RYKER
> Okay, well, we lost defamation because the
> judge wasn't convinced we suffered damages.
> Which, well, okay.
>
> And he said Will Roy does have the right to
> believe Odo is the antichrist, so long as it
> doesn't pass the boundary of belief. The
> judge *did* say that he found this to be
> abhorrent, even if Mr. Roy had the right to
> believe it. (laughs)
>
> But we got harassment. And Will Roy did *not*
> get intimidation.

Ryker briefly throws up his hands, and then lets them
drop.

                    OWEN RYKER

        So it's bittersweet, but yeah. We won.

Ryker gives a shrugging nod.

before: 1970

BIGGER COULDN'T SLEEP. It wasn't just the humid night or the sounds of nocturnal creatures and the trees and the men crying and trying not to be heard. It was that every time he closed his eyes, he saw the shadow of the thing he'd closed his eyes against, embellished grotesquely by his imagination. It sent lightning all through his head, down into his neck, bright, burning, agony.

He could hear the clicking songs of the crickets and the frogs. He couldn't stand to try closing his eyes again. He got up. A few of the men on night patrol had fallen asleep, bored, but Silk was awake, staring into the trees. Bigger made a noise as he approached, to let Silk know it was him. Silk didn't jump. He could hear that kid's manic heartbeat from six paces away. Bigger settled down next to Silk.

They're sleeping on their shift.

Silk shrugged.

Don't matter. There's nothing out there. Not tonight.

You never know. Things seem to go bad real quick.

That's the way it is. Shift's almost over, anyway. I'm up, ain't I?

Bigger shuffled closer to Silk, spoke in an urgent whisper.

I did it.

What you talkin about, man?

I got Bo Weevil and that rabbit killed. *I* did it.

What *are* you talking about? You had nothing to do with it.

Bigger shook his head. It swam painfully. He licked his lips. They tasted like metal.

You don't understand.

I sure don't.

I closed my eyes, get it? I must've moved. On accident. I stepped on the wrong carpet.

Silk broke his gaze off of the trees to glance at Bigger. He looked again, studying the man closely. Silk could feel heat radiating off the kid. He was like a radiator.

Hey Bigger, you all right?

I did it, you get me? *I* killed them.

Silk reached over to grab Bigger's arm.

Christ, you're burning up. Listen. You ain't thinking straight. You're sick, all right? You didn't kill anybody.

Bigger's vision was all red. He nodded, the pain knocking from one side of his skull to the other.

Yes I did, you're not getting it, I did.

Stop that. Cmon. You'll be all right, you just need the malaria pill. We'll get the medic.

Silk cursed himself. He should've known. He'd seen enough soldiers get fever-crazy off malaria. Even Crazy Horse had gotten it. Preach would've known. He hauled Bigger up by his elbow.

You'll be all right. Just a little jungle fever. Come on. Move your feet.

But Bigger dug in his heels, smiled a madman's smile.

You were right, Silk. Preach *is* still with us.

That's right. He's watching over you.

No, no. He's right there.

Creeped out, Silk looked over at the trees, where Bigger was pointing. No enemies there. No friends, either.

That's enough. Let's go.

He's there, he's *there*. He's right there.

Bigger jerked out of Silk's grasp and fell to the ground, convulsing. Rose-colored foam seeped out from between his lips. Silk dropped to his knees beside him, snapped at the nearest dozing soldier to get the medic.

Shit, man. Shit, *shit*.

Silk held Bigger's lolling head between his hands as the other soldier, alert now, sprinted to wake the medic.

But Bigger was above his own body, looking down, watching. He could see himself there on the ground, and Silk holding him. He could see the soldier running for help. He could see them all, some sleeping and some awake, some frightened and some full of rage, some of them full of fire. And now he was not himself, but a tiger. Ravenous.

Between Silk's hands, Bigger's head went still, his eyes open a sliver and his mouth wet with the rose-colored foam. The medic cursed when he reached them. Quiet, off-key, Silk began to sing with the part of him that was Preach.

> *My brother's body lies a-peaceful in the grave*
> *He is gone to be a soldier in the army of the saved*
> *My brother's body lies a-peaceful in the grave*
> *But his soul goes marching on.*

Brother Ned remembered the explosion like glass shattering, and then the bodies being thrown up, silhouetted—dark stars in a molten, steely sky. And then them coming apart in the air, but incompletely, so that, for a fraction of a moment, it looked like Bo Weevil and the good-ol-boy were holding hands.

The good-ol-boy's friend remembered the sound of thunder, nature's cackle, and then the two bodies being blasted away from each other, the good-ol-boy's limbs flapping like he was a paper doll in a storm. And Bo Weevil's eyes were open, two white circles in his black face, already empty.

Crazy Horse remembered nothing of sound, only the men shooting up and back toward the trees so that it seemed for a moment that they might get tangled there, like kites. Bo Weevil's face was already ruined because he had been crouched still when the bomb went off, and the good-ol-boy was missing a foot, the other dangling by a thread.

Silk's memories were gangrenous with guilt. He'd seen the wildness in Bigger's eyes right before the Bouncing Betty went off. He should've known then. Part of him *had* suspected something was wrong. He should've done something. He bucked momentarily at this responsibility. Christ, can't a brother make one mistake? But he answered himself: Not in the jungle, he can't. He'd failed. Useless. And yet, it is Silk who smells the mortar attack before it begins. Even as he dives, yelling for the others to take cover, he is reassured that this gift, this mystic fragment of Preach he's inherited, has not wholly abandoned him.

The world lights up like a hellish disco and then quickly smokes over. Each soldier peers into the chaos of dust and smoke and catapulting shreds of foliage, trying to discern the enemy's location. Bullets join the mortar rounds. The sky comes crashing down.

Crazy Horse, crawling through the violence, drags Bullwhip down with him, narrowly pulling him out of the way of a bullet that seems to whirl toward his head in slow motion. Before Bullwhip can say anything, Crazy Horse spots Brother Ned. The white boy is wildly swinging his rifle back and forth, three soldiers down around him. Cursing, Crazy Horse signals at Silk to cover them, and he begins to fight his way over to Brother Ned, making his way through a tunnel of blood and sound, though when he thinks of Preach, of the photo of Preach's sister Brother Ned carries in his pocket, the sound disappears, leaving only blood.

Crazy Horse shouts at Brother Ned to get down, but before the rabbit can obey, he takes a bullet to the thigh that *puts* him down. Crazy Horse curses again, and Silk, covering them with a spray of fire, begins to pray.

Bullets wreck the ground immediately to Crazy Horse's right and he rolls away from them. Half blindly, he reaches out and finds Brother Ned's leg. He clamps down like a vise and pulls Brother Ned toward him. He's got hold of the bad leg—Brother Ned lets out a warbling shriek. Crazy Horse keeps pulling.

Least you're not dead, brotherman.

Once Brother Ned passes out from the pain, it becomes much easier to move him. Crazy Horse carries him, dodging and crouching, and drops him at Silk's feet. Inside Crazy Horse whole oceans converge, their currents churning together in agony, in fury. The feathers in his helmet are great, malevolent wings; they lift him up above the blistered earth. It runs red.

Silk watches Crazy Horse charge back into the thick of the fire and shakes his head.

Crazy motherfucker.

He keeps covering him until he can't see him anymore. The mortar attack levels trees and men; bullets do the rest. Even over the sounds of battle, Silk hears the whining, guttural roar, getting closer. Puff the Magic Dragon—they'd called in air defense. Silk's breath hitches, and he stoops down to drag Brother Ned to cover. Problem with Puff is his angry fire sweeps everything in its path.

Silk bends himself over Brother Ned's body as the noise of Puff's initial blast claps through the air. Brother Ned is awake again, but in shock, his eyes like little ponds and a glistening mustache of sweat above his upper lip. Silk presses a hand against the wound in his thigh, and Brother Ned hardly seems to feel it.

Puff breathes his fire for something like fifteen minutes, and when he retreats, he pulls the smoking air behind him, leaving an uncanny silence. The scouts go out to count the dead. Silk can see no sign of Crazy Horse, doesn't want to think about it, so he focuses on slowing Brother Ned's bleeding with his hand, perhaps pressing too hard. Brother Ned's eyes are squeezed shut, but he is whispering. No, singing.

Going home, going home. I'm just going home.

Silk nods, presses his hand into Brother Ned's bloody leg.

Don't you forget about Missy when you see all them pretty nurses—Preach wouldn't go for that. And you write just as soon as you get to Philly, you hear?

Missy's there expecting me, Mama's waiting too. Lots of people gathered there, all the friends I knew.

Promise you'll write, you got that? Promise me you'll write. I wanna come to that wedding.

By the time the medic reaches them, Brother Ned's shock is wearing off. The medic offers him morphine, but he refuses it—he wants to remember being lifted out of this country. Silk clamps his bloodied hands over Brother Ned's mouth as the medic extracts the bullet from the muscle of his thigh—until the scouts return with their tally, they can't be sure how many Vietnamese are dead, and how many might be hiding, waiting.

Moving quietly, like a stalking cat, the grunt picked through bamboo and elephant grass, scanning for signs of the Vietnamese. He was a little over two kilometers out now, and so far, he'd counted two dead Viet Cong. He froze when he heard movement, his pulse a tribal drumbeat. Achingly slowly, he reached for his gun, his jaw tightening painfully. But when he crept out of his cover, he found not the enemy, but Crazy Horse, who was standing over four more dead Vietnamese.

Relaxing slightly, the grunt began to approach. Crazy Horse did not seem to notice him. He seemed, in fact, to be praying. But as the grunt drew closer, he heard that Crazy Horse was not praying, but reciting the names of their dead. Now the grunt grew uneasy. Crazy Horse's gun was at his side, but his eyes were strange vacuums, and his recitation seemed to sway his body slightly.

The grunt reached out a hand, and, swallowing, touched Crazy Horse's shoulder. Crazy Horse turned to look at him, reinhabiting himself. The next thing he said was his own name.

It took the scouts about an hour to drag the Vietnamese bodies out into the open. Fourteen in total, and nine dead Americans. A win, they told each other, though it didn't feel that way to anyone. A bird came to take away the fallen and injured, and Crazy Horse found Silk, the two of them watching Brother Ned get loaded into the helicopter. Silk didn't ask any questions. They just stood side by side, the oceans inside Crazy Horse circling down a drain, and the blood on Silk's hands drying.

As he lay half reclined in the chopper, the throb in Ned's bandaged thigh reached pulsing tentacles down to his feet, up into his lower back, his balls, his stomach. He was surrounded by dead men. He struggled not to writhe as the bird jerked higher into the air, sweat creeping down from his hair and into his eyes. He craned his neck to watch Vietnam shrink underneath him. It was the tainted green of turning produce, with chocolate milk rivers and tarnished smog, growing smaller and smaller, evaporating like a nightmare. He pulled Missy's photo out of his pocket— a corner was brown with blood—and pressed it to his lips, his chest.

today

MINH-AN'S FACE WAS a full moon above his in the darkness. Faruq blinked up at her.

"Mare duty?"

"Mm-hm," she said.

The mare was Candace, a great white horse with doll-like black eyes. Gabe told Faruq that she was the last of their foaling mares, and he felt an inexplicable grief at the news. The night was unusually hot, and Candace's haunches were streaked with sweat. Faruq was sweating too, his shirt clinging to his back. Minh-An sat as stoically as always, unbothered.

Candace let out a great sigh from where she was lying on the floor and rolled onto her back, her muscular legs kicking. She tossed her big head, glancing balefully at her own hindquarters. Faruq swiped sweat from his forehead with a wrist. When the mare's water finally broke, Faruq sat back with relief, knowing the foal would come soon. The air in the stall was close and sticky.

But one of the foal's front legs was bent, flexed at the knee. Candace grunted and huffed, her muscles rippling with effort, but the foal would not emerge any further. Faruq looked to Minh-An, and she met his gaze, one eyebrow raised.

"It's stuck," she said.

Faruq scowled at her and pulled out his phone. Google told him that he needed to push the foal back in a bit and then see if he could reach in and straighten its legs. Great. He groaned. There were no gloves around that he could see, but he slipped out of the stall to thoroughly wash his hands at the metal sink. Minh-An made no move to assist in any way.

Candace eyed him warily as he approached. He crouched down behind her. Gingerly, he touched his palm to the foal's head—its eyes were black slits, its mane matted to its neck.

"Sorry buddy," Faruq said.

Planting his hands on the foal's shoulders, he began to push. Progress was slow, partially because Faruq was terrified of injuring the newborn, and partially because Candace was still having contractions. Once the foal's shoulders were back in, Faruq, sweating profusely now and coated in viscera, worked an arm in until he could feel the foal's knobby, bent knee. Candace let out something like a growl, a noise he didn't know horses could make. Her legs kicked out tiredly, a hoof catching him in the thigh. It would leave a bruise.

He summoned more patience than he knew he had to carefully work the leg straight. There was a faint tremor in the foal's muscles, and Candace whipped her head back at him twice as though to bite him. But in time, the leg came straight. He wiggled his arm out of Candace's birth canal, and immediately, she sprang to her feet. With a great contraction, the foal dangled out of her, its legs hanging limply and its tongue coming to peek out of its mouth. The rest of the birth went quickly.

The filly was pure white like her mother. She was exhausted—it took her some time to gather the energy to get to her feet. Then she stumbled sleepily to Candace's teat. Sweat dripped into Faruq's eyes and he could not wipe it away with his soiled hands.

Minh-An watched him wordlessly as he washed and rewashed himself as best he could at the stable's sink. He itched under her scrutiny.

"You know," he said, "no one's ever given me a real answer as to why Odo put me on mare duty in the first place."

Minh-An made no answer.

"If it's an attempt to convert me by making me witness the beauty of life, you might want to reconsider the part where I stick my entire arm *inside* a horse."

He'd meant it as a joke, but he could see right away that it was a mistake. Minh-An's sunken face went ice-cold.

"You know, Odo sees all your smugness and thinks you're beautiful anyway. And *all* you do is squander the gifts he gives you."

"Then what am I missing? Please, speak plainly to me. What is it I'm not seeing?"

But Minh-An only scowled at him and stormed out of the stable. He heard the sound of the golf cart they'd driven to the stables as it started and then drove off. He groaned. Hopefully he'd get lucky and find a bike or something out in the darkness. He shook the excess water off his hands and dried them on the thin towel by the sink.

He increased his speed through the woods, but the wolf's ghost footfall underneath his own kept pace. Faster, he ran. Still, the wolf easily kept up. He broke into a sprint. Now the wolf's footfalls were louder—leaves crunched and twigs snapped as it loped with him. He could see snatches of its gray fur through the trees. It was closer, faster. For the first time in a while, he felt fear. He heard the wolf grunt, and he pushed himself into an even faster sprint. He could almost feel its exhilaration, as if, all this time, it had been waiting for him to *fly*. It outpaced him, making the woods ahead of him sing with its breath, branches bending in its wake, gray fur strobing through the trees. Flying. For the first time in a while, Faruq was in the woods alone.

"What's my tithe today?"

Faruq, his hair still wet from the shower, was sitting across from Odo at the dining room table, his cell phone already recording audio, and a burning hot mug of coffee teepeed between his hands.

"Why don't you tell me, scholar?"

"I don't know—want me to recite another poem?"

"No, I don't. I want you to tell me something true."

To have something to do with his hands, Faruq tried to take a sip of his coffee. It burned his lower lip. He set the mug back down and pretended to swallow.

"Like what? Did you have a specific question?"

Odo only stared. Though he hadn't mentioned it, Faruq was sure Odo knew about the faux pas with Minh-An. Somehow, Odo not saying anything left Faruq feeling especially chastised. But he hadn't done anything *so* wrong, had he? Just a dumb joke.

"Minh-An's angry with me." An unnecessary confession.

"Does that bother you, scholar?"

"Well, yes. I don't want her to be mad at me."

Odo smirked. "Can't you tolerate it?"

Faruq was about to say something defensive, but stopped himself. Why *couldn't* he tolerate it? He couldn't tolerate his father's disappointment, so he hid his atheism. He couldn't tolerate his aunties' disapproval, so he never brought up his mother in front of them. *The wet face, wet tendrils of hair escaping the hijab*—he couldn't even tolerate his own memories. He was sick of being weak.

He took in a slow breath.

"When I was twelve, my mother drove off of the Throgs Neck Bridge."

Odo leaned forward almost imperceptibly.

"Her death was ruled an accident, but—I don't know. I always wondered what she was doing on the Throgs Neck Bridge. We lived in Brooklyn. And her family—they're upstate." Faruq shrugged. "I don't know. Anyway, after she died, my father's family stopped speaking about her. My father would close up like a clam if I brought her up. The accident made the news, but just a week later, 9/11 happened, so—everything was eclipsed. And it was just my father and I, and—I don't know, everyone hated us. Everyone thought we were monsters. It was like my mother never even existed."

"But she does," said Odo. "She does exist."

Faruq nodded heavily.

"Tell me about her. The whole complicated, uncomfortable, *beautiful* truth."

Queasiness rose up in Faruq like fire. But he decided that today was the day he'd speak through it. Faruq gave Odo the complete picture: His mother had a ready smile, an open laugh. His mother loved music, loved to dance. His mother bought an American cookbook, and, in secret, she and Faruq tried as many recipes as they could. She made the best fried chicken and the worst pancakes. His mother only ever told him she loved him in English. His mother insisted on holding his hand just about everywhere they went. His mother sometimes didn't sleep for days, would wake him up at odd hours, sometimes by vacuuming, turning on all the lights in the house, having loud telephone conversations with her sisters.

She'd start giggling during prayer, and his father would scream at her. Once she'd gone outside to sweep the stairs with only a kitchen towel covering her hair and his father had screamed at her with tears in his eyes. She'd go blank, limp and gray, and Faruq would be terrified that she was dead. He'd hug her tight, trying to press his life into hers. He'd hold her deadweight hands. He'd call her in every way he knew how: *Mom. Mama. Ammu. Fatima.* When she came back, it was never because of anything he did.

"She wasn't as conservative as my father," Faruq continued. "Religiously. And that caused a lot of problems. I don't think they hated each other, but they definitely didn't understand each other. He was always lecturing her about being a better Muslim, always telling her she fell short. And she'd rebel like a teenager."

His coffee was cool enough now, so he drank. His hands were shaking.

"I knew something was wrong with her, even as a little kid. I mean, sometimes she was fun and sometimes she was scary. But I think she was, like, really sad *all* the time."

He brought the mug back up to his lips. Some of the coffee missed his mouth, dribbled onto the table. He wiped it away with his hand. Still shaking.

If he was going to write this, he needed to be able to speak it.

"My father and his sisters called in an exorcist."

He waited for Odo to react, but the other man's face was perfectly still.

"They thought everything going on with her was evil spirits—jinn. They didn't see it as mental illness until later. Until they'd already done their damage. My father drove us out to his sister's house in Queens. He told us we were just going for a visit. But when we got there, his sisters were waiting with the ustad. My father told me they were just going to pray with my mother. He sent me to play with my cousin Danish. I did. I was eight."

Faruq shrugged.

"Me and Danish ended up fighting about something—I don't remember. I went to go tattle." He chuckled mirthlessly. "But the grown-ups weren't downstairs. I heard voices in the backyard, so I went out. At first, all I could see were my dad, my aunts, and the ustad, all gathered in tight. They were praying. I heard crying. No one was paying attention to me. I got closer."

Faruq closed his eyes. His mother's face, eyes wide, lashes clumping wetly, mouth shut tight, vein throbbing at her temple, hijab clinging and the wet tendril of hair escaping, and the muffled crying coming through those closed lips.

"They had her in the kiddie pool. My aunts were holding her in the water, but she wasn't fighting them. They were all reciting verses and holding her down, and the ustad was pressing a prayer mat onto her chest. Her face was wet, but I could tell she was crying. But she was—limp. I thought they were trying to drown her and I thought I was going to do something. I thought I was going to save her. But then she looked at me, and her face—I ran away."

Faruq looked down at the coffee. He squeezed the sides of the mug until he was sure it must shatter in his grip. It held.

"It didn't work. The exorcism. If anything, she got worse after that. And then, just a few years later . . ." Faruq shook his head. "I never believed it was an accident. I mean, she was in the car alone, but my father might as well have been the one driving her off that bridge." He glanced up at Odo. "That's what I thought."

"Is that what you think now, scholar?"

Faruq rubbed at his eyes with his palms. "I don't know what to think. I loved my mother. I—I loved my father. He made it difficult, but I did, I loved him. It's complicated. Or maybe it's not. She needed help and she didn't get it."

Odo nodded slowly. It was making Faruq seasick.

"Anyway," Faruq said, "there you go. Tithe."

"Don't distort, scholar," Odo chided. "*You* needed that. Not me. Nuh-uh."

Faruq laughed harshly. "I don't know about that. I don't feel any better, if that's what you mean."

"But you didn't run away this time," Odo said. "Faruq, if you don't look away, if you keep your gaze steady at death, the distortion wavers like a mirage. It'll slip away. And then you can see the beauty that was there all along."

Faruq stood abruptly. "I can't do this. Okay? I just—I need a break. We'll circle back or something later. Okay?"

Without waiting for Odo to answer, Faruq took his phone and left the dining room, left Odo's house, walking out into the Forbidden City with nowhere, really, to run.

He'd been trying to take more pictures of the foals, but they wouldn't stay still, the lighting was off, and the photos weren't coming out the way he'd imagined them. The confusion about which colt was Asher and which was not still unsettled him. He didn't know why it mattered so much, but it did. So now he was all around frustrated. He left the pasture, drove toward the Persian Garden.

The walled garden was a prism of silence and color. Faruq didn't see anyone else around. He stalked to the gazebo, thinking he might sit for a while, try being idle. But the gazebo was occupied. Minh-An was there, dancing.

Upon seeing her, Faruq thought he should apologize, but he didn't want to interrupt. There was no music, and Minh-An wasn't wearing earphones—she was dancing to silence. Her body moved like the answer to an ancient question, declarative and calm. Faruq wished he knew more about dance so he could articulate what awed him. Right now, Minh-An didn't look dilapidated. She was a pulse.

Her dance reached its conclusion and she let herself crumple. Faruq approached.

"It was all wrong," she said, her voice full of air. She swallowed audibly. It sounded dry. "When I first performed that piece, I was nineteen. I can still remember what it felt like in my body, then. But now—ugh. Now I'm nearly fifty, and frail."

Faruq sat down next to her. "It looked pretty damn good to me."

"No, you don't understand. I have no balance—there are supposed to be these little pauses, but I can't hold a shape. And forget about the jumps." She squeezed her eyes closed. "But I'm being a perfectionist. And I *know* better. I don't know why I'm clinging to distortion."

Faruq thought she might cry, but when she opened her eyes, they were dry.

"It's wonderful," she said. "All this beauty." The space between her eyebrows seemed to crinkle, but in a flash it was gone. "Help me up."

Trying to be gentle, Faruq pulled Minh-An to her feet. She was unsteady, winded. He kept his hands loosely cupped around her broomstick arms, just in case.

"I should go rest," she said, barely above a whisper. She didn't move.

Faruq kept his hands where they were, ready to hold her up. A slight breeze stirred his hair, swayed Minh-An's body. She looked up at him. The crease between her eyebrows was back, and her eyes were dark liquid. A rare glimpse of something vulnerable.

"Did you think it was beautiful, scholar? Even with the mistakes? Even though I can't dance it right?"

"Yes," he assured her. "It was beautiful."

"I should go rest," she repeated, and this time she stepped out of Faruq's hands. She didn't meet his eyes again, but she touched his arm before walking away. She walked as though through sand, pausing at every stirring of the wind. Faruq saw that, though her hands were at her sides, she was reaching her fingers out, spreading them, letting the wind flow through them like a current.

It had been awhile since he had infiltrated the group meditation Odo led every Saturday afternoon in the house of the nameless. He didn't really like going. It reminded him too much of Friday afternoons, when his father would collect him from school and take him to the masjid. That feeling that, at any moment, he'd get called out as an imposter. But this Saturday, his curiosity won out. He wanted to see if meditation would feel any different now that he'd shared things he hadn't even let himself think about in so long. The Deep were there, at the edges of the room, the black clothing stark against everyone else's red, their faces serious and still. They held nothing in their hands.

"I was made to do violent things," Odo was saying. "But I am not a violent man. I was *made* by the government to do violent things, yes I was. These hands"—he reached out to touch his fingertips to a follower's cheek, and she closed her eyes and swayed into the touch—"these hands were bloodied over in Vietnam. And these eyes were bloodied too. My, my, my."

Odo was quiet for a while and Faruq looked around. His followers were rapt, unflinching.

"Death," Odo continued. "I saw death everywhere. And back then, well, I was still despairing at it. Oh, I was a poor mourner all the time. I saw a man step on a Bouncing Betty—that's a kind of bomb they'd bury, and you'd trip it if you stepped on it. Well, this soldier stepped on one. We all heard the click, but it didn't go off. But the moment he moved his foot, he'd be done for, you understand? Well. This other soldier tried replacing the brother's foot with a rock. Didn't work. The bomb went off, and it sent both of them flying. They died up in the air, holding on to each other."

Faruq tried to picture such a thing, but his imagination kept getting snagged on details he didn't have. How high were they blown? Would they have lost body parts? Was there a spray of blood? What did they look like? What were their names?

"Now. A year later and I'm out of that war of distortion. I'm hipped, my eyes are open. And the nameless god shows me Their face and speaks to me. They leads me to a witnessing. I found a doe laboring under the cover of some shrubs. It was twins—my, my, my. The one was struggling to its feet while the other emerged, wet and raggy. That little one came loose and let out a cry mightier'n a thunderclap. Scared me."

Odo and his captivated audience laughed.

"Well, that doe jumped up and got to nuzzling on that new-born. Then the two of those fawns started talking—*ehh! ehhh!* Something human in the way that they sounded. And that's when I knew—they were those two soldiers. I'd watched them fly up, holding on to each other, and now here they were again, born together. Do not despair at death."

The followers echoed. *Do not despair at death.*

"Do not despair at death."

Do not despair at death.

"Do not despair at death."

Do not despair at death.

"Do *not* despair at death."

What the hell? Faruq joined in. *Do* not *despair at death.*

The room filled with the static of rapid breathing, whispering of the 18 Utterances. Faruq was mildly disturbed to realize he now knew them by heart.

there is no god but the nameless
Odo is the messenger of Mow Vutu
all suffering is distortion
strip yourself of distortion
sacrifice
create Beauty
get hipped to Oneness
love freely
meditate to the vibration of Vutu and the World

pray regularly
see only Beauty
do not despair at death
train the Other Sight
hip all beings to the nameless
create order in chaos
correct distortion
harness gosah in pursuit of Wholeness
seek the face of Mow Vutu

Faruq held his breath with everyone else, and then released it, waiting for an impact, a vision. Waiting to be moved. But nothing happened. He fell asleep and was startled awake by exaltation—followers crying, cursing, moaning, bleating. He smiled to himself, reassured. It was out of him now, what had been repressed. Those things he'd felt before—they were all in his head. He lay still for a while, enjoying his own weight, his body's passivity.

But noise ruffled the room as followers began to gasp, whisper to each other in awe. As though from far away, Faruq could hear Odo softly intoning, "Do not despair at death." Confused, Faruq sat up. The meditation was usually over once followers began making their strange, exultant noises. Faruq couldn't see Odo, but the followers were crowding toward the front of the room. Faruq stood.

Standing did not help his vantage point—the followers were crowding in so close he still couldn't see what all the commotion was about. He pushed forward, his curiosity burning. Followers glanced at him as he squeezed by them, their eyes full of enraptured light. Too bright. Too wide. Too open.

At the front, a shrouded figure walked slowly across the room, Odo following with his intonation. A woman in something long and flowing, with her face shadowed and her hair covered. Except for the wet tendrils that escaped her shroud.

Do not despair at death.

The eyes wide, the lashes sticking wetly to each other, mouth clamped shut—

Faruq narrowed his eyes, part of him not wanting to believe what he was seeing. He stepped a bit closer. Odo was not looking at him.

Do not despair at death.

Hijab clinging to the skull, wet tendril of hair escaping, muf-fled cries—

The shrouded woman was silent, her wet hair hanging down from the fabric that covered her head, her face hidden, shoulders rounded forward.

Do not despair at death.

The throbbing vein at the temple, the wet hair like a small serpent—

Odo was not looking at him. The woman did not look at him. Her hair dripped water at her feet.

Do not despair at death.

"What the *fuck* is this?"

Faruq had not meant to yell. His voice silenced the room, stopped Odo and the shrouded woman in their tracks. Now they were looking at him. They were *all* looking at him.

"Is this what you do?" Faruq continued. "Use people's trauma to—what? Humiliate them? Make a spectacle out of them? You're a fucking psychopath."

"Faruq," Odo said in that infuriatingly calm voice, "nobody's trying to hurt you. You're safe. It's like I said before—you're see-ing patterns and connections everywhere. That's a sign that your Other Sight is awakening."

And now, in this moment, Faruq didn't care about burning bridges anymore. He didn't feel curious. His hands burned. He stepped forward, toward Odo. "No, fuck you, man. Patterns and connections my dick. I've been letting you play your games be-cause I was interested. But it's not complicated, is it? You're just a sick fuck."

Odo shook his head minutely, his mask not falling. "Your anger is coming out of distortion, scholar."

Faruq took another step closer to Odo. "*You* are distortion.

You are grotesque. All these people—you've taken their weaknesses and . . . and *twisted* them to suit your own, fucked-up agenda. You think you can do it to me too? Fuck you." Faruq threw his hands up, gesturing emphatically like his father used to when he was angry.

He heard gasps, felt the followers around him step away from him like he was a detonating bomb. He glanced around the room. A chorus of mostly white faces, looking at him like *he* was the monster. Like *he* was the dangerous one. Violent. Barbarian. *Terrorist*.

He felt sick to his stomach, his burning hands shaking.

The woman pulled the shroud off of her face.

"Faruq," Kaya said quietly, fear in her voice. "It's not what you think."

Faruq took a step back. He was either going to punch Odo or vomit. What were they seeing as they looked at him now? Surely they were thinking that *his* mask had fallen, that he was truly what they feared he was. His legs itched to run.

"Faruq," Kaya repeated, "I know what you must be thinking. We weren't trying to upset you. This"—she gestured to the shroud—"is just a costume we use to represent the distorted view of death. You know, like the Reaper?"

No matter how many of these followers he'd gotten to know, no matter how unintimidating he tried to be, no matter how many times he professed his atheism—one show of rage and they all saw only that. The rage. The danger.

But didn't he have a right to be enraged? Was this really just more weird, performative nameless shit? He wasn't sure anymore. He took two more steps back.

"Scholar," Odo said, holding out his hands as though to lay them on Faruq. "Hey, it's all right, scholar."

Faruq continued backing up. Odo stepped forward as Faruq stepped back, as though chasing him in slow motion. Or as though herding him.

"That's all right, scholar. It's *all right*."

He was still aware of the stunned, fearful faces around him. The followers backed away from him as he passed. Only Odo stepped toward him.

"Look, don't worry about anything. It's all right."

Faruq had reached the door. He remembered those early years of running, when he'd felt the city air scratching at his cheeks, and he had no history, no family, no religion, no weight. He was alone. He was nobody. That brown, motherless, godless boy was crumpled on the stoop of his father's brownstone.

He couldn't think anymore. He couldn't talk. He couldn't fight. He could only run. He turned and took the first wide stride out, away.

He did his best not to be seen by anyone for the next couple of days. His thoughts were no more sorted as a result. If Kaya had been telling the truth, he'd humiliated himself for no reason. If she'd been lying, he'd been justified, but he'd still humiliated himself. To keep his mind from spinning in circles, Faruq wrote. The words came easier to him now, because they were something else to focus on. He described his neighborhood, his childhood friends, his secret girlfriends.

But when Faruq sat down to write about his mother's exorcism, he found that words were inadequate. How to articulate the trauma, the horror, the irreparable indignity? How to explain how he did not pity his mother afterward? How to explain how he could still love his father?

Blocked, Faruq looked up from his computer. Odo was there, in the doorway of his bedroom, watching.

"Faruq. Minh-An has returned to the World."

"What? You mean she died?" Faruq laughed, as though this must be a joke. "No—I just saw her. I just watched her dance. She was—no."

Odo only watched him, face unreadable.

"I mean, I know she's sick, but—I don't believe you."

"Scholar."

"She's dead? Shit. She's really—?" Faruq closed his laptop. "Shit."

He couldn't explain his grief. In the scheme of things, he'd only known Minh-An a little while. Months. And she'd been chilly toward him for most of that time. But still—those dinners spent watching her not eat, those late nights next to her in the stables, her obvious love for Odo, the dance, the glimpse of her vulnerability. Why did life always end so abruptly? Even when you knew someone was dying?

He found himself pressed into Odo's shirt. He wanted to pull away at first—hardly ever in his life had he been this close to another man—but Odo's arms were firm and now Faruq was crying, actually *crying*, so he couldn't pull away, couldn't let Odo see him break down like this again. Damn Odo to hell. Faruq knew what he was doing. He wouldn't forgive him. But he needed him right now, didn't he? Odo's arms were bands holding him in place. And Odo smelled like the forest, earthy and green and, deep underneath, something like wild game.

Instagram Post #386

@thenamelessmvmnt: A close-up of Odo's face, off-center. He is wearing a skullcap, a nearly black purple, and his hands, clean and long-fingered, are at his mouth, eyes meeting those of the viewer, slightly wet. Either nirvana or quiet lament.

#Odo #heartoftheWorld

132,687 likes | 3,028 comments

Nero

BLACK SCREEN:

SUPER: "As a result of the lawsuit, the nameless are
awarded $50,000, plus legal fees."

                                              FADE IN:

SUPER: "The nameless donate the money and abandon their
Texas expansion project, leaving the land they'd
purchased in Burning Hill vacant."

                                         FADE TO BLACK.

INT. CWE NAVE—MED. SHOT—WILL ROY

                    WILL ROY
          The whole thing was a big 'fuck you.'

                    ROY'S WIFE (O.S.)
          William!

Roy holds up a placating hand.

                    WILL ROY
          Sorry darlin'. I apologize. Jesus will
          forgive me.

Roy lowers his hand.

                    WILL ROY
          Really, though, I think of it as a victory.
          All that media—we exposed him. And true
          believers will know the deceiver when they
          see him. They won't get led down the
          primrose path.*

          I'll always stand up in the face of evil. I
          will always challenge the antichrist. And in
          the end, God will reward me for it.

INSERT—FOOTAGE

Silent footage of Owen Ryker and Odo walking side by
side outside of the courthouse, their backs to the
_____
    * Music: fade in, Pièces Froides—Airs à Faire Fuir (Satie)

camera. Odo glances over his shoulder, looking directly
at the camera. The footage slows to half-speed. Odo
smiles, an eerie knowingness in his eyes.

                                              DISSOLVE TO:

INT. GREENHOUSE—MED. SHOT—MINH-AN

              MINH-AN
     We couldn't stay there. Even after hitting
     them in their pockets, the pall of those
     false allegations against Odo hung over
     everything. He was vindicated, sure, but the
     atmosphere in town was ugly.

INSERT—FOOTAGE

Cell phone footage of Odo walking on Burning
Hill's Main Street, flanked by followers. A car
pulls up alongside them, and a man leans out of the
window, yelling. For a moment, Odo scowls, his face
contorting with anger before going abruptly blank.
The followers guide him away by his elbows (audio
removed).

              MINH-AN
     I think the whole thing made him . . . sad.

INSERT—FOOTAGE

Cell phone footage, shot through a window, of CWE
congregants gathered on the street chanting "Go home"
over and over again.

                                              DISSOLVE TO:

INT. GREENHOUSE—MED. SHOT—MINH-AN

              MINH-AN
     Odo doesn't hate the distorted. He loves
     them. He empathizes with them—we all do.
     We mourn for those without the Other
     Sight.

We never wanted *money* from Will Roy.
(chuckles)

We took it and made beauty—we handed out
stacks of cash to the hungry, the poor. We
didn't need it. All we ever want is to make
beauty.

Minh-An shrugs, and then nods.

          MINH-AN
After everything, Odo was called to strip
himself and retreat into the wilderness. He
went West, into the redwoods. For a while he
didn't talk.

Well, we followed him, of course. We found
land—16,000 acres. Bigger than Manhattan.
And we built up a city, a community, all
around him.

Minh-An smiles. ZOOM in slowly on Minh-An's face.

          MINH-AN
The nameless is only growing. More and more
people want to see. It's so, so beautiful.

Minh-An gazes into the camera's lens.

                              FADE TO BLACK.

INT. GEORGETOWN OFFICE—MED. SHOT—FATHER SCHUYLER*

          PRODUCER (O.S.)
So, do *you* believe Odo could be the
antichrist?

          FATHER SCHUYLER
Well, ah—

Father Schuyler reaches up and touches his collar, then
adjusts himself in his seat. Clears his throat.

_____
* Silence.

FATHER SCHUYLER
Well, I think the more interesting question
is, What does Odo really want? What's
driving him?

Father Schuyler licks his lips and looks into the
camera for a long, uninterrupted moment.

FADE TO BLACK.

ROLL CREDITS*

---

* Music: Evil Blues (Mance Lipscomb)

before: 1970

SILK WAS SINGING THE BLUES.

Well the old world's a-callin me, ever I go
Time in Hell's getting short, that's fo sho
Mm-hm hmm, Mm-hm hmm
People is waitin there, Mama'n them
Caint wait to see their lil' ol face again
Mm-hm hmm, Mm-hm hmm
Well this ol land's a-crumblin down to ash
Gotta get outta here 'fore they smoke my ass
Mm-hm hmm, Mm-hm hmm

Crazy Horse solemnly danced along—a Vietnamese dance, hands like wind-lifted leaves, neat, compact twirls, his feathered helmet mask, then sun, then fan. At first Silk's singing and Crazy Horse's dancing was a kind of joke, but by now it had become something serious. Every man's pulse recalibrated itself to Silk's beat.

Ghosts out here is following me, ever I go
Caint stand that funky jungle at all no mo'e
Mm-hm hmm, Mm-hm hmm
If Charlie shoot me up he gonna hit a heart of gold
Time's getting short, and I'm getting old
Mm-hm hmm, Mm-hm hmm

They were thinking of home, of hot meals, of sex, of dry, starry nights, of the molasses bliss of opium, of baked sidewalks and fire hydrants, of soft perfumed arms, of real maple syrup, of fresh corn and butter, of laughter, of shelter. Now others were humming along. The nearby grunts digging a foxhole stabbed into the earth along with the rhythm. Crazy Horse's face was a still pond.

> Rich men die easy, and a poor man too
> Killin ain't hard, whatever you do
> Mm-hm hmm, Mm-hm hmm

The water buffalo were wallowing, rolling their bloated-tick bodies in the milky mud of the rice paddies. They ground their square teeth, flicked their ears against flies and mosquitoes. They knew who was a native child of this land and who wasn't. When the soldiers came, they stood, became stones. They stared with nothing in their eyes, neither recognition nor fear.

One of the soldiers pointed his gun at the water buffalo, and then, tired, lowered it. They sweated and sloshed through the rice paddies, heavy monsoon clouds muting the sun's light, but not its heat. The wet sky bulged down toward them, great sackful of water, a threat. They were the only people around. Slimy carp slithered around their ankles, leeches found purchase and burrowed.

Up ahead, stringy brown ducks take dumb flight, and some see opalescent ghosts fly up with them. Then the machine-gun fire. The water buffalo amble away, in no particular hurry. Men crouch down in the mud, cigarettes smoking at their lips, to return fire. Some are close enough to semi-solid ground to take cover in the high grasses. The carp twist themselves away from soldiers' frantic ankles, theirs a world of lapping silence and dull brown light.

Crazy Horse and Silk see the brother get hit at roughly the same time, and from opposite directions fight their way toward him. The brother has been shot in the shoulder, in his arm, and, as far as Silk and Crazy Horse can tell, he's been grazed near his groin. He should survive, provided he doesn't lose blood too quickly. He is emitting a mechanical-sounding drone, his teeth clenched together.

Silk loops one of the man's arms around his shoulder, and Crazy Horse takes the other. Doing their best to stay out of the fire, they drag him out of there. Bullets hurtle past them, some of them dangerously close, whining like fever mosquitoes. The brother, delirious with pain, rubs his face into Crazy Horse's shoulder. They drop him off in the high grass, where some of the other wounded have crawled, and he collapses into the sodden ground gratefully.

The bulging monsoon clouds rip open and, through rain like shattering glass, Crazy Horse and Silk run back out. Crazy Horse fires into fire—the net is starting to take shape; the rain has beaten down some of the smoke and he can make out where the Vietnamese must be hiding. Silk covers the medic as he hurries to another fallen soldier, but then the medic too goes down. Silk swears, waves at Crazy Horse to get his attention.

Hey, we gotta go get em.

The medic and the fallen grunt aren't far, but they are in the thick of the whining bullets. Both Silk and Crazy Horse fire into the net, hoping to create a hole that lasts long enough for them to retrieve the fallen men. The rain swiftly pulls the rice paddy water up to their shins, dulling their movements. It is like they are running in a dream. As soon as they deposit the medic and the grunt into the tall grass, a bullet crashes into Silk's arm, just above the elbow. It hits with a pop, a current of fire, and then he can't feel it. He looks down at the black hole in his sleeve, the rain already diluting the blood.

Hey, man, you all right?

Crazy Horse is studying that black hole too. Silk grins.

I'm invincible, baby.

They laugh manic laughs. Silk spots a slender body in a crouching run through the tall grasses, aims, and fires. The body jerks and falls. Silk feels the flush of victory. He imagines it's the mother-fucker who shot him. Crazy Horse claps him on the back.

Look there. You can see where they're hiding. We can sneak around the rear and ambush them. Our side'll drive them back, right into our barrels.

Crazy Horse reaches out an arm and sweeps it in a slow arc to indicate the positions of the Vietnamese. Silk's heart fills with adrenaline.

Ambush the ambush. All right. I like that.

Together they crouch, sneaking around the net of gunfire. Even outside of the rice paddies, mud sucks at them, begs for their bodies. They fight it, make their way to the bushes at the edge of the paddies. From here, they can hear the Vietnamese. The rain carries sound strangely—shouts are muffled, conversations sound like they're happening right over their shoulders. They surprise a Vietnamese soldier hiding on a little rise, and Crazy Horse smokes him, climbs up himself to see what he can see. He gestures at Silk.

They are behind the Vietnamese now, can see them crouching in the greenery, rescuing their wounded, joking with each other, firing. Crazy Horse can understand snatches of their conversation, and so closes his ears to them. He and Silk get down onto their bellies, poke the barrels of their guns through the shrubs, and, as quickly as they can, begin to pick the Vietnamese soldiers off. They drop in agony and rage.

Before the Vietnamese can locate them, Crazy Horse and Silk clear the area immediately in front of them. Return fire breaks into their general direction, but they are already slinking to a new hiding spot, keeping the cover of foliage. From their new vantage point, they snipe as many Vietnamese as they can before they have to sneak away to another spot. They are laughing with each other like two boys stealing Santa's cookies on Christmas Eve.

The American soldiers are using the chaos Silk and Crazy Horse are sowing among the Vietnamese to advance. They call Crazy Horse and Silk out so they can finish clearing out the horizon with their grenade launchers. Silk and Crazy Horse scramble to find a new path out. Their spot is hot now—the Vietnamese are watching the foliage. By dumb luck, one of them hits Silk in the leg, and the impact knocks hot sensation back into his arm.

Son of a *bitch*. Why I'm the only one getting shot?

You the war hero, brother. Just think of that Purple Heart.

Fuck, *fuck*.

Hey now, we ain't got time for that. C'mon now—we're *tigers*.

They manage to break out of the foliage, angling back through the sucking mud toward the paddies. Behind Silk, Crazy Horse stumbles, falls forward. Silk hears his shout and whirls around in just enough time to catch him. An angry wound in his shoulder. Silk shakes him gently.

Aw, man, that's just a flesh wound. Now, we tigers, ain't we?

Through a soggy fog of pain, Crazy Horse growls. Silk laughs, shooting into the foliage. They hear the zip-*thwap* of Thumper, the grenade launcher, and watch smoke and fire blossom in the bushes. They smile to each other—that ought to get them. They run toward the rice paddies, Silk loping along with a limp, and Crazy Horse clutching his shoulder. The Vietnamese fire has quieted.

Just ahead of them, a Vietnamese soldier rises from a mound of mud like a mythical sea creature. His face is slick with mud and rain, his teeth bared. He fires. One of his bullets punches into Crazy Horse's gut, and the other rips into Silk's side. They fire back, their fingers jerking their triggers. The Vietnamese soldier stumbles back, hit in his gut, his chest, his neck. They all fall down.

Rain drives into Crazy Horse's eyes, up his nose, the mud holding him like flypaper holds a lightning bug. He calls out for Silk and receives a weak growl in response. Silk reaches out, feeling only hot rain, mud. They can hear the Vietnamese solider wailing in pain, until eventually the rain swallows his agony, his blood, and he is quiet. Silk heaves himself up onto his knees and crawls, the hit leg dragging, pain making his body heavy and slow.

Crazy Horse feels a hand take his and opens his eyes. Silk is there. He squeezes Silk's hand, not letting go. They look at each other through wet, slitted eyes.

That motherfucker dead, Silk?

He dead. And we're alive. Tigers?

Tigers.

All right then. We're getting outta here, man.

They'll just ignore us, Silk. Just like before. Like nothing ever happened.

Nuh-uh. Not me. I'm not nothing. Can't wait to see all of them fine nurses, neither.

Just make sure they don't see you, brother. Else they'll put you outta your misery.

Crazy, one look at *your* face, and they'll send your monkey ass back to the jungle.

That right? Least they won't make me sit to piss.

That a dick joke?

Sure is, brother.

All right, well your dick is so ugly, they invented rubbers just for you.

Your dick is so small, you and your mama share panties.

Your mama so broke, she thought a dollar was a type of dog.

Your mama so stupid, she bake you a birthday cake every Sunday.

Man tell me why when you were born, the doc tried to throw you back in

Saw you coming and tried to spare me

And you a skinny nigger too, lookin like a burnt chicken wing

Least I ain't got them big ole lips pullin my head down

Your hairline makin you look surprised all the time

You try to take a bath and all the water dries up

And your hair's so nappy, all your combs got a union

Right now, the president's addressing the nation about your breath, brother

You so tall, I heard your shadow done quit

You got a license for them big feet?

That penny in your wallet's been putting out personal ads

That head got you lookin like a weather balloon
So skinny the doctors use you to teach anatomy
Your mama can't spell *anatomy*
Heh, yeah . . . skinny . . . brother
What's that, man?

Crazy Horse knew Silk was dead before the hand grew cool in his. He blinked up into the rain. He could feel his body leaving an impression on the soft earth, and the monsoon rain driving him down into it. He thought he felt the touch of something feathered, some fragment of the last of his friends. And then something sharp. Writhing muscle, venom. A python of fury. He opened his mouth, wide. But it didn't crawl out into the wet air. He was its home—this powerful fury. This power. He swallowed. The python twisted inside him, inhabiting his body, distorting to fit inside.

today

ODO'S AND FARUQ'S faces were close together. Faruq was sweating, and he could see a thin film of perspiration on Odo's brow too. They were in a hot storage room in the house of the nameless. Faruq hadn't even realized this room existed. It seemed all the heat from sunlight and meditating bodies got driven down into this windowless room and trapped, creating a kind of dry sauna.

Around them, the reason Odo had brought him here: boxes of photographs, hundreds of hours of audio and video recordings, all dating back as far as the eighties. A treasure trove.

"We're working on digitizing all this," Odo said. "Minh-An wanted to make a kind of nameless Netflix."

"So a subscription service?"

"That's right. But until then, scholar, you're welcome to it. Whatever you think'll help you write."

"That's amazing—thank you."

Odo smiled. Faruq thought it looked almost sad. "I can't just sit in this place anymore, scholar. Vutu is calling me back out. People need me."

"You're leaving the Forbidden City?"

Odo chuckled softly. "As above, so below. Just as the ten Tintan were meant to govern the chaos of the universe, so too am I meant to restore beauty to this world. And just as the World was always home to the ten Tintan, so too is the Forbidden City home to me on Earth. I'll be back."

"Where are you going to go?"

"We're planning a big thing in LA. A little glitter in the eye of the world."

With that, Odo winked, stood, and left Faruq alone in the sweltering storage room. Faruq looked around at the packed shelves around him. There was no way he'd ever be able to make his way through all that footage, not with the time he had left here—the last time they'd spoken, Anita said that it was time for him to come home for his own good. They were long past the initial, agreed-upon six weeks.

He stood, scanning the shelves. One side of the room was dedicated to videotapes, and the other side to cassettes. The videotapes were carefully labeled and arranged in chronological, then alphabetical, order. He selected a tape labeled 1988, MAY 10: HIPPING HARLEM. He snapped it into the VCR that sat on a small table at the back of the room and turned on the projector. Odo's smooth, ageless face, looking much the same as it did now, filled the walls, the image distorted here and there by the angles of the room. The camera zoomed out. Odo was wearing a black beanie, jeans, a denim shirt. He was in a wood-paneled room with thirty or so people, most of them Black, who were listening intently, with occasional self-conscious glances at the camera.

BROTHERS AND SISTERS, WHEN YOU LOOK AROUND AND WHAT YOU SEE IS UGLY, THAT'S DISTORTION. MY, MY, MY. DISTORTION FROM LIES ABOUT YOUR HISTORY, LIES ABOUT WHERE YOU COME FROM, LIES ABOUT YOUR BEAUTY, LIES ABOUT YOUR WORTH. YOU'RE SICK AND TIRED? WELL, THAT'S BECAUSE YOU'RE NOT LIVING IN REALITY. NUH-UH. REALITY IS BEAUTIFUL, BROTHERS AND SISTERS. YOU JUST AIN'T SEEING IT. YET. BUT YOU DON'T NEED NOBODY'S PERMISSION TO ENJOY THIS LIFE YOU'RE LIVING. AIN'T LIFE BEAUTIFUL? (YEAH). YEAH. DON'T LET NOBODY TELL YOU YOU AIN'T BEAUTIFUL. I LOOK AROUND THIS ROOM AND I SEE A BUNCH OF BEAUTIFUL PEOPLE—DON'T YOU?

. . .

Fine shards of rain got in his eye. The mist was thin and sharp—it hissed through the woods. But still, he thought he could hear the wolf following, that sound-beneath-sound. The beach was gray, the waves churning in thickly. He slowed when he reached the shore, turned to watch the line of trees, muted as they were by the fog. He stopped. Waited. What if, all this time, the wolf really had been a figment of his imagination? A hallucination. A delusion. A distortion. What if he was crazy?

By the time his breath slowed to normal, the wolf still had not emerged. He turned to the water. Waded in. He imagined a great wall of water rising, coming to swallow him whole. He walked forward. Salt water soaked into his sneakers, drenching his socks. It cupped his ankles, climbed up his legs. He flinched when it reached through his shorts for his balls, and then it was lapping at his stomach, spreading across his chest, closing around his neck. A wave swelled forward, coming for his head. He closed his eyes.

After three and a half hours of watching nameless footage in that close storage room, stepping out into the sunlight was a shock. Faruq blinked into the brightness. He'd been making his way through footage from the late eighties through the early nineties. Mostly the footage was of Odo talking to groups of people, talking about beauty, freedom, the Other Sight. But there were also recordings taken at lavish parties, poetry readings, college campuses.

He'd found a brief video of followers happily painting the house of the nameless in Brooklyn, another that featured several followers being interviewed, one of the Fall Day procession of 1991. What struck Faruq was the conventional attractiveness of Odo's followers—that had remained consistent over the years—and the way they all seemed to be missing something that they thought Odo provided them with. One woman described Odo casually breaking her down when they first met until she'd cried. She described it with happy tears in her eyes.

Faruq walked through Ewa Park, his eyes taking their time to adjust. He knew Odo was near because followers were hurrying excitedly to the Waterfowl Pond. Odo was sitting cross-legged on a rock, looking out over the water. He wasn't speaking, but still, his followers' faces shone on his like suns. Odo seemed to be largely ignoring them, but when he glanced up and spotted Faruq, his entire face lit up.

"Ah, there's my scholar. Hey, I'm tired of talking. *You* tell us something now."

Faruq stopped in his tracks. "Me?" he said, but the followers' faces were already turning to him, bright and expectant. "Oh— okay. Well, I don't really know what I'd say. I guess—well."

The followers had all turned to him now, their doll eyes bright. He thought of his mother, wide-eyed in that kiddie pool. They probably all knew the story by now. Nothing confidential in the Forbidden City. He thought of his father, his stern face softened only during prayer. He thought of his father in that hospital bed, his body heavy and slack, none of his fastidiousness left. He thought of the brownstone, his home, which wasn't quite his. Faruq swallowed. He thought of Minh-An, her body passive, covered with flowers.

"You—you ever see someone you love stumble? Or, uh, fall? And it hurts *you*?" He swallowed again, licked his lips. "Maybe it makes you feel kinda sick inside. But—but it's not just that you don't want them to suffer, you know? It's, uh, well, it's not just empathy. It's the *indignity*."

The word "indignity" came out with a harshness he didn't intend. He tried again. "The indignity. Like they—they fall in front of your eyes and they fall *in* your eyes. A little. It doesn't matter how much you love them. Or how much you respect them. In fact, that makes it worse. I think that's part of the reason people mourn death, you know? Seeing someone die—it's like seeing them demeaned. I guess you all would call that distortion." Faruq shrugged. "I don't know. Not despairing at death . . . that'd be—that'd be . . . God, that'd be such a *relief*."

When he was done talking, followers surged up, closing in around him. They thanked him, touched his arms, hugged him. So this was what Odo's power felt like. To Faruq, it was stifling. Hot as breath. Hot as his father's gaze, his aunties' meddling, the followers' creeping, Odo's weighted watching.

He tried not to squirm. He breathed easier when they cleared off, went on about their days. Odo remained, smiling like a proud parent. He drew himself up from his rock, came up to Faruq.

"Not bad, scholar."

"What was that for?"

Odo lifted one shoulder. "Like I said, tired." He placed a hand on Faruq's arm. "I know you're going to leave here soon, scholar." He squeezed his arm, regarded him silently for a bit. "You'll be back, I think."

Faruq didn't know what to make of that. He didn't answer.

Faruq packed away his T-shirts, his jeans. He packed his laptop, his camera, his notes. He left his running shoes—between the mileage on them and his dip into the ocean, they were dead now. Before leaving the bedroom in Odo's house that had been his, he stared at the Allama Iqbal book on the dresser for a long time, both pulled to it and repelled by it. Finally, he packed that too.

His body was sore and heavy, and he hadn't slept well. He couldn't wait to get back to his own bed, to Muezza, but he also didn't know how it was going to feel to reemerge into the noise of New York City, into the silence of his father's brownstone. He didn't know what it was going to feel like to inhale exhaust fumes instead of salt on his morning runs, to sit down for breakfast alone, trying not to stare at the spot where his father used to sip his black coffee, squinting at the Pakistani newspaper, *Dawn*, on his outdated iPhone.

Odo was waiting for him outside, along with the car that

would take him to the airport in Eureka. A follower was already waiting behind the wheel. Two more took his bags and loaded them into the trunk. Both Kaya and Thea were there to hug him goodbye, and Gabe dapped him.

Then Odo stepped forward. Faruq thought he was going to say something, but instead, he clasped Faruq's face in his hands and stared. Faruq did not look away. One last test. Odo's hands were warm and dry, his eyes the deep brown of loam. He didn't blink, his gaze steady, unfathomable. Odo's fingertips dug into his cheeks, trying to hook into him, trying to claim him and not let him go. Faruq didn't flinch, didn't look away. His eyes burned. Was this a kind of love or a kind of hate?

Finally, Odo released him. "You know," Odo said, "you fought me, scholar, you did. But in the end I wound up understanding you after all."

Faruq pursed his lips, something tightening in his jaw.

"You were seduced, Faruq. I hope you put that in your article. That you weren't above all this. That, deep down, you know, you could've found your home here."

Faruq narrowed his eyes at Odo. He looked—not malicious, but *earnest*. Almost like he was pleading. And that word— "home"—scraped up against Faruq uncomfortably. The brownstone, its doors ever porous to his aunties. Something inside rose, hot, close, muscling up his throat, forcing the tightness out of his jaw.

"I know what you want," Odo continued. "And I know—"

Faruq let his jaw release, let his mouth open wide. He howled, the sound round and full. His eyes wide. Odo flinched, and Faruq took even more breath, Odo's breath, to fuel his howl. The mask had slipped. *He'd* made Odo's mask slip. The power of that carried him through the discomfort in his lungs. He was in control.

When Faruq's howl petered out, there was a brief moment of silence, true silence. Faruq felt gloriously empty. He held his lungs, letting them burn before he breathed in. Odo, recovered, mask back in place, laughed. Faruq could see the fillings in his back teeth. But he wasn't fooled. Faruq still felt power and adrenaline tingling in his hands, his feet, his throat. So Faruq laughed too. He matched Odo's volume and they laughed together, Odo near mad, and Faruq full of his own power.

Odo stopped laughing and regarded Faruq, waiting. Faruq could see the slightest bit of wariness there, and he could also see that Odo was trying to hide it. Faruq saw things in Odo he'd never noticed that much before: the way the skin bunched up underneath his eyes, the fine twitching in the right side of his jaw, the tendons in his neck like frayed ropes, the way his nose flared subtly as he breathed, as though he were scenting the air.

"What I want," said Faruq, his voice, he thought, deeper than before, "is to finally, *finally*, be left alone."

Odo smiled slowly. "No place in the world you can get that, scholar. Why you think I moved all the way out into these woods? Look what happened." He swept an arm out, encompassing the followers who were gathered, watching. He laughed again.

Faruq shook his head. "You love it."

"That's right, scholar," Odo smirked. "You do too. Ain't that great? It's *all* love."

Faruq smiled and turned to get into the car.

"Hey, scholar?"

Faruq turned back around.

"Whatever you must write, let it be the bare, beautiful truth."

As the car drove down the main road, Faruq thought he saw a glimpse of the Deep's black, in the distance, half obscured. He fingered the scarf tucked in his pocket. Odo watched him be driven away, still as a stone. Faruq watched too, out the back window, until a curve in the road swept Odo out of sight.

Faruq stood in goggles and a helmet he'd borrowed from one of his father's contractor friends. This same friend had walked Faruq through determining whether the wall was load-bearing (it wasn't), and whether there was any electrical or plumbing rerouting to be done (there wasn't). But this part, Faruq had wanted to do himself. When he'd returned home, he'd found a neat pile of mail stacked on the formica dining table, with his father's AirPods placed tidily on top. The place had smelled of lemon wood-cleaner and his aunties' perfumes. This time around, he'd decided, he wasn't going to bother changing the locks.

He stared at the thin black groove in the wall. Muezza, sensing a disturbance, slinked away, his paws so light he barely even crinkled the plastic draping as he left. Faruq chuckled to himself, imagining what Auntie Naila would say if she were to walk in right now. *Let her come,* he thought. *Let them all come.* This was just his house. *He* was his own home, impenetrable, full of quiet, and lit with a wild, benevolent power that buoyed him when his mother died, showed his father only what he wanted to see, carried him through long, hard runs, and howled in the face of tricksters.

With a whoop, he raised the sledgehammer above his head and swung, knocking a hole into the black groove, breaking through, into the wall. Making more space, more air, more light. Moving the mountain of memory, of time. Again and again, he swung his sledgehammer, and the wall crumbled before him, leaving behind only its framing. Wide open. Faruq breathed in, hungrily.

ACKNOWLEDGMENTS

Thank you to the veterans who were willing to talk to me about their experiences in the Vietnam War, those who guided and aided me in my research into Islam and Pakistani culture, and those who were willing to share their experiences with high-control groups and organizations.

Research is achieved in the trenches of texts, and understanding is rounded out in the mouths of those who share their stories, their oral histories.

Thank you to my family for their support and understanding, and all the people who helped me polish, fact-check, and mold and remold this book.

ABOUT THE AUTHOR

Nicole Cuffy is a proud Brooklyn emigrant living in DC. She holds a BA in Writing from Columbia University, and an MFA in Fiction from The New School. She does her best writing when she's writing by hand, and she is a high-functioning book addict. Her work can be found in *Chautauqua*, *The Masters Review Volume VI*, *Blue Mesa Review*, and the *New England Review*, and her chapbook "Atlas of the Body" was an editor's choice and finalist for the Black River Chapbook Competition, and winner of the Chautauqua Janus Prize. Her previous novel, *Dances*, was released in May 2023 through One World. Nicole can be found muddling her way through Instagram and life in general here: @nikk2cole.

ABOUT THE TYPE

This book was set in Sabon, a typeface designed by the well-known German typographer Jan Tschichold (1902–74). Sabon's design is based upon the original letterforms of sixteenth-century French type designer Claude Garamond and was created specifically to be used for three sources: foundry type for hand composition, Linotype, and Monotype. Tschichold named his typeface for the famous Frankfurt typefounder Jacques Sabon (c. 1520–80).